"We are living free
Though there's blood been shed
And we'll always be
Be Chicago red. . . ."

"What's that mean?"

"It's talking about the rebellion," said the man who was now Chris-John but would soon be known as Chicago Red.

"What rebellion?"

"The one that must be, against the Crown. It means we were meant to be free. It means tyranny is only a temporary unnatural state that cannot last, because it is unnatural." He swallowed, blinked his eyes. He was trembling. "It means even after they executed all those people in the Chicago purge—even if Chicago is a river of blood—people would stand up and declare freedom. It means— oh, my God—" And because he was still Chris-John and not yet Chicago Red, the future which he could suddenly see made him begin to scream and then he could not stop. . . .

"Strong . . . full of pulse and purpose . . . R.M. Meluch writes about tyranny and ignorance in a nightmare America with a fiery pen."

—Janet Morris

Ⓥ **SIGNET SCIENCE FICTION** (0451)

DISTANT BATTLES

☐ **ANACHRONISMS by Christopher Hinz.** When the starship *Alchemon* brings a strange alien life-form aboard ship, systems start to malfunction and the crew begins to behave oddly, and a simple mission of planetary exploration is suddenly a war against psionic madness.

(162358—$3.95)

☐ **WAR BIRDS by R.M. Meluch.** A husband and wife space warrior team attempts to save their planet from a hostile invasion. A technological race to accelerate space travel raises the stakes as interplanetary war erupts creating a deadly universe. (161122—$3.95)

☐ **YESTERDAY'S PAWN by W.T. Quick.** Garry gains possession of a rare artifact dating back to the ancient, long-vanished Kurs'ggathan race, and unknowingly has acquired the secret to Faster-Than-Light time and space travel. He also has become the most wanted man on the planet.... (160754—$3.95)

☐ **SYSTEMS by W.T. Quick** A data bank reveals secrets that can topple his world, unless the government catches Josh Tower, a Defense Intelligence Agent, first. (163427—$3.75)

Prices slightly higher in Canada.

Buy them at your local bookstore or use this convenient coupon for ordering.

NEW AMERICAN LIBRARY
P.O. Box 999, Bergenfield, New Jersey 07621

Please send me the books I have checked above. I am enclosing $_____
(please add $1.00 to this order to cover postage and handling). Send check or money order—no cash or C.O.D.'s. Prices and numbers are subject to change without notice.

Name_____

Address_____

City _____ State _____ Zip Code _____
Allow 4-6 weeks for delivery.
This offer, prices and numbers are subject to change without notice.

CHICAGO RED

by

R. M. Meluch

A ROC BOOK

ROC
Published by the Penguin Group
Penguin Books USA Inc., 375 Hudson Street,
New York, New York 10014, U.S.A.
Penguin Books Ltd, 27 Wrights Lane, London W8 5TZ, England
Penguin Books Australia Ltd, Ringwood, Victoria, Australia
Penguin Books Canada Ltd, 2801 John Street,
Markham, Ontario, Canada L3R 1B4
Penguin Books (N.Z.) Ltd, 182-190 Wairau Road, Auckland 10, New Zealand

Penguin Books Ltd, Registered Offices: Harmondsworth, Middlesex, England

First published by Roc, an imprint of New American Library, a division of
Penguin Books USA Inc.

First Printing, October, 1990
10 9 8 7 6 5 4 3 2 1

Copyright © R. M. Meluch, 1990
All rights reserved

 Roc is a trademark of Penguin Books USA Inc.

Printed in the United States of America

Without limiting the rights under copyright reserved above, no part of this
publication may be reproduced, stored in or introduced into a retrieval system, or
transmitted, in any form, or by any means (electronic, mechanical,
photocopying, recording, or otherwise), without the prior written permission of
both the copyright owner and the above publisher of this book.

BOOKS ARE AVAILABLE AT QUANTITY DISCOUNTS WHEN USED TO PROMOTE
PRODUCTS OR SERVICES. FOR INFORMATION PLEASE WRITE TO PREMIUM MARKETING
DIVISION, PENGUIN BOOKS USA INC., 375 HUDSON STREET, NEW YORK,
NEW YORK 10014.

To Jim

CHICAGO RED

Prologue

I.

Chicago Red

THEY SAY IT BEGAN THE NIGHT CHRIS-JOHN STANTON cut Henry Iver's body down from the scaffold. The rebellion was actually quite old by that time, but that night in the dark of a thunderstorm its leader, its rallying flag, was born. It was the beginning of Chicago Red.

Henry Iver had gone before; he had already crystallized an idea, putting dissatisfaction into words, and instilling the hope of freedom in the people and in the one who would be Chicago Red. For that his carcass hung on Potter's Hill for two days and nights, a royal edict promising death to anyone who took him down. A soldier was posted in Dunhelm Tower to keep watch.

For two days no one came near. Then came the thunderstorm. It was difficult to see from the tower to the top of the hill in the driving rain, but the guard swore no one could possibly approach it without his notice. He still swore that no one had. But when the rains let up, the body was gone.

Chris-John Stanton had been hiding under the scaffold since the first crowds gathered for the execution. He'd heard Henry's bootheels clomp loudly on the wooden planks over his head with those huge feet of Henry's. Then he waited helplessly through the proclamation, through Henry's pardoning the hangman, through the drumroll; then the wooden trap swung down with a clatter and creak, and those big feet came bouncing through and dangled in the air over Chris-John's head. Chris-John fainted.

He was under the gallows two days until the weather changed. He had run out of water the day before—he'd only brought a small skin. He'd brought no food; he could not have eaten in the stifling heat with the stench of death and all the flies. All he had was a copy of Henry Iver's banned seditious book, which he clutched close as a Bible.

When the heavens broke open on the third day and the rains turned noontime dark as night, Chris-John crawled up the scaffold. He threw his head back and drank the pelting rain that stung his mouth and his face. He drew his knife from its wet leather sheath, grasped the stinging hemp rope that suspended Henry's body, and set himself to sawing through the fibers. Henry's neck was black where the noose tightened around it. They hadn't given him a hood. Chris-John would not look at his face. The body swung away from him once, Chris-John's hands slicked with rain, but he caught it again and carved through the rope. He tried to keep hold of the corpse as he cut it free, but it got away from him, fell down through the trap, unbalancing Chris-John, who fell down with it and landed on top of it. Whether from the fall or the horror, or whether he'd seen Henry's face, Chris-John could never say, but he lost consciousness, part of his memory, and part of his sanity ever after. Later he couldn't even say what he had done with the body. He must have buried it under the scaffold, for that was the only conceivable way he could have disposed of it so quickly and unseen. And later when Scottie Deerborne revisited the site, he in fact found a shallow grave in the vicinity where the gallows had once stood. There were many unmarked graves on Potter's Hill, but those were six feet deep, not one.

At any rate, those were the bones Scottie Deerborne

took away with him, and those are the bones that now
rest in the Rebels' Field beneath a gold cross.

Chris-John woke numb, emotionally dead. He could
not even be alarmed by his circumstance, naked and
tied facedown, spread-eagle on a bed. The room was
small and shabby, with smeared windows and a broken
skylight covered by a bent metal grid through with sunlight streamed. The place was clean-swept and as neat
as it could be with its broken furniture and peeling
paint.

A reluctant toilet flushed behind one of the thin
walls, and from the bathroom came a shirtless barefoot
young man with tight-curled blond hair, narrow canine
eyes, sharp canine teeth, and a many-times broken
nose. He was zipping up the fly of his corduroy trousers when he glanced at Chris-John on the bed. He did
not look surprised on seeing Chris-John. He said, "Oh,
you're awake."

Chris-John tried to swallow. His mouth was dry.
"Let me up," he said.

The young man barked a short mirthless laugh.
"You're funny," he said, and Chris-John guessed that
the youth was not here to rescue him. Chris-John lowered his face back down on the pillow and closed his
eyes wearily.

"Hey, don't go under again," the youth said, coming to crouch by the bed, his face level with Chris-
John's. Chris-John opened his deep brown eyes, his
eyelids smooth and soft as the petals of a dark rose.
Chris-John was beautiful, startlingly so, and the youth
caught his breath. "You're not from Farington, are
you."

Farington. The black pit of the Kingdom. "Is that
where I am?" said Chris-John.

"Well, where do you think?" The youth thrust his
hard palm over Chris-John's bound prone figure in a
gesture of presentation. There were not too many places

one could expect to wake up tied to someone's bed.
Chris-John must've gotten lost in the rain. He hadn't
meant to come here. No one came to Farington on purpose.

It was a safe bet anyway that the king's soldiers would
never find him. No one would ever find him. Farington
was the end of the road.

Farington, not surprisingly, was the closest town to
Potter's Hill. Other towns raised great public outcries
at the mere suggestion of allowing gallows and criminals' graves near their city limits. The most civic interest Farington ever showed was coming out en masse
to witness executions of state criminals, and cheering.

There were other cesspools in the Kingdom. But it
was difficult to imagine another so bleak and vicious;
and this one was within riding distance of the Capital
itself.

Farington's notoriety came from its ferocity and per-
version, and of course from its most famous son, the
king's assassin, General Tow. It was said that Farington
ate soldiers alive, and no one knew if that was figura-
tive or not, because military police were sometimes
sent in but never came out of Farington.

"I guess I got lost," Chris-John mumbled very
faintly.

"I guess you did. Good for me, bad for you," said
the youth enthusiastically, and unzipped his fly again.
"Look at this."

"I have one, too, only it's smaller," said Chris-John,
and turned his head away.

"How can you be so blasé about this? You're supposed to scream and beg."

"I can't."

"You're weird. I've never done this before, but you're
weird. Well, let's get to this." The young man jumped
onto the bed, bouncing the tired springs, and scrambled to kneel between Chris-John's spread legs. And
he immediately folded. He sat back, bare buttocks on

his heels, disconcerted. He sucked at his lower lip and scowled at the dirty windows. He waited for something to happen. Nothing did. Not a twinge. "Don't feel like it right now," he mumbled, and climbed off the bed.

"May I have something to drink, please?" said Chris-John.

"Want to drink from this?"

"No, thank you," said Chris-John.

The youth rolled his yellow eyes. "No, thank you, he says. This is a rape. Why don't you scream or something?"

Chris-John stared forlornly at the baseboard. He didn't feel like screaming. He didn't feel much of anything. Thirsty.

"Why don't you politely ask me to let you free?" said the youth sarcastically.

"No such thing as freedom," said Chris-John.

The youth threw up his hands. "A philosopher. I want begging and screaming, he gives me philosophy." He slapped his thighs and went to the bathroom. He returned with a glass of water, sat on the edge of the bed at Chris-John's head, held the glass for Chris-John, and let him drink.

When Chris-John lowered his head, the youth set the glass aside on a wobbly night table coated thickly with layers of chipped white paint. He ran his hand down Chris-John's smooth light brown back. "God, you're a pretty thing. I love how clean you are. No one's clean here."

Chris-John could not have been clean when his youth found him. The youth had given him a bath. By "clean" he meant unblemished, and undiseased. "Don't you even wanna know why you're here?"

Chris-John shrugged in his bonds, an approximation of a shrug. It was little more than a sigh.

"A clean fuck," said the youth. "All mine and always here. Anything that's willing always has some disease that could eat a bus."

"You didn't have to do this," said Chris-John.

The youth crouched by the bed and brought his face close to Chris-John's. "I'm ugly, aren't I?"

His cheekbones were too high, crowding his face up near his yellow eyes. His once-noble nose was crooked and thickened, and there was a thick scar on his thick lips over pointed teeth. "Yes," said Chris-John. "But you're not that ugly."

"Bullshit," said the youth. "I may be inbred but I'm not an idiot. I'm not letting you up." He slapped Chris-John's bare behind. "I never raped anyone before," he said. He was still soft. He frowned, then stood up and zipped up his trousers. "But I'm not worried, though. I'll get you later, when I'm in the mood."

Chris-John asked for a blanket.

"Cold?" said the youth.

"Yes," said Chris-John.

"I'll warm you up," said the youth, climbed onto the bed, lay over him, spoke low with his lips against Chris-John's ear. "Better?"

"I would rather have a blanket," Chris-John confessed.

The youth got up abruptly. "Don't get me angry." He stalked to a closet, pulled out a blanket, and threw it over Chris-John. He put on a shirt, went to the door, and unlatched the five locks. He looked back as he was leaving, "Don't go away."

Eight rebels gathered in a forest glade and held a small makeshift service for their fallen hero, Henry Iver. They hadn't a priest in their number, so they chose Scottie to lead the Mass.

The Crown did not permit many people to learn Latin; only those people authorized to become priests and doctors could learn the ancient Beforetime language. Scripture and medical books were written in Latin so that the common people could not misinterpret things that were properly beyond their limited understanding.

Scottie Deerborne had been sent to the Royal Academy to become a doctor. But, once educated, Scottie still had the heart of a common person. And as soon as he'd finished medical school and he was summoned to practice for the Crown, Scottie Deerborne drove his car—few besides doctors could drive the rare automobiles—over a cliff and escaped the Crown the only way a man of his education ever could.

Except that Scottie hadn't been in the car.

Free and without identity, Scottie took refuge with a band of rebels near the Capital and undertook the task, a hanging offense, of translating the Bible and the medical books into common Americanese. Henry Iver had always said information should be in the hands of the people; ignorance was tyranny.

So now, in a wild green cathedral, Scottie read his translated words in memory of Henry Iver. It was all the rebels could do. They hadn't a body to bury—for someone far more courageous than they had defied the royal edict and spirited the corpse from the gallows. They were ashamed that they hadn't done it. They dared not even leave a marker here. They felt helpless, directionless, outraged, and lost.

Scottie closed his handwritten book after the last words were spoken and turned his dark haunted eyes to the others, with an almost meek set to his broad shoulders. He didn't know what to do. His size made him feel all the more obvious and awkward. He was tired and felt ancient. He was not yet thirty years old.

The sound of a woodpecker drumming came from deep in the forest. Dappled sunlight filtered through leaves of silver birchs and maples, their boughs knit overhead to form the high roof of their woodland cathedral.

The rebel hideout was nearby, a deep plastic-walled bunker built in the Beforetime and provisioned against some disaster none of them could fathom—something even more violent than a tornado. But none of them could imagine any force as devastating.

The bunker was well hidden, set in a field within a forest, out of sight of the road, miles from any building, but within a few hours' horseback ride of the Capital's walls, and less than an hour by car. The rebels had possession of two of the precious automobiles, which they kept in camouflaged shelters in the forest. Keeping the automobiles fueled and maintained, and driving them without challenge, were perennial difficulties. Keeping them hidden was no problem. Travelers quickly passed through this stretch of wooded road to get to somewhere else. They never stopped.

Until today.

"Hist!" Little Detroit suddenly demanded silence and held up one finger.

The sound of a car was rare enough, but this one came to a stop on the road just beyond the trees. Detroit raised her black eyebrows, half comment, half question.

Then a woman's raw screams made all the rebels shrink down and dart glances at each other like a group of startled deer. The screaming grew louder and closer, and soon the heavy stomping of feet became audible, crashing through the underbrush toward the rebels' glade; and, all at once, all eight outlaws bolted for their underground shelter. Scottie and Lark, the last ones in, crowded together at the top of the ladder to peer out of the hatch.

Lark saw them first—a movement in the woods and the drab green color of military uniforms hardly distinguishable from the surrounding brush and trees but for the flash of pale pink between them.

"Soldiers!" Lark hissed.

Two of the king's soldiers came dragging a struggling young woman between them. They stopped at the field, looked around them, nodding as in satisfaction, and they began stripping off their prisoner's dress, the

pink uniform of a palace maid. They took her white
shoes and the mother-of-pearl combs she wore in her
hair, leaving her in her white slip and torn stockings.
And it came clear to Scottie what was happening. This
was more than an assault. It was a covert execution.
The soldiers were taking her dress so no one would
trace the body to the palace.

Scottie started to climb out of the bunker. Lark
caught the sleeve of his black sweater and shrieked in
a whisper, "What are you doing!"

"I have to help her."

"It's too close to the bunker!" someone whispered
from down below. "You can't bring soldiers here!"

But Lark released her hold on Scottie. "They'll kill
her," she said. "We do have to help her." For if they
didn't help the king's victim, then all their talk of freedom and rebellion was nothing more than heated air.

Before she finished speaking, Scottie was out of the
hatch and running empty-handed to the rescue. Lark
scuttled out after him with a tire iron.

The soldiers were surprised to find anyone out here,
much less an enormous dark bulk charging at them like
a bull and yelling like a maniac. They hadn't time to
let go of the girl and draw their guns before Scottie's
big fists hammered one soldier's face in and drove up
under the other's rib cage.

The two of them crawled on the ground, slow and
helpless; they could not even breathe. Scottie towered
over them, menacing with his fists, snarling at them as
if he meant to kill them.

But Scottie was a doctor; Scottie could not finish it.
The crazy rage was already leaving him, and he was
only swaying there, posturing. He had never killed.
Lark had; and before there could be any debate, she
smashed the skulls of both soldiers with the tire iron.

The half-clad palace girl was stumbling away through
the underbrush, crying without sound. Scottie caught
up with her in a few long strides and laid a huge, gentle

hand on her bare shoulder. The girl whirled, her mouth
distended in a mute scream, and she backed away from
him in horror. She turned and ran to one side, straight
through a rose thicket. "Stop. Stop. Stop," Scottie
cried in pain for her. "You're hurting yourself."

The girl's movements only became more panicked
and thrashing. She ran into Lark, threw her arms
around the rebel woman, and clung to her. Her mouth
was open, her eyes flooding tears, but no sound came
forth but her ragged breath. Lark swayed as if cradling
a baby and she stroked the girl's hair. "It's all right.
It's all right. Nobody's going to hurt you now."

Scottie was standing in the brush like a stunned
beast, his bruised hands at his sides. He couldn't believe the girl was cringing from *him*.

By then Detroit had climbed out of the bunker and
come running. She was a tough ragged little twenty-
five-year-old, who stood fully five-one in her block-
heeled black boots. Detroit grabbed the mute girl's pink
dress, white shoes, and combs from the dead soldiers,
tugged on Scottie's arm, and hissed at Lark, "Come
on! There could be others!"

Scottie returned to the bunker, and Lark coaxed the
palace servant along, while Detroit covered their retreat, crouched in the field grass, scanning the woods
with a drawn revolver. When the others were inside,
Detroit jumped down the hatch and capped it over her
head. "I didn't see anyone," she reported. She spoke
to the palace girl. "I think we made it."

The girl still would not talk, could not. She was palace soft, slender, her fair skin crisscrossed with thorn
scratches, her plain-pretty face bruised and red with
crying. Her eyes were hazel, her hair straight and light
brown. Scottie wished she would stop shrinking from
him. He felt enormous and awkward around petite
young women.

She was not only afraid of Scottie but of all the men.
It was cool inside the bunker and she was shivering

in her sheer snagged white silk slip. Lark poured some
whiskey into her and put her own torn khaki jacket
around the girl's narrow shoulders. Lark was not a big
woman but the jacket was roomy on Lark, and the di-
minutive place maid was swimming in it. There just
wasn't much to the girl.

Eventually Lark calmed her enough to answer questions with nods or shakes of her head. Was she from
the palace? *Yes.* Had she committed a crime? *No.* Were
the soldiers going to kill her? *Yes.* Was it an official
order? *No.* Was she being silenced? *Yes and no.* Did
she know why she was being killed? *Yes and no.* Was
it an order of the king's? *No.* Did the king know? A
dubious *no.* Had she been raped? That was Lark's
question, and the girl broke down and could not answer
anything else for quite some time. Lark took the response as a *yes.* Did she know who ordered her death?
Emphatic *yes.* And with that, the girl smoothed a clear
space on the table and traced three letters with her forefinger.

"Well, there it is," said Detroit, to no one's surprise. "The king's viper."

TOW.

The letters seemed to persist after the drawing was
done. The king's assassin. Brigadier General Tow.

But she'd said it was not an official order. "What is
this, then?" said Scottie, puzzled. "Just pure evil on
Tow's part?"

The maid's green-brown eyes darted sideways, wide
with fear and suspicion, to the big dark man. Her lips
were pressed together and tucked in, and drawn down
into an exaggerated frown with deep creases on her
brow. Her expression would have been comical if it
hadn't held such pure fear. Eyes fixed on Scottie, she
nodded very deliberately. *Yes.*

There was a long silence.

"Well, didn't we always know that sort of thing went
on?" said Lark.

"We always suspected. Now we know," said Scottie.

"The king closes his eyes to a lot General Tow does."

The Crown was blind to anything convenient for the Crown to be blind to. The inequalities, the injustices were all-pervasive. Otherwise there would have been no Henry Iver, no incipient rebellion.

"What is your name?" Lark asked the girl.

She traced on the table again: *Terese.*

"You're safe here, Terese," said Lark, patting the maid's torn hands. Lark's hard long-fingered hands were callused and reticulated with deep dry lines. The palace girl's skin, around the scratches, was soft as a baby's. She was in a different world out here. "But I should tell you, you really can't go back."

Terese shrank away, shaking her head. She had no desire to go back. She got up suddenly and cowered into a corner of the bunker, wedging herself between two footlockers, daring anyone to try to pry her loose. She wanted to stay here.

Detroit was drumming on the tabletop with a dried-up pen in nervous tattoo. At length she tossed the pen aside and spoke. "If it's Tow, there probably aren't any other soldiers out there. Just those two henchmen." She turned to Terese. Terese confirmed with a nod. Detroit turned to the others. "We have to move that car and those bodies. Tow is the last man in this kingdom we can afford to come looking for us."

"That gives me an idea," said Scottie. "The good brigadier has the answer."

"Tow? What answer?"

"The best place to lose or find a dead body. No one would blink twice. Least of all the brigadier."

Detroit scowled a moment, then nodded in comprehension. Tow's hometown. It was perfect.

"Farington."

* * *

Chris-John had dozed off. He woke at the sound of the five locks unlatching and the door opening. The ugly youth smiled. "Happy to see me?"

"Yes," said Chris-John.

"Bullshit," said the youth, set down the bag he was carrying, and redid all the locks. Smell of food filled the small room.

"I thought you had been stabbed or shot and I would spend the rest of my life like this," said Chris-John.

"Good point," said the youth, coming to the bedside. "But then you might do that anyway." He reached into the bag and brought out a chicken leg. He bit into it, then got up and went searching for something to wipe his hands on, the drumstick still clenched in his teeth. He came back with a towel, turned on a radio, sat by the bed, and settled down to eat. He tore off a piece of chicken and popped it into Chris-John's mouth. Chris-John chewed slowly. His stomach had shrunk and he didn't really want food anymore, but there was nothing else to do with it.

The youth was sitting on the floor, his back resting against the bed. What varnish was left on the floorboards was aged black, but most of it had been scratched and worn down to the bare wood. The place was cluttered but there was some kind of order to it. The youth himself was clean; his clothes fit well on his strong build; there was no dirt under his fingernails. He was ugly but he had a style—a subterranean creature with a vague instinct for something better.

He was thumbing through the soggy book Chris-John had been clutching when the youth had found him. "Can you read?"

Chris-John swallowed. "Yes," he said. The youth popped another piece of chicken in his mouth.

"Where are you from?"

"Delancyville," said Chris-John.

"We-ell-ell," said the youth with a grand, pompous frown and a strutting shift to his shoulders with each drawn-out syllable. "I could've guessed, you know. The clothes would've fooled anybody else. Not me. It's the way you talk." If there was a class Farington despised, it was the upper-middle class, the likes of Delancyville, even more than royalty. Because the upper-middle class was made up a commoners like themselves who dressed, acted, were treated, and thought they were better. Royalty was royalty, a breed apart, inaccessible, not within reach even of envy.

Chris-John had been dressed like a poor commoner in a pullover sweater and corduroy trousers, not in his native frock coat, waistcoat, breeches, stockings, silver-buckled shoes, and tricorne hat. Chris-John had been a student of Henry Iver too long to dress like that. He wore no wig and his black curls were short and completely unarranged.

The youth offered Chris-John another bite of chicken, Chris-John couldn't take it. "I'm full."

"Eat it," said the youth, and popped it in his mouth. Chris-John chewed very slowly.

"Want some milk?"

"Yes, please."

"Please? I can't stand it!" the youth cried. He reached into the bag and pulled out a carton of milk and a straw. "I brought this for you, see? I don't drink the stuff myself. You look like you do." He opened the carton and set it on the bed, and put the straw in Chris-John's mouth. For himself he'd brought a bottle of liquor.

It was growing dark. The youth lit a lantern. There were no light curfews in Farington. One did what one had strength to get away with.

Chris-John heard voices outside in the street. They sounded a few stories down. Chris-John guessed that the outer walls were sheer, for there were no bars on the side windows.

Someone was calling. "Phoenix! Hey, Phoenix! I wanna screw!"

The youth, Phoenix, got to his feet and threw open

a window. "Screw yourself, pisscock! Who needs you!" he yelled, and slammed down the window. He turned away, muttering Farington curses. With common use, the words lost their impact, so he had to string a lot of them together to get any effect. He sat down and finished his dinner.

He let Chris-John up to use the toilet, keeping hold of him the whole time, not that Chris-John was going anywhere. There was really nowhere to go. The street held for him the same or worse. And even if it hadn't, Chris-John had no will of his own anymore. He went where he was led, and he meekly lay down and let Phoenix tie him back to the bed.

Phoenix reached into his bag, "I brought you something else." He brought out a jar of petroleum jelly, and he crumbled the empty bag and threw it away.

Chris-John looked at it, uncomprehending.

"Something to make your life easier," said Phoenix, and caressed Chris-John's buttocks. Growing excited, Phoenix quickly took off his clothes and climbed to sit astride Chris-John. "This is it, kid. Beg for mercy. I'm gonna do you all night."

Chris-John didn't beg. Chris-John didn't do anything.

And Phoenix did not stay hard for a moment. He became incensed that he couldn't keep it up. He told Chris-John to scream. Chris-John lay still in futility.

Phoenix threw the unopened jar of jelly across the room. He jumped off. "That does it. When you get it, you're gonna get it hard. You wait," He sat on the floor in an angry pout and unstopped his liquor bottle.

He changed the radio station. There were only two. He couldn't figure why radios where made with so many numbers on them.

After a time he calmed. He glanced aside at his captive and his gaze held.

Chris-John was one of nature's stunning beauties, eternally young, lineless, not masculine, not really feminine, simply lovely youth. His skin was a rich light brown, with a luster like ivory, like polished wood, like velvet. His body was slender, mostly hairless, and taut, with fluid curves to his calves, his thighs, his rounded ass—to which Phoenix's focus always returned—his shoulder blades, and the femininely smooth muscles in his arms. His hair curled in tiny black ringlets, one fallen across his sweet brow like some kind of angel child. Phoenix felt low stirrings but was becoming afraid to try again. He had a horrible thought stowed away at the rear of his consciousness that he was not really cut out to be a rapist. It just wasn't possible. Not with his breeding.

He cleaned the milk from Chris-John's straw and offered him a drink of liquor. Chris-John took a half-hearted sip.

Phoenix cracked the book again and leafed through its ripply watermarked pages. "Is it filth?" he asked Chris-John.

"Sedition," said Chris-John.

"You wrote it?"

"Henry Iver."

"They hanged him," said Phoenix.

"I know," said Chris-John.

Phoenix came to the handwritten inscription in the front. He held it open for Chris-John. "What's this say?"

Chris-John read, " 'To my dear friend Chris-John.' "

"Is that you?"

"Yes."

"No kidding. I never knew anyone who wrote books. Don't know too many people who can write their names." He pointed to the poem printed beneath the inscription. "What's this say in the blocks?"

Chris-John started to read, then his vision blurred and he was reciting from memory, his voice wavering:

"We are living free,
Though there's blood been shed,
And we'll always be,
Be Chicago Red."

"What's that mean?" said Phoenix.

"It's talking about the rebellion," said Chris-John shakily.

"What rebellion?"

"The one that must be, against the Crown. It means we were meant to be free. It means tyranny is only a temporary unnatural state that cannot last, because it is unnatural." He swallowed, blinked his eyes. He was trembling. "It means even after they executed all those people in the Chicago purge—even if Chicago is a river of blood—people would still stand up and declare freedom. It means—Oh, my God—" Chris-John started screaming.

Phoenix jumped at the sudden outcry. "O no," he said. He got up and hesitated over the hysterical boy, completely at a loss. "No. Don't, honey, don't." He stroked Chris-John's smooth back, felt all its muscles tightened, drawing in breath in great quavering gasps. Chris-John screamed and screamed, shrill and raw, his face red.

In a panic, Phoenix untied all his bonds, gathered him into his arms, and held him tight to keep him from clawing himself and pulling out his own hair. Chris-John shrieked, crying wildly. Phoenix stroked him, rocking him in his arms, talking comfort. He paused once to ask, "What the hell am I doing?"

Chris-John was screaming. Phoenix was not aroused at all.

"Oh, what the hell." Phoenix pressed Chris-John's face against his chest and petted him.

When Chris-John was too exhausted to cry anymore, he curled up in a ball with a sheet in the bed, his eyes seeping tears.

Phoenix swore up a blue streak. "Who am I gonna fuck now!" He stormed to the window, threw it wide, and yelled, "Fuck me! Fuck me!"

Hoots and catcalls from a few strays in Farington's midnight streets answered him. He slammed the window shut with a resolve. He turned to Chris-John. "If I can't have you, no one else will either."

In the early morning, in the gray light before dawn, Phoenix strapped a set of brass knuckles to his hand and slipped a throwing knife into his boot. He cast a cold yellow eye at Chris-John, who quietly assumed he was about to be killed.

Phoenix slid open a drawer and took out Chris-John's clothes. He threw them on Chris-John all in a wrinkled wad, clean and smelling faintly of cheap harsh soap. When Chris-John hesitated, Phoenix snarled, "Well, go on, dammit."

Chris-John dressed. As he slipped on his shoes, Phoenix unlatched the five locks on the door and peered out. "OK." He signaled for Chris-John to come.

Phoenix turned once on the wooden stairs as they descended. "God, you're loud."

"Sorry."

Phoenix glanced down disparagingly. "Those are stupid shoes." He continued down, Chris-John tiptoeing after him.

He pushed through the door to the dank narrow street. Tall blocky buildings cramped one against the other. Old, they were all old, and so many of them, one could only think there must have been a whole lot more people in the Beforetime in the Kingdom of America than there were now.

Chris-John stepped out where he could look up between buildings to glimpse the last stars in the dingy twilight sky. A rough hand on his collar jerked him back against the shadowed wall. Thick lips against his ear hissed, "I'm surprised I didn't have to teach you to piss. Jesus H.R.M. Christ. Follow me."

Phoenix led the way, walking close to walls, crossing streets in black shadows. He whispered, "Unless you're the strongest man in town, you better give a shit who knows where you are. Stay out of sight, but if someone sees you, you don't want to look like you're hiding."

Chris-John tried to imitate his manner. Phoenix moved with the smooth belligerence of a carrion crow, arrogant but quiet about it.

Past the city limits, on the Capital Road, Phoenix became jumpy, looking over his shoulder, casting apprehensive glances at the woods on either side. Chris-John grew frightened to see the cocksure street soldier becoming so edgy; he'd thought it was becoming safer.

And it *was* safer. Phoenix was simply out of his element. The forest frightened him. Open space and civilized roads frightened him.

As Chris-John relaxed, Phoenix was unraveling. When the road turned, threatening to take the steel and concrete buildings out of view, Phoenix broke down; he could not go any farther. "You're on your own, kid," he said, already starting to trot back the way he'd come, as if pulled by a magnet. He turned once to shout—still walking backward. "And don't you dare tell anyone about this! Anyone asks, I screwed your brains out!" And he turned around and ran back to the streets of Farington, *home*.

Chris-John had walked two miles, hugging his book. He was crossing a stretch of road through once-cultivated fields where grapevines now grew wild, when a cloud of dust appeared up ahead, and too fast for Chris-John to take cover, two military cars came cresting over the hill. Chris-John froze in the road, holding his seditious book, wide-eyed and doomed. He had cut down Henry Iver. The Crown would have its way with him now.

His brown hands whitened on his book and he

breathed like a prayer, "We are living free, though there's blood been shed, and we'll always be, be Chicago Red . . . Chicago Red . . . Chicago Red. . . ."

The cars were upon him, army green horrors, roaring damnation at him with choking exhaust and flying dust.

They passed him by.

Chris-John turned in disbelief and watched them disappear in their dust clouds, bound for Farington.

"Chicago Red . . . Chicago Red . . . Chicago Red . . ."

"This is far enough," said Detroit. "Stop the car, Scottie."

They had been seen by one witness already—the kid back there in the road, in the middle of nowhere. Detroit had looked out of the rear window of the car to see the boy turned around in the road and watching back with a look of utter astonishment in the most beautiful pair of eyes Detroit had even seen.

Scottie slowed the car to a stop. The follow car, driven by Lark, swung around in front a few hundred feet and came to a stop. They were within Farington limits, though not yet to the jungle of its congested buildings. This was quite far enough.

Scottie positioned the dead soldiers in the front seat of their own car. He took all the things a Faringtoner might take—the car's battery, the radio, and the soldiers' purses, which were heavy with gold; Tow paid his men in advance. Scottie siphoned the fuel out of the tank and put it in the rebel car. He shot the soldiers' guns empty and threw them in the ditch; it would brand the killing as rebel work to keep the guns; Faringtoners did not keep what they could not reload.

Then he set the soldiers' car on fire and ran.

Detroit sighed at the heartbreaking waste of a fortune in rare equipment, but no price was too steep, no action too cautious when they were dealing with General Tow.

Automobiles were Detroit's passion. She always wore black because she was always grease-stained. She always smelled slightly of motor oil with a thick overlay of cheap lilac perfume, which was making Lark motion sick right now.

Scottie turned the rebel car around and drove quickly out of Farington. The gunshots and fire would soon attract the town's scavengers.

"What about this kid up here," said Lark as they approached the place where they'd passed the slight young man carrying a book.

"Leave him," said Scottie.

"Pick him up!" Detroit cried. Something in his eyes. "He's not Crown and he's not Farington. I'll swear it." He'd been scared to death when he'd seen the military vehicles coming at him. And he was walking *out* of Farington. Detroit sat on the edge of her seat and pointed. "There he is."

Scottie slowed the car. The boy froze in the road as the military car drew alongside. He was clutching a book to his chest and mumbling with his eyes shut. Detroit jumped out of the car and caught his last two mumbled words: "Chicago Red."

"OK, Chicago Red," said Detroit, circling around to face him, her fists on her hips. The boy-man was nearly as short as she was, though not nearly as sturdy. Like the waif Terese, he looked like he might blow away on a wayward breeze. "Where are you headed?"

Before Chris-John could stammer out an answer, Scottie leaned out of the car window and cried, *"Chicago Red?"*

"That's what he said," Detroit called back.

"His book," said Scottie. "Detroit, what's the book?"

Detroit looked at Scottie queerly, then pried the book loose from the petrified Chris-John, who held it as in a death grip. Detroit read the title and crowed, waving the book in the air, *"Freedom for America,* by Henry Iver. He's one of ours!''

Chris-John opened his beautiful eyes in startled wonder.

"Good thing we got you before some real soldiers did.'' The dark-haired girl Detroit was talking to him. Then she pushed him. "In the car quick,'' she ordered.

Chris-John let himself be ushered into the car. He felt lost without his book, which the three rebels passed around among themselves in reverent eagerness. They thought all the copies of Henry Iver's book had been destroyed. They ran their hands over it and read passages aloud to each other. Lark found the inscription. She asked if he was Chris-John. He told her yes; and Lark and Detroit were in instant awe of a personal friend of the legendary Henry Iver. Scottie was not happy. Alarms were ringing for Scottie, who did not like this mumbling lost-child fanatic at all. "Where can I take you?'' Scottie growled.

"I don't know. I can't go home.''

The rebels took Chris-John back to their bunker against Scottie's better judgment. The bunker was a closely guarded secret. They would never find another like it should they lose this one to soldiers. Scottie did not like to bring in wild-eyed strangers. Fate had brought Terese to them. They didn't have to bring this Chris-John themselves.

The others immediately found Chris-John captivating, and even Terese was not afraid of him. There was a visionary quality about him. And Scottie never trusted visionaries.

"Why can't you go home?''

Chris-John lowered his long lashes, placed his hand upon his book. "The Crown will be looking for me.'' Of course he couldn't go home. Not while any monarch ruled America. His eyes focused and the lost-child look was replaced with an air of purpose.

"What are you wanted for?''

And in the midst of a directionless, disheartened knot of rebels in need of a totem Chris-John told them very quietly that he had cut Henry Iver down.

And so it began.

Part One:
The Kingdom

I.

The Crown

THE FARMING VILLAGE OF GRAINVILLE CORNER HAD been short in its taxes two years running, so this year the Crown impounded the entire corn crop before the stalks were knee-high. To isolate the town, its train stop was eliminated, and to make certain the villagers did not neglect the Crown's corn, a garrison of soldiers moved in.

It was midnight, in the height of summer. A lonely whistle of a passing train sounded through the cornfields.

In the morning the soldiers of the garrison woke to find the town empty. The gold-green sea of young cornstalks waved in the wind around a ghost town.

The Crown ordered the unhappy soldiers to tend the corn themselves since they had let their workers get away.

At the end of a long hot season, on the eve of the harvest, the soldiers woke to find the cornfields stripped clean by a silent horde come and gone in the night.

The story was repeated all over the land like a folktale.

Asked who had done this, the name they were given to say was Chicago Red.

Scottie Deerborne was a practical man. He had been the closest thing to a leader that the rebels had before they pulled this babbling lost waif off the Farington street two years ago. In those two years Chris-John had taken over as if the rebellion belonged to him, as if he had invented it, and Scottie wondered if they could not just put him back where they'd found him. Pandora's box was one of the few legends that the Crown allowed to survive from the Beforetime and encouraged the retelling. The tale was on Scottie's mind often of late.

He preferred simple reason to wild dreams and emotional appeals. But people responded to dreams and symbols.

Starting with Grainville Corner, Chris-John/Chicago Red organized a series of raids he called "backfire sanctions." Scottie called them dumb stunts and was appalled that these were what drew people to the cause more than the commonsense fact that self-rule was better than tyranny.

In the town of Edgecliff, whose main industry was a paper factory, a child broke the light curfew.

The Crown had a practice of punishing an entire town for a failing of a few of its residents—the idea being that if everyone was liable for the crime, then everyone would take better care to keep his brother in line. For the violation of the light curfew, the regional governor confiscated the whole town's lamps. Soldiers patrolled at night to make sure there were no lanterns in Edgecliff.

Upon their arrival one night they found not darkness but lights, hundreds, thousands, lining all the streets and walks and the river edge, like heaven turned upside down, all the lights on the ground instead of in the sky. The townsmen were wandering the streets in astonishment like wide-eyed children, and folk were coming from miles around to view this wondrous sight. They strolled the light-lined lanes and climbed the tallest buildings to see the land mapped in white lights.

It was so breathtaking that the soldiers did not dare touch it. They signaled their commander, and he came right away.

He stormed out of his car, brandishing a swagger stick. "Who did this!" He grabbed a strolling townsman. "Who did this!"

The officer's wrath confused the townsman. "They were here all day, sir. They came in cars pulling wagons. We thought—" He foundered. Of course they thought nothing amiss. Only Crown officials drove cars. So some of the villagers had actually helped the strangers.

Daylight. They had done it in broad daylight.

The commander yelled, "Where did all those lanterns come from!"

"The-they're not lanterns, sir."

The commander stalked to one of the softly flickering lights. "Bags!"

Each light was a candle set inside a white paper bag, such as the factory produced.

The commander swept the makeshift lantern away with his swagger stick. The white paper burst into flame and burned out in a moment. "Paper bags!" The commander shrieked for them all to be put out.

Townsmen stared, and soldiers hesitated. "It's grand pretty, sir."

"Burn it! Burn it!" The commander kicked over bags, picked them up, and hurled them at the buildings. "They want fire? Burn everything."

The first house was beginning to take the flame when it began to rain.

That was divine intervention if ever anyone saw it. A lieutenant called the governor and managed to get the commander recalled before he could get them all struck by lightning.

So the lights of Edgecliff gave divine sanction to Chicago Red. Never mind, thought Scottie Deerborne, who had misplaced God quite some time ago, that if the soldiers had just stayed calm, God would have rained on Chicago Red's candles instead of on the Crown's conflagration.

But the daring deeds worked miracles. Chris-John fired the imagination. He gave heart to Henry Iver's words of freedom. From such things armies were raised, and within two years after the arrival of Chicago Red, the Revolution found its legs and began to run.

Meanwhile Chris-John was working on wings.

The summer sun beat down on the Capital, gleaming off its picture-pretty buildings and the horse-drawn carriages and polished automobiles of the royalty. Gentlemen tipped their tricorne hats to ladies dressed in full skirts and carrying parasols, strolling down tree-lined promenades along red-brick garden walls topped with white stone borders and framed between ornamental piers. The brick or cobblestone streets were lined with charming little shops with their wares displayed in leaded-glass picture windows. Even the twenty-five-foot-high perimeter wall rising in its whitewashed stone courses around the Capital with soaring guard towers at every corner was pretty.

The folk of the common classes sweltered in the summer heat, filling orders for the gentry, bringing in produce from the outside in their mule carts, while the craftsmen and merchants went bustling about the day's business, trying to stay out of the sun.

Storms brewed inside the cooled walls of the red-brick Capitol building, where the officials and generals of King Edward III's council conferred inside a spacious room under a painted ceiling between dadoed and pilastered walls with white cornices. Condensation was forming on the wide windows behind sheer damask curtains. Along one wall, a tall clock was beating out the hour again. The ten men were growing irritable. Their pacing foot tracks pressed crossing paths into the carpet.

Commander General Lindy was baffled that these stupid officers and politicians could not agree with him on the obvious course of action. He was baffled that the king should expect him to consult with lesser beings at all.

"Gentlemen," Lindy began again in a strained, overly polite voice. "The rebellion is a shallow one— obviously. Of course they were successful at first in overthrowing the local governor and militia in Seattle— they used all their resources, but that was the full extent of their power—obviously. They planned only so far, now they've all gone underground again simply because they didn't think any further ahead. They weren't prepared for the arrival of the Fifth Army. All this is obvious."

"Care to get on with it?" said Secretary Shie. His round face and shiny bald dome shone brilliant red within the snowy wreath of his hair. "You've been repeating that for the past two hours; now what do you propose to do with this 'obvious' situation."

Lindy opened his hairy hands and nodded. "I know you're all tired—"

"Obviously." The voice cut in from the far side of the room. "Sir."

The others turned to look at who had spoken.

The brigadier lounged in a wing-back armchair near the door. A refined, trim figure, always well groomed, he was just under six feet tall standing up, with boyish hips and a waist slim as an athlete's. His hair was fine, light brown, clipped very close to his well-shaped head. His face, his sloping brow, straight nose, and high cheekbones looked carved, perfect as a statue and as cold. Aristocratic hands rested lightly on his chair's wide arms.

Commander General Lindy narrowed his black eyes at him. "That's the first thing you've said all afternoon, Tow. Too bad it couldn't have been constructive."

"Thank God someone is spare of words today." General Martel sighed, leaning heavily on his knobby cane, and he rolled his eyes to Tow in almost gratitude.

Tow returned a slight nod to the old gentleman-general and lifted his hand partly from the arm of his chair in languid acknowledgment.

Then the Council officials were quick to turn away from the brigadier again and return to the problem of the erratic rebel activities in Seattle.

Brigadier General Tow was silent, sitting back, watching, bored, sometimes wryly amused. He was the youngest man in the room except for the two aides flanking the door. He was outranked by everyone else in the room—except for the aides—but in these conferences rank mattered for little.

Tow turned his attention to the two aides at the door. The imperious and starched-looking fresh-scrubbed college boy was Chancellor Franklin's aide; the other was Secretary of State Shie's new aide, a lad of twenty named William Stanton. Tow chuckled to himself as he watched the latter's bewildered expression at the proceedings. Tow soon ignored the arguing officials entirely and watched William's reactions to the heretofore-believed-dignified generals and statesmen, the most powerful men in the Kingdom. Though on the verge of laughter, Tow's expression remained cool, almost contemptuous as always.

As he watched, Admiral Kester's voice rose above the others, punctuating his speech with less than polite language, which, to judge from the young aide's startled expression, William had never heard before, and Tow turned away, suppressing a smile. Genuine naïveté was hard to find.

William had no idea he was under observation, and mutely stood in his place, watching the generals yell at each other. The lad was nothing like his father, the dusky demonic-looking overbearing Colonel Stanton, whom Tow despised. The son was of more poetic build, large-boned but willowy, medium tall, gentle-eyed and fair. His hair was light brown, straight and fine. He had a look of intelligence but extreme innocence. He was skinny, his exquisite bones showing clear, which only added to his wide-eyed look. No, there was nothing of the father in the son.

Colonel Stanton would have been at this long-winded meeting but he was in Seattle, commanding the Fifth Army.

Tow sat back drowsily, wondering with a vague curiosity what it would be like to shoot Lindy. Probably the same as anyone else, he thought, and yawned. Tow never said much in conferences, and he wondered why he had to attend them—as he was sure Lindy and the others wondered also. They hated Tow. They hated him because he was a lowly brigadier counted among their august number, they hated him because of his origins. Unlike most of them Tow hadn't come from a wealthy family that bought him through the military academy or some fine school. Tow had been picked off a Farington street to be hanged and had ended up somehow as the king's triggerman instead. Most of all they hated him because they were afraid of him. When someone displeased the king, that someone sometimes disappeared, and the officials had a good idea who was behind the disappearance. But what frightened them was that Tow did not restrict his victims to those King Edward designated.

Tow's steel gray eyes drifted across the room. At one side, heavyset Lindy was shaking his hairy fists at Franklin as if he would hit the calm, elderly politician. Franklin's composure never failed him, the picture of a venerable statesman with crystal blue eyes. Lindy turned scarlet with rage, his lips purple, his thick black hair matted with sweat on his broad brow, and he sprayed saliva as he talked. *Some*one ought to shoot him, thought Tow. For aesthetic reasons, if nothing else.

On the other side of the room Admiral Kester was scorching the air blue. The ramrod-backed martinet was clamoring for a chance to use his feeble navy against the insurgents in Seattle. Since the consolidation of the northern tribes, America was the only country on Earth—according to royal edict—and had little use for its navy. And since it was forbidden for ships to go out into open ocean, the navy spent its time pulling yachts and fishing boats off the shoals. A useless entity and a useless officer.

Secretary Shie was intently not listening to him, for which Shie had a great talent.

William Stanton was staring toward the crystal chandelier. Tow looked from William to the chandelier then back again, wondering what it was the boy saw. *Where are you?* he thought, looking at the young man's wistful pale brown eyes. *Far away from here, apparently.*

Suddenly the great walnut double doors swung wide and everyone stood and snapped to attention as the king stormed into the center of the room. Even Tow uncoiled from his armchair and stood. He noticed the boy William Stanton stiffen bolt-straight, his eyes huge. The boy had never been in the royal presence before and still regarded Edward III as something of a god.

And Tow knew the king could be impressive on first sight—or on one-hundredth sight—a tall man, with square lofty brow, and noble Roman nose. He carried himself with royal bearing, and his anger was frightening, though excessive rage diminished him. He wore no wig today. His hair, pulled back with a satin ribbon, was brown with silvered blaze at his temples. His frock coat was white silk, glittering with zircons round its embroidered edges. Snowy cascades of ruffled lace made up his jabot and his cuffs. Once a great ladies' man, he still made hearts beat fast at age sixty-two—being monarch could do that, had he all the presence of a toad, or a General Lindy. But Edward III had little time for dalliance these days.

The king whirled at the table to face his council, and he brandished a fistful of papers at them. "Chicago Red."

"Sire?" Shie queried uncertainly.

King Edward threw the papers on the carpet. "What is Chicago Red!" he demanded, furious at finding himself utterly in the dark about something he suspected he really ought to know.

"Sounds like a brand name." Lindy shrugged.

Franklin spoke. "It's a code name for a . . . what should I call him—a demagogue, a revolutionary, a rebel leader."

Secretary of State Shie gave a disdainful smile. "Of what rebels?" he said.

The king wheeled on Shie. "Don't you do that to me!" The flat of his hand boomed on the walnut table and shook all the glasses. "Don't you *ever* hide things from me!" his command thundered. "What am I? A common subject to be dazzled with your rosy propaganda? Talk to me!"

"There are a growing number of rebels—right here near the Capital," Franklin answered. "This Chicago Red seems to be their rallying point."

"So who is he?" said the king.

"No one knows, sire," said Shie. "That's the reason for the idiotic name."

"Not idiotic," said Franklin. "Ominous rather. He is to be taken seriously."

The king scowled. "He is to be taken" was a diplomat's way of giving an order to a king; "*you* must take him." The only person with the nerve to come out and speak bluntly was Tow.

"Ominous? How so?" said the king.

"Those are the last two words of a seditious poem praising the dead in that Chicago bloodbath three years ago," said Franklin. "It was written by Henry Iver."

Henry Iver. Edward III clenched his fists to hear that name again. The man was dead and still he was a plague. *Die, for God's sake, die, Henry Iver!* "What poem?" said the king.

Franklin answered, "I believe it goes thus." He cleared his throat.

"We are living free,
Though there's blood been shed,
And we'll always be,
Be Chicago Red.''

The king turned to General Tow. "What do you make of that?"

"Singsong tripe," said Tow, bored.

"Do you have anything else to offer besides literary criticism, Tow?"

"Yes, sire," said Tow. "If you like. I told you you should not have executed that man in public. Now you have a martyr and the rebels banding around his legacy. *You* created this Chicago Red, sire.''

"Mind whom you're talking to," the king growled.

"Mind who *you* are talking to," Tow returned, leaving the others aghast, holding their breath. Not only rude, it sounded like a threat, but then Tow continued, simply rude, "If you wanted a polite, well-educated yes-man with genteel manners, you can pick them out of any college—I see you've already got a room full of them—you didn't have to look where you found me."

The king took Tow aside to one corner of the wide chamber and whispered harshly, "Watch your tongue or—" He stopped before he said something absurd.

Tow finished for him. "Or you'll point me out to your assassin? I am your assassin. And if you're thinking of hiring a new one, remember what happened to the old one. I can keep my job the same way I got it.''

"Tow, you can be disposed of. It would take fourteen men, but you can die like anyone else.'' Tow's gun held thirteen rounds—one in the chamber, twelve in the clip.

"You are going to kill me, then?" said Tow.

"No, and don't look so smug about it. Speak to me so frankly only in private—you *are* aware that some things are fit only for private, are you not?"

Tow did a lot in private that the king preferred to

ignore, and would continue to ignore as long as Tow was discreet.

"Yes, sire."

"In front of others you will be civil—and don't tell me you haven't learned how. You are able to pass for royalty if it pleases you."

"Yes, sire," said Tow, pleased at the comment on his impersonation of class. Those who did not know better assumed Tow was an aristocrat.

"And I expect an apology before them." The king motioned to his staff across the room.

That command was pure power play. None of these men was deceived as to what Tow was; no one expected, wanted, or would believe an apology from him. An apology would be just to prove that the king could make him do it.

"Do you want me to grovel?" said Tow.

"A simple apology will do. I trust you remember what the floor tastes like."

Edward looked for Tow's cheeks to blanch or flush, but there was no change, and not a flicker in the eyes that were as cold and still and hard as a viper's. But the king needed no reaction to know he'd hit target. He knew Tow—had almost created him—and knew anyone else would have died for that remark. Knew that he might yet. The king's control of his creation was weakening as the creature took on more and more a life and will of its own. Edward knew he should kill Tow, now before it was too late, but he couldn't—and didn't know why.

Tow turned back to the others and announced to all in the room, "Majesty, gentlemen, if I have offended, my apologies." And he snapped his heels together and gave a courtly half-bow.

The king nearly sighed, defeated. Tow had done it again. He could take what would mortify the others and make it a thing of pride. Most of the king's high officials would gag on the humble words, strangle on their stiff collars, and they would mumble and sweat. Tow pulled it off with the grace of a prince, nothing lost. How, when he was in reality the underside of humanity?

The king returned to the matter at hand. "Chancellor," he barked.

"Yes, sire," said Franklin.

"You tell me this Chicago Red is a local criminal."

"Yes, sire."

"Then tell me why his name has appeared in Seattle!"

The blue-eyed politician was at a loss. "I don't know, sire. The rebels simply are not that organized. Not coast to coast. It's impossible."

The king made the beginnings of a stoop to reach for the papers he'd thrown on the carpet, and immediately the five nearest men dove to retrieve the documents for him. Tow remained aloof, watching the five rear ends suddenly stuck up in the air. *What are all these asses I see?*

The king took the papers, which were transcripts of rebel radio conversations, and shoved them at Franklin. Chicago Red was named in all of them. "These are from Seattle. Tell me impossible!"

Franklin looked through the transcripts. He held his ground. "There's nothing to indicate that this is the same local Chicago Red. It must be rebel vogue for a leader to adopt that name. There is no centralization of command to this rebellion. I still have to say impossible, sire."

The king turned to Lindy. "Impossible?"

"Yes, sire," Lindy concurred. "The rebellion in Seattle folded up at the first appearance of the Fifth Army. They've gone to earth. There's no organization there. A few punitive measures and they'll never raise their heads again."

The king turned to Tow. "What do you think of that?"

Tow shook his head. "Something doesn't smell right."

Lindy scoffed at such a nonsensical statement and appealed, smiling forbearingly, to the king. "Sire."

"My brigadier has a good sense of smell," said the king without humor.

Lindy's smile withered, and he backed down in the face of the king's support for what Lindy mocked. "Sire, how can I answer you?" said Lindy, abashed. "He's wrong. Dead wrong."

"As you say, General," said the king, giving Lindy the benefit of the disagreement. "What is your proposed course of action?"

"Attack," said Lindy. His gestures became jerky, quick, and excited. He wiped beads of perspiration from his upper lip with the back of his hand, even in the cooled room. "Send the Fifth Army in there to flush out the rebel core. Put the city under martial law. What rebels we don't find, the citizens will turn over to us when they see what trouble they've caused them. It's obvious the rebels have fed the good people with all kinds of promises. When they see the reality of what the rebellion means, they'll want done with them quickly and have their life return to normal."

The king glanced to Tow, who shook his head. The king made his final decision. "Give the order, Lindy. It's your project."

"Thank you, sire!"

And the king adjourned the meeting. General Tow was first out the doors, before even the king.

Chancellor Franklin watched him leave. He detained the king a moment, "Sire, I beg you to get rid of that man. The sooner the better. He's a creature."

"He is *my* creature," said the king. "And I will decide what is to be done with him when, understood, Chancellor?"

"Yes, sire."

* * *

"You must be proud of your father, William," said Secretary Shie absently behind his expansive desk. The secretary of state looked like a round, middle-aged pixie, with a wreath of white hair round the back of his head from temple to temple and springing in a little tuft on top in front. He played the palace Santa Claus at Christmastime.

"Yes, sir," said Will, standing by the window waiting for orders.

Shie scratched behind his ear with the blunt end of his pen. He was not actually talking to Will. Aides were nonpersons, functional pieces of equipment, conveniences. The only time they received direct attention was when they malfunctioned and needed replacing. Shie was merely thinking aloud. "Military governor of Seattle," said the secretary. It was a position Shie thought he would enjoy. "I suppose he'll get a promotion after this is all over," he said without warmth. Bryon Stanton was the hero of the day, the man who had quelled the Seattle uprising with his mere approach. A promotion was inevitable. And promotions other than his own discomfited Shie.

William waited, quiet and inobtrusive as the woodwork. He gazed out the window toward a little fruit stand down in the street where two soldiers were helping themselves to the wares while the owner protested, waving his arms and shouting. The soldiers were laughing and taunting the little man, though Will could not hear them through the closed windows. The vendor grew more irate, and the soldiers overturned the fruit stand into the street. Will was astounded. He could not imagine anyone hurting another human being for fun. He watched the little man scurrying around in the street trying to rescue his fruit while carriages rolled over them, and horses and people trod them. Some little children ran off with some oranges. Finally the owner just sat down on the curb, his head in his hands. Will was upset.

"Your father must be proud of you, William," said Shie vacantly. "You've done well for yourself."

No, my father is not proud and I haven't done anything, thought Will. Bryon Stanton had been a captain of the cavalry at age twenty. Bryon Stanton made sure his son knew that. At age twenty Will Stanton was a palace aide, with the rank of lieutenant and the duties of a sergeant orderly. A glorified servant. It was all he was good for. Bryon said his son had the heart of a girl.

Will was aware that the secretary did not want a real answer. "Yes, sir," he said. Will was naive but not unperceptive.

"Any other boys in the family?" said Shie.

"No, sir. Not really."

"Not really?" That was a peculiar answer. Shie looked up with his first real interest.

"I had two brothers," said Will. "One is dead. The other is missing."

"Missing?" said Shie cautiously. "Missing" was a bad word these troubled days. " 'Missing' as in 'missing in action'?"

" ' Missing' as in 'on the suspected rebels list,' sir," said Will.

Shie was gravely alarmed. He shuffled through the records in his desk quickly. "I didn't know that. How did you get palace clearance with a rebel in the family?"

"Suspected rebel, sir. My father got me clearance."

"I see, I see," said Shie in great consternation. This was bad business, this was. Association could drag a name down very fast. Shie made it a point not to associate with the wrong people. Shie did not get where he was by accident, and he hoped to get further. Chancellor Franklin could not live forever. The secretary cleared his throat, stammered around. "There's a grievous mistake in here somewhere. *Ahem.* Yes, a mistake." He straightened a stack of papers on his desk. "I'm afraid, my boy, I'm going to have to let you go. You understand, don't you, lad?"

Will understood. He understood what his father was going to do to him.

Secretary Shie did not look at Will. He set about reordering his desk. The boy was still standing there. Shie grew irritated. He looked around the room for an excuse to get out.

It was then that he noticed General Tow standing in the door. The sudden sight of the handsome figure chilled, the dread familiar army green jacket without medals. Tow never presumed to gentry's clothing—or else he disdained it. His appearance was always cool simplicity, like the clean lines of his automatic. Shie hadn't heard the assassin come in. How long had *he* been there?

Whatever Tow had to say was best heard without witnesses. Shie gestured impatiently to Will. "Leave us."

"How dare you give orders to my aide in my presence," said Tow evenly.

"Your—" Shie sputtered, taken for a momentary loss. What was his game? *I hate this man.* Shie's thoughts raced. What was Tow doing? Why did Tow need an aide? Didn't he have an aide? Tow went through aides like bottles of wine. All the palace officials did— except that Tow's were seldom seen again. Tow wanted Stanton for some reason. What was this strategy? Was there an advantage that Shie had overlooked? Perhaps he'd been too hasty dismissing the lad. "Actually I haven't let him go yet officially," said Shie.

Tow laughed. Shie cringed inwardly. Few things were as terrifying as Tow's laughter.

Perhaps Tow knew something about the elder Stanton that Shie did not. The Stanton name must be held in high regard by the Crown to survive the damage of a suspected rebel son. Higher regard than Shie had first thought. Yes, that had to be it. This weasely climber out of Farington was going to attach himself to a rising name. Shie turned to Will with a nervous condescending smile. "William, my boy, you know what I said wasn't official."

Tow's eyebrows were high, his lids low, and he made sideways eye contact with Will—the gesture making Shie's words sound very very lame. "Come with me," Tow said.

"Stay, that's an order," said Shie as Will started to move. Will froze, torn and uncertain; he looked to Shie, looked to the young general. Shie never looked directly at Will. Tow was looking him straight in the eyes. Tow cocked his head in a beckoning gesture, a wordless *Let's go*.

Will moved toward him, definitely this time, and he felt an enormous dull weight lift from his soul—a weight named Shie—and he kept walking, feeling incredibly light, even as Shie's bellowing pursued them all the way down the corridor.

Scottie Deerborne sat on the dusty couch that had been falling apart for a long time. A single kerosene lantern with its wick turned low shed its yellow light in the bunker. Scottie frowned at the small ethereal figure of the one they called Chicago Red seated cross-legged on top of the table.

It had been two years since they had found Chris-John in the road outside Farington. Chris-John was a siren. He was immune to age. How long could a boy stay at the bloom of youth like that? Two years had done absolutely nothing to him—except make him a legend—the rebellion's dark-eyed god. Soft voice spoke and it was done. Eyes enchanted. He was the only male the mad girl Terese would come near. Scottie called Terese mad because she still did not talk, and because she worshiped Chicago Red.

Scottie and Chris-John were alone in the bunker just now, and Scottie watched him in growing aggravation.

Do something.

If the rebels of the Kingdom must wait for Chris-John's every word with held breath, then Chris-John could at least say something to them.

Chicago Red's Pacific-coast contact called himself Atlantis on the radio. In case of surveillance the name might point the Crown's bloodhounds in the opposite direction. Atlantis did not make a move without approval from Chicago Red.

But the last word Chris-John had sent to Atlantis in Seattle had been weeks ago, at the approach of the king's Fifth Army. It was time for action, and Chicago Red was strangely silent.

Chris-John sat on the table, drawing circles in the dust, his tight dark curls fallen forward from his bent head, shadowing his face. Finally he looked up, as if feeling Scottie's eyes burning holes in his side. Scottie was surprised to see tears on Chris-John's face. "Help me, Scottie."

"What do you want?" said Scottie.

"I am acting like the king," said Chris-John.

Scottie was puzzled both by what he said and how he said it. Chris-John's habit of speaking in royal plurals was a constant irritation to Scottie; to Chris-John everything was "we this, we that." So it was odd to hear him now say "I." It sounded very lonely. And now that he did speak in singular, he said he was acting like the king. Puzzle and puzzle. "How is that?" said Scottie.

"All that is happening in Seattle is happening because I won't tell the people to fight," said Chris-John.

"That's true," said Scottie coldly. It was all his fault. Scottie wasn't going to pretend otherwise. "And the solution is very simple, Your Majesty. Give the word and our people will beat the Fifth Army out of there and into the ocean."

"My father is in the Fifth Army," said Chris-John.

Scottie paused, without answer. Just when he thought

he'd found one, Chris-John specified further, "My name is Stanton."

Scottie's answer abandoned him. In fact it exploded. There was no answer. Scottie was wordless, astounded.

My father is in the Fifth Army. So simple how he said it, understated to a point where it was nearly laughable. His father *was* the Fifth Army.

Scottie felt physically dizzy, a maelstrom within that could only be rivaled by what Chris-John was going through. And confusion was compounded by the fact that Chris-John chose *him* to tell such a secret. *Any* of the other rebels were closer to Chris-John. Scottie didn't even like Chris-John.

Chris-John bent forward over his crossed legs so his forehead touched the table, and he wept. Curled up, he looked even smaller than he was. Scottie got to his feet and hovered over him, feeling as clumsy as with a weeping girl, and uncertainly placed a giant hand on his back, felt his ribs through his cotton shirt fragile like a small bird's. "Um . . . Chris-John." Scottie never called him Chicago Red. "Your father is a beast."

"I know," said Chris-John into the table.

"Something has got to be done in Seattle."

"I know," Chris-John wailed.

But even Scottie couldn't ask Chris-John to do it. The boy had asked for help. "Can I use your name?" said Scottie.

Chris-John didn't answer. He couldn't even do that much. Scottie took the failure to reply as default affirmative. Chris-John would have been quick to say no if he wanted to say no. But he could not say yes. He put his hands over his ears as Scottie went to the radio and made contact with the nearest rebel relay station. He used Chicago Red's ID code and sent a message to Atlantis in Seattle. "Use own discretion. Do what must be done."

He glanced aside at Chris-John curled in his ball on

the table, hands over his ears. Scottie signed off. He swiveled in the squeaky chair toward Chris-John, who mumbled into the table, ''What if they kill him?''

They would kill him. There was no doubt.

''Cancel the order if you want to,'' said Scottie. ''Try. I'll sit on you if you make a move for this radio, though.''

Chris-John lifted his head and stared at Scottie with smoky ringed eyes. He'd stopped crying; his face was tracked with wet streaks. Scottie met his stare with level return. He meant what he said. He couldn't read all the shifts of writhing emotion behind Chris-John's expression that scarcely changed, except his eyes grew wider and wider. He climbed off the table and went to the radio.

Scottie was ten inches taller than Chris-John, and seventy pounds heavier. And maybe that was why he tried. Maybe it was why Scottie offered. Chris-John never reached the radio. Chris-John screamed at Scottie, beat him with useless fists, tried to pry his way out of steel-banded arms, and eventually cried himself into an exhausted sleep in his lap.

Colonel Bryon Stanton strode through the town square, snapping his riding crop against his thigh with every other step. He was disappointed that there had been no fighting. He had publicly bludgeoned a few malcontents to death just to make certain the people knew who was in charge here. The town was shuttered and bolted in fear. Cowards. The whole district. Nothing but cowards. So where was this mythical uprising he'd been sent to quell?

Ahead of him the signal tower matted its red-brick rectangle against the dull white sky. Colonel Stanton was startled to see a woman up there, a tall striking willow of a wench. She saw him, smiled. With a long white arm she reached out and hung a red lantern on an iron hook.

Well!

When had Seattle's signal tower become a brothel?

She was not dressed like a lady. One could say she was not dressed. Bryon Stanton decided to go up and teach her a lesson.

She had no curves. None. But, Lord, she was tall and she moved like a swan's neck. Could be interesting.

He hoped she did not think he was paying her. This town and everyone in it belonged to him. Actually he hoped there would be a misunderstanding, a little resistance to be put down by force.

She hung out a second red lantern, and another.

Colonel Stanton reached the foot of the tower and did not see that the lanterns formed an arc like the letter *C*, all in red. He did not notice at first the sound of doors opening. He noticed only that the door to the signal tower, when he tried it, was locked.

Bitch.

He pulled his revolver, took aim, and shot at the lock five times.

The wood around the knob splintered. Colonel Stanton tried it again. The lock gave, but the door was bolted from within. The hinges were also on the inside. He did not know whether to burn the tower down or lay siege, drag the stumpet out, and whip her to death.

He stepped back to look up, noticed now the red arc. Noticed the forest beyond it beginning to crawl, heard tramping footsteps on cobbles, sounds an army would make.

Scattered gunfire erupted from somewhere like green wood popping in the fire. And chanting. He did not make out the words until the last line, *"Be Chicago Red."*

Hell, thought Colonel Stanton, *you think Chicago was red, wait till you see how Seattle looks in fire and blood.*

He turned.

Doors were slamming back off their stops.

"We are living free."

The colonel yanked on the signal-tower door, bellowed, "Open in the name of the king!"

Laughter from high above, pretty laughter like a bell.

"Though there's blood been shed."

All those voices. They didn't sound human. More like a rushing wave. There could not be that many people saying those words.

"And we'll always be . . ."

He turned just in time to see the King's flag and the Fifth Army's pennant run down the pole at the far end of the promenade. Run up instead was a red letter C.

"Be Chicago Red."

He took a step in that direction as the first mass rounded the corner into the square. Then from the sides. Then from the forest.

Seattle poured into its town square with pitchforks, scythes, logging hooks, pokers.

And a hangman's noose.

Lindy was wrong. Dead wrong. No, not dead. Edward III did not dispose of generals like empty soup cans because of an error they made, even a colossal one.

The police action in Seattle had been an unqualified catastrophe. The Fifth Army had been defeated, run out of Seattle, and humiliated in the eyes the entire Kingdom. General Lindy had sadly underestimated the rebels' power. Obviously.

The king created a position of cogeneral of the army and elevated Lord Martel into it, a de facto demotion for Lindy.

For good sense and experience Martel was worth the rest of the lot put together. He'd been born into one of richest, most respected families in America; he'd fought the northern tribes when he was a very young man; and his father had been a general for Edward II. Martel would be a natural for general of the army. But Martel didn't want it. He said he was just a crotchety old war-horse who wanted to go home and tend his rose garden. The king told him his roses would have to wait. So here Martel was yoked with the blustering, saber-rattling, field-burning Lindy.

Martel had opposed the military investment of Se-attle, as had Tow, but the king was not going to pro-mote Tow, not on his life.

Edward III did not eat crow well, but realities must be faced. He ordered what was left of his Fifth Army out of Seattle. His armies had grown soft since the last savages had been beaten back from both borders in the reign of Edward II. Without enemies, the armies had forgotten how to fight. And the rebels were stronger and more numerous than anyone had thought—or any-one had cared to tell the king.

Rebels. For the first time Edward III had to face publicly that there existed such a thing as a revolution-ary force—an organized one. Denying its existence hadn't helped at all. It had been a full-scale disaster.

If he could have resurrected Henry Iver, he would have. What a mistake that had been. *Henry Iver, come back, and call off your Chicago Red!*

Then there was the death of Colonel Stanton to deal with. The rebels had hanged him in a Seattle square. Loss, yes, it was a grave loss. There was in that, how-ever, the smallest consolation. Now the king did not have to worry how he was going to get young William Stanton from Brigadier Tow's clutches. The king had been very troubled by that situation—it was a danger-ously ticklish one. He had never rescued anyone from Brigadier Tow's web before—never really dared—but this was a colonel's son! Dammit, how could he? But now the boy had no father and the problem resolved itself. The king needn't trouble himself over the boy's fate any longer, whatever should happen to him. Brig-adier Tow committed atrocities upon his aides.

Sometimes he killed them.

II.

The Highwayman

THERE WAS IN THE CAPITAL AREA ANOTHER LEGEND-
ary hero of the commonfolk besides Chicago Red. In
fact this one was closer to the common heart than was
Chicago Red because he was strictly a local phenom-
enon, he had been around for a much longer time than
Chicago Red, and he dealt less with ideology than he
did with immediacies like food and money for the poor.
He was called the Devil Rider. He was a masked highwayman on a black horse who robbed from the rich
and gave to the poor. General Tow called him Robin
Hood, after a Beforetime tale that was on the list of
forbidden literature that was available to the assassin
but not to the public. Beforetime lore was riddled with
masked outlaws, usually of noble birth, who champi-
oned the downtrodden against a legal authority presented as being cruel. There were Zorros and Scarlet
Pimpernels by the bushel in the Beforetime. And the
new Kingdom of America had grown one of its own,
the highwayman. The Devil.

The Devil Rider's favorite haunts were the long
stretches of open highway seldom traveled by the peasants, feasible only for the wealthy in their carriages and
for the very richest and most favored in their automobiles. The Devil Rider liked automobiles.

When both front tires blew out, Scottie nearly lost
control of the car. Chris-John, who had been sleeping
in the backseat, rolled onto the floor. Lark, in the pas-

senger seat, shrieked and covered her head in a useless
gesture—the trunk was full of explosives.

Scottie brought the careening automobile to a stop
and gave an unsteady exhalation of relief. Lark crossed
herself and pulled her nurse's cape around her as if she
were cold. Chris-John pulled himself off the floor and
peered over the front seat. He was about to ask what
had happened, but instead he pointed through the front
windshield. "Look."

Beyond the bright pool of the car's headlights loomed
a rearing black horse without a rider. "Oh Christ!"
said Scottie. It was the Devil's horse, a huge black
stallion with a white streak on its forehead, standing
up against the storm sky, pawing the air, its nostrils
flaring, its mane flying in the wind. All around it, black
shapes of trees were tossing and bowing in the face of
the coming weather, so that the forest itself seemed to
be closing in around them. The car had halted in the
middle of the Black Forest, isolated.

A sharp rap on the driver's-side window made the
three rebels start. Scottie turned his head to see two
long pistols pointed at his head through the glass. One
motioned for him to lower the window.

Scottie rolled down the window, the rush of leaves
becoming loud, and moisture-laden air spilled inside.
A tall menacing figure all in black holstered one pistol,
reached in with a black-gloved hand, and turned on the
inside light. The rebels could suddenly see the black-
hooded head, the face covered by a grotesque gas mask
from the Beforetime appearing like a very monster or
a vision from hell.

"Ah, a doctor." The voice came strained through
the mask's filter, but not so changed as to disguise the
sneering on the word "doctor." Scottie always wore
the caduceus when driving, in case he was stopped by
soldiers. "How is business." It was not a question.

Doctors were trained and licensed by the Crown and
their fees were set by the Crown, but doctors were no-

torious for bleeding the desperate dry. The Devil Rider was notorious for bleeding rich doctors of their profits. Scottie didn't answer.

The Devil stepped back and motioned them out of the car.

He'd struck a wide stance, ready with both pistols, the layered capes of his black carrick snapping with storm gusts. Overhead a gibbous moon was winking in and out behind fleet clouds in wild, wind-whipped sky. The Devil searched the three of them and made them lie facedown on the ground. He searched inside the automobile. He found no money.

He pointed one pistol down at Scottie. "Open the trunk, doctor."

Scottie stopped breathing—the trunk held their forbidden cargo—and he turned his head to Chris-John, who said calmly, "Open it, Scottie."

It must have struck the Devil odd for a youth to give orders to a doctor, because he gestured at Chris-John with one pistol and growled at Scottie, "Who is he?"

"He's the boss," said Scottie, and slowly started to rise.

The Devil Rider placed one foot on Scottie's back and pushed him back down to the ground. "Then he can open the trunk," said the Devil, and motioned Chris-John up.

Chris-John took up the keys. He was very small next to the highwayman, who towered six feet or more and grew still more in the terrified imagination with his swagger and strength of movement, his broad shoulders padded even bigger than they actually were, his torso widened with the added bulk of a bulletproof vest. The gas mask made him inhuman.

Chris-John opened the trunk to reveal the load of dynamite. He turned his beguiling eyes into the gun barrel and said quite evenly, "Does it mean anything to you that even if you don't kill us, the king's soldiers will when they find us out here in the road with this?"

The Devil Rider holstered his pistols, leaned on the car, and drummed his gloved fingers, absorbing the import of this. Rebels. He'd held up rebels. His hooded head turned from Chris-John to the dynamite to Chris-John. The Devil was annoyed. He nodded as if to say this was a fine mess. Then he reached out and cuffed Chris-John's curly head, not hard. Chris-John gave him a sheepish smile and a shrug.

The Devil circled the car with long tramping strides, fists on his hips, his massive shoulders hunched.

He whistled for his steed, and the great black stallion came trotting to the summons. The Devil loaded the incriminating cargo of explosives into his saddlebags, mounted, and rode away.

Chris-John stood in the middle of the desolate road listening to the hoofbeats diminish.

Lark and Scottie stood up and brushed off the leaves and dirt. None of them was quite sure what happened, but they were stranded.

It started to rain.

It was the hour before dawn, and Lark was struggling in vain to patch the punctured tires together well enough just to get them to the nearest rebel underground station—wishing to God that Detroit were here—when headlights appeared up the road. Chris-John and Scottie hid in the woods, leaving Lark with the disabled car. A lone nurse stranded in the driving rain might get more sympathy and help and less suspicion from the king's soldiers than the whole trio of them. And, if not, Lark was handiest with a tire iron.

The car slowed and came to a stop. It was a long car, the longest Lark had ever seen, and sleek; raindrops beaded and rolled off its smooth painted body that glistened in the smallest light. The windows were smoked, so she could not see inside. The vehicle was not military. On the hood was the cross and ensign of the clergy.

This was wonderful. Lark picked up the tire iron. She was not above stealing a priest's car. Priests were often as greedy as doctors—and a person had to wonder about a priest who traveled in a car four blocks long. This was the stuff of royalty.

Lark waited by her jacked-up automobile with a winsome smile of distress to draw out the long car's occupants.

The door opened and the black-robed figure stepped out. A weird filtered voice said, "You are going to hit me, my child?"

Lark dropped the tire iron. It was the Devil Rider.

The highwayman moved to his automobile's middle door—there were three sets of them—opened it, and bounced out two tires of the proper size.

Lark could do nothing for a moment but gape, dumbstruck. Then she called into the woods, her voice wobbling with relief and surprise, nearly laughing, scarcely daring to believe, "Uh, Chris-John, I think it's a friend of yours?"

And the Devil Rider spent the hour before dawn helping Chicago Red change tires.

When they were done, Chris-John requested his dynamite back. The Devil Rider refused. "Children shouldn't play with explosives."

Chris-John shook his head. "Mister, you don't know who you're talking to, and it's too bad we can't tell you."

General Tow lived on the third floor of the palace in the east wing. Several of the king's top officials also had rooms here to be near the Crown because their estates were rather distant. Of course Tow had no estate of his own, and these rooms were his only home. The main room was large, with three streetfront windows on the south face. The opposite wall, where the door to the hall was, was all bookshelves. There was a hearth, a huge bed, a sofa and chairs, and a grand piano. There were two bathrooms, a royal one for Tow, and a small one for the small side room that was occupied by his aide William.

The boy was different. He had a gentle sensitivity that was often called feminine but was hardly common to all females nor exclusive to them. This boy was case in point. He was fully twenty years old, still boyish, even childlike, soft-eyed and slender; and he had a certain delicacy even with his big-boned shoulders and hands that gave him his masculine edge. He was intelligent, if painfully naive. Tow hated stupid people, even pretty ones. Tow enjoyed having the boy around. And when he began to be bored with him, he would enjoy crushing him and seeing horror in the gentle eyes.

But the boy was different. The first thing that set him apart, really set him apart and make Tow notice, was that the lad treated the piano like the hallowed thing it was.

There was a small scratch on the top of the piano from a past servant, whom Tow had ordered taken out and shot. He would have shot her himself on the spot but the king had told Tow never to kill anyone in the palace. It was the only time anyone had ever seen Tow in a real rage, or roused any degree from his snakelike cold composure. How anyone that cold could play the piano with such passion was a mystery. And sometimes he would sing, sing beautifully. Tow's tenor voice was renowned throughout the Kingdom. More than as the king's assassin, Tow was known for his music. Outside the Capital, people who did not know what Tow was knew he could sing because there were a few recordings from when Tow had been persuaded to perform at palace balls, and those were played on the radio with great popularity. But Tow did not really enjoy performing. That was not what his music was for. He despised all people and did not care what they thought of his beloved music. Tow played and sang for Tow.

Will seemed to know without being told that the piano was holy. He set nothing on it; he never used it as a writing surface. The current maid never touched it because she'd been told not to. She had, in fact, been told graphically what she could expect if she touched it. Will, seeing it neglected, took it upon himself to dust the piano with a clean soft cloth. The first time he'd done it, Tow held his breath, ready to kill him, his eyes following the boy's movements without a change in his face; but the boy did nothing stupid, and Tow relaxed, watching his hands move lightly on the instrument through the dustcloth.

He beckoned Will to him. "Give me your hand."

Will uncertainly extended one hand, and Tow laid it across his open palm. He compared their reach. Will's was bigger but baby-skinned, his long fingers bony and gawky things next to Tow's aristocratic hands. The general murmured a wish that he had Will's span. Tow struggled to reach over one octave.

"Do you play?" said Tow.

"No, sir," said Will. The boy listened. Tow had heard the door of the adjoining side room softly crack open whenever he began to play.

And the boy was useful, as it turned out, and that was pleasant to have, for once. An ornamental and functional, nonirritating aide. So helpful and oblivious to peril. A fresh innocent fluttering around a flame. That excited. The boy thought Brigadier Tow was a well-bred aristocrat and a fine human being. That was funny. Such innocence was rare. He would be beautiful in terror. Others did not see Will's looks as striking; and they were really not. Just something caught the pit viper's particular fancy.

The telephone rang once.

"Shall I get that, sir?" said Will.

"Let it ring. It's probably Lindy," said Tow. It was probably Princess Juliet.

The phone rang five more times and was ignored.

After three more rings the general asked, "Does that bother you?"

"Yes, sir," Will admitted during the tenth sounding.

"Answer it."

Will did so; his eyes widened, he covered the mouthpiece and whispered urgently, "Sir, it's the king!"

The general signaled for the phone. "Yes, sire."

"Why did you not answer!" demanded the king, impatient.

"I did not know it was Your Majesty," said Tow.

"Who else ever calls you, Tow?"

"Your Majesty does not want me to answer that."

The king paused. No, he really didn't want that answer. He pressed on with the reason for his call. It was the Devil Rider and Chicago Red. Could they be the same person?

Tow considered. "From instinct only, sire, I don't think they're related. I don't think they even know each other."

One was a down-with-the-Kingdom revolutionary. The other a bleeding-heart philanthropist.

"I want them dead. I want them both dead," said the king.

Tow glanced aside at Will. "Your Majesty knows he has only to show his servant a face."

"Ah, would that I could. I would to God I could. The day will come."

"I am certain, sire," said the assassin. "I will be there when it does."

The ten-year-old prince held his nose up at a haughty angle. He had a cold. He was trying to keep from sniffling in church. If he kept his head tilted back, the phlegm would run back down his sinuses instead of out his nostrils. Royalty did not sniffle. Royalty did not kick down itchy woolen socks. Royalty did not shift in a seat or yawn or fall asleep during Mass. Royalty never burped or passed gas or made embarrassing noises.

Young Prince Edward was sure there had to be a mistake; he knew, just knew, he was really a peasant who'd been mixed up with the royal child when they were both babies. Royalty's nose did not run. The prince tilted his head back further and gazed up at the stained-glass roundel in the high-vaulted ceiling. Lace-cuffed shirt and velvet jacket worked not at all well for wiping one's nose. He wished the Mass would end.

He was relieved when the congregation began to sing. He took advantage of the volume to try to clear the clot in his throat.

Then he sneezed. Sneezed big, all over his hands and down his face.

Princess Juliet rolled her eyes; Princess Catrina giggled; Princess Trisha crossed her arms and made a face of ultimate adolescent embarrassment; and young Prince Edward contemplated spending the rest of his life as a hermit in the Rockies while the queen kept on singing "Onward Christian Soldiers."

Then, into the prince's gooey hands appeared a handkerchief as from heaven, snowy white and embroidered with the initials "EIII." Prince Edward looked up. It was his father, the king. The king had passed him the handkerchief without commotion or frowning or excess attention. The king had already returned his attention to his hymnal to find his place in the song, thereby reducing the incident to insignificance. The child's gratitude was unbounded and he felt adoration for the distant lofty figure. It was almost sacrilege to sully the pure white embroidered cloth. Of course he had to—though he supposed it would be tempting fate to try to blow his nose in it. He cleaned his face and hands, and pocketed the soiled handkerchief.

The Mass ended. Heavenly voices in the choir loft raised the recessional hymn to the highest vaults as the archbishop exited down the aisle between the cathedral's Byzantine clusters of columns. The king waited, symbolic acknowledgment by the Crown that there was a higher power.

Outside the great wooden doors of the cathedral the archbishop turned to greet his parishioners. The king was first out.

They faced each other. "Peace be with you," said the archbishop.

The man was a magnetic presence, with an imposing frame, strong-voiced, and masculine, handsome in a craggy weathered way. It was difficult not to like the pontiff—though he was a little more forgiving of the rebels than the king would prefer.

Gregory Vandetti, born aristocratic and risen to head of the Church of America, had never lost the common touch. There was always great temptation for the archbishop of the Church of America to make a second king of himself, or even to equate himself with the One he served. That never happened to Gregory. His Eminence was still and always would be Father Greg, accessible to the humblest. And only at high Mass did one even see a miter covering his dark close-cropped curly hair like a tall crown.

He kept company with the poorest; he received the most important personages from all over the Kingdom; he regularly played chess with General Lord Martel and tutored Martel's daughter Lady Marion. A gentleman. An eminently civilized man. Still the pontiff knew how to use a pistol. When brigands had ransacked the peasant widow Jenny Stile's home while the archbishop was visiting there, Father Greg stayed very quiescent and accommodating to the villains until they tried to misuse Mrs. Stile. Then, like an archangel, with his eyes all afire, strong and calm, he commanded, "In the name of God, stop." The brigands cackled, and Father Greg said, "Then God receive your souls." And with that the archbishop drew a pistol and shot the both of them, one fatally. He did no penance for it. The Bible said only: "Thou shalt not commit murder." No one called that murder; and the widow Stile was obviously in love with the man ever after. The king asked him how he happened to be carrying a firearm that day. Father Gregory said he always carried one on his country rounds in case he met with feral dogs. And it was true enough that there were many vicious wild dogs in the woods and fields around the Capital—not to mention the highwayman who haunted the Capital Road.

The king faced the archbishop outside the cathedral. The king clasped his broad shoulders, drew him into him in ceremonial embrace, and spoke into his ear. "Greg, I want to talk to you."

The tall rough-faced archbishop nodded. "Yes, Majesty." And the king moved apart while the cathedral was emptying. He went to his carriage to wait. From there he could watch the parishioners come out, lords and commoners alike; Greg drew a mixed crowd. Edward did not like to interfere with this part of the ritual. It was the nicest part of the week, Father Gregory and his flock.

His eye was caught at once by General Lord Martel's daughter Marion. She was with her sweetheart, a young captain of the palace guard who had been courting her. This suitor had lasted longer than all the others, and maybe the young lady would settle for him. She was not going to find her equal, thought the king, not anywhere. Marion was a slender girl of exceptional grace with a smooth polite alto voice. She held her head and back like a man—no, not merely a man, an officer. She practiced fencing with the king's son, young Prince Edward, and she rode like a cavalryman. Raven-haired and fair of face, never painted, she had a fresh healthy peasant's look, not unappealing but not really suiting a girl of her station. Edward knew his own famous and widely imitated daughters were quite plain without all the art. Marion's unconventionality troubled her father. "How am I to get her married?"

That was a problem. King Edward would marry her

himself if he were free. Edward III worried about the succession after he was gone. If Lady Marion were queen, he would have no worries. He even considered putting his own wife, Queen Gertrude, away just for that reason, but the soundness of his judgment would be questioned if he divorced his queen of forty years and mother of his children in favor of a girl nearly a third his age. So he worried, and hoped he lived long enough to secure a smooth transition after his passing.

From his carriage the king saw his heirs, the royal family, climb into the second royal coach.

There was Queen Gertrude, a solid woman but no monarch. Three years his senior, she might not outlive him. Ruefully he watched the footman assisting her stout figure into the coach.

Then there were his daughters. He remembered General Lord Martel had told him once, "I wish my Marion were more like Your Majesty's daughters, sire."

His daughters? His daughters. Soft, plump, shallow, snipping showpieces. They spent hours before mirrors and in shops, wearing a fortune in silk and baubles and perfume. Princess Juliet, of song and sonnet, had whored all his generals—anything in a uniform. They all denied it of course—except for Tow, whom King Edward pointedly never asked because Tow would not deny anything and the king really didn't want to know. He did not want to execute his generals and disgrace his daughter. He wanted denials. Why did she do everything to break his heart?

Though he adored them, as heirs his daughters were worthless; *Juliet* was, and Juliet was first in line. She was the reason the king had put his wife through two more daughters and three miscarriages until he had a son. He needed some excuse to pass over beloved irresponsible Juliet.

Young Prince Edward, he of the runny nose, was helping his sisters into the carriage. He looked so small and slight standing there. The young heir apparent showed some promise but Edward III wanted more than promise. Edward III wished the child would grow. He wanted Edward IV to be an adult, now, immediately. The king had a terror of dying without a proper order behind him. Especially now with the rebels in such force. The child took the blunt end of the king's worry. As a father, the king was strict, aloof, and never pleased. The child could not please—he was a good ten-year-old boy; he was a bad full-grown and educated administrator, which Edward III was looking for in him.

He watched the young prince assist the last of the royal princesses into the carriage. Princess Trisha disdained to take her brother's offered hand—not after he'd sneezed on it—and she climbed into the carriage herself. The little prince kept a stoic face, a bit paler perhaps, and he climbed in after her. He was a good boy, the king caught himself thinking. Edward III really ought to give him a gentle word. He would have to do that one of these days.

At length the church crowds dispersed. The king bid a lackey send Father Gregory to him.

A footman held the carriage door for the archbishop. Gregory gathered up his long vestments, ducked his mitered head, and climbed in.

"It is good to see you, sire." The archbishop smiled. "Will we be seeing Your Majesty every Sunday now?"

"Ah, Greg, you know better. I've come here to see *you*. I can never reach you on the telephone—not even in the middle of the night. I tried last night, did you know?"

"Mrs. Tass's son has pneumonia," said the pastor.

"Tass?" The king searched his memory for a Lady Tass. "Tass?"

"Peasant, sire."

"Oh." The king dismissed it. How had the archbishop time to worry about every last peasant? And how did he remember all their names? "I wanted to talk to you about Seattle."

The pontiff folded his hands. "A bad situation."

"I made it so."

"I didn't say that, Majesty."

"You didn't have to Greg. I know you. I know what you're thinking. And I know it's true. If you'd been at that Council meeting, you would've talked me out of Lindy's damn police action."

"Yes, I would have tried," said Gregory.

"So I am telling you: from now on, you are on the Council, Archbishop."

"Sire?" said Gregory, a surprised, amused wrinkle to his brow, a sparkle in his dark eyes, on the verge of smiling at a joke.

"No arguments," bade the king. "It's done."

Father Greg laughed.

"Funny?" said the king.

"Me on the Council is funny, Majesty," said Gregory. His smile was warming.

"I need a plain talker besides Tow," said the king. He was fond, truly fond of this man. Yes, he thought, this was a good decision, and he was becoming more pleased with it as he spoke. "As long as I have a representative from hell on my staff, I may as well have a priest, too. That's my decision, Greg." When the king made up his mind, there was nothing more to say.

But he didn't know who he was talking to. And it was too bad Father Greg couldn't tell him.

Lady Marion donned her riding cloak, much to her father's alarm. Dusk was the worst time for a lady to be going out. "This is the hour of the outlaws," said Lord Martel.

"The deer come out at twilight," said Marion. "Please."

Lord Martel grumbled. Well, she had the shotgun slung over her shoulder in plain sight, so no one ought to accost her. And if they did, Lord Martel had taught her daughter how to use it. "Stay on the estate," he relented. And he insisted she take his biggest stallion, the great black war-horse with white feet.

Marion kissed his bristly cheek and rode across the fields.

Marion kept riding—out the back of the estate and onto the Capital Road.

She hid the shotgun in the folds of her voluminous skirt and riding cloak, and took out of hiding the jewels her mother had left her. She slid gem-studded combs into her thick raven hair, put on the heavy lapis-and-diamond necklace and the gaudy rings that flashed even in starlight. And she went for a ride through the haunts of the Devil Rider.

All of Marion's friends—if she could call the aristocratic ladies who whispered behind her back friends—had been held up by the highwayman at some time, or else someone in their families had. Marion's father, General Lord Martel, had never been stopped. His carriage driver shouted once that he thought he saw the brigand up ahead, but the Devil never showed.

Marion's carriage had never been stopped, so she decided it was time she went looking. The tales she heard were so incredible, she just wanted to see him once for herself. If all he wanted was her jewelry, then he could have it. They said he gave what he stole to poor people and she never wore the stuff anyway. If he wanted anything else, she still had the shotgun.

The Devil did not show that night.

It became of habit of Marion's to go riding "around the estate" at twilight. She would stay on the lonely highway into the darkness. She saw plenty of deer. No Devil Rider.

She began to suspect he must have spied her shotgun. It was perfectly concealed, but what else could be the problem? It was very disappointing.

Finally one night she circled her steed in the road

and shouted to the trees, ''Damn you, highwayman, am I not rich enough for you!''

Marion was used to being left out and uninvited, but she never dreamed she would be passed over by a bandit. She was going to be the only lady in the Kingdom who could not get herself robbed.

Marion Martel always scared men off. The outlaw hero, it would seem, was no different from the rest of them. ''You'd think I was a holy relic,'' she muttered, and headed for home, closer to the truth than she knew.

III.

Return to Farington

THE PLAN WAS COMPLEX. THERE WERE TOO MANY VARiables for it possibly to be safe. "Safe is not what we are about," said Chris-John—he often said "we" when he meant "I"—and he delegated the dangerous part for himself.

The target was yet another converted factory. Rather the factory was slated for conversion. If the rebels waited until the Dunhelm plant was actually ready to produce weapons, it would be so heavily soldiered, no one could get near it.

As it was, there was a guard station very nearby, Dunhelm Tower, on the other side of Potter's Hill. There was nothing else in the area but forest—and Farington. A saboteur attempting to flee would be caught between the king's soldiers and Farington's—"soldier" was what Farington called its street creatures.

And there was the railroad. The train came past twice a day, but had no scheduled stop near Farington. But this particular line was rebel-operated. Today, Chris-John announced, there would be a stop—ostensibly for a cow—at six o'clock, directly next to the lightning-blasted elm tree that had fallen and been moved off the tracks last year. The train's engineer knew where it was.

Dunhelm Factory closed regularly at 5:30. Chris-John said he would steal inside after everyone was gone and set the dynamite—he had a new supply—at fifteen minutes before the hour. That gave him fifteen minutes, plenty of time, to get to the train tracks. At six Chris-John would board the train. At five minutes after the hour the factory would blow up. Chris-John would get off the train at the Manxville station and meet Scottie at the tavern called the Red Stallion (Lark called it the Red Gelding because they watered the drinks), and Scottie would drive him home. That was the way it was supposed to go.

Scottie stayed a brooding silent hulk at the end of the table in the bunker while Chris-John explained his plan to the other rebels. Scottie frowned, the color deepening in his dark reddish skin. Dark eyes loured from under his moody brow, watching the others listen, enthralled, to this lunacy. That Chris-John should be speaking lunacy had ceased to amaze Scottie. It was expected. Chris-John was always fanatical; now he was suicidal. Scottie suspected he was punishing himself for his father's death.

The others did not know that Chris-John's name was Stanton. They did not know who really gave the order to Seattle that had decimated the Fifth Army and Colonel Bryon Stanton with it. Chris-John never confessed to anyone else. It was a deadly secret between them. And Chris-John was a bit diffident around Scottie ever after, as if Scottie owned a piece of him.

Scottie rested his high cheekbones on his two fists, his elbows on the table, and he listened to Chris-John discourse to the others. The others were nodding and saying, "Yes, Chicago Red." Chris-John was getting excited, animated as he talked, with that other-world shine to his eyes.

Dammit, the plan stank and Chris-John was going to kill himself.

Scottie abruptly stood up, seized Chris-John's narrow wrist, and yanked him around to look at him. "Chris-John."

Meeting Chris-John's eyes directly was always electric; Scottie thought Chris-John did it on purpose, but who could figure out how? He touched all chords of emotion, could inspire love, pity, trust, zeal. He was innocence and extreme sensuality but ever untouched and inaccessible.

Chris-John cloaked himself in vulnerability now, looking very small. His wrist felt so thin in Scottie's huge grasp that the fragile bone under his smooth dark skin might snap at a rough turn. Black curls haloed his siren face. Just a slender wraith, he looked breakable, his frightened eyes asking not to be broken—as if Scottie would betray his horrid secret. Scottie demanded in low baritone, "Why are you doing this?"

Chris-John's eyes were all bewilderment; why was Scottie so angry? "We have to," he said.

Suddenly Scottie's big hand was on Chris-John's face, holding his jaw closed. "Shut this *we*, Chris-John. I'm talking to you."

He slowly released some of the pressure on Chris-John's jaw so he could talk—if he started spouting fanaticism, Scottie would shut it for him again—and Chris-John's voice was high sweet and small. "Why are you trying to stop me?" There was a hitch in his voice before he said "me"; he had almost said "us."

The others in the bunker had been staring all the while, confused to silence. Scottie and Chris-John could have been talking another language as far as the others could tell. They could not understand what going on between them. Finally someone thought to break in and ask. Balt asked why Scottie was being so hard on Chris-John.

Scottie turned to look at them, the ring of staring rebels. He could read their faces, they didn't understand. They couldn't understand. All they saw was great big Scottie bullying little Chicago Red. Scottie opened his mouth but couldn't find anything to say to them.

Carrie answered into the void. "He's jealous."

Comprehension washed over all the perplexed faces, and that summation was easily accepted. It became truth, surely as written in stone. Scottie couldn't erase it, no matter what he said. All their expressions had relaxed into wise knowing. Tina and Meredith were nodding *of course,* and Terese was scowling defensive hatred at him.

Scottie released his hold on Chris-John and held his hands over his head like a gunman giving himself up. "Fine," he said, sharply, angry. "Fine. You win. You want me to help him, I'll help him do whatever he wants." *He wants to kill himself.* He turned to Chris-John. "You want me to pick you up at 6:30 at the Manxville station. I'll be at the Manxville station. All right? All right?"

The others just looked at him.

Chris-John, ever the sweet angel, said with voice of forgiveness, "All right."

Scottie grabbed his doctor's bag and coat and climbed out of the bunker. He didn't want to be there a moment longer, and they didn't want him there. The air inside was thick with quills all pointed at him. He stalked through the woods to the car with the caduceus, got in, and started it. He would be at the goddamn Manxville stop at 6:30. He'd be there early, probably drunk as a skunk, but he'd be there. He only wondered, would Chris-John?

At 5:30 Chris-John successfully dodged the guard at the door to the Dunhelm plant and slipped down the corridor to the boiler room. He wired the explosives and set the timer running when he heard footsteps. He ducked behind the furnace and listened.

The guard ambled down the corridor, stopped not five feet from the boiler-room door, leaned against the wall under the "No Smoking" sign, and lit a cigarette.

Chris-John waited. He prayed. He broke a sweat, looked at his watch. It was 5:50. He had ten minutes to reach the tracks a half mile away. He gnawed on his knees.

The cigarette smoldered slowly. The guard did not move. Chris-John closed his eyes. In two minutes he would have to do something—run screaming, "It's a bomb!" and hope the guard panicked and ran as well, not thinking that it would have to be Chris-John who had set the bomb. That was a long shot. Or he could fight the guard. He didn't know which was more unlikely.

The bomb could not be defused. Detroit purposely made them that way; in case one were ever discovered, there wouldn't be much a guard could do about it.

Two minutes passed.

Trembling, Chris-John edged to the door.

The guard began to stroll, ever so slowly, down the corridor, and around the corner.

Chris-John bolted from the boiler room and ran toward the outside door.

And met with a metal-mesh barrier.

When had they added this? It was not in the blueprints.

Now he panicked. He seized the mesh and shook it with all his might. Chris-John weighed 110 pounds.

The guard came back around the corner, and Chris-John wheeled, his back against the barrier.

The guard chuckled.

Chris-John shut his eyes.

"Fell asleep, did ya, kid?"

Chris-John opened his eyes. The guard was reaching into his pocket for keys. He thought Chris-John worked here.

Chris-John nodded, mute. He could not speak. His throat had closed in terror. Had he made a sound, he would have screamed.

The guard strolled, chuckling, to the gate, shuffling through the many keys on the ring, pausing to shake his finger at Chris-John. "Sleep at night, young man, not on company time. Stay out of the taverns."

"Yes, sir," Chris-John whispered. He glanced at his watch. He had four minutes.

The guard placed the key in the lock. He tried to turn it. Nothing happened. He jiggled it. "Oh, damn," he muttered, and shuffled to the next one.

Chris-John closed his eyes again.

He heard a key in the lock, heard a click, and the mesh behind his back began to fold open.

The guard started to say, "There you are—" but Chris-John had bulleted through and charged out to the open field toward the train tracks. He had two minutes and a half mile. In the distance he could already hear the engine's whistle.

Brigadier Tow gazed out the window at the passing countryside. Beside him his young aide William Stanton was growing sleepy with the easy swaying of the train car on the tracks. The front door to the car slid open, and a roly-poly man with a jaunty hat on his balding head and heavy coin changer at his belt called for tickets. Halfway down the aisle he came to Tow. The man's jolly face drained of color with recognition. "Sir!"

William blinked awake, looked up at the conductor, looked at Tow.

The conductor was rattled. "There's room in the first-class car if you like, sir," he said nervously.

"Thank you, I may move," said Tow. "Then again I may . . . not." He looked out the window.

The conductor wrung his sweating hands and hovered by the brigadier's seat. "Expecting trouble?"

"No," said Tow coolly. "But you never know these days. If there is, I am more than ready." He leveled steely eyes on the perspiring conductor, making him squirm.

"That's good to know, sir," he said in a strangled voice with a wilted smile. He worked a fat finger into his collar that was suddenly too tight.

"Of course this train has never been hit by a rebel bomb," said Tow.

"That's true, sir!" the man said proudly, expanding his chest and his already expansive middle, some color returning to his plump cheeks.

"Due to no effort on the part of your security men," Tow continued, "since this train has never even been attacked. It does however break down quite a bit—but only for a few minutes at a time."

"Sir?" The man deflated again.

"There is no safer mode of travel these days than on the rebels' own line."

Will's eyes widened, and the conductor said, "Sir! You can't mean—"

"But I do," said Tow. He dropped his insouciance and sat forward, his voice becoming quiet and lethal. "This train is the main artery in and out of the Capital City. I'm sure half of the people on it are rebels, and were it up to me, I would shoot them all just to be rid of that fifty percent. But lucky for you it's not up to me. But I will say that this train had best not make any unscheduled stops or be held up in any way, because in a shoot-out I would *not* be concerned with innocent bystanders, since there is a fifty-percent chance that they are not innocent. So you tell whoever is flashing those signals out there to give it up." He nodded toward the window, never taking his eyes from the conductor.

"But I don't know what you're talking about—" The man spoke at the top of his register.

"Then find out who does, innocent bystander," said Tow.

The man abandoned his ticket collection and scurried back up the aisle and through the door.

The other passengers, who had heard only part of the words, were upset. An elderly woman with a bag full of gaily wrapped baby presents at her feet, leaned across the aisle and said to Tow, "Sir? Are we in any danger?"

Tow smiled charmingly at the woman and said loudly enough for others to hear, "We should be perfectly safe now."

The grandmother smiled. She knew who he was. He was the handsome young king's man who sang so beautifully on the radio. She sat back in her seat, reassured.

Between Farington and Potter's Hill the train began to slow. There was some yelling, too muffled for words to be distinguished, and the train abruptly picked up speed again.

"There goes another would-be rebel stop," Tow said nonchalantly, loud enough only for Will to hear, his arm around the back of Will's seat.

Will was awed, as if the general had done something major and heroic. Then he asked tentatively, "If you know there are rebels on the train, why don't you arrest them?"

"They're like cockroaches. You can swat at the ones you see if it makes you feel better, but for every one you see there are nineteen others in the woodwork perpetuating themselves. I don't want the one. I want the nineteen."

Will knit his brow, and admitted he knew nothing about cockroaches. He'd never seen one.

Tow laughed aloud. He ruffled the boy's hair.

Chris-John ran till he felt his heart and lungs would burst. The train was slowing toward the lightning-struck elm and Chris-John was not there yet. He fell once, over an ancient rusted barbed-wire fence sticking one strand out of the ground. His palms skidded in the grit as he caught himself. He scrambled back to his feet and *ran*.

Wind whistled in his ears, his feet had grown wings, and he flew over the remaining yards.

But already the train was picking up speed.

"No! Wait! I'm here! I'm here! he screamed.

The engines quickened, the smokestack belched coal billows. Chris-John kept running, made it to the tree before all the cars were past, and he waved his arms and yelled into the noise of metal wheels speeding on rails.

The train sped on. It hadn't stopped. It hardly even slowed.

As the caboose flew past, Chris-John dropped his arms and stared after it. He looked around for the rebel signalers always in contact with the train, but they had fallen suddenly and strangely dark. Something was drastically wrong.

Behind him, the factory was going to blow up in five minutes. He had five minutes to get to a place of safety before the searchers came out with their bloodhounds. But Chris-John knew, because he'd studied the map, that there was no place of safety near here. The only escape had just passed him by.

He started running. To Farington.

Far past midnight Scottie climbed down the ladder into the rebel bunker, his black hair disheveled. He looked hung over, eyes locked in a squint, barely kept open, his brow knotted. He dropped his doctor's bag. He was alone.

The other rebels received him in stone silence. They wanted to know where Chris-John was. Scottie looked to see that they were all there: Lark, Detroit, Balt, Carrie and Meredith, Ezra, Tina, Terese. He was only going to say this once. "The six o'clock never made its Farington stop. Tow was on the train."

"The bomb?" asked Detroit, gnawing on her hair. Detroit had made the bomb.

"The bomb went on schedule."

"And Chris-John? said Lark.

Scottie shook his head and sat heavily. "God knows."

"They didn't catch him?" said Detroit.

"They were still searching the woods at one o'clock."

Lark jumped up from the table. "We have to find him first!" She threw on her torn khaki jacket as the mute Terese opened the bunker's hatch. Scottie sprang out of his chair and stopped them. He grabbed Lark's arm. He knew better than to try to touch Terese. Terese stopped when Lark did.

"Find him first?" said Scottie. "They'll find *you* first. There are soldiers all over. Do you think you're invisible?"

"Well, *you* didn't look for him!" Lark shouted back at him.

"I looked for him!" Scottie cried out. "I've been looking since 6:30! Where the hell do you think I've been!"

Lark sat down with her jacket still on. Terese was watching her, still waiting for someone to come with her. The others looked at each other, searching for a decisive voice to follow.

"For God's sake, what are we supposed to do?" said Lark.

"We wait," said Scottie. He moved to the hatch—Terese scuttled out of his way—and he shut it roundly. He was a powerful man and the angry slam rang through the bunker, making the others wince.

He was exhausted, sick; he'd inhaled a lot of smoke. He was feeling like a pariah. He was lonely and he could have used some comfort and pity and loving concern for himself, but he was finding none. He was angry at Terese's running out of his way like that as if he were going to rape her. Admittedly he would have liked nothing better than to take that girl's slim naked body in his bed and make love till the springs broke, for petite little Terese with her sweet fragility, her tiny neat figure, and brown eyes was physically everything he wanted in a woman, but he would never hurt her. That she seemed convinced that he would made him furious.

And he was angry at the blind loyalty that would have them all rush out and be caught for a useless display of love for Chris-John. He was angry that he himself had almost done just that. When Chris-John hadn't shown up in Manxville, Scottie had gone right to the demolished factory, where the king's soldiers were thick as flies on dead meat. Scottie had walked into the thick of them with his doctor's bag and said, "Is anyone hurt? I thought I could help." And he'd stayed there in the lion's mouth through sunset, listening for rumors and stray talk of soldiers as he treated fire fighters' burns. Then as they were searching the smoking rubble, the soldiers called the doctor over to a pile of charred bones that nearly stopped his heart, and they asked him if they were human. They were human and they were male. But the teeth were bad, not Chris-John's pretty white. So Scottie had come home.

He told the others none of that. He moved apart from them in the bunker, to behind the curtain where they kept the food. There was room enough for one or two people back here. The curtain was no real barrier, but it afforded a semblance of solitude and separation. He found dregs of tea in the pot.

He poured himself a cup, leaned on the counter made of stacked crates, and covered his eyes.

He could hear the murmured discussion on the other side of the curtain. At least their talk was making sense now. They had listened to him even if they didn't like him.

"If Chicago Red gets caught, we'll free him," Detroit was saying. "We have to wait for some word of where he is. We can't just run out looking for him. He's trying *not* to be found right now."

"Where do you *think* he went?" someone whimpered, grasping for hope.

No one answered. In his corner Scottie shook his dark head. *I hope he didn't go to Farington.*

Chris-John crept down the cold street, his lungs on fire. There was a pain in his thigh like a burning coal, and he hadn't realized till he stopped to look that he'd been shot. Blood caked round the tattered hole in his trousers at the fleshy part of his thigh. It had not pierced through. The bullet had been spent when it struck him.

The street was dirty. Chris-John was certain he would die of something horrible. He felt sick to his stomach.

Bare steel girders of gutted apartment buildings clawed at the skyline and crouched over the alleys with jagged arms. Rats scurried away at Chris-John's limping approach. Farington rats were unusually wary of people, and one had to wonder what they knew.

Light hurried footsteps made him huddle into the black shadows behind some garbage cans at the opening of an alley. He watched as a lone female figure darted across the open lighted space, glancing over her shoulder. She was a hard woman, still young but without youth, black-haired and buxom like Detroit. She wore the low-cut dress and apron of a tavern girl. One of Farington's survivors, she was making her nightly attempt to get home from work.

Chris-John moved behind the garbage cans and the girl stopped dead. "Who's there!" her voice was hard, if frightened.

Chris-John stood. The crouching position had driven daggers of fire into his thigh. Standing up made him feel suddenly faint.

The girl swore and threw a brick at him. She missed. Chris-John swayed, caught the wall, and groaned.

The girl squinted to distinguish the form in the dark shadows. She was not going to venture any closer to the alley. "What kind of act is that?" she said, sneering. "I missed you."

And Chris-John crumpled into the street.

* * *

King Edward III tore his hair. General Lindy trembled. Chancellor Franklin paced. General Martel frowned, shaking his head. Secretary Shie smoked incessantly. Admiral Kester swore incessantly. Father Greg sat silently with his hands folded. And William Stanton stood discreetly behind the serene Brigadier Tow.

Lindy had sworn that the Capital line of the railroad was firmly in the control of the Crown. Why was he so sure? the king asked. Well, because the rebels never dared attack it. The king exploded. Never dared? Never dared? Why was Tow the only one with the marginal sense to realize that the Capital line was a rebel train?

And with that, Lindy was kicked from his lofty post down to lieutenant general. He was assigned an army and he was going to be sent into the field at the next uprising.

Chancellor Franklin was put in charge of Capital security. "Unless you bungle, too," said the king. "Then I won't be as gracious. Politicians aren't as indispensable as generals!"

It was a bad thing to say. Even if true, it was a very bad thing to say. One could add, *and kings are not immortal.* Father Greg crossed himself.

Finally the king dismissed them all, but he detained Tow, who in turn detained his aide. King Edward would have objected, but he had learned that Tow goes nowhere without his aide, and he was not in the mood to fight the assassin.

For a moment the two just looked at each other and Will wished he were invisible. For all practical purposes his wish was granted; neither the king nor the brigadier gave him the slightest glance. Tow studied the king calmly. Tow would have been the logical man to put in charge of Capital security. Tow's instincts were uncanny; he was ruthless; he was capable. But the king could never promote Tow past his present rank. That was understood.

Who would think a lowly Farington ditch could have so much power? The king's eyes fell on Tow's fine aristocratic hand that touched piano and trigger with equal art. Edward III wouldn't put it past Tow to turn on him in the proper situation. *But I'll outlive you, Tow, I swear I will . . . Foolish. You're half my age.*

"Majesty?" said Tow. That was politeness; breaking the silence first, he ceded dominance to the king. He usually did. Minor transient victories were not worth the winning. Tow took a very long view—rare in the gutter-bred; he knew it was in his best interest that the king stay the most powerful man in the Kingdom. When Tow began ignoring him, Edward would know he was dead.

"The saboteur of the Dunhelm plant hasn't been found," said the king. "I think there are places my men don't want to search. Do you think that bombing has anything to do with the incident on the train."

"Possible," said Tow. "I suspect the train might have been meant as a getaway for the saboteur. I should have let him board." There was little or no regret in his voice. Done was done. Twenty-twenty hindsight was a fact of life. Tow was not going to mourn over a missed step.

The king drove a fist into his open palm in impotent frustration. He turned to his brigadier. "Tow," he began, and stopped, glancing for the first time at the boy William Stanton. He had been about to say, *I realize you are a killer, not a hunter,* but more delicate words seemed in order in front of an audience, no matter how insignificant the audience was. "Tow," he began again. "I realize executing definite commands is more in keeping with your usual duties, but if you could lend any aid to the search party . . ."

He glanced to William. The words went completely

over the boy's head. He looked to Tow. Tow knew what
was being asked of him.

Tow was not accustomed to having to *find* his tar-
gets, only eliminating them. But this was a special case
and he nodded. "Yes, sire."

Tow would search where the soldiers feared to go.

Phoenix was lying on his bed, half-asleep, when he
heard shouts in the street. "Soldiers! Soldiers!"

He thought it a peculiar thing to be shouted, because
there were *always* soldiers in the streets. "Soldier"
was what Faringtoners called the street boys with the
knives.

From the alarm in the voices, it occurred to Phoenix
that they must mean *soldiers,* real ones, king's men.
And he was startled to hear the stairs creak. His stairs.
Someone had come through the outside door. Phoenix
knew he'd locked it, but he'd heard no sounds of breaking. Still someone was coming up his stairs. He jumped
off his bed and stared at the door to his room.

The solo set of footsteps stopped just outside. Phoenix watched the five locks open, unforced, one by one.
Someone with keys. Phoenix had lived here all his life.
His mother and sister were dead. There was only one
other person who had ever lived here while those locks
were on the door, and Phoenix hardly expected the
likes of him to keep his keys where *he* had gone. And
not after sixteen years.

The door swung open. It wasn't a soldier. It was a
brigadier.

"Welcome home," said Phoenix.

IV.

Stephanie's House

PHOENIX HAD BEEN SIX YEARS OLD ON THEIR LAST meeting; still he would have recognized the man even if he hadn't seen his picture in the newspapers from time to time. The face held a vague similarity to the image Phoenix saw in the mirror, would have been said to look like Phoenix's had Phoenix been handsome.

The brigadier walked into the room, steel eyes taking in the shabby surroundings—the springs hanging out from under the chair, the torn bedspread freshly washed but still stained, the curling wallpaper, the warped floorboards. He ran his leather-gloved hand across the top of a bookshelf, which contained no books, and regarded his still-clean palm with a curious arch of his eyebrows. Even in this rattrap an instinct for better ran in the family.

That face did not. Tow touched his fingers to Phoenix's chin and frowned. "Age did not improve you."

"Must be in the genes," said Phoenix.

"I don't understand," said Tow. "Mother was beautiful."

"Musta been my father," said Phoenix, and Tow pushed the ugly face away. He walked to the window. The king's brigadier made an odd refined portrait at the broken pane with his trimmed hair, his leather gloves, his light wool military jacket with every thread in place, his handsome unmarked face. He moved the tatter of a curtain aside with the back of his hand and gazed down at the street, where was parked an equally incongruous long shiny green-black car without a driver. He'd come alone into the midst of the cutthroats. And the cutthroats were wisely cringing.

Tow turned to Phoenix, moved so his back was not to the window, and said, "Chicago Red."

Phoenix remembered those words—and a strange beautiful boy running from the gallows with a holy book and a purpose, long before there was any rebel named Chicago Red. The rebel leader Chicago Red was reputed to be lovely; and there was never a lovelier creature than the one Phoenix had tied to his bed and let go two years ago.

Phoenix blinked quizzical yellow eyes at Tow. "Soda pop?"

"Don't pretend innocence," said Tow, pulling his gun, that imfamous thing with a long barrel that gleamed in the light, steely like his eyes. "You weren't innocent when you were born."

"Get outta here, I'm not a rebel either," said Phoenix. "Yeah, I heard of Chicago Red. What else am I supposed to know? We got no politics in Farington, Davy, you know that."

"Somebody has politics in Farington," said Tow. "I want an outsider. Arrived yesterday after six or today."

Phoenix shook his head. "Dogs ate someone last night by the dump, but I think that was a vent man. Did you check the lynching tree?"

"That's an old corpse and it's wearing an army uniform."

Phoenix shrugged.

"You were smarter when you were a child," said Tow.

"My kind's supposed to be idiots."

"I should have drowned you when you were a puppy," said Tow, and went to the door. He cracked it and peered out to the hallway before exiting. His Farington instincts hadn't dulled with palace living. If anything, the palace had sharpened them. Farington wasn't the only dangerous place in the Kingdom.

He turned, pointed his gun.

Phoenix dove behind the bed as Tow fired and left.

Phoenix peered over the edge of the bed at the smoking hole in the mattress. Tow hadn't missed. Phoenix had never known him to miss. That was a simple reminder.

Phoenix went to the door and locked all the locks. His hands were trembling.

He *had* heard of an outsider recently arrived in Farington. It was said that the Screaming Rabbit had picked up a *very* pretty stray with a wounded paw last night very close to here. Now the king's hit man came looking for Chicago Red, and Phoenix had to wonder if that pretty stray were in fact the beautiful Chris-John and what the hell was Chris-John doing coming back to Farington? Had he been coming here?

Was that why Phoenix hadn't told Tow? It was the biggest of risks to go against David Tow. And for what? A raving Delancyville-soft outsider. *Why am I protecting his pretty ass?*

Phoenix heard shots in the street. That would be David reasserting himself with the locals. How soon they forgot. Phoenix hadn't forgotten. And he castigated himself for a true idiot for not telling Tow what he knew. All for a pretty ass.

Whatever the reason, Phoenix had already decided in favor of Chris-John. There was no backtracking. Now he was committed. He put on his jacket.

He took off his jacket.

Wait.

If Chris-John were indeed in the Screaming Rabbit's bastion, then he was safe enough against all but Tow; there was no purpose in rushing. Phoenix sat on the bed and turned on the radio. In a few days, if the boy hadn't been caught, Phoenix would get him out. If Tow found him first, well then, so be it. Such were the fortunes of the eternal Farington War.

When Chris-John was coming to consciousness, the first thing he did was call out for Scottie. But then he was silenced by wonder of where he was. As his mind grew clearer he realized he was in bed and, on opening his eyes, found himself in an unfamiliar room. But more disquieting was the realization that he had forgotten to whom the name he had called belonged.

At once he was aware of the presence of one close by and he turned his head slowly, painfully, to look. He was looking up at a black-haired girl of twenty-three.

"Am I supposed to know you?" he asked in a daze. He felt awfully stupid not recognizing her, since it seemed if she was in his bedroom, he must know her. The next question sounded unreal, but he just could not remember. "Are you my wife? I don't . . . seem to . . . know . . . anything . . . anymore."

The girl laughed and said, "No. Stephanie. I'm not your wife. Guess I can never mind asking who you are."

Chris-John blinked his rose petal lids over horrified eyes. "I don't know."

"Kinda looked that way," said Stephanie.

"If you're not my wife, what are you doing in my room?" said Chris-John.

"Oh, proper type we are. For one thing, puppy, this is *my* room. As to what you're doing in it, honey, you're a *long* way from home from the way you talk."

"Who is Scottie?" he said suddenly, "I called him, I think. But now I can't seem to remember."

"Your boyfriend?" she suggested.

He scowled darkly.

"Well, this town is packed with ditch boys."

"What is a . . . ditch boy?"

"Oh lordy, you aren't from anywhere *near* here. You

musta fallen from the sky and landed on your gorgeous head.''

When Chris-John had fallen out of the alley at Stephanie's feet, Stephanie was going to leave him there on the cobbles for the feral dogs, but a stream of moonlight had caught his young face, his lips parted, his eyes closed as if sleeping. Stephanie had never seen a face like it in her life, not in her dreams. And as fortune would have it, he was not too heavy for her to carry up the stairs to her fortress apartment.

There came a yowling out in the street below like mating cats with distinctly human voices. Stephanie went to the window and let loose a barrage of obscenity and abuse to rival the worst.

"Aw, you can do better than that," said a male voice from below.

Another sang, "Rabbit's got a soldier. She doesn't love us anymore."

Stephanie unleashed another torrent to hoots and hollers down below.

Chris-John sat up in the bed. He spoke softly. "You know if you don't say anything, they'll get bored and go away."

Stephanie turned her head. "Yeah, I've heard that. But if I don't scream at them, I'll lose my mind."

Chris-John hardly heard her answer. The edge of his eye caught a movement. "Oh." he said.

"What is it?" Stephanie came away from the window. Chris-John was staring.

"I—I was going to say I know him." He pointed at his image in a mirror pointing back. "But I guess I ought to. That's me." He was disappointed.

"Hey, honey, don't worry, you'll remember," said Stephanie. "You're a little shook up is all. You remember things. You were talking in your sleep."

"I was? What did I say?"

"Names mostly. Scottie. Lots of Scottie. Lots of

Terese and Lark and Detroit. A few Ezras, a few Balts. Oh, and Walt. You screamed Walt.''

"Walt.'' He looked in the mirror. "Maybe that's me.''

"I don't think so, buns. How often do you call your own name?''

"Oh,'' he said, crestfallen. "It just seemed the name went with the face.''

He lay back again, dizzy. His thigh was numb. *Who am I? Who am I?*

He stared at the cobwebs strung delicately across the dirty ceiling cornices. He spoke. "I think I'm from Chicago.''

Tow put a fresh clip in his pistol. He was only five shots down, and there were four bodies in the street as warning to any other challengers, but he would not be caught short in Farington. He chided himself for wasting a shot on Phoenix. The shot had been a wish, a frustrated one. Tow wanted Phoenix out of existence.

There was only one way to realize that wish, but filicide—or was it fratricide?—was equally bad as the creature's existence. Both were a shame to him.

Shame. Since when had Tow ever been touched by shame? He did not have a conscience with which to feel shame. If he didn't want the monster to live, why not just make an end to him? For that matter, why should it bother him that such a creature existed?

Oh, would that the creature had never been born!

Tow looked both ways down the street, then crouched, supported himself with one hand on the ground, and checked beneath his car before getting in. He was, after all, on the trail of a rebel who used explosives. It did not pay to be careless.

He had no driver and he had not brought Will. The boy would not have survived five minutes in this town away from Tow's side. And Tow would not have the boy with him to see that thing up in that room where

Tow used to live, where he'd been born. He hadn't even told Will where he was going. Tow was not accountable to his help, he thought with nettled pride. But he hadn't told the boy because he did not want to be even *thought* of in this place, not by a boy who had never seen a cockroach. The boy thought Tow was aristocracy. Let him go on thinking.

Tow started the car, stepped on the pedal once so the engine ran slower. Curtains of tenement windows parted at the sound that was so unusual in this city. He placed his hand on the shift, hesitated, retracted his hand, sat.

Tow was angry. Why should he care what a pale Delancyville boy thought of him?

He gripped the wheel and bowed his head to it in defeat. *I do.* He shuddered at the thought. *I do.*

Tow, who had lived his life mocking God, felt God mocking back.

He drew his automatic again, just to feel its familiar deadly cold steel, bringing him back a sense of comforting cold routine and purpose. He was here to find a rebel.

Instinct told him this particular rebel was an important link in the rebel hierarchy—though Tow had no suspicion that he was close on the trail of Chicago Red himself. He only knew that this rebel was worth capturing. The train had been arranged to stop for him, which indicated that he—or she—was valued. The fugitive had eluded the search parties, and since the bloodhounds had lost the trail at the outskirts of Farington, then he must have come to Farington, which indicated strength and cunning. Or stupidity. At any rate the quarry was on Tow's ground now. The rebel's days, his hours, were numbered. Tow was angry for having to come here, and someone would have to pay for it. Tow had begun to view himself the way Will did, as an honorable man, and Tow liked the illusion. Returning here was a rude reminder otherwise.

Well, if this rebel forced Tow to remember, then Tow would damn well remember for him who Tow was.

He put the car in gear and started down the street, running over two of the corpses sprawled in his way.

"I'll show you something." Stephanie pulled at Chris-John's arm. "I never get to show anyone anything."

"I feel sick," said Chris-John, hanging back in the bed.

"Come on." Stephanie tugged.

Chris-John rolled onto his good side, the right side; his left thigh had been shot. His whole left side hurt. He could barely stand.

Stephanie picked up a lantern and led him to a door that opened to a closet. She pushed her clothes aside and lifted off the back panel to reveal a secret staircase.

Chris-John questioned the lantern. It was very late. "Is that legal?"

"Nobody enforces light curfews around here, bingo. Come on. This way."

He had difficulty following her down the two flights of dusty wooden stairs. There was no opening at the first-floor landing; this passageway was accessible only from the second floor and the cellar.

The cellar was dank, the weeping cinder blocks hugging a chill even on the warm summer night. Nocturnal creatures scurried out of the lantern light. Chris-John waved a web out of his face.

Stephanie brought the light over a wheel like a vault lock in the floor where the concrete gave way to some other material underneath it. Chris-John squatted with his right leg, his left sticking half-bent out to the side. He swept the caked-on dirt off the smooth surface below the wheel lock, a sturdy unweathered Beforetime substance like fiberglass or plastic. "Another bunker," he said in surprise.

"Another?" said Stephanie. "Another? You've seen something like this before?"

"I—I don't remember," said Chris-John. But he *was* beginning to remember. He'd had losses of memory before, but they seldom lasted. Chris-John was given to hysterics.

"What's a bunker? Is bunker good or bad?"

"Bunker is good, I think."

"Help me open it," said Stephanie. "I can't turn it myself."

Neither could Chris-John, who was still very weak—and getting weaker, he thought. He felt hot. He took a two-by-four and tried to use it as a lever on the wheel, but the beam was rotted and broke—though not before it loosened the lock enough for Stephanie and Chris-John to make it turn.

The hatch opened to reveal a ladder. Before Chris-John could warn her about foul air, Stephanie started down and took the light with her. The light did not fade and Stephanie called up in a healthy voice, "Look at this!"

Chris-John did not want to climb down the ladder, but it was now pitch dark up here in the cellar and he heard rustling along the dank walls, so he lowered himself into the subcellar bunker.

It was filled—filled—with books.

The air was dry, very dry; Chris-John had noted that the rungs on the ladder were not clammy to the touch, and the air, if stale smelling, did not cling to him as it did in the damp cellar. The books were brittle, some crumbling, but there was no decay. The books in the best condition had a plastic feel to the pages.

Chris-John scanned some of the unfamiliar titles: *The Plays of Shakespeare; In Search of Identity* by Sadat; *The Holy Bible,* King James Version (James?), translated into Americanese or something like it; two sets of Encyclopedias; the *Oxford English Dictionary* (what was English?); Thucydides' *The Peloponnesian War*, translated; and the *2004 Physicians' Desk Reference*.

On the first pages of all of them were printed those eerie four-digit dates of the Beforetime, like 1985 and 2004.

The present year was 217, counting from the consolidation of the Kingdom out of the savage anarchy that had gone before.

And the books all said: "Printed in Great Britain"(what was Britain?) or "Printed in the United States of America."

United States?

Then he found an atlas. It took him a while to figure out what he was looking at—a map of the Kingdom before the wicked cites sank.

Then he turned the page and found a map of the world—he only knew it was the world because it said so—and the world was huge!

To Chris-John the Kingdom of America *was* the world. Atlantic and Pacific were names of *coasts,* and the Ocean was the Ocean; there was only one.

Chris-John was overwhelmed to find himself very much mistaken. The Crown had *lied*.

Chris-John scanned a book called the *History of the United States* and, just when he thought he could not be shocked anymore, learned that America had been a democracy.

"Oh, my God. Oh, my God," he said. He had remembered who he was by then.

Stephanie wrinkled her brow at him. They were both sharing the sphere of the lantern's light to see the pages of their separate books. Stephanie was looking at pictures because she could not read. "Maybe you better not read this stuff," she said, growing worried. "It's a hanging offense to learn Beforetime stuff."

Faringtoners did not worry much about offenses, even hanging offenses, but this one was different. Murder was usual. Reading Beforetime information was bigger than that. It had a mystical flavor to it, like black magic. It was treason. "Come on; let's go up."

She took the lantern, so Chris-John had to follow. But he grabbed a pamphlet before he went, with the intriguing title *Civil Disobedience*.

When he was back up in bed, and Stephanie asleep in another room, he lit a candle and read:

> *I think we should be men first, and subjects afterward. It is not desirable to cultivate a respect for law, so much as for the right. The only obligation which I have a right to assume is to do at any time what I think right. . . .*
>
> *All men recognize the right of revolution; that is, the right to refuse allegiance to and to resist the government, when its tyranny or its inefficiency are great and unendurable.*

The whole essay set him on fire. He decided he would memorize it. Later. His eyes were tired and he blew out the candle. He settled his head into the musty pillow and dozed off, with visions of a glorious revolution glowing in his dreams.

Chris-John woke to Stephanie's screaming. Stephanie was always screaming.

Chris-John turned over in the bed. He was drenched with sweat. It was dark still, or again. He tried to fall asleep again. Stephanie screamed.

Chris-John bolted awake.

The sound was coming from *outside*. Stephanie was screaming *outside*.

Stephanie twisted in the grip of two whip-thin, half-toothed Farington soldiers. They weren't doing anything to her yet, just holding her, as if waiting for the rest of their gang before the party began. She kicked, spat, screamed, yanked, and pushed.

Chris-John fell off the bed and crawled to the dirty window and peered down. He was too weak to run

down and help her. He'd been sinking by the day. He
slept all the time. His thigh was all puffed and ugly.
There was still a bullet in it. Nothing had been done
for it. Stephanie was not a doctor.

Chris-John dragged the window open, heard the ominous sound of an automobile somewhere in Farington's streets. Stephanie screamed.

Chris-John fumbled for something to throw. He
grabbed a clay pot with a dead plant in it, threw it
down, threw perfume bottles, shoes, a broken clock—

"Hey!" an angry voice sounded from down below.

—a wine bottle, a pillow—didn't matter if it was
hard, whatever he could grab. The night table—he
pushed it out and it dropped with a crash. At that, the
soldiers jumped out of the way and lost their grip.
Stephanie bolted.

The two beasts made to chase her, but just then an
automobile without headlights turned the corner, and
the two soldiers faced the car warily.

The military car stopped. The man emerged
smoothly, dressed in general's uniform without medals,
handsome, with the coldest eyes in Farington. The kid-
leather glove on his right hand was not for warmth on
this summer night. A .357 automatic had a recoil like
a cannon.

The beasts pointed up at the window. Chris-John
sprang back. He hadn't thought he could jump like that.
It was a convulsion of fear.

At the sight of Tow and the sound of the front door
breaking, courage failed. Chris-John fled the room
through Stephanie's closet to the secret passage. He
replaced the back panel behind him, and carrying an
unlit lantern, he crawled in darkness as softly as he
could down the two flights of creaking wooden stairs
toward the cellar. On the other side of the thin wall he
could hear footsteps mounting the main staircase up to
the second floor, then prowling overhead through the
rooms where he'd just been.

Once in the cellar, Chris-John lit his lantern with quivering hands. He opened the bunker hatch and lowered himself, gripping his lantern's handle between his teeth. He tried to pull a piece of rotting pressboard over the top of the hatch to cover it as he let the hatch close over his head.

Then he crouched, cowering amid all the books, shivering from the cold and his fever. And still he was looking for a place to hide.

He held his lantern to all the bookshelves, along the walls of the bunker. The light caught on the shape of a wheel low on the wall. He held the lantern closer. It was a hatch like the one that opened the bunker from the top. It was a peculiar thing, not part of the original structure. Chris-John could see the cuts in the wall where it had been added later by someone who wanted a second entrance. Or exit.

It was a strange arrangement, custom-ordered for a revolutionary.

Chris-John tried to move the bookshelves clear of it, and the whole rack tipped, spilling books, and fell over with a clatter, knocking over another rack, and tilting the books out of another.

The noise made him jump but it did not horrify him. He knew from living in the rebel hideout that these bunkers could absorb a lot of racket. What disheartened him was that now the wheel was exposed to plain view. Even if he covered it again, the row of fallen racks pointed the way toward it like an accusing stack of toppled dominoes.

So, with a feeling of sacrilege, Chris-John overturned *all* of the racks in the bunker in all directions, making a chaotic obstacle of heaps of books and metal racks. Then he leaned the nearest empty book rack to cover the hatch, and placed a brittle carpet over that.

Having so hidden the wheel from view once more, he tried to open the hatch.

His arms were weak, his hands quaking. The wheel stuck fast.

Chris-John fell to one knee. He leaned against the wheel and wept. It occurred to him now that there was no building next to Stephanie's on this side, the rear side of the house. This hatchway—whatever the circumstance had been when it had been added—now had to open to nothing but solid earth.

He screamed, "No! No! God, you can't! You can't!" until his throat was sore and harsh. He cried wildly, tugging at the wheel, then he fell on a heap of books and sobbed.

Phoenix had been watching the bastion apartment of the Screaming Rabbit all day, waiting for a chance to do something, he did not know what. He'd seen Stephanie captured, caught a glimpse of Chris-John coming to her rescue with the damnedest barrage of missiles from the upper-floor window, and he'd seen the arrival of his deadly kin Tow. Phoenix hid around the back of the building, behind the dried-up wishing well under the spreading branches of the weeping willow tree. Then he saw lights up on the second floor, saw a familiar coldly trim silhouette at the window, and Phoenix sighed in defeat. It wasn't fair that David get hold of the beautiful Chris-John. Rumor had it that David had lots and lots of pretty things of either sex at the palace. And goddammit, he killed them. To have so many that he could just throw them away like that and get a new one just like that. Life was not fair. Phoenix wished he were like David—ruthless. If Phoenix were ruthless, he never would've let Chris-John go in the first place; and he could be screwing his brains out right now instead of crouching behind this stupid well, watching the overprivileged David move in on what was rightfully his.

Suddenly, from very close by—it was deep within the wishing well—there was a squealing like metal on metal or an unoiled wagon wheel in the same timbre as fingernails on blackboard, making Phoenix reel back in fright.

The raucous squealing came again, like a wheel turning. Then came a crack, a thud, a grunt, and a gasp.

Phoenix ran.

Tow stalked through Stephanie's apartment with drawn pistol. He found nothing. He glanced out the front window. His eye caught a moving light a few blocks away. Headlights of a car.

A car in Farington.

And the fool had his lights on. The assassin's instincts goaded him to investigate this irregularity. But instinct also told him to stay and find his quarry before it slipped his noose.

Finally Tow ran down the stairs and barked at the two street soldiers. "Search this building. Hold anyone you find. *Don't* let anyone out past you."

The goons grinned. "Yes, sir."

Tow climbed into his car and drove toward the moving lights.

Lark squinted at all the shadows through the window as the rebel car slowly threaded the streets of Farington, as if she really expected to find Chris-John this way. Scottie had warned her that the possibility was slight, so slight he refused to call it a possibility. The only reason he had consented to this driving tour of Farington was the possibility that Chris-John might see *them*. A real search would necessitate their getting out of the car. None of them was about to get out of the car.

"You know who they say hid out here once?" said Detroit.

"The Agassiz hatchet murderer?" said Lark.

"Henry Iver," said Detroit.

"I find that difficult to conceive," said Scottie, slowing the car.

"Why are you slowing down?"

Scottie nodded at four corpses in the street, two of them crushed. "Check these carefully as I go by. I'm not going to stop."

Lark and Detroit held their breath and looked hard. None of the four corpses was Chris-John's. Lark breathed a sigh of relief. But Detroit demanded, "Stop the car, Scottie. Let me out."

"Do you see Chris-John?" said Lark.

"No," said Detroit quickly with an urgency approaching panic. "Something is real wrong. Let me out. I'll just take a second."

Scottie stopped and Detroit sprang out. She ran to the two uncrushed corpses, looked at them carefully but hastily, turned them over, then she ran back to the car, jumped into the seat, slammed the door, locked it, and cried, "Get out of here, Scottie. Fast as you can. Now. Yesterday. Last week. Go go go."

Scottie started away. "What is it?"

"They were shot. One shot each. Hollow points. Go in this big, come out this big. Coulda stopped a bull moose. Those are tire treads on those two."

Someone had a big gun and a car. Guns and cars were rare and expensive. Accurate shooting took a lot of practice and a lot of precious ammunition. And assassination with one telling shot was a trademark of Farington's favorite son.

"Jesus," said Scottie, and his hands became unsteady on the wheel.

"Get us out of here," said Detroit. "God, God."

Scottie had just noticed the dark movement in the rearview mirror when suddenly a set of automobile headlights flashed on directly behind them.

V.

Cross Double Cross

DETROIT JUMPED WITH A GASP. LARK SANK DOWN IN her seat, hands over her heart. Scottie brought the car to a stop and whispered, "What should I do?"

"I'll talk," said Detroit. "Scottie, you just grunt. Don't you say a word; you talk like a doctor."

The long green-black sedan pulled alongside the rebel car. The driver's-side window rolled down. It was Tow.

Detroit rolled down her window. "Yeah?"

"Who are you? What are you doing here?" the beautiful tenor voice sounded in calm demand.

"Security, Dunhelm plant," said Detroit. "We're looking for a terrorist bomber."

Tow waited as if expecting more, but Detroit had answered his questions and would not be pressured into gibbering. Steel eyes bored into her. Silence suffocated. If is was meant to unnerve, it succeeded. Detroit scratched her head.

Finally he seemed satisfied. "You want to look for a rebel, you follow me," said Tow. His window rolled up and the long dark automobile pulled in front of the rebel car.

"Oh Christ. Oh Jesus," said Lark. Her face had paled, so her faint freckles showed dark and clear on a pasty ground.

Scottie swallowed, stepped on the accelerator, and followed the brigadier's car through the claustrophobic streets to Stephanie's house.

Detroit inhaled for courage and got out. She turned up the collar of her black leather jacket even though the night was warm. Rain on the cobbles had left a slick sheen to the street. Soggy trash collected in gutters under the curbs. Sour smell lingered over everything, keen in the damp air. Detroit kicked a sodden cardboard box from her boot, and walked, hunch-shouldered, toward the house with Tow.

She started at the sight of a skinny razor-hard Farington soldier snarling at her from the doorway.

Tow addressed this creature: "Didn't you find him?"

The beast shook his scraggly head.

"Maybe if you looked," Tow suggested in silken voice.

Sunken, diseased eyes shifted uneasily, and the beast withdrew into the brick building.

"You will find two such creatures inside," Tow instructed the bogus security team. "You are looking for something pretty."

Pretty? Lark's brows lifted convulsively as her heart leaped.

Her reaction did not escape notice. "Yes?" said Tow.

Lark smirked nervously. "Just seemed bloody unlikely." She shrugged as if dismissing the thought.

Tow's eyes were fixed levelly on her, and she suddenly remembered that Tow was from Farington and she wondered if she had insulted him. There was no telling how a viper's mind worked.

There came a rapping from above, fist on windowpane, and all of them looked up to see one of the dragoons motioning from the second floor for Tow to come.

"Go see what that junkhead has found," said Tow.

Detroit, Lark, and Scottie went inside the front doors and up the stairs, Tow at their backs with drawn pistol.

The Farington soldier had found the false back to Stephanie's closet. The girl's clothes were thrown on the floor along with the back panel; and the dragoon directed a shaft of lantern light into the closet to illuminate the wooden staircase beyond. He beamed a half-toothed grin at Tow, like a fawning mongrel dog expecting a treat.

Tow turned his aristocratic head to Detroit and her companions and the mongrel. "Follow it," he said. He posted the other Faringtoner as guard at the head of the steps to make sure no one came up past them. Then he lit another lantern and followed the others down the steps.

The beast found the hatch in the cellar floor and he howled with delight. He pounced on the wheel, but Tow motioned him away with his gun barrel. "You." He pointed the gun at Scottie, then nodded to the hatch. "Open it."

Tow kept his pistol trained on the hatch as Scottie turned the reluctant wheel and lifted the hatch. He stepped away.

Nothing sprang out. All was dark below.

Tow nodded at the beast and motioned to Scottie. "Give him your lantern."

The street soldier gave Scottie the lamp, and Tow sent the three rebels down into the bunker.

"What do you see?"

"Books!" Detroit called back. "Piles and piles of books."

And no Chris-John. They'd all been certain he would be here and wondered with heart in throat what they could do to protect him from Tow. Or what they would do if Chris-John joyfully cried out their names.

But he wasn't here.

"What kind of books?" said Tow.

"Can't read," said Detroit before one of her companions could do something rash like read off a title. "Here." She handed one up the hatch to Tow.

Then she waded over the heaps of books and found the side hatch underneath the carpet-covered book rack.

Silently she motioned Lark and Scottie over to see. She muttered, "If we get him down here alone, I'm taking him. Be ready to back me up if he's faster." And she moved away from them.

"What have you got down there?" Tow called again, hearing curious a murmur and silence. They had found *something*.

"Uh," said Detroit. "Something. I'm not real sure, sir. No rebel but, well, I'm not sure what it is. It's under a ton of these fuckin' books."

Tow made a sound of impatient disgust, set down his lantern on the edge of the hatch, and gripped the top of the ladder.

And he froze where he was.

Tow made mistakes. His instincts were good but sometimes he erred. However, about one thing he was never wrong; concerning this, his instinct was infallible. Tow always knew when someone meant to kill him. He knew, just knew, if he went down that ladder, he was dead. The wrong feeling that had first struck him on seeing the headlights of their car roaming Farington's street broke out full force. He felt death down there.

He looked down the hatch. The leather-jacketed little talker was looking up at him expectantly, her ragged cut black bangs fallen across an upturned nose that was nicked by an old scar. The lanky blond in the big khaki jacket was tramping over the books, trying to keep her balance. The big dark man was standing casually against the wall; something wrong about him. He wore a moth-chewed black sweater over his lean big-boned frame, black trousers, and worn shoes; he had a starved look, shadowy deep hollows of his skull showing through dark reddish translucent skin. He was looking at the books, his head cocked sideways to look at the spines lengthwise. He was reading titles. Tow stood up straight.

Detroit was waiting for him. Tow uncapped the kerosene well of his lantern and turned the wick up till it burned with a leaping huge yellow flame that licked over its blackened glass. ''I see a room full of treason,'' he said, and hurled the lantern down into the pile of brittle dry books in the bunker and he shut the hatch as the fire roared up and the bunker filled with smoke.

The Farington street soldier with Tow was giggling in evil glee, jumping up and down in the lanternless dark of the cellar like a maniac. He thought Tow was marvelous, it never occurring to his rotting brain that the viper could turn on him as well, with as little provocation. But Tow merely said, ''Go upstairs.'' And the soldier stumblingly obeyed. Tow followed more slowly, with cautious steps in the blackness, listening for where his vanguard tripped.

At the head of the stairs Tow took the lantern from the guard he'd posted there and he went back out to the street.

Tow's car was still there but the rebel car was gone.

Tow turned to the Faringtoner who had been his rear guard. ''You didn't see anything?''

The Faringtoner mumbled no. He said he'd been watching the stairs.

Tow looked into the creature's bloodshot eyes, vapid like his smile. He was high.

Tow was furious. A cold fury. He shot the creature. The impact carried his body back four feet, and the other beast just giggled. Tow did not waste a bullet on that one. He was feeling soiled and frustrated and wanted to be gone.

He checked his own car very carefully for sabotage before he drove away.

Chris-John came to consciousness and thought he was delirious. Everything he felt was impossible: sense of motion, the bouncing of a car on a poor road; smell of Detroit's cheap lilac perfume overpowering his own unwashed stink and the car smells. He leaned over the side of the car seat and threw up on the plastic mat.

The car stopped. The driver turned around and looked down at Chris-John.

"Why did you have to do that? You know you're not pretty anymore."

It was Phoenix.

Chris-John *knew* he was delirious now. "I was . . . I was in a pit. . . ."

"You were in a wishing well. I made a wish. I should know better than to make wishes, I might get what I ask for. Shouldn'ta come back."

Chris-John dragged himself up to look over the back of the car seat. They were parked at a small building surmounted by a cross and flying the flag of a red cross on white ground. This place was a little hospice far from any other sign of civilization. Phoenix had ventured out of Farington to find help. He had also figured out how to drive a car.

Phoenix started to help Chris-John out of the car, but Chris-John feebly hung on to the doorframe. "No. No. I know this car. Where are they? Where are they?"

Phoenix's blond brows shot up. "Those were friends of yours? A big bony giant; a black-haired little girl with big—" Phoenix finished with his hands. "And a skinny sort of blond sort of ordinary—"

"Yes! Yes! Where are they!"

"Hate to tell you, friend, they joined the other side," said Phoenix. "They came with Davy."

"Davy?"

"Tow. Brigadier David Tow."

"No. Oh no. We've got to go back—"

Phoenix laughed. "*I* ain't going back! Davy'd kill me. And you ain't going back 'cause if I let go of you, you'll fall on your butt."

"Let me go. Let me go," said Chris-John.

Phoenix let go and Chris-John fell on his butt. He howled with pain.

"Told you," said Phoenix. He hefted Chris-John up and carried him into the hospice.

Inside the little wayside sanctuary, Phoenix's Farington bravado faded. His yellow eyes darted over the walls, the religious pictures, the candles, the donation box, and he held tight to Chris-John—less to keep the boy on his feet than just to hold on.

He swallowed dryly at the approach of a brown-robed man with sandaled feet, a beaded belt tied round his waist. The monk lifted his hood away from his shaven head and looked to Phoenix questioningly, without fear.

"Um, you have to help us," Phoenix commanded, but all the threat his voice was supposed to convey stayed behind, and the words came stumbling out like soldiers without guns.

The monk regarded them dispassionately, two wild things come out of the nearby woods with hunters' traps on their paws. The monk's blue eyes lowered to Chris-John's brown-crusted thigh. His benign face twisted into anger. "He's hurt!" the monk said like an accusation, his tone so sharp Phoenix jumped like a guilty person. "How long did you let that go like that!"

"Um . . . I don't know," said Phoenix in confusion.

The monk scolded, "You wait till maybe he'll lose that leg, then you come here in an automobile and tell me I have to help you—"

"Hey look, I just found him myself, OK? And as for the car I stole it, OK? An' I don't even know how to drive!" Phoenix yelled back. "You gonna help him or do I beat your stupid head against the wall?"

"Beat away," said the monk, and folded his rough hands.

Phoenix rolled his yellow eyes heavenward and said helplessly, "Shit. This guy's nuts. Shit, God. He's a nut."

The monk stepped forward and took Chris-John from

Phoenix's arms—almost had to wrestle him for him.
"What you gonna do?" said Phoenix.

"I am forbidden to turn away the helpless," said the
monk. "Or to ignore anyone who prays, no matter the
crudeness of the form."

And the monk—his name was Brother Thomas—
carried Chris-John to the dispensary to see what could
be done for his wound.

Phoenix and Chris-John spent the rest of the night
in the hospice in a small high-ceilinged room whose
only window was a small skylight. The room was clean,
stark, monastic ("Fancy that," said Phoenix), with two
cots, a washbasin, and a toilet. And in the morning
Phoenix discovered that the single heavy oak door was
bolted from the outside.

"Chris-John. Chris-John. Wake up. I don't like this
at all."

He liked it less when he put on his jacket, searched
his pocket for his knife, and found it missing. "Fuckin'
monk. Chris-John, wake up."

Chris-John blinked awake and lay in the cot, sick to
his stomach. His fever had broken, but the monk
Brother Thomas had used sodium pentothal to put him
under while he dug the bullet from his thigh, and the
drug made Chris-John nauseated.

The drug had also made Chris-John babble. That was
why the door was now locked.

Phoenix pounded on the door and hollered, "Open
up! Open up! Do you hear me! Brother Thomas!
Brother fuckin' Thomas!!"

Chris-John sat up, cleared his throat. "What is it?
He's not going to hurt us." He blinked at the breakfast
of hard rolls, jam, oatcakes, and water set on the night
table.

"He's calling the cops. I know he is."

"Priests can't do that," said Chris-John.

"Then why are we prisoners!" Phoenix beat on the

door. He yelled at the skylight. "Why did I ever get involved? Oh God, why did you make me an idiot!"

He broke into strings of obscenity and kept up such a din that he hardly heard the bar being lifted away when Brother Thomas came at last to open the door.

Phoenix immediately rushed at the small monk, but suddenly a much larger monk appeared from behind him, lifted Phoenix off the floor, and threw him back across the room. Behind the big monk was yet another monk, a tough-skinned farmer with a long staff that could be a handy weapon to one who knew how to use it.

Phoenix groaned on the floor. "They called the cops. I told you. They're turning us in."

Brother Thomas shook his head. "I would that I could. I despise a rebel." His blue eyes turned angrily to Chris-John. "Chicago Red."

Chris-John blinked his enormous brown eyes in shock.

"The sins committed in your name are past number," Brother Thomas said. He turned to someone in the hall. "Bring the Marcos baby."

The Marcos baby was brought squalling in the arms of a monk. Brother Thomas pulled back the baby's blanket for Chris-John to see a blistering red letter *C* burned into the tender skin on the infant's stomach. "There's for you, Chicago Red. This child committed the grievous crime of being born to a woman loyal to the king. Why do you wish such disorder and wickedness on our peaceful Kingdom? Why?"

Chris-John opened his mouth. His mind was still foggy and he hadn't been prepared to defend his creed. He stammered. All he could say was, "My people aren't supposed to do things like that. I never wanted that."

"This is what you have, though, Chicago Red. And I won't let it go on."

"You've notified the Crown," said Chris-John.

Brother Thomas shook his shaven head. "No. You came to me as a man of God. I will not turn you over to secular powers."

But before Chris-John could express relief, Brother Thomas repeated harshly, "*I* will not. I have called upon a higher authority than myself, and perhaps the shepherd of our flock will see fit in his wisdom to make decisions that I cannot." And with that, Brother Thomas and the other monks withdrew and barred the door behind them.

"What'd he just say?" Phoenix hissed to Chris-John.

Chris-John answered dully: "It means he's calling in a bishop." He lowered his face into his hands. "He's gonna let the bishop turn us in."

Phoenix groaned. "Davy's gonna kill me."

The door opened again. The farmer monk came in and rapped the butt end of his staff on the floor like a chamberlain for the entrance of the king. There was a scuffling of sandaled feet out in the hall, a hush of voices, and the strong striding of a single pair of hard-soled feet with the rustle of a cape, and the pontiff swept into the small room.

They hadn't just called a bishop. It was the arch-bishop of the Church of America, member of the King's Council, His Eminence Gregory Vandetti.

VI.

Holy Alliance

THE ARCHBISHOP ORDERED THE OTHER HOLYMEN OUT of the chamber. The monks protested for his safety, but the archbishop carried a revolver next to his breast and assured them he knew how to use it, so they withdrew.

Gregory turned to the skulking yellow-eyed ugly Phoenix and thought him vaguely reminiscent of Brigadier Tow. Then he turned to the beautiful sick boy on the bed. The archbishop's dark eyes widened; the look was—but couldn't be—recognition. Gregory's mouth spread into a surprised smile and he nearly laughed. "Chicago Red?"

"That's what Brother Thomas says," said Chris-John. He gazed up at the archbishop's craggy rough attractive face. He sensed strength, more strength than he'd ever encountered in a man. Chris-John felt compelled to hope, though he knew this man was on the king's own council, was a personal friend of the king and acquaintance of the dreaded assassin Tow.

The archbishop drew near the bed, noted Chris-John's wrapped thigh. "What did you do?"

"What's it to you? You're just going to turn us over to the king anyway."

"Child, you don't know who you're talking to and it's too bad I can't tell you."

Chris-John's jaw dropped. He reached out over the side of the bed and grasped the edge of the pontiff's cape, fell off the bed, and knelt at Gregory's feet. Chris-

John stared up, his beautiful face touched with holy awe witnessing a miracle. He gripped tight on Gregory's cloak and pulled. "You. You." He kissed the archbishop's rings.

The archbishop smiled, his forefinger before his lips begging secrecy.

Phoenix was watching them, bewildered. Chris-John turned his head and shot Phoenix a joyful smile that took Phoenix's breath away. Phoenix supposed that meant they were safe, though in that instant, caught in the radiance of the blinding smile, he didn't care if he died.

Gregory lifted Chris-John up. He beckoned Phoenix closer and spoke in a low confessional drone, the kind whose words were impossible to overhear. "Try to look dejected and repentant when we leave here, can you?"

But Chris-John blurted in a whisper, "Father, General Tow is after us. He'll find out you helped us. There's more of us in trouble with him, I have to get back to Farington—"

Gregory cut him short. "You can tell me everything in the car," he said, hurrying, but without undue haste, serene and assured. He drew his revolver, left it uncocked. "I'll arrange everything. Just come with me now. Fold your hands and bow your heads."

Tow was driving back to the Capital on the road through the Black Forest when he saw the long, long clerical car stopped on the roadside, appearing abandoned, with no one in sight. Tow slowed down. It was the archbishop's car.

Tow pulled alongside Father Greg's car and got out.

He discovered Father Greg bound and gagged in the front seat. Tow undid the gag, then stood back amused at His Eminence's predicament.

Mister Tow, if you will," said Greg.

Tow untied Greg's hands, chuckling. "Who did this to you?"

"The highwayman. The Devil Rider."

"The *what?*" said Tow. "I thought you had Chicago Red!"

"I did," Gregory grumbled. "Then the Devil came out of the—how did you know I had Chicago Red!"

"I just know," said Tow. He was not feeling informative. He was not going to say that he'd extorted the information out of the monks back at the hospice to which he'd tracked the rebel car.

Tow backed away from the archbishop's automobile and looked around. Yes, this was the Devil's favorite stretch of road. The Devil loved automobiles. And he loved clergymen. The outrageous irony of it. "The Devil Rider!"

"As God is my witness," said the archbishop, untying his own feet. "He has little enough respect for God's servants."

Greg was showing little enough alarm, being very sanguine about the whole episode. It would have struck Tow odd had the archbishop displayed any nerves or horror. Greg was an unflappable man.

"I could have sworn that Chicago Red and the Devil Rider were in no way connected," Tow mused, narrowing his eyes hawklike at the overhanging tree boughs.

"I would agree with you," said Greg, rubbing his wrists. "They both seemed genuinely surprised to encounter one another."

Well, thought Tow, if they were not connected before, they certainly were connected now. "Are you going to tell the king that you let Chicago Red go, or shall I?" said Tow.

"You may," said Greg, not fearful of the king's wrath. "Or I will when I get back to the Capital this evening. Thank you for your assistance, Brigadier."

Tow climbed back into his own car and drove toward the Capital. He was out of sight when Greg let Chris-John and Phoenix out from the compartments under the second and third seats of his car and asked where they wanted to go.

"You suppose we could give the area a last search?" said Scottie. His dark face was greasy with salve covering his burns.

"That would be your fourth last search," said Lark flatly, then moaned because she'd split her lips open again.

Detroit just coughed and held a cool wet rag over her eyes. Her eyebrows had been singed off.

Ezra had found the three of them wandering Farington's streets, automobile-less, blistered, coughing up soot, and half-blind. They had escaped from the bunker beneath Stephanie's bastion via the side hatch. None of them had ever heard of a bunker with a side exit. Tow hadn't, and Tow had seen many such bunkers in his time, so he never suspected that the three rebels could possibly escape from their smoky tomb.

The three of them had stumbled out into the wishing well and shut the hatch fast behind them so the fire would die for lack of air. Later, much later, they would go back and get the books that were left.

Now, safe in their own bunker headquarters, they were not thinking about books. They were hurt, they'd lost a car, Tow had seen their faces, and still they had no trace of Chris-John. They did not know if Tow had caught him.

They monitored the radio for some report on the Dunhelm saboteur, but the Crown stations were silent on the subject.

"What if he's still in Farington?" said Carrie.

At that moment there came a tap on the bunker's hatch and everyone froze—because they were all there, everyone who knew the location of this bunker: Ezra, Scottie, Lark, Detroit, Carrie and Meredith, Terese, Balt, and Tina. Everyone except Chris-John.

They held their breath and the tapping came again.

The code was right, and Detroit whispered in smoke-hoarsened voice, "Chris-John!"

The hatch opened and Chris-John clambered down the ladder, jumping the last two steps to land on his unwounded leg. When he straightened up, he hardly seemed to know where he was. There was a smear of dirt across his face where he'd brushed away tears with a dirty hand.

Mute Terese ran to him and kissed his soiled hands. Carrie cried, "Chris-John! Oh Chris-John, thank God!"

Detroit hugged him hard. When released, Chris-John swayed like a dazed fawn. He looked up at Scottie, who shrugged at him. "How are you?"

"Fine," said Chris-John, and he broke down sobbing. His legs buckled and Scottie caught him as he was sinking.

Chris-John cried into Scottie's wide chest, then suddenly lifted his face, drew himself together in shaky approximation of normality, and said as if he'd forgotten, "We—I brought somebody." He sniffed and dashed a few straggling tears from his face with the heels of his palms. The black handprints made him look like a woeful raccoon. His brows drew together. "Um . . . he's a friend."

"You brought him *here?*" said Scottie. And suddenly he was struck by a more alarming thought yet: "How did *you* get here?"

"The Devil Rider let us off," said Chis-John.

"The Devil!" Carrie cried. "Why didn't you bring *him* down here?"

Chris-John hesitated. "Um . . . he's also the archbishop."

"The—" Scottie started, then cried, "You showed Vandetti the way here!"

"Yes," said Chris-John. "He's a friend. He's the Devil."

"Have you lost your mind!"

"A little I think," Chris-John said, childlike.

"He's the archbishop, Chris-John!" Ezra cried. "The arch-bish-op!"

Lark put a protective arm around Chris-John's narrow shoulders. "Oh, for God's sake, if Vandetti turns us in, we'll turn him in. He's got to know that. How much safer can we be?"

Scottie's jaw moved like an agitated cat's tail twitching. He could not give in, but neither did he have any arguments left.

A pounding at the bunker's hatch broke the stalemate and a coarse voice yelled down, "Hey! It's starting to fuckin' rain up here, dammit! What if I get eaten by a bear!"

"Who's that?" said Scottie.

"That's my friend," said Chris-John. He had forgotten about Phoenix. Phoenix was afraid of the forest. Chris-John called up the ladder, "You can come down now."

Phoenix jumped down and paced across the bunker with a surly Farington swagger, strutting his yellow-eyed, fat-lipped, pointed-toothed ugliness for an appreciatively stunned audience. "This is Phoenix," said Chris-John to his rebels. Phoenix sneered for them. "He's from Farington. He's staying with us."

Out of nine sets of dubiously staring eyes Phoenix met Scottie's. "You got a problem with that?"

"Why not stay in Farington?" said Scottie. "We could use a friendly base in Farington. We found that out." He dabbed his greasy burns gingerly with his middle finger.

Phoenix wagged his head. "I can't go back. Davy'd kill me."

"Who?"

"Tow!"'said Phoenix impatiently. "The goddamn brigadier assassin."

Detroit broke into an amazed grin, her hairless eyebrows lifted high. "Davy? *Davy?*" She didn't believe

she'd ever heard the brigadier David Tow ever called
Davy before.

Lark giggled as well. "Davy?" She started coughing.

Phoenix shrugged.

Scottie shook his head. "How's Tow going to know
you're one of us?"

"The priest'll tell 'im," said Phoenix.

"I thought Vandetti was supposed to be a friend of
ours," said Scottie archly. His dark eyes slid aside to
Chris-John.

"He doesn't have a choice," said Chris-John. "He
has to give descriptions of us to the king. He's not the
only person who saw us. There's some monks. They
saw us and they saw Gregory see us. If his description
isn't like theirs, his own head's in the noose."

Phoenix agreed. "You can't tell too many lies to
Davy."

"The king's going to know what Chicago Red looks
like!" said Scottie. He threw up his hands and nodded
with an ironic bitter smile on his burned face. "Wonderful."

"This is my fault. I ruined the Dunhelm raid."
Chris-John gazed at his feet. "Scottie, I'm sorry I
didn't let you talk me out of it."

People moved out of Tow's way as he mounted the
wide white steps of the palace. Most people never cared
to cross Tow's path at any time, but sometimes they
gave him a wider berth than others.

Today he looked all wrong. There was a smudge of
soot on his high cheek; his clothes were not so fresh,
as if he'd been out all night; a fine light stubble glittered on his chin in the morning light. One just didn't
see Tow like that. Steel eyes smoldered dark. He was
tired, dirty, outwardly contained, but with an subcur-
rent of anger. The palace stairs cleared as he started
up, his back straight, shoulders square and military.

The king received him right away, not in the audience hall, but in his private library. Edward III had just come from his bath. He was fresh and lightly scented with powder. He wore white breeches, a silk shirt, and black shoes with silver buckles. Silver threads lined his blue brocade coat. He sat in the red velvet wing chair and waved his hand for Tow to be seated as well. He ordered coffee for both of them.

Tow sat wearily in the other wing chair, rested his elbow on the arm, his stubbled cheek on his fist, and he looked at the king in flat defeat.

"Ah, my poor assassin," said Edward in mild spirits. It was odd to see Tow so grubby; Edward knew Tow loathed it. "The old hometown does not agree with you anymore."

Tow shook his head to concur; no, it did not.

"I notice your aide is absent. I was just getting used to seeing him tag along wherever you went," said the king. "You never had much use for an aide before."

"I've had useless aides in the past," said Tow shortly.

Stanton was useful? Good. He might live awhile.

The pretty maid returned with their coffee on a silver tray. She started to pour, but Edward motioned: "Bring it here." The maid set it on a table by the king and he sent her out. Tow hadn't even looked at her. The king poured the coffee himself. He set Tow's before him black. "So what happened? You look like a very sad assassin."

Tow lifted his eyes to the painted ceiling. "We had him. In custody. On the Capital Road." He closed his fist as around an invisible bird. Then he opened it with an incredulous look at his empty hand, seeing his bird had flown. "He got away."

The Dunhelm saboteur? One can always console oneself imagining he was no one," said the king.

"One could," said Tow. "Except we know he was Chicago Red."

King Edward spilled his coffee.

Ordinarily an error of this dimension called for a tirade against incompetence, but not to Tow. For one thing Edward had never known Tow to be incompetent; and even if he had been, the king would not berate him to his face. Not Tow. "Well," said Edward soberly, setting his coffee cup aside and sitting back in the chair. "Tell me what happened."

Tow told his tale, leaving out Phoenix and a few bodies, and ended with finding Greg on the road, bound and gagged in his car.

"His prisoners overpowered him?" said Edward.

Tow shook his head no. "It seems the preacher took the wrong road home."

Edward frowned, tried to think of what Tow had just told him—where he'd found the archbishop's car. In the Black Forest on the Capital Road. "No," he said. "Oh no."

Tow nodded.

The king's mouth worked as if building to an explosion of rage. Then he started to laugh. He roared. "Oh God, Tow, it's horrible." Tears rolled down his cheeks. Tow made a droll expression and a shrug. He was too tired to laugh. He had failed, been made to look ridiculous, been forced to do all manner of things he did not want to do, and all for nothing. He was weary, sick. He was dusted with a patina of soot, his shoes were scuffed, he felt a slimy film on his face. He needed a bath and a shave. His gun needed cleaning. His clothes were beginning to smell. He had killed, and he was not feeling right about it. Unease persisted about the existence of the creature Phoenix, whom he now wished he'd killed while he'd been exterminating the other vermin and had done with it. He rested his forehead on his hand.

The king dried his tears, still smiling. He was in an unusually magnanimous mood this morning. Besides, he could not be angry with Tow. Tow had come closer than anyone, except for that damn archbishop, who hadn't the brains to call for armed assistance in bringing Chicago Red back to the Capital. "You never actually saw the man Chicago Red."

"No. Vandetti did. The monks did."

"We'll have a description of him now anyway." The king sighed.

Tow's lips twisted into a wry half smile. "It's quite a description," he said. However, it was the description of Chicago Red's *companion* that was alarming to Tow. *Ugly,* the monks had said. About that Tow said nothing. He was afraid to think about it.

The king rose. Tow stayed seated. They were rarely formal in private. Edward came around behind Tow's seat, patted the top of the chair as he would have Tow's shoulder except that he never never touched Tow. "We'll find him."

Tow took no encouragement from that. He couldn't tell the king that finding Chicago Red would make very little difference in combating the rebellion. If Tow had learned anything in this farcical goose chase, it was that the rebels' strength was not in any particular powerful leader but in their scattered interconnected numbers. They were not even like cockroaches—more like ants, a cohesive colony of little beings that accomplished feats beyond the ability of its tiny individuals. Chicago Red had not escaped from Tow because of any skill or cunning of Chicago Red's. Tow was infinitely more skilled and cunning than his quarry. Chicago Red had gotten away because he had help, lots and lots of help from several people in several places. And that made him a more formidable opponent than the assassin. Tow said nothing.

The king moved to the window and spread the curtains to the cheery morning light. The day would be brilliant. "Get some rest," he said to Tow. "Send me a full report at your convenience."

Tow rose, relieved to be done with this dismal affair,

even if he'd failed. He left the study and mounted the
stairs to the third floor of the east wing, disgust and ill
feeling slipping away as he neared his chambers. He
could already see his sunlit rooms, airy, clean, the
muted carpets, damask curtains, a shower, crisp sheets,
his piano, a soft-voiced boy to pour a glass of sherry.
He was singing by the time he was at the end of the
hall.

Part Two:
The Power

I.

Harvest

MARION WHISTLED A LITTLE GIN TUNE CALLED THE
"Devil Dance." Her father's stallion stepped high,
thinking they were on parade. Its long tail brushed
Marion's skirt as it whisked away flies that swarmed
thick in the Black Forest in autumn. Marion had never
strayed so far from home on the Capital Road.

She reined in her mount and her whistle died. All
around her the birds had gone silent in the evening
gloom. *Did I do that?*

A jay screamed. As some people told, the harsh
notes cried, "Thief! Thief!" and Marion had to wonder if the bird spoke true. Every shadow in the nodding
trees was alive.

Suddenly came a crashing and dark shapes rushing
at her from the underbrush—common brigands who
knew nothing about horses, for even as they dashed at
her, her stallion spooked and reared, its hooves slicing.
Marion seized its mane and held tight. The scarecrow
of a man grabbing at her reins staggered backward,
another danced away crab-stepping. Marion kicked the
third away from her with her boot and she tried to reach
under her cloak for the rifle while still keeping her seat.
The stallion bucked and Marion fell across its neck.

Pistols cracked. Marion's pulse froze. They had
guns. Rebels.

But as Marion struggled to sit up in her saddle she
realized she had not been hit and that the three brigands were running, yelling in terror. Tattoo of hoof-

123

beats neared from behind her and out of the dark
swooped a giant figure on horseback, black cape flapping like a great raven, its face a hellish mask. The
black stallions screamed at each other, eyes rolling, as
the Devil flashed past. The edge of his cape snapped
against Marion's hand.

The brigands scrambled for the bushes and the hoofbeats thundered down the road.

Marion got her own bolting steed under control and
put a hand to her heaving, still-bejeweled chest. The
Capital Road was quiet again.

Marion blinked wide eyes. "Well!"

Down the road, a peasant boy accosted Marion.
"Ma'am?"

Marion answered, surprised to hear her voice trembling so, "Yes?"

"A scary man said to give this to a lady who came
riding this way." He held up a note that was crushed
from being held in a small boy's sweaty grip.

Marion reached down for the note and gave the boy
a coin. The boy took it, then said guiltily, "He already
paid me, ma'am."

"Then give it to someone you love."

She opened the note.

*Woman, I am a THIEF. I don't take donations. If
you want to get rid of your jewels, give them to the
Church. I understand It will be glad enough to take
them.*

Marion laughed. More like a royal guardsman than
a highwayman, she thought. There must be a revolution, the whole world is topsy-turvy.

Marion returned home, flushed. Her father noticed
it. "I could swear you've found a sweetheart on the
side?" said Lord Martel.

He sounded almost hopeful. For God's sake, he
wished she would fall in love with someone. He would

buy a title for a stable boy if that's what she wanted, if she would only chose someone.

But she just smiled. "A mild flirtation is all."

Time came again for the king's October harvest party. He was advised perhaps he ought to subdue it this year. He would not hear of it. So on the afternoon of the fete, carriages drawn by glossy horses with beribboned manes drove up to the palace, bringing ladies in velvet and satin gowns and men in their handsome brocades and silk cravats and tasseled canes. Lords doffed their tricorne hats of velvet or fur, some with feathers, edged in gold lace, or sporting a single jewel. Ladies blushed behind feathered and carved ivory fans. They were all in powdered wigs, the men's curled neatly into rolls at the sides and tied at the nape of the neck with silk ribbons, the women's piled high with feathered aigrettes and diamond tiaras or strands of pearls and autumn flowers. They all wore colors of the harvest, straw gold, autumn leaves, browns of earth and trees, evergreen and rusty brown of dried field grasses.

Beginning in the early morning, common folk gathered outside the palace, lining the streets and crowding all the windows of the buildings across the street to watch the aristocrats arrive in their finery and parade between a long double row of footmen in splendid scarlet livery flanking the walk from the street through the garden courtyard to the palace's grand main entrance. "You see," said the king. "They enjoy the spectacle, too. It would be very dismal for them to see us all in burlap."

The peasants enjoyed when a lady arrived with a pet squirrel monkey on her arm, tied to her bracelet with a golden leash. The creature panicked at the cheering crowds and went into a climbing, screeching frenzy, pulling off the lady's wig and defecating on her escort, who tried to come to her rescue. The king chose not to remember that incident.

Among the guests was General Tow—not because he was on the Council and not because he lived in the palace, for Tow was still, before all else, a commoner of dishonorable birth. He was here because the king felt need of guards and Tow was inconspicuous—he blended in well when he wanted to—and he was still the most efficient marksman the king had ever seen.

Tow's inclusion caused the king a bit of concern, though, because Edward had invited a soprano to perform for his guests. "Be kind to her," the king warned Tow. "Her voice pleases me."

Tow was an artist, recognized Kingdomwide. The greatest masters never faulted him, and some even counted him in their ranks. His musical opinion was highly regarded.

At best Tow endured sopranos. He never liked them. He had once killed someone, long ago, for daring butcher a song. Lately he was mellowing, or learning how to behave in society. Now he was just frostily abusive to the transgressor. He would applaud if they managed not to offend him. His applause was mocking. He had no use for soprano voices. Normally expressionless, Tow would wince in real pain at the harsh edge to a high voice, and the king had even once seen him suck air between his teeth in involuntary reaction of pain at the cutting edge. Boy sopranos were the same. He hated them all. "Razors in the silk," he called them.

The king remembered Tow's encounter with a singer years past. The young lady had foolishly pranced up to the brigadier and asked him if he did not think she sounded like a very nightingale. Tow, with more tact than he generally showed, dodged the question. "That song wants a tenor voice," he'd said.

"You?" said the soprano, a little miffed.

"I do passably well." That was how he described his piano playing and his marksmanship.

"And I?"

"You're a soprano," said Tow.

"What does that mean?"

"If it were up to me, all the sopranos in the Kingdom would be lined up against the wall and shot."

The soprano had left the palace and never looked back.

So now for harvest festival Tow sat as if in a dentist's chair. Gray eyes turned beseechingly to the king and begged, "Must I?"

"Brigadier, if you don't find her painless, I will grant you any wish your heart desires."

Tow's eyes flickered and the king knew he'd just made a mistake. Tow had decided to be evil, and for a moment the king was genuinely afraid. Tow could be very evil. He had been civilized lately and lulled Edward into a false sense of complacency.

And Tow's request was dangerous, even alarming, but not as bad as it could have been. "A command," said Tow.

The king was surprised. Tow was a loner. He was an assassin, not a real general, not a leader. What use had he for a command? But the king was stuck. He had promised. And with luck he would not have to grant it. "Very well."

Tow's eyelids lifted momentarily over steel eyes to see the king agree. "Confident, aren't you?"

"I am," said Edward. "I think I am."

But he was beginning to doubt. Edward was not a musical expert. He only knew what he liked. This wager could be a big mistake, knowing how Tow felt about sopranos. Still, Edward had an idea of what Tow found offensive in the female voice, and he knew this girl was different.

The singer was a tall, slender, very young lady, draped in flowing white. Actually she was not a lady, being a peasant orphan of no birth or breeding, but for her talent she'd been dressed and ornamented as a lady to entertain the guests of the king. Her honey-colored hair was pulled back from her face, crowned with a circlet of autumn flowers, and it fell loose down her back like a maiden's. She was only seventeen; her voice should not yet have been mature, but the people who cared for her in the orphanage said that her voice had never been immature. If she did well, she would never have to go back to the orphanage.

As she stepped beside the piano, the king wished at her, *Sing like an angel, my dear.* He glanced over his shoulder at his viper as the girl was about to begin.

She took a deep silent breath, her wide rib cage and thick diaphragm belied by slender form, and the first pure note like a delicate bell took flight. She sang prettily, her middle tones a sweet silky lyric voice, soaring into the higher register as a silvery effortless coloratura. It was said that her usable range was higher than the highest notes ever written for the human voice, so there was no strain, no edge on the high notes of her song.

Tow stood up abruptly from his seat.

Oh no. The king lowered his eyes and put his hand to his brow.

But as the music faltered to silence, and everyone stared at the outraged brigadier, Tow growled, "That's wanting a different accompanist."

The king laughed into his hand in surprised relief. It was not the girl who offended. It was the pianist. The king clapped his hands together, laughing, and no one knew what was funny. He nodded at Tow and motioned toward the piano with his open hand for him to do as he willed.

Tow chased the pianist from bench—the gawky, bespectacled little man could not get away fast enough—and the recital was ready to resume with Tow at the keys. The young orphan singer looked nervously to the king, to Tow. Tow gave her the cue with a nod of his handsome head, and she sang.

Everyone was delighted and applauded at the finish.

Tow gave a silent nodding bow of acknowledgment for his part, but said not a word about the girl.

Afterward, as the party moved to the banquet hall, the king caught up with Tow. ''Well?''

''Pretty,'' said Tow.

The king was shocked. ''Pretty'' was better than he could've hoped for. It meant he'd won his bet. ''I am relieved.'' By God, that little girl would never have to worry about money ever again, the king vowed.

Edward had gained from that gamble. He now knew that *Brigadier* Tow wanted a command to go with his title. The king hadn't been aware of that before. Very well, thought Edward. This was interesting and curious. It didn't pay to assume too much and turn his back on his viper.

He went to his table, satisfied.

For the banquet he had arranged for General Lord Martel to be seated at the king's table, because Martel was his best friend—*only* friend, he thought sometimes—and highest-ranking general. Also because Edward wanted Marion at his table.

Lady Marion Martel was still an unmarried beauty. She wore less embellishment than the other ladies. Instead of wearing jewels, she had tied a brown velvet ribbon around her neck and arranged a spray of silk flowers in her hair, which was dressed up and back and arranged in smooth lovelocks, strikingly black among all the powdered white, because it was her natural hair. Her gown fit snugly at her narrow waist, and Princess Juliet pouted that the girl was never in fashion. Fashion did not become Marion, so she made up her own.

Tow was seated at Princess Juliet's table because Juliet requested it, and as the chamberlain pointed out, there wasn't much choice since neither of them had escorts. Juliet was going to dance with every man present anyway; though she liked to be seen with Tow—as some people liked to show off pet jaguars.

During dinner, the orphan girl played the harp for

the king's guests. Princess Juliet called the girl skinny
and funny looking. The maiden did have an unusual
face with disproportionately huge gray eyes—which
were not unattractive. She was long-waisted, thinner
than the generous figure that was in vogue. It was Juliet
who set the fashion and Juliet was voluptuous. But Tow
was looking at the harpist more than at Juliet and
needed to be reminded.

After the banquet the orphan musician was sent
home, and an orchestra played for the dancing.

Tow came to the king's table and asked Lord Martel
if his charming daughter would care to dance.

Lord Martel had been leaning over his knobby cane,
conferring with the king. At Tow's request, Martel
straightened up in his seat, a little startled. Brown
bushy eyebrows raised and he met glances with the
king. Edward gave a slight nod to assure him that everything was all right. Edward knew why Tow wanted
Marion. The triggerman had no interest in the lady
himself. Tow had asked her because there was music
and Marion could dance. Tow was a splendid dancer
and almost as much as bad sopranos, he loathed dragging an inept partner across the floor, distracting him
from the music.

"Go, Marion," Martel bid his daughter. As much
as he disliked Tow, it would not do to anger the king's
assassin. Besides, Marion already knew more about
politics than a young lady really ought. She should be
dancing.

They looked beautiful together on floor, the brigadier and the lady.

Carried away on the tide of the music, Marion closed
her eyes and let herself glide within the man's arms
encircling her, moving with him, feeling for the subtle
changes in pressure from the warm hand at the small
of her back that would tell her which way to go. It
became effortless and she needn't even think, only feel
the music the way he did and she became the brightest

star in the ballroom with him. Anything touching music
Tow could make unspeakably lovely. The man himself
made her skin crawl.

He was handsome, no doubt, with his beautiful facial bone structure, and fine hair and smooth hands.
He was slim and youthful, his body strong. And he was
a cold-blooded viper. Thank God he was beneath her
station, thought Marion. Not that her high station was
any *guarantee* of her safety. The one Marion really
pitied was the harp player, an orphan of no rank. Marion had seen him look at her. She also pitied Tow's
young aide, who seemed to have no idea whom he
served. The creature was omnivorous.

Marion opened her eyes and met his cold gray eyes,
gazing down at her with a knowing smile, half-lidded,
and she shuddered, as if he had read her mind. She had
heard that some serpents hypnotize their prey with their
eyes. And she could not look away, finding a deadly
fascination in his coldly attractive face. After a few
glasses of wine her blood rushed to be in his arms.
Sometimes their bodies brushed and she was too aware
of his hard masculine form.

I'm drunk.

She was very glad that her father and the king were
there. Nothing would happen. But that thought gave her
no peace either. Her blood still ran hot and she was
frustrated past civilized words.

But it was not Tow she wanted. He was simply
there—now. Neither did she want some nebulous fantasy prince. She knew who she wanted. She could not
have him, but that did not stop the wanting.

She wished he were here. Then her flesh wouldn't be
melting to this reptile. But just as she could not expect
to have him, neither could she expect him to be here.

Because an archbishop did not dance.

The garden room of the Martel house was built with
a rustic bent, its stone-gray-tiled floor uncarpeted, a

hunter's horn and trailing plants in hanging baskets hooked to rough timber ceiling beams. Potted apricot and fig trees had been brought inside here before the first frosts. There were windows all around three walls, and French doors with wide beveled panes through which to survey the estate and see out to the horses in the fields.

It was late morning after the harvest ball. The sun was very bright. The windows were thrown open to the brisk autumn air, and Marion wore a long knit jacket over her day dress. She was sitting in a white wrought-iron chair across from Archbishop Gregory and squinting at the chess set on the glass-top table between them, her one hand around a steaming demitasse of strong black coffee, the other hand propping up her forehead. The archbishop had taught her this game when she was a little girl. She had since become difficult to beat.

"You've been linked romantically with the brigadier," said Father Greg.

"My God!" Marion choked.

"Not true?" Greg asked.

"Most definitely not true," said Marion.

"I'm glad," said Greg. "How do these rumors get started?"

"I danced with the man," said Marion, distraught. She pushed her black hair off her brow. It fell free around her shoulders, unkempt. She sat back and squinted out the window, fingering the ends of the knit belt of her sweater jacket. "My God, I just danced with him."

"All evening?"

"The man is an eel. He's Farington incarnate!"

Greg nodded. "I'm surprised you know that." Well-bred gentlewomen weren't supposed to know about such things. "It's true."

"I'm not stupid," said Marion.

"I never said that."

"And I'm not a child. I'm not blind and I'm not naive."

"No," Greg agreed with a speculative turn to his voice. "Unpleasant, perhaps. Touchy. Churlish—"

"Hung over."

"Hung over." Greg nodded. "Marion, you drink too much. And you shouldn't go riding on the Capital Road looking for the Devil. You keep inviting trouble. Check."

Marion moved her king. "I'm desperately unhappy."

Greg moved his queen. "Check. You ought to marry."

Marion moved her king again. "Then what do you care whom I dance with! If you are so eager to have me married. Whose problem will that solve? Mine or yours?"

Greg moved his queen. "You are in foul temper this morning. Check. I think we have a stalemate here."

"I think so, too," said Marion, and stood up. She retied her sweater's belt. "I don't feel well. I'm going to my room. Good day, Father."

She was in bed before the thought caught up with her. She opened her eyes with a start. Who told Greg that she rode on the Capital Road? Who could have, when absolutely no one knew?

The king had given his orphan songbird a little cottage just beyond Capital City's walls. She lived alone. The cottage was not so much given to her as she was installed in it as a pretty fixture. Someone would come. That she knew. She did not know exactly who or how many, and it was not for her to question. The rap on door she received with a sense of inevitability.

She opened the door and admitted him without a word. He asked where her bedroom was and she led him there. There was no fight. It was not good fortune to be called upon by one so high, but it was not to be resisted. One could only accept them when they asked. She was no one; he was from the palace. And there were lots older and uglier who could've come for her. She supposed those would come also in time. This was the first.

She lay back on bed under the pressing weight of his body, her arms loosely around his neck. He pulled up her long dress. There was nothing of clothing beneath it; patrons never wasted funds past the surface when dressing up peasants for show. She felt warm hands on her naked thighs. She let him between her legs, and he took her with all their clothes on.

Tow lifted his head and watched the girl's face, saw pain. He was not big, so she must have been a maiden. And he found himself being almost gentle with her— gentle for Tow. He came hard, long-pent. He hadn't had anyone for months. Odd for him, who could do it several times a day if he had his way. He had brought no one to his room since Will had become his aide and moved into the little side room. Before that, it had never bothered Tow who heard or saw him fornicating what. He felt funny around the boy. He had come here as to a port in the storm.

He got up and went to the bath to wash himself and straighten his immaculate clothes and hair. When he came out, the girl was smoothing her gown. There had hardly been any blood and there was no stain on the white. Her enormous eyes were dazed and swimming. He knew that childlike look on her cheeks was going to fast fade.

He remembered the king had told him to be kind.

Kind? Well, the best that could be said was that it had been over with quickly, and now she would have a measure by which anything to follow could only seem slow and romantic. It could only get better. Then he thought of Lindy, Franklin, or one of those other goats coming here. It could get worse.

And he felt an impulse to the most kindness Tow had ever shown. "Listen to me."

"My lord?" she said.

"I'm not a lord. Listen. If someone else comes to your door and you don't want to let them in, don't."

"Who am I to say who may come to me?" She lowered her gray eyes submissively. She was nobody and had been taught accordingly. She existed to please her betters.

Tow had never lent his power to anyone before. But he had come to this girl instead of to Will, and somehow she and Will were becoming fused in his mind, as if doing this for her was doing for the boy. "You tell them the brigadier told you not to let them in. They won't come in. I promise you. I don't care if it's the king."

She lifted her eyes.

"You let him in if you want to." Tow wouldn't be surprised if the king did come to her door. He would have bet on it in a younger day, but the king was slowing down and becoming straitlaced. "But if you don't want him, you tell him what I said."

"How can you be supreme to the king?"

"I am not," said Tow. "I am very very mean."

The girl folded her hands in her lap. They looked very soft, but the ends of her fingers were callused from the harp. "I don't believe that," she said.

"You and someone else are sadly mistaken."

William Stanton was born yesterday.

The lad was alert and attentive but too gullible and idealistic. He had the faith of a child. He had mistaken attention for benevolence and he thrived in it, oblivious to the death trap, grateful like a fatted calf might feel toward the one who fed it.

Till somewhere along the way, Tow came in for a shock. He suddenly realized that Will was not the one mistaken. *He* was. Because Tow realized he didn't want to hurt him. He didn't want to see him hurt.

Tow had been possessive and protective of him from the beginning, that he knew. But that was because—he'd thought it was because—Will was *his* aide, *his* victim. Tow let no one else abuse the boy; Tow never let someone abuse a target he'd marked for self. But then he didn't hurt the boy himself. He had thought he was waiting for the proper moment, when the horror and betrayal would be sweetest. The night of the party, tired of abstinence, he had decided that he had waited damn well long enough and he was going to take this silly deluded lad and throw him into his bed like he'd intended to from the first. But then he'd gone to girl's house and taken her instead, and was a little puzzled as to why.

He realized that if he took the boy, it would be the last he would ever see of him, and Tow was not sure he wanted that yet. In fact he knew he didn't want that yet. So the decision was that he could either take him or keep him. He decided he still wanted Will around. He was tired of the long string of mindless aides; this one had insinuated himself into Tow's life and Tow would find it annoying to go back to doing without.

And he just liked having him around.

"Don't ever get yourself promoted," he told Will as the boy turned on the radio for the one-o'clock news report and set Tow's pen, notepad, and telephone within reach without Tow having to ask. "I should fall apart. Utterly."

Will smiled.

"That's the first time I've ever seen you really smile," Tow said, and Will's smile faded into confusion. Tow laughed and said, "Were you always this nervous?"

Will mumbled around nervously and Tow laughed again.

"Will that be all, sir?" Will asked, mustering enough courage to sound indignant.

"No. I'm sorry. I don't make a habit of laughing at my aides."

Tow was in the habit of *shooting* his aides. He'd never apologized to one.

The boy was born yesterday. Tow was just waking up.

Despite rebel hindrances, the Crown managed to get some factories converted and working. The damned rebels were unpredictable in their movements, while the Crown, so it would seem, was very predictable. At least the rebels always knew what the king's armies were about to do next.

Then in their most devastating push to date, the rebels struck in the Great Lake, struck hard so that the government of Michigan Province was on the verge of collapse. The rebel leader there was Alan Cervany, acting on orders from Chicago Red two hundred miles away. Such unity and organization was hideous to contemplate. The crown could not afford to lose Michigan; the rebels would control the Chicago isthmus and the Seaway. So the king sent a secret force of guerrilla fighters. It was anticipated and ambushed. As if they had known. As if they had known.

It was becoming apparent that Chicago Red had an information tap very high up. The king strengthened security around his council meetings, banishing all extraneous persons from them—recorders, servants, and aides, including Tow's. Rather he tried to exclude Tow's aide. Tow stood adamant; when the aide wasn't there, neither was Tow. Finally the king relented because it was inconceivable that information was leaking out that way. The boy had all the guile of a doe, and it was hard to imagine anyone squeaking information out from under Tow.

"All right, Tow," he said, piqued. "Bring your boy-friend if you have to."

The blaze of anger on the brigadier's face was terri-fying. The king was stunned by it and had to back down quickly. "Irritation. Unmeant."

Tow turned away. The king stared after him, baffled. He had seen anger. Pure real anger. Tow was seldom so transparent. The king had touched a nerve. Those were usually hidden and deep—if Tow had any at all. This one was bare and sprang at a touch. The boy was a dangerous topic, the king gathered. And it came to him in a lightning flash of incredible revelation.

Good night! He's in love!

II.

Janus in the Mirror

DAILY THE REPORTS CAME IN FROM MICHIGAN, EACH successive one more grave than the last. The Crown would soon lose control of the entire province to the rebel Alan Cervany, who had gained the backing of majority of the people.

"What do they want!"

The king exploded, his arms thrown wide to heaven. He let his hands drop and turned to face the archbishop, who was listening with his perennial, infernal serenity, his great hands folded. Greg wore his usual simple white cassock with short cape, nothing on his head in deference both to the king and to the teachings of St. Paul.

"*What?*" The king repeated his bewildered demand, this time at the archbishop.

"Do you want me to answer that, sire?" said Greg.

"If you can! Tell me there is a rhyme or reason to what these rabble outlaws are doing!" he cried out as if it were an answerless question. And as Greg began to speak, the king was chagrined to hear that an answer was actually forthcoming. There wasn't supposed to be one. Edward wanted his archbishop to tell him that the rebels were all insane, and nothing more substantial than this.

"They want a bit of security for one," said Greg. "These peasants work the land with almost every waking breath. But they live eternally as in the shadow of a hanging rock that could fall any given moment. The land is theirs only so long as the Crown hasn't other use for it. If Your Majesty or one of his governors decides to create an estate to reward a nobleman, then these poor people are driven off the land which they have lived on and worked all their lives. And even if it never happens to *them*, only to someone they know, still they live with this threat every day. They just want to know that if they are diligent, they will have a home, enough to eat, and clothes for their children. They want to know that anyone who tries to take it from them will be punished by the same law that protects the noble class." Edward III was listening, his dark blue eyes narrowing, his square jaw thrust forward. His voice was coldly quiet when he spoke again. "Is that all?" His tone let Greg know that Edward thought it already a great deal.

"A little dignity, sire," said Greg. "They want to be thought of as more than a faceless resource of labor, taxes, and produce."

Jaws clenched, the king breathed through his nose, deeply and angrily. His eyes shifted to Brigadier Tow, who was lurking, seated off to one side of the room. At the king's glance, Tow raised one quizzical brow as he did when expecting an order to kill someone. The king had only to nod. Edward III never spoke orders for high assassinations aloud.

But this time the raised brow only incensed the king more. He had no intention at all of having Greg killed. "Tow, leave us."

Tow rose, leisurely uncoiling. He brought his heels together and bowed slightly, and he walked out with his dignified military bearing and cold ungodly good looks.

When the assassin was gone, the king said to Gregory, "I am going to forget I heard what I just heard. You almost sound like you are defending the rabble. There is no excuse for lawlessness. There is no excuse for treason. Do not try to exonerate anyone to me because they were born poor. Nobody dies of hunger in this kingdom—not because they did not have a place to work. I have many factories—and lots of work *rebuilding* factories nowadays," he added with a bitter humorless smile. "Owning land is a privilege, not a right. If a peasant has a piece of land for a while, he should feel lucky he was allowed to have it for a while, not complain because his unearned good fortune ran out. As for the rest, I will say only to you this, Archbishop: *Ye have the poor always with you.* You may go now."

The pontiff took his leave with a bow of his head, and found his own way out of the palace.

He stepped outside into sunlight. The monumental front stairway led down to the palace's courtyard, the wide space embraced between the sprawling east and west wings, a place brilliant with roses and late-blooming flowers. The autumn air was filled with their fragrance; and the pontiff slowed his pace and walked among them with the sun on his face.

He did not regret what he had done. He was only sorry that the king was so unbending that it needed to be done. The rebels did in fact have an information source very high up—next to God, as it were. Chicago Red sent a rebel woman named Tina into the Capital to confession regularly. Tina confessed to the archbishop that she needed guidance, and the confessor advised her and her friends where the dangers lay.

When Gregory came at last to the street, he found Brigadier Tow waiting. The brigadier did him the courtesy of untethering the pontiff's steed for him, and he held the stallion's bridle as Greg mounted. The stallion was a big black without markings. Tow patted its unmarked brow.

As the archbishop rode away, Tow looked at his hand. It was clean. He rubbed his fingers together bemusedly. He had been expecting black grease or paint to cover a white streak. He was mildly put out not to find it.

But the stallion's pure black brow proved nothing to Tow. Just as a marking could be covered, so a white streak could be added where there was none. It just made the Devil harder to catch. Tow chided himself for supposing it might be easy.

He went inside and found the king where he'd left him. Tow could tell from the monarch's pensive demeanor that Edward had already forgiven the archbishop. The king was never so angry and unreasonable as when he was confronted with a truth he would rather not face. He was regretting his wrath now. Tow had hoped to find the king still angry. "Why was Vandetti put on the Council?"

"He's my conscience," said the king, and looked at Tow. "So *I* put him on the Council."

"Security has gone to hell from the day you did," said Tow. "The rest of your military and political advisers are too fawning to say anything. And you, I don't know why you don't see it. A child would be suspicious."

The rebels seemed to know when and where the king's armies were coming. They bombed the railroads that transported the troops, or they evacuated the site before the troops ever arrived. As if they knew the Crown's every plan.

The king was angered. "I dragged you off a Farington street, *General.* You were over your head in capital offenses for which I could still have you convicted."

Tow laughed.

"What is so funny?"

"Your Majesty will not execute me."

"Do not be so certain."

"Sire, when I find I am no longer needed, then I shall vacate before your new assassin can find me."

"You think you are needed?"

"Would you keep me here if I weren't?"

Absolutely not, thought Edward. "You have me all figured out, you think, General?"

"I will never understand Your Majesty," said Tow.

Sincere, Tow? Sincere? Edward III sighed heavily. "So what am I to suspect of my archbishop?"

Tow shrugged. "There's no white streak on his horse's nose."

The king was astounded at the implication. "You think he's—"

Tow lifted his brows and made no argument.

Past events took on sinister colors in this new light.

Greg had let Chicago Red get away.

Greg had been stopped by the Devil Rider, he said.

Greg was forgiving of the rebels.

Greg knew what they wanted.

Greg was on the king's council, and the rebels appeared to be privy to council information.

The king frowned. "Are you sure?"

"He still breathes," said the assassin.

Tow was not sure.

The king nodded. He said nothing more to Tow. But he had much to think about.

Lady Marion Martel and young Prince Edward came out of the exercise room with their foils in hand. The prince pulled his mesh fencing mask off and shook his head. The lad's cheeks were cherry red. Marion's raven tresses came tumbling loose as her mask came off. They were both breathing hard, heat radiating up from their heavy padded jackets. Marion presented her back to young Edward. "Get me out of this." She couldn't get her heavy canvas-sleeved arms to reach around to the buttons between her shoulder blades.

The prince was setting his gear down to help her out of the padded armor when the front door chimed. The Martels had no servants in today, so Marion went to answer it, her foil and mask tucked under her arm, ten-year-old Edward dogging after her.

She opened the doors; the prince and the lady were

struck still and wide-eyed like a pair of deer caught in the headlights of an automobile. It was the king.

Young Edward bowed, and Marion dropped onto one knee to the floor.

The king looked down upon Lady Marion's bent head. She was a truly beautiful woman. He was mystified how anyone could look so pleasing, so feminine in a fencing jacket that obscured her slight figure, and a man's white breeches, with her hair in uncombed perspiration-matted disarray, her face red from exertion.

Old man, you are smitten. Edward III bid them rise.

The king had come to the Martel estate, without attendants, only the coachman who waited outside with the carriage. "Where is your father?" he said to Marion.

"Immediately, sire," said Marion, and whispered to young Prince Edward, "Tell my father."

The little prince ran to do her bidding, and Marion ushered the king into the drawing room, apologizing for her looks and the lack of servants. She settled the monarch into a chair with a view out to the horses on the hill pasture. She asked what he would like, then ran out to make some tea.

The king chuckled. He liked this house, its rustic flare, its bare wood beams, always full of light. Hunting guns stood in their racks; a hunter's horn hung on the rough plastered wall. The general's favorite hound, now blind, curled up by the red-brick fireplace. The woodpile Lord Martel had chopped and stacked for himself. The palace's sated opulence could be oppressive; Edward never realized how much until he came out here and breathed the fresh air.

He saw his son, Prince Edward, running outside toward the garden to fetch Martel. The boy was strong-limbed, but cherub-faced with thick dark curling locks. The boy was too pretty. Would he never grow? It was well that the prince decided to spend most of his time out here at the Martel estate. For some reason the king could not fathom, degeneracy thrived back at the palace.

Shortly, General Lord Martel came running from the garden in his overalls and broad-brimmed sun hat, pulling off his brown work gloves as he came. He took off his woven hat as he came inside, bowed to the king, apologized for his appearance, said he would change and call some servants. "Marion!" he bellowed.

But the king beckoned him into the drawing room. "Sit. Don't dress."

Martel wiped his boots on the mat and came in. He sat gingerly.

Said the king, "I want it said I just stopped in to see my old friend and maybe look in on my son."

Lord Martel rested his elbow on the end table and spoke low and seriously into his hand: "And what *did* Your Majesty come for?"

"Bad business," the king said, shaking his head. "Bad business."

Marion came in bearing the tea service. She'd thrown on a calf-length white linen dress, white shoes, and brushed her hair and tied it with a white ribbon. She set the tray on the table between them and poured first for the king then for her father.

The king watched her go out. "You mean it doesn't take them an hour to put on a dress? My daughters had me convinced that it did."

"My Marion is careless as a peasant. I keep thinking if she had a mother, she'd know about perfume and stockings and all those other things ladies are supposed to know and I don't know what or how to tell her."

Marion did not walk in a wave of gardenias or honeysuckles like the royal princesses, and her legs from the hem of her dress to her shoes were coltishly bare. Edward found it appealing but one didn't tell a lady's father that.

"How can I serve Your Majesty," said Martel.

"You know Michigan must be dealt with soon," said the king by way of preamble. "We have little choice."

"Yes, sire." This much everyone knew.

The rest was more difficult. "I want a plan," said the king. "I want you to make the best plan you possibly can. You. Only you. Consult no one. Dispatch the orders in code at the last possible moment."

Martel's brown bushy eyebrows drew together. "Without going through Council, sire?"

The king raised his beringed forefinger. "For Council I want another plan. A good one, but in no way like the real one. You will say I have approved this latter plan, and unless there are major arguments, this, you will say, is *the* plan. No one is to know there is another. You will then anticipate where, if you were a rebel, would be the best place to ambush this announced expedition and you will send some of our guerrilla troops to attempt an ambush of an ambush. Do you understand?"

"I'm afraid I do. Sire, you think there is a traitor on Your Majesty's own council?"

The king frowned deeply. Tow's words kept returning to him, insidiously, and eating at him from the inside like an ulcer. "I can hope not. You know I am sick about this. But I need to know."

"Can Your Majesty tell me whom he suspects so—"

"No. Because I hope to God I'm wrong. Trust no one."

"Yes, sire," said Martel, rising as the king rose.

The king went to his carriage. Martel left off his gardening, put on his reading glasses, and began to draft his plan at once. He called no secretary. He didn't want to trust one. But finally, by evening, he was going cross-eyed. He needed someone to write for him. He put down his pen, took off his glasses, and pinched the bridge of his nose between his thumb and forefinger.

He squeezed up his tired eyes and bellowed, "Marion!"

Scottie climbed down the ladder into the bunker, agitated and full of news he could hardly wait to share. Assured that Chris-John was not there, he faced the rebels in the hideaway.

"What is it?" said Detroit. "Scottie, what's wrong?"

"Him," said Scottie.

"Who? Chris-John?"

When Scottie took that suspicious angry tone anymore, it was always Chris-John. Still they asked, "Who?" and Scottie said, "Good question."

Scottie was unfolding a news clipping as Chris-John came down the ladder into the bunker.

Chris-John perceived the electricity in the air at once, and saw strained faces around him, felt the silence. "What is it?"

"Just in time," said Scottie, and planted the news clipping on the table for all to see. No one came forward to look, so Scottie told them what it was. "It's an obituary. May twenty-third, 209. Do you want to know whose?"

The one called Chris-John didn't have to look. From the way his dark face paled to ivory white, Scottie could tell he knew. He was caught in a lie and he knew. It was an eight-year-old death notice for a certain Chris-John Stanton of Delancyville.

Scottie stalked over to him, lifted him roughly by the shoulders to pin him against the wall. "Stanton, hmm? I believed you. Do you know I felt so sorry for you? Sorry for you! I *worried* about you. What a horrible thing for a kid to have to live through. What a chump I was! And you can shut off the thousand-candle eyes; I'm not falling for it anymore. You're not Stanton, goddammit; now, who are you?"

Chris-John's eyes started to roll up as if he were about

to faint, but then he recovered slightly, still shaken,
dazed, and very pale. "I am . . . Stanton." He swallowed. He searched wildly all around for something,
someone safe to look at. There was no refuge. "My
name is Stanton . . . the problem is the Chris-John
part."

He covered his face with his hands so he wouldn't
see everyone staring at him, but he could not blot out
the visions coming to him, because that attack was from
within. He saw a soldier. Several. And a beautiful
child. He spoke in feeble cry: "We were—I—I had a
twin."

Scottie snorted in dubious disgust and dropped him.
Chris-John huddled on the floor and said, "Walt."

Scottie snatched up the obituary from the table. That
claim was easy enough to check. And Scottie was surprised to see that the deceased Chris-John Stanton was
in fact survived by two brothers, Walter and William.

Scottie's tone softened a degree. "So what the hell
is going on?"

*Two fifteen-year-old boys. Dusky children, silken
brown skin, tight-curled short locks tossed over smooth
brows. Velvet-fringed bright eyes, straight little nose.
Sweet mouth. Pretty things.*

*A drunken soldier enforcing the curfew, finding two
wayward children in the midnight street. Grabbed one
twin under either arm and crowed jubilantly at his
catch. "Lookee what I got!"*

A lewd voice saying, "But are they boys or girls?"

*"I don't care! There's more than one way to fuck a
cat."*

*No one fucked anyone. One twin wriggled free, lithe
as an eel, picked up a shovel, and swung it at the soldier's legs. "Let my brother go!"*

*The soldier roared, dropped his other captive, lunged
at the twin with the shovel, grabbed it away from him,
and brought it down on his pretty face.*

The twin died two days later.

The other one ran away and became the disciple of Henry Iver.

But which twin was he? Lark spoke slowly: "Well, Chris-John, did they make a mistake or did you take your twin's name? Which one are you?"

Chris-John kept his hands over his face and trembled. He thought hard, then answered in horror: "I don't know."

Tow poised his pen over a document. "What's the date?"

Will checked the calendar, made a small expression of surprise. "Oh." Then he said, "October tenth."

Tow looked up. "What is it?"

Will mumbled an apology, said it was nothing. "My brothers' birthday."

Oh yes, Tow remembered Will had had two brothers, one dead, one missing. "Which one?"

"Both. They were twins."

"Were they lovers?"

Will blinked in shock, then, in a moment, felt a flood of incredulous relief to hear a long-secret shame spoken with such frank normality. Like asking about a shepherd dog, *Is it black and tan?* Weren't most of them? *Were they lovers?*

Will felt suddenly light, his worst shame lifted. Pale brown eyes turned to Tow with adoring gratitude for taking that from him.

Will remembered when he had discovered the two of them together. He had heard those sounds from his brothers' room, thought someone was sick. He'd opened the door to shock and shame. He couldn't eat or sleep for days afterward. In his extreme youth it was something so horrible, and somehow stuck to him because they were his family. An unholy, capital crime.

And here now the offhand question as usual as pouring wine. *Were they lovers?*"

And there came to him a rush of love for this man,

and simple shameless answer, "Yes." The awful weight, set free, rid him of itself and flew away, light, on wings.

Tow made no expression of comment or even acknowledgment that he had heard Will's answer. He was already thinking of something else, looking for something on the table that wasn't there. "Where's my seal?"

Will took the brigadier's seal from his desk and gave it to him. It was a simple one, with a single bold Roman *T* and no border at all.

"Any sisters?" said Tow.

Will almost laughed. "No."

Tow glanced up at Will as he gave him the document to deliver.

Colonel Stanton's youngest son had none of his father's duskiness. Even when he was younger, it was obvious he was going to be tall. He hadn't the feline grace of the smaller twins. Will was too awkward and gangly to be catlike. Not that Will was clumsy exactly, but he was too lanky, his shoulder bones and hands too big, and he was not so purely androgynous as his older brothers. He was more masculine, but Father favored the twins. Will hadn't their spirit, spunk, or fire. He was a good boy, obedient, kind, and quiet, never in any trouble. Colonel Stanton had hardly noticed he was even there.

Will checked his watch. He spoke a soft reminder: "It's 10:25, sir."

Tow sat back in his chair and put his fine hand over his eyes, an elegant gesture the way he did it. "It's too early to listen to Lindy."

It sounded like Tow was going to duck out of this one. Will gently, nervously reminded him, "The agenda is the Michigan situation. The memorandum says imperative."

That meant attendance mandatory.

"Is the king going to be there?" said Tow.

Will checked. "No, sir."

"Then Martel's plan has already been rubber-stamped. We're not going to do anything at this meeting." He let his head roll on the chair's headrest toward the window. Sunlight was streaming in. "The last nice day of the year," he murmured. "The Ocean is warm. I want to go to the coast." He looked to Will. "How does that sound?"

Will almost smiled in disbelief.

"Don't look so frightened. You're not going to get in trouble. I am," said Tow. "That does it." He got up. "We're going."

"Where, sir?"

"Not to Martel's meeting. Comment, Lieutenant?"

Will was nervous about the consequences. Aides were at least half-responsible for getting their officers where they were supposed to be on time—fully responsible if their commanding officers decided to put the blame there. But Tow didn't want to go, and Will would be damned if he would try and make him. It came down to a choice of consequences.

Finally Will smiled shyly and shrugged. He said, "I guess there's not too much worse than General Lindy's voice at 10:30 in the morning."

The meeting began at 10:45 when it became apparent that Tow was not coming. "Where is he?" said Martel.

"In hell I hope," said Admiral Kester.

"Seconded," said Secretary Shie. "Can we vote on that?"

Then they furtively looked around to make sure Tow was not in earshot, inwardly chiding themselves for being cowards all.

Admiral Kester was fuming. He had yet another grudge against the worm-spawned brigadier. The admiral had gone to the cottage of a certain young harpist and had not been welcomed. The name Tow had been mentioned and Kester had gone away cold.

General Martel presented a plan for the military occupation of Michigan, to be effective that very night. The Crown's troops would be on the province's border by tomorrow evening. Speed, said Martel, was essential to the plan, if they hoped to catch the rebels unaware. "As you know," said Martel, "We've had some security problems in the past."

"Ought to be no problem this time. I think our leak is absent," Kester growled.

There was a unanimous intake of breath, as if Tow were here and they would all be shot for Kester's loose comments.

Martel frowned. He considered Kester's implication. Martel had not been told whom the king suspected. If it were Tow, then this ruse was for nothing.

But then if Tow were a rebel informant, he would not have missed this meeting. Tow tended to be rather cavalier regarding official matters. No, the traitor wasn't Tow, as much as any of them might wish. Martel could think of no one—with the possible exception of Lindy—whom he would rather see off this council and hung from a tree on Potter's Hill.

And the king had seemed so distraught about the suspect's identity. That Tow might be a turncoat would cause no one to be heartsick, only frightened. The king had not been frightened. He was heartsick.

Martel surveyed the faces. The suspected traitor was one of these.

Franklin, Lindy, Shie, Kester, Mack, Howe, Salten, Archbishop Vandetti . . .

They all approved the plan, except the archbishop, who made an impassioned plea against use of military force. "I beg you, no." He said lives would be lost on both sides, and in the end the innocents would suffer most. And suffering innocents, he pointed out, turned into rebels. If the Crown were to employ a different tack to quell the dissatisfied among the population, there would be no rebellion, no need for rebellion. Marching against one's own citizens was madness.

Martel countered that these people were claiming *not* to be citizens. The madman Alan Cervany, Chicago Red's arm on the lake, was calling Michigan an independent state. If they did not want to be the king's subjects, then they forfeited the king's protection.

"Is this the king's wish?" said the archbishop, seeing he was getting nowhere. They were not even trying to listen to him.

"Yes, Your Eminence," said Lord Martel.

The pontiff bowed his head. "Then how can I speak against my king?"

Father Gregory sat within the confessional, wishing a breath of air might stir the heavy purple curtain hung over the small window cut in the door. It was close, hot, and dark in here. He had been in here a long time. He could be here for hours more and still there would be penitents to be heard. People seemed to think they would have a closer connection with God if they confessed to the archbishop than to a simple priest. So there was an endless stream of them.

He checked his watch. He had another half hour to go, and the rebel Tina was not here yet. He listened for her familiar voice through the divider each time he slid the inner panel open. She was due tonight. And it was imperative that she come tonight. He had to tell her that the Crown was going to strike in Michigan tomorrow. Sunday.

Tina had to come soon. Maybe this next one. Gregory slid the panel open and spoke quietly through the gauze-covered lattice window: "Go ahead."

The voice that came was not Tina's, but he knew it well. "Bless me, Father, for I have sinned. . . ." It was Marion Martel.

Greg sat back, letting the girl's words fly past. Marion never did anything. She came regularly to have her petty transgressions absolved.

This time she said she had stolen something. She was in anguish over what to do. He told her to return it; she could not be forgiven while benefiting from the sin.

"I can't," said Marion. "I don't actually have *it* anymore. It's a secret plan to trap a suspected traitor. I made a copy of it. I won't feel right unless you have this, Father."

A folder came sliding under the lattice.

Greg opened it. Inside was a plan for the invasion of Michigan. It was nothing like what had been discussed in the council meeting.

A secret plan to trap a suspected traitor.

Astonished, Gregory blurted out her name. "Marion! Do you know what you're doing?"

"Probably not. I'll go now. I'm not really sorry, so I can't say the contrition." There came the sound of rustling fabric, Marion gathering up her skirts to go.

He called after her in hissing whisper, "Marion!"

But already he heard her footsteps outside the confessional as she fled, and he could not go after her.

The kneeler on the other side of the barrier creaked with another parishioner coming in.

Greg closed the shutter to wait a moment, hand on his heart. Shaking.

III.

Tangled Web

GREGORY DREW IN A SHUDDERING BREATH. A TRAP. The girl had just saved his life and the life of the Michigan rebellion.

And there was something else implicit in Marion's "confession." Marion knew who he was. Either that or she knew he was suspected and she informed him just in case he was guilty. She would sell her soul for him.

He leaned his forehead on the sill with a sense of numbness and guilt. He opened the lattice shutter, and the next penitent's sins numbled through him, unheard. He was lenient in meting out penance. He was lenient to the next three. The fourth was Tina.

"Greg, it's me."

Gregory lifted his head. "Tina. Thank God."

Lord Martel passed Tow in the foyer in the evening as the general of the army was leaving the palace and the errant brigadier was returning. Martel greeted him coldly. "You were missed at the council meeting, Mr. Tow."

Tow answered him breezily, "I took a holiday."

The brigadier appeared youthful, refreshed, and sunburned. And everyone was surprised that his aide was still with him, alive, still as unwary and dumb naive as ever. Will followed the brigadier up the stairs carrying his day pack.

Will simply assumed that the general was fond of

him in a paternal way. Associations with darker things never crossed Will's mind. Farington desires were so far removed from his sphere of experience that it never occurred to him, no matter how obvious.

For himself, Tow was becoming disturbed and not a little bewildered by the situation. Wanting and not daring to take was new, alien, to Tow. He had never cared what his intended thought. He did now.

Why you?

A total lack of art or guile. A sensitivity.

Five years ago those qualities would have meant little to Tow. Ten years ago, nothing.

I have changed.

And he was not altogether pleased with what was happening to him. The sense of things happening beyond his control was unsettling.

But they *were* beyond control.

His eyes followed Will across the room as the youth was opening the windows that had been shut all day. A fresh evening breeze parted the damask curtains.

If only I could stop loving you . . .

Sunday morning after church, King Edward III addressed members of the radio and press corps in the Capitol building next to the palace. He was flanked by Royal Guards, and at a short distance stood the brigadier Tow without his aide. Eyes like a viper's scanned the crowd to make even the hottest blood run chilled.

The king made scalding remarks directed toward the rebel Alan Cervany of Michigan, warning that the rebel was to surrender or else. The king was full of confidence and fire. *Or else.*

And with the final warning ringing in the air, the king returned to the palace, hounded by droves of reporters who wanted further explanation, but the king's soldiers kept most of them backed off.

It was at the top of the palace-entrance stairs that some unbearable clod with a microphone from the ra-

dio corps blundered into Brigadier Tow, and both fell
against the wall.

Tow drew his pistol and emptied his full clip into the
man.

The crowd scattered, screaming, and dove into
niches and bushes and behind the low stone wall in
front of the palace.

When the shooting stopped, tentative eyes peered out
again. None of the spectators had been hit. All the
bullets had gone in one direction.

The king's guard had taken cover and now looked
out, clutching their guns, uncertain where to point
them. At the brigadier?

Edward III came back outside. Everyone gasped for
his safety, but the monarch exhibited no fear, if he felt
any.

The king never approached anyone directly in public. He now descended the stairs and came to Tow, who
had turned to the wall and let no one see—not that
anyone wanted to come that close to Tow even with an
empty clip.

The king was allowed to see. It was Tow's left hand.
He'd broken a finger. Edward looked into his assassin's
steel gray eyes that actually let emotion show through.
Tow was genuinely frightened.

Ah, his music.

The king carefully took Tow's hand so it rested across
his own palm—like taking a wolverine's paw while the
thing was all snarling and rolling eyes and bared yellow
fangs. The ring finger was already blue and ballooned
twice its size. The other fingers were slender, even, and
artistically tapered, with short well-groomed nails and
smooth skin unknown to manual labor beyond killing
with a trigger. And caressing a piano.

"You will have my personal physician," said Edward to calm the beast. Then quietly, not for his guards
or for the press that was inching closer and taking doz-
ens of pictures, he said, "You will play your beloved

piano again, my dear viper. Don't panic on me. Not in front of them.''

The king was a little concerned with the carcass at their feet. Stupid stupid commoner. Tow's inability to play would be a great loss to the music world, besides that Tow without his music and his immaculate hands would be a vicious viper indeed.

The king snapped to his guards, "Remove that."

The guards jumped to obey, quailing only briefly at the aftermath of thirteen point-blank shots from the Magnum into a single body. The guards covered the remains and whisked the corpse from the palace steps. The servants would have to hose the blood away.

The king made no statement to the reporters concerning the shooting. There was really nothing to be said about a thing like that. And maybe it would put the fear of God into some careless people. It was best left uncommented on. The king could weaken himself by explaining things to commoners. Later, if need be, he could have his director of information, Hugh Salten, gloss it over. For now, let that be a warning.

On Sunday night the king's armies were routed, their planned ambush was ambushed, and the whole Michigan Province fell to the rebels.

Monday afternoon, an emergency session of the king's council was called.

The meeting room was strangely silent, with none of the usual arguing or idle chatter that went on before the king's arrival. An air of doom hung over them, awaiting the thunder.

The council members were aware now that the king had suspected a traitor in their midst since he had not trusted them with the real plan. They were aware that General Martel had been the only one of them to possess the true plan. And the true plan had found its way to the rebels.

Of course no one thought Martel so stupid as to hand

the secret plan over to the rebels when he was solely responsible for its secrecy. Even so, when the king was angry, his wrath was likely to fall without reason. Martel sat in the wing chair with his rough hands clasped between his knees, contemplating the gallows.

Kester was swearing softly to himself.

Tow was leaning on the windowsill with his good hand, gazing outside to the street. He had left Will behind this time. He did not want Will seeing him get a tongue-lashing from His Majesty.

Archbishop Gregory was watching the others. He knew whom the king had suspected and he knew who had planted the suspicion of him in the king's mind. Tow. The brigadier had a street dog's instinct for survival. He smelled something not right. Even with Marion's providential interference, given time, Tow would figure everything out. The Devil Rider would have to lie low for a while. But then even that would look suspicious to the assassin. Greg knew he was not out of danger yet. He had merely escaped one trap, and very narrowly at that.

The doors flew wide. The king entered with an armed escort of four Royal Guardsmen, who fanned out to stand in the room about the king. No one was accustomed to having them inside the palace, and not in a meeting with the king's highest statesmen and military officers. Edward III was furious.

The king lashed out at his council for the Michigan debacle. The Crown had lost the Great Lake. The rebels controlled the sea route between the Mississippi and the St. Lawrence. "How!" He spun on General Martel and roared. *"How!"*

Martel sighed helplessly. "They must have broken our radio codes."

"Then change the codes!" the king bellowed, purple in the face. "Isn't that obvious to an imbecile!"

All of them winced to see Martel so belittled.

Tow started to speak. The king whirled on him.

"Nothing out of you! You are missing your step anymore. In fact, stand over there, I don't want to have to look at you."

Tow made no facial expression; and a bolt of fear passed through the others at the way he held his right hand, his trigger hand.

But Tow silently went to the side of the room where he had been told. And his acquiescence was terrifying in itself.

The king turned back to Martel. "I thought I could trust generals more than politicians. But generals are just politicians in uniform."

A palpable ill wind was blowing through the chamber as he demeaned them all.

"Sire, I haven't betrayed you," said Martel with deep emotion, his bushy brown muttonchop side whiskers vibrating, and the others were afraid the old general was going to turn over his sword.

Suddenly there was an uproar out in the streets, which made them all turn. One window was open and they could hear the clanging bell of alarm, and they rushed to see what was happening.

A black-clad figure on a galloping black steed scattered townsfolk off the street in its path straight down the main avenue in full daylight. The demon carried a pumpkin raised over its head. As it drew near the palace, the Devil stood up in the stirrups and hurled the pumpkin into the palace courtyard. The face that looked up as it rode under the council chamber's window was an inhuman mask.

The king appeared on the verge of apoplexy. He looked around at the men with him. "Tow!"

The triggerman was not at the window. Tow was in the corner where he'd been sent. The ringing of the outlaw's horse's hooves had already become distant. The king stalked over to Tow in sputtering rage. "Goddamn you, why didn't you shoot?"

Tow drew his pistol and spoke low and cold. "Why don't I?"

Everyone stopped breathing. The king and Tow locked mortal stares. Tow's pistol was pointed up toward the cornice, a threat but not a commitment. The king was in a rage at the threat, rage that the Devil had gotten away while damned Tow sat in the corner in childish obedience to the king's order. His order. The king was vaguely aware that he was wrong in this matter, but this viper dared draw on him. This was treason.

It was Tow who defused the confrontation and gave the king space to back down. Half still a threat, but half changing emphasis of the drawn weapon that was pointed nowhere, Tow asked, "Whom should I shoot?"

"It's too late," said the king, and turned his back on Tow, asserting that he still had control enough to show his back to the creature.

And Tow holstered his gun.

The others breathed. No one treated the king like that. No one treated Tow like that.

The king glowered at his Royal Guards. Untried young men, they had frozen at their weapons when the crisis had come. God, if Tow had been at the window! The Devil would be dead in the street now. As it was the villain was somewhere laughing at him.

The king was looking for a place to lay blame. Part of it was due to himself, but he could not take it now. Tow. What were assassins for! But it was unwise to turn on Tow. So he turned to these other . . . idiots!

Martel ground his teeth. "He mocks us, sire."

The king exploded. "He mocks *me!* Don't flatter yourselves! You are standing in here in my chambers agitating a lot of air, wearing your uniforms and medals and your chancellors' bronze," he sneered and flipped Franklin's medallion. "While Michigan falls to rebels and the Devil Rider is breaching the walls of my capital and throwing pumpkins on my very doorstep in broad daylight! Get out of here! Get out of here, all of you! This meeting will reconvene when someone has something useful to offer me!''

The officials filed out silently, the archbishop last. The king caught his sleeve as Gregory reached the doorway. Greg turned. He was surprised to see the king's face furrowed and lined, suffused with other emotions than wrath, almost to tears. The king croaked, ''My old friend.'' And he let him go.

Greg went out, heard the door shut behind him. He let his head fall back and he breathed guilty thanks to heaven. He was cleared on all charges.

Trouble was, Greg had no idea who was on that black stallion.

The rebels could be surprisingly clever, and this maneuver had been an effective and audacious move. But Greg remembered that none of Chicago Red's rebels could ride. That kind of horsemanship was the province of aristocrats like Lord Martel.

Lord Martel's daughter was a fair mount.

Marion.

Lady Marion was in the garden room with her fiancé, Frederick, a young captain of the Royal Guard whom her father had arranged for her to marry. Frederick asked where Marion had gone that morning; he had come to call on her earlier. She said she had gone riding.

She was just bidding him good day when the archbishop arrived.

No one else was there to see how different was Marion's face when she was alone with the archbishop than when she was with her betrothed. Lights came on in her black eyes.

The archbishop was not smiling. He strode in with a powerful current. He did not sit down. He was gruff and direct. ''Marion, what in God's name do you think you're doing?''

''Are you the Devil Rider?'' She cut him off.

"Why are you asking me that?"

"How do you know it was me and not the real Devil Rider this morning?"

She'd caught him there. If she'd only suspected before, she knew now. "Marion, don't get involved in this."

"Greg, why won't you see what you mean to me? I'd do anything for you."

He half smiled. He spoke more gently: "You haven't already?"

"Anything, Greg."

"Marion, you're an aristocrat, for God's sake. What have you to do with the rebellion? You have a station."

"Oh, yes, I'm a proper lady. I am suffocating. I am not a jewel to be stored in someone's box!"

The archbishop walked to the window and gazed out to the wide fields of the Martel estate, his arms crossed. "You've never been hungry. You've never been in prison. You've never lost your land. These are the people I have to defend. They are my flock, my responsibility."

"You wouldn't have anyone at your side?"

Greg kept his back to her. "I'm not the man you think I am."

"Do you think I care?" She was all ready to forgive his human failings. She *wanted* him to be flawed so she could forgive. She thought she understood the situation. She thought the only thing standing in their way was his concern about the danger to her, and his vows.

She rose from her chair and drew near, came around to face him, smelled his faint smoky scent. She stood as tall as his chin. She bent her head, her dark hair falling in a curtain around her face. She touched his chest lightly, above the gold cross. She spoke softly: "Don't worry about me. You've seen I can take care of myself. Greg, don't tell me you don't have feelings like a man. I'd do anything. Do you think God would mind so much?"

Greg was vexed. He spoke as if annoyed at a child. "And do you think rebel women are not as comely or willing?"

Marion's voice froze up. Shock. Sick. Shame of a child suddenly discovering how really naive she was. It was not his vows in the way. He'd broken those long before and often. When she had been still toddling in diapers.

Her stomach flip-flopped. Her cheeks burned. "I . . . oh. *Oh.*" She had to sit down.

She sank into her chair, trembling, trying to hold in her tears, but they escaped and splashed on her cheeks. All inside was aquiver, her world tumbling apart. She'd thought she'd had it all figured. Things were not going right at all. Finally she asked with trampled spirit, "Am I not comely?"

"Of course you are."

"Then why are you turning me away?"

Gregory was astonished. She couldn't still want him. "Marion, you can't—"

"I can't? Why won't you take me? Do you think I'm fragile? Do you think you'll ruin me? Are you trying to tell me I can do better?"

Gregory did not like to see her crawl like that. But it gave him enough anger to answer her. He stood over her and took her chin roughly in his big hand and tilted her face up to look at him straight. She was still so very young. "Don't try to tell me you're not a maid. I know you are. You are comely. You have a mind, you have talents, you have a heart and *you have a station.* And yes, by God, you can do better!"

"Stop being paternal!"

"And what is wrong with a priest being paternal! It's what I'm *supposed* to do. This is my answer to you: Under no cirmcumstances! Leave the rebellion to the peasants and leave sin to the already fallen!" He let go of her and walked away from her.

In insult, Marion found her pride. She drew herself

up to sit straight, her hands clasping and unclasping on the chair arms, quick and angry. She snarled, baring white teeth, "I could be queen of this land! Do you know that!" She was not blind to the interest of the king.

"I daresay you could."

"I could—" she began in threat.

Greg met her angry hurt heartbroken eyes. "Yes?" he prompted.

She choked on the words she would say. Greg turned away and let the threat hang empty in the air. All that came out of Marion was a cry and a flood of tears.

Gregory walked out of the house, his receding footsteps striking loud on the wood floor. The door shut hard and he left her bent over in her chair, sobbing.

IV.

Brothers

SCOTTIE WAS FEELING VERY LOW. HE WAS SICK TO HIS
stomach and forlorn.

The others had gone out to the Red Stallion in Manxville to celebrate the liberation of Michigan. Scottie
stayed behind in the bunker. He said he didn't feel well.

He had been alone in the bunker that morning with
Terese. He considered it a major achievement for Terese
to let herself be alone with a man, and Scottie knew
better than to try to talk to her. So he pretended to
ignore her entirely and simply enjoyed her presence.
He just liked having her there with no one else around.
Sometimes he stole a short glance when she was occupied with something and in convenient sight line of
something else Scottie could possibly be looking at.

The morning went smoothly until she came near.
Scottie was sitting on one side of the couch with a
book. Terese curled into the opposite end of the couch
with a sweater of Chris-John's and a pair of scissors in
her lap, and a threaded needle in her mouth. She started
to mend a hole in the sweater. Scottie hardly dared
breathe. She was growing used to sitting on the same
piece of furniture with him, even if she was curled way
against the far arm. This was nice. He could smell her
faint scent, something she used on her hair. He was
taken with her petite figure, the feminine way she
moved her hands. Palace women were so pretty. His
skin warmed at her proximity. The girl glanced over,
noticed he had an erection—with Scottie it was hard to

miss. She slapped his face hard and scampered up the ladder and out.

Scottie felt sick the rest of the day, a dull lump in his stomach that would not go away.

Of course Terese told no one. Terese didn't talk. But it was obvious when the others returned that Terese was frightened of Scottie and was avoiding him, scowling at him all over again, as when she had first come to the bunker. Phoenix spouted out, "Scottie, what'd you do to her?"

Scottie said nothing. Nothing Phoenix said needed answering.

Scottie stayed in the bunker when the others went out that evening, because Terese put another person between herself and Scottie at all times and peered from behind her chosen shield like a hunted creature. Scottie could not celebrate like that, and it was obvious Terese would rather not have him around. So he claimed to be sick—he really was by then—and stayed behind.

The king summoned his archbishop to the palace. Gregory was apprehensive, wondering what the king could want. In these days there were no social calls anymore.

Edward III received him in the council chamber. With the king was Hugh Salten of the information corps, a man with a dazzling smile with huge white teeth, a strong cleft chin, and a shock of wavy blond hair. His title was "director of information." Hugh Salten was director of propaganda. Gregory bowed to the king.

Without preface the king gave him a charcoal drawing.

Greg studied the picture in dismay. It was a fair likeness of Chris-John. The mouth was ill drawn and the texture of the skin could not be captured on paper, but the eyes were those magical luminous eyes of Chicago

Red. Someone just might be able to recognize Chris-John from the drawing.

"Well?" said the king.

"It's an accurate rendition. I'm surprised."

"Brother Thomas is quite an artist. Here. What do you think of these?"

The king gave him two more drawings, executed by a different hand. They were both more or less Chris-John but one was too dark, the hair curled tighter and frizzy looking. The other was too light, and the curls were too big and loose. "No," said Greg. "This one is too dark. This one is too light." He could not lie. The monks would contradict him.

The king gave the light picture to Hugh Salten to give to the press liaison. "Distribute this one in the black towns. This one"—he gave him the dark picture—"to the white towns. And this one"—he gave him the accurate picture—"to the police departments."

The king shifted his eyes to Gregory with a look of devious triumph, a curl on his mouth.

Gregory frowned and said nothing. It would be difficult to identify Chris-John from the pictures the newspapers would be running, and that was good. But the king was not hoping for an identification from the common folk. He was playing a much more underhanded game here. He was preying upon prejudice. He had no hope that the common folk would turn over their hero. He wanted to subvert their hero any way he could. The king could be cruel.

Gregory nodded. It eased his conscience when the king was like this.

"Must we stoop to this?"

Hugh was about to leap to the defense with something flowery and circumlocutory, but the king waved the propagandist silent and said bluntly to his archbishop, "They hanged my governor in Michigan. They are throwing the port control authorities into the lakes with their hands and feet tied. I am not stooping. I thought it was a good idea. You may go, Archbishop.''

Greg bowed stiffly and left.

William had been running errands for the general in town. He had seen the newspapers, seen the black face looking out at him from the front page on the stands, and thought nothing of it. Nothing registered beyond that it was a black face.

He returned to the general's rooms and restocked the wine and liquor cabinets. He refilled the decanters with sherry and cognac, then polished the apples and put them in the bowl. Apples were beautiful this time of year. There would not be many more of them to be had, since a great part of apple country was in rebel hands.

Lastly he brought out a bag of aromatic coffee beans. The brigadier had expensive tastes. Whether it made Will an errand boy or not, Will liked handling fine things. He put the coffee in its canister in his own side room, where the coffee grinder was kept by the small range and squat refrigerator. Will's chamber left little room for Will himself. But it had a huge window overlooking the picturesque street, and Will did not need any space.

He had bought a newspaper for Tow. Tow did not usually read them, but since his hand had been broken, Will was looking for distractions for him.

Tow thought the front page was very amusing. ''That fox. That old hell fox,'' he said.

Will paused in his duties, wondering if he'd been spoken to. He hadn't, but Tow beckoned his aide to him. The general took a picture from his desk drawer and showed Will a face the same yet different from the one in the paper.

Will inhaled sharply through his nose, like a small gasp.

A reaction like that did not get by Tow without an

explanation. And Tow extracted from the boy that the picture, the eyes, looked a lot like his brothers, the twins.

"I fail to see the family resemblance," said Tow, looking from the drawing to Will.

"There isn't one," said Will. He went to his little side room and brought back a picture of the fifteen-year-old twins Walt and Chris-John.

They were beautiful dusky children, nothing like Will, except perhaps the delicacy that touched Will was outright androgyny in these two.

And they looked very much like the drawing Tow had taken from his desk. The eyes.

"May I have this?" The general looked up at Will. Will gulped.

"You had better say yes, because I'm going to take it," said Tow.

Will stammered, "Yes, I didn't mean, I . . ." The boy was on the brink of tears and he was lovely. Tow nearly lost his train of thought.

"Don't become alarmed until I see if alarm is in order," said Tow. "Do you really think your brother is capable of being Chicago Red?"

Will shook his head and spoke with tears in his voice: "I don't know. You know, I really don't know which one died." He laughed helplessly, though he thought nothing was funny. "We *thought* we buried Chris-John and Walt ran away. If Walt's alive, he's no Chicago Red. If it's Chris-John . . ."

"I see," said Tow, rising. He put on his coat.

"Should I bring your car, sir?"

Tow shook his head. "I'll drive myself."

Will was being left behind. He paled to white and looked as if he would faint.

Tow was seized by an impulse to hold him. He turned quickly away, went out the door, leaving Will standing there looking frightened.

* * *

Upon the rebels' return from the Red Stallion—they were all a little drunk—Phoenix wanted to know what was wrong with Terese. The squirrely girl didn't talk.

Phoenix was told that Terese had had a confrontation with Brigadier Tow with ugly results.

Phoenix chuckled. "Yes. He gets ugly results." Phoenix gave an ugly grin.

Scottie scowled at the ugly Faringtoner significantly. He remembered an exchange earlier that day. Someone had reported that Brigadier Tow's hand was broken. Lark had asked which hand and Phoenix said, "Don't matter, Davy can shoot with either hand."

Scottie spoke up now. "You seem to know him well."

Phoenix barked a laugh. "Didn't anybody ever tell you my name?"

"Phoenix," said Scottie.

"Nobody's got one name, jerk. My last name. Tow. Phoenix Tow."

Lark dropped something.

"Jesus," someone said.

"He had nothing to do with it," Phoenix snapped.

Terese was shrinking away from him in horror. Phoenix snarled at her. "Oh, get out. Who wants you, you skinny little rag?"

"Don't talk to her like that!" said Scottie.

Phoenix's brow cinched. "What do you care? She spits on you, you stupid doormat."

Scottie seized Phoenix by the shirt and pulled back a big fist to smash his face. He smelled whiskey and focused on Phoenix's scarred lips and crooked, thickened nose.

Suddenly there was a different face there, other than Phoenix's. Beauty instead of beast. Little Chris-John had eeled in between Scottie and his target and looked up with luminous eyes.

And Scottie started to laugh. Because he would just as soon smash Chris-John as he would Phoenix, and now here was Chris-John putting himself in harm's way like a nun with a cross. Scottie let go of Phoenix, laughing. "You're all polluted. Go to bed."

Phoenix oozed down into the couch. Lark slid onto the couch with him. "So what are you to Tow?"

Phoenix hesitated. "Half-brother."

There were so many stories about Tow that the man was nearly legend. It was hard to tell what was true and what was not. All of it couldn't be true. No one was that evil. "Did he really rape and murder his sister and his mother?" said Lark.

Phoenix laughed. "That's funny. That's not true. Davy did a lot of things, but they arrested him for something he didn't do. Well, I'm not quite sure about the sister. She was gone before I got there. But the way I hear it, *his* father raped the sister when Davy got too big and mean to pick on anymore. Davy killed his *father.* As for raping Mama, she was kind of willing, at least by the time I arrived on the scene. Our mother was a really sweet person. He didn't kill her. Someone did. We don't know who. Davy killed—" Phoenix paused to make a mental body count, then threw up his hands and said, "Gobs of people. Killed about half of Farington and a few of the king's men besides. Figured he'd get Mama's killer somewhere in the pile. When the king's soldiers finally got him under arrest, Mama's blood was the only blood on him—see, he picked her up. But everybody else he killed at long range—no blood. So they charged him with Mama's murder. Bunch of jerks. The king had sent his assassin after Davy. Davy got him. Got his job, too, I guess. He's not on the end of the rope. He gets away with, well, murder."

Detroit wrinkled up her nose. "He actually killed your father?"

"*His* father," said Phoenix.

"What happened to your father?" said Chris-John.

Phoenix looked at him queerly. "I'da thought you'da

figured that out by now, bright eyes. Davy is my father.''

Tow returned to the palace. He had gone to the hospice to see Brother Thomas and the other monks who could identify Chicago Red. As the brigadier climbed up the east-wing stairs to his chambers he saw Admiral Kester start out of a room and dodge back inside at Tow's approach. The admiral kept his back always rigid straight, his movements stiff as if his clothes were overstarched, and for Kester to move quickly made for a comical image, like a wooden duck in a shooting gallery. The analogy appealed to Tow.

Kester did not live in the palace. So why was he here and why was he hiding? It could not be simply that he disliked Tow. Here was a man with a secret. Tow would get that out of him in proper time. He had other things on his mind now.

He went to his room, took off his coat. "William."

Will came out of his side room. He moved to take the general's coat.

"Leave it," said Tow, letting it drop on the sofa. "The monks identified your brother's picture."

A sound like a cry. Like a sob. Will's hands flew to his gaping mouth. His pale watery eyes rounded. Shoulders heaved and he backed away, shaking his head.

Tow took a step toward him. "Will."

But the boy ran and locked himself in his room.

Tow tapped on the door. "Will. Will, open up." He tried the knob. It would not turn. He went out into the hallway and tried the other door, but it was also locked.

Tow came back to the inner door between their rooms. By now he was growing angry. "Will, open this." He rapped with the side of his good fist. Tow never used his hands for heavy work. He became incensed when there was no response from inside. He drew his automatic and shot the lock off.

He kicked the door open and stalked inside. Will wasn't there. If he'd gone out through the hall door, Tow was going to kill him, but that door was still bolted.

Will was in the bathroom, throwing up.

Tow came in, gun in hand. Will, already sick, backed up against the bathroom wall, hands fluttering, nose running. He saw the gun and Tow's anger and was seized with redoubled terror and couldn't stop throwing up again. His bladder was empty or he would have let that go, too.

Tow holstered his automatic and held Will's head— the boy had half missed the bowl. He inhaled wrong with a sob and coughed till he couldn't breathe. His face was purple until he stood up, and then it was ashen. He was shaking like an aspen in the wind. He sank to the tiled floor and Tow knelt with him, took him in his arms, and held him.

Will's thin arms circled round him and Tow warmed to his ears and burned in his groin. It surprised him a little. The lad was a mess, and this reaction? He was touched with an extreme tenderness he had never felt, and desire. He barely stopped himself from stroking him and kissing his hair. He did not dare for fear of how Will would receive it. Tow couldn't bear it if he touched the boy that way and he threw up.

With his left arm crooked around his sobbing aide, Tow reached for a washcloth with his right hand and wiped away Will's tears and the vomit from his runny nose. Tow thought it strange he should ever do that. He remembered his mother with the infant Phoenix, cleaning the baby while young Tow stood apart in the doorway as if to leave, his arms crossed, facing sideways and regarding his mother and the messy infant over his shoulder, frowning and dubious. He had watched with morbid disgust and curiosity. His mother flushed the used tissue down the toilet. "Why don't you flush *it?*" said Tow. He was young, fastidious, and baffled by why the woman bothered with the squalling little beast that did nothing but eat, cry, shit, spit up, and sometimes sleep. But Mother was humming and serene. She could love a toad if she'd given it birth. She had. Phoenix was a toad. Tow had turned away. ''Ugh.'' Mother was humming.

Within Tow's arms Will was returning to his senses. The aide remembered himself and started to pull away with an abashed apology, called Tow ''sir,'' groped for a rag under the sink with which to clean the bathroom.

Tow snatched the rag from him with a flash of rough anger and told him that that could damn well wait.

The youth's eyes poured tears and he curled back into him, arms around his waist like a child.

Tow stared at his own slightly trembling hand. He had not been ready for reestablishing that barrier of rank and order and propriety. If he couldn't have him, he at the very least wanted to sit here and hold him awhile longer.

Finally he had to let him go. The boy had quieted and there was no more excuse. Anyway, the place was beginning to stink and Tow didn't know if he could tolerate it much longer.

Will stood on wobbly legs, his eyes bloodshot, his face swollen and blotched red. Tow still felt a pain in his groin on releasing him. He wanted him. Tow went out before it could be noticed. Will set about the soothingly mindless task of cleaning up. Tow changed his clothes.

Tow gave Will a glass of sherry when the aide dauntedly peered out into the big room again. Will asked what was going to happen.

Tow had been thinking about that. If reported, there would be much action taken and no good result. Knowing that Chicago Red was Chris-John Stanton would in no way help to apprehend the rebel leader. Chris-John had maintained no contact with his family or old acquaintances, and those would be the people to be questioned and grilled and tortured. Not that Tow ever cared about the Crown's inquisitions disrupting innocent lives. But they would take Will from him. For nothing.

Tow knew that the rebellion was more than Chicago Red. Killing Chicago Red could possibly be the worst thing the Crown could do right now—as killing Henry Iver had been, but the king hadn't listened to Tow when the brigadier had told His Majesty that either. Better that the Crown know the nature of him who was leading the opposition and deal with him accordingly. The king wouldn't understand that. Well, the king wasn't going to know. Neither would any of the other officials. There was not one of them Tow trusted. And to make matters worse, the king had recently insulted all of them in front of each other at the last meeting. Things were bad. This volatile information was right where it belonged and no further.

Tow looked to Will. "Where's your loyalty?"

Will gazed at the floor and mumbled. "The Crown."

"Look at me," said Tow. The brigadier came face-to-face with his aide. Will lifted his eyes timidly, and Tow had to catch his scattered thoughts; the eyes knocked his mind blank. He couldn't talk. The boy spoke: "Rebels killed my father at Seattle. Chicago Red gave the order. I guess I know what Chris-John thinks of family ties." His lips quivered. He blinked his eyes fast and dropped his gaze from Tow's.

Tow moved away, feeling light-headed. At last he said, "Only those who need to know will know. Nothing will happen to you or your mother. Chicago Red, of course, is in grave trouble if he's ever caught. This matter will be taken care of."

Will looked immensely relieved and grateful.

The matter, thought Tow, would be buried.

V.

Storms of a Darker Season

THE SEASON WAS TURNING. CRISP BURN SMELL OF fallen leaves carried on sun-warmed cold-edged breezes. Scottie had left the bunker's hatch open. A gust of pleasantly cold air swirled through the underground chamber and fluttered the newspaper clippings tacked on the note board—two different pictures of Chris-John, one black and one white; they were the drawings that the Crown had distributed in the white towns and the black towns of the Kingdom.

Chris-John drowsed on the broken couch. Scottie sat at the table, redrafting an old map of the Capital City. He could hear a passing flock of northern geese calling like baying hounds. Then he heard the *rush rush* of someone stepping through the fallen leaves outside. Scottie checked his wristwatch. It was too early for Tina to be coming back from confession, so who was coming?

Scottie nudged Chris-John's foot. Chris-John sat up, listened. He climbed the ladder and peered out.

It *was* Tina.

She climbed down the ladder and unwrapped the black wimple from her head.

Chris-John asked her, "What happened?"

"Couldn't get into the Capital." She took off her black gloves. "They want to see your pass. They want to see your ID. 'Who are you? Can you prove it? What's your business in the Capital? Can you prove it? You can't? Why not? Confession? Which church? What minister? Where are you from? Don't they have churches there? No, you can't be admitted. Next.' "

"Good God."

"They made me feel like an outlaw," said Tina. "Never mind that I am one, they really made me feel guilty."

"Any idea what made them suspicious of you?" said Scottie.

"Nothing. That's just the point," said Tina. "They're doing it to *everyone*. It's because of Michigan."

In the wake of the fall of Michigan, the king's reign had turned harsh.

"Go into any town, you never saw so many soldiers. They're even going into houses and arresting suspected sympathizers of rebel sympathizers."

"How is he paying for all this?"

"O yes," Tina said, remembering. She withdrew a handbill she'd stuffed up her wide sleeve. She held up the proclamation for her friends to see. "Dig deep. Taxes are going up."

"Again?"

"Someone has to pay for all those police and soldiers and censors, not to mention all those tax collectors. It's never been so bad."

"Good," said Chris-John, and his companions looked at him curiously.

For a time the repressive measures would make life very difficult for many unoffending people, but the more restrictive the monarchy became, the more people would be irritated out of complacency and take favorable notice of the rebellion. The middle-of-the-road part of the Kingdom was hard to move. Chicago Red had not been able to reach those people.

Chris-John smiled his winsome otherworldly smile. "I knew we could count on the king to win the fight for us. He's going to alienate everyone. Everyone."

* * *

Brigadier Tow had two telephones in his chambers; one was an interpalace line, one was an outside line. He was always slightly surprised when the outside line rang, so he picked it up himself instead of letting his aide answer for him. It was the king. His voice was agitated.

"Tow, come to my study. Hurry but don't show it. Leave your aide. Don't tell anyone."

Tow was puzzled. "Where are you, sire?"

"I'm in my study," the king hissed angrily. "Get here." And the connection went abruptly dead.

Tow returned the receiver to its cradle, puzzled. The king was making an interpalace call on the outside line?

Spies, thought Tow.

Or a trap. One never knew. And one never assumed.

Tow looked to his aide. Clear brown eyes were waiting curiously for an order. A gentle young man. Tow did not want to leave him here. If someone were coming after Tow, then his rooms were a bad place to leave anything he valued.

Tow pulled a piece of stationery from his phone desk. "William, go to the printer; have a new order of this made for me. Everything the same except make sure it's gray on gray. He gave me black ink last time. Tell him I didn't like it."

"Yes, sir," said William. He folded the paper and slid it into his inside breast pocket. "Anything else, sir?"

"No," said Tow. "Go."

Tow made sure the boy was clear of the palace before he answered the king's summons. He went to the king's study, but not through the door. He came in through the big window and swept the drapes aside with the barrel of his automatic.

The king had been watching the door. He turned at the sound from the window, saw Tow, the gun, and started back with a gasp. The king was alone in the room. His face was gray as ash within the frame of his white wig and he said, "God, not you too."

Tow holstered his weapon. "No, not me." Tow had been right; there *was* a plot afoot, but it was not against Tow.

The king put his hand to his breast and let his breathing return to normal. At last he said in a near whisper, "Actually I am glad you chose that entrance. I take it you were not seen."

"No, sire."

"Good, good," the king mumbled to himself, wringing his hands and pacing the room. He noticed Tow had wrapped his wounded hand a second time, as if expecting it to be jostled. He was prepared for violence; good.

The king's pacing took him to a bookcase. He moved something, Tow did not see what, and the étagère swung out on a hinge like an opening door—which was what it was. Beyond it was a secret passage. The king looked back to Tow and motioned him through. "Brigadier."

"After Your Majesty," said Tow.

The king's ashen lips twitched in a thin smile and he swept through the secret door. Tow followed, and the shelves swung shut behind him.

The narrow passage led to a small windowless room, its ceiling as high as any on the first floor of the palace, and Tow was trying to picture exactly where it was. He figured out that it was sandwiched between the pantry and the firewall that backed the kitchen servants' quarters.

A bed took up most of the space in the closed chamber. There was a deep pile carpet and a very small adjacent water closet.

Tow started to laugh, threw himself on the bed. "Is *this* where you take them."

He knew the king was in real trouble when he did not react to the mockery. "Tow, get up. Look at this."

Tow sat up and took the folded packet of documents

that the king had pulled from the deep gold-buttoned pocket of his brocade frock coat. Tow slouched against the wall and flipped through the documents as the king paced the narrow confines of the room, looked back into the passageway as if he suspected he were followed, pulled his gold watch from his waistcoat pocket, opened it, checked the time, wound it, returned it to his pocket, and paced.

Tow recognized the documents. They were simply memos and minutes from past council meetings. Parts were circled and annotated in red pencil in the king's characteristic scrawl. Those places were the trivial extraneous parts that usually went unnoticed, invoice numbers, document numbers, all the numerical filing codes that littered every piece of paper in the government. But on second look the innocuous marks were not filing codes at all. They were *code,* all right. Numbers that should have been dates were impossible; filing numbers had too many digits and were out of order. Tow read the king's tentative deciphering marked in red pencil, and the numbers all fell into neat order and messages.

Most of the messages, lacking antecedents, remained incomprehensible. Many were evidently instructions on where/when to find more detailed messages or perhaps where/when to leave a reply. Some were more ominous.

To Hugh Salten: *How many K guards are ours by now?*

And to Admiral Kester an inquiry regarding a load of blanks in sufficient quantity.

The telling line was to General Mack: *Remove Ashton.*

The very capable Lieutenant Ashton of the palace guard was distant kin of Edward III and as solidly a king's man as anyone could be. Tow knew that Ashton had only this week been promoted captain and given a field command in a remote part of the Kingdom—on order of General Mack. Before this, it was assumed to be a rather natural assignment of one of the king's most promising officers to a difficult post.

Remove Ashton.

Tow sat up and whistled. "It's a coup."

The memos were the only way to get messages between men who could not afford to be caught talking to each other outside Council without raising eyebrows. Tow rechecked the copies to see who was all implicated. "Mack, Howe, Salten, Kester, Shie," he said, marveling.

The king was fidgeting, rocking on his heels. "And."

Tow resifted the documents, searching for the name he'd missed. Not Martel. Not Lindy. Not Vandetti. Not himself. At first he started to shake his head, drawing a blank, then it came to him, the man to whom no messages were sent because he was sending them all. Tow spoke incredulously: "Dr. Franklin."

The king nodded. He was shaking slightly.

From the documents there was no way of knowing when or how the mutiny was to take place. And it did not matter. What was needed was a preemptive strike. Now.

"Get them, Tow."

Tow rose, uncoiling, a hard deadly look on his handsome features, in the eyes of living steel. "Yes, sire."

The king took off his ring and placed it in Tow's palm. "You may need this." Then he slumped to sit on the bed. "That I should come so to depend on you," he murmured in despair. "Tow, I no longer have the power over you I once did. I will not deny that—that would be fooling only me. You could seize this opportunity to be free of me. Of course you would be on the hit list of whoever comes to power after me, but I have no doubt as to your powers of self-preservation. You could escape and live somewhere well enough. No doubt in the shuffle for power that would follow my assassination—not to mention the unrest among the populace—there would be little time to look for Tow. Unless someone knows you to be as dangerous as you are, though I doubt that. Only I know you for what you truly are. And I am staking my life on your desire to preserve the status quo and remain in the palace. In fact I am willing to go so far as to give you that command you wanted, you whom I swore I would never allow an inch higher.''

Tow paused, cherishing his power, then he said, ''I will ransom you this time, because, as you say, I like my life the way it is. And I don't want the command.''

The king's eyes widened, surprised by the opportunist he thought he knew so thoroughly. ''Why ever not? You asked for it?''

''Only to know I could get it,'' said Tow lightly. ''Why not should be obvious,'' he continued as he was leaving. ''The higher you go, the better target you make''—he looked back at the king hiding in his secret retreat—*''sire.''*

Tow waylaid William in the palace entrance hall. The boy had returned from his errand and was on his way back up to the brigadier's chambers, the receipt from the printer in his pocket. ''William.''

''Yes, sir.'' The boy turned toward the voice and lifted soft brown eyes to Tow's.

Tow crossed the wide marble floor. ''Will.'' He encircled the boy's narrow waist with his right arm and drew him close to him. Will felt the general's heart racing and was alarmed.

''Don't go to the room,'' said Tow low and close so his breath disturbed Will's hair. ''Don't go anywhere near anyplace we usually go. Hire a carriage, don't take a car, and go to your mother's and stay there. Don't ask questions and don't answer any.'' He paused to glance about the foyer. If anyone saw him, he looked more like he was propositioning the boy than preparing

for a bloodbath. Will's nervous confusion, his trembling, and hasty departure would all be dismissed on
that assumption. "Don't take anything with you. Just
get out of here. I'll send for you in a few days. Go."
He released him, and the boy started away. Will looked
back once and Tow's lips formed the word "go."

Tow watched till he was safely clear of the palace.
There was no telling how many or which of the king's
guards were in the insurgents' pay.

Not till now. Now was the time for declaring one's
allegiance.

Admiral Kester marched down the palace hallway,
twisting his waxy mustache, swearing under his breath.
This was dangerous work, unseating a reigning monarch. Proper timing was essential. So why the hell
wasn't anyone where he was supposed to be when he
said he'd be there?

Kester was coming after General Mack and telling
that man if he couldn't keep a schedule, then Kester
wanted no part of this affair. They would all see the
end of a rope before they got to the throne.

He opened the door to Mack's office and entered
cursing.

His voice stopped. Just stopped. And for once he
could not think of anything, not an imprecation, to say.

Mack was there. The papers on his desk stuck in a
spreading pool of blood still seeping from his head that
was shot half away.

Salten was there also, facedown on the floor at the
end of a trail of vomit, a neat hole precisely in the
middle of his back. In front, most of his chest was
gone.

Kester backed out of the room with an oath.

The elderly statesman Chancellor Franklin was
seated behind his desk, his snowy wig arranged on his
head, and a mantle of solemn dignity upon him, befit-

CHICAGO RED 185

ting a man of very high office. He looked up with blue
eyes, peeved, when Kester burst into his wide octago-
nal chamber babbling, his collar undone, eyes wild as
a madman's. The stiffer they start, the worse they look
frothing at the mouth. The man had fallen to pieces.
Franklin knew that Kester should not have been counted
in their number. This endeavor called for level heads.

Kester lurched over Franklin's desk, supporting himself on both straight arms, and gasped out, hysterical,
"He's found out! Mack and Salten are dead!"

Franklin took his pince-nez from his nose and slid it
into his pocket at the end of its fine gold chain.
"How?"

"*Tow.*" Kester choked. Those had been his style of
execution. One shot each, no warning, just done, in
the back, in the head, done. And the ammunition he
was using turned his already lethal automatic into a
cannon. "It's his work. The bullets go in this big and
they come out this big. It's a purge, Franklin!"

Franklin gathered up his papers, put them in a metal
wastebasket, and tossed in a lighted match. He went to
his cabinet and took out some more treasonous documents, his motions hasty but methodical. "We'll make
this work for us." He pushed the papers into the flaming basket. "This is the justification we need to make
our overthrow legitimate to the people. The king has
become murderously paranoid. As long as there's nothing to convict us, there'll be no opposition."

"No opposition!" Kester nearly screamed. "What
about Tow!"

"We shall just have to survive Mr. Tow."

Kester looked over his shoulder. "He's probably on
his way right here right now!"

"Undoubtedly," said Franklin. He picked up his gilt-
edged white interpalace telephone and dialed 99 for the
palace guard. "Yes. Chancellor Franklin here. I want
to declare a full alert. Brigadier Tow has made an attempt on the king's life. General Mack and Director

Salten are dead. Stop Tow at all costs, do you understand?''

He depressed the button and made a second call, to his own people within the guard. ''It's begun. Get Tow above anyone.''

Franklin hung up the phone and looked to Kester. ''That should slow his progress, don't you think?''

Kester was mopping his face with his handkerchief and licking his lips with a tongue gone dry. He coughed from the black smoke rising from the trash can.

The door opened. It was Tow.

Kester screamed. A bullet caught him in his open mouth.

Franklin, always quick-witted and still spry for his advancing age, had jumped out the bay window.

Tow darted to the window, sat on the window seat, and leaned to look out, but Franklin was evidently skirting the wall behind the palace hedges because he was nowhere to be seen. The sun was going down. Tow lined his gun barrel up with the outside wall, but could not bring himself to shoot blind. Tow never missed.

Tow moved from the window, kicked over the burning can of documents, and threw a heavy rug over them.

He heard the heavy clumping thunder of running guards. He was not deceived as to whom they were coming for and he quickly quit the chamber. Now that the mutineers were alerted, the game had changed. Tow was on the defensive and had to think how the serpent would think, where would they strike. It was not difficult to anticipate. Tow knew serpents.

He made his way to the chambers of the royal family, Queen Gertrude, the royal princesses.

And Prince Edward IV.

Marion Martel was filing some of her father's records when she noticed that her father's copy of the minutes bore a different date than those given Secretary Shie. She had Shie's minutes because General Martel had asked for written suggestions at a meeting, and many of the Council, as was their practice, had scribbled their opinions on the back of their minutes from the last meeting.

Trying to find which date was correct she cross-referenced Admiral Kester's copy, found that it gave yet another date, a nonexistent one. She looked for Salten's copy of the minutes, but Salten, an inveterate margin scribbler, had abruptly changed his ways and had turned in his suggestions on a fresh sheet of paper. So had Mack and Howe. Was there something in those minutes that they did not want to let out of their hands?

Marion was suspicious of everything these days, ever since the king's visit. She immediately set to looking for anomalies in the records available to her. Always good at puzzles and the maneuverings of the chessboard, she discerned a pattern right away. The key was the name Vandetti. She looked for it in clouds, heard it on the wind, so of course she pulled it out of the cipher immediately and constructed from there.

One message read: Wat[c]h Vandetti.

Something was happening of which her father was not aware. Worried for her father's sake and for Greg's, she determined to find out what the Council's secret was. She had hoped it somehow involved a threat to Greg from which she could save him and make the man realize he needed her.

There was not enough here to work with. So it was that she rode to the Capital and sneaked into the palace this night of all nights.

The small candle guttered in its shuttered lantern where Marion placed it atop Secretary Shie's oak filing cabinet. To the young woman trying to be invisible, the tiny flame seemed a beacon blaze. The drag of the drawer opening smoothly on well-oiled rollers sounded like crashing cymbals.

She took a deep breath, pushed back her black hood, and set herself to her task of searching Shie's confidential records and piecing together the stray bits of coded messages she found there.

Absolutely not Martel.

Tow will be removed proper time.

The first shots were not close enough to make her jump. They sounded somewhere across the courtyard, in the other wing.

She knew roughly what was happening. She had discovered enough in Shie's strange records to know there was a conspiracy. She guessed from the odd timing that something had misfired and gone vastly wrong. And she knew she was not supposed to be here, stolen past the palace guards at an unseemly hour into a locked office—a very unfortunate circumstance when bullets and charges of treason started flying.

Heart in mouth, Marion pulled up the hood of her black cape, doused the light, climbed out the window, and stole through the blackening shadows.

The night air was cold and damp. She crept along the hedges until they ended and she would have to dash across the wide cobbled courtyard to the street. She heard shouts, clashing swords, and gunshots within. Royal Guards were firing at each other, divided in two factions. One could not recognize the enemy on sight; one could only declare one's loyalties aloud and prepare for a shoot-out if he declared wrong, and pray his side prevailed when it was all over.

Marion closed her fist around the gold crucifix at her throat. Its hard edges bit into her hand. She breathed a prayer and ran for the street.

Suddenly, from around the wall and through the main gate from the street, more guards came running. Marion froze in her tracks and with sinking heart saw Frederick, her fiancé, captain of the guard. Her face burned in horror of discovery, a bitter sting in the back of her mouth. Caught in the act. It felt worse than she could ever have anticipated. With a cry she ran toward him, her arms out to embrace him, to keep him from shooting her. Frederick stared as he saw her coming. "Marion!"

She reached him, her arms wide, and at the moment a bullet pierced her midback and she came up on her toes with a squeak, the black clouds swarming before her eyes. Frederick caught her against him as she went limp in his arms.

Tow knew he would find Franklin near the royal chambers. The chancellor would be looking for a hostage. The brigadier caught him in the corridor, raised his gun for a straight easy shot—Franklin was five feet from any door—but someone else stepped into the hall between them.

Tow would have shot anyway, but it was Prince Edward.

The royal child looked left, looked right, saw men on both sides of him, one with a gun. Franklin and Tow. He froze, knowing he'd made a very bad step. He was not too young to know what treason was.

One of these men would be loyal to his father. One was a traitor.

Tow's automatic was leveled in his direction. The muzzle looked like a cannon. It looked like a crater. And it was on level with his eyes. The voice behind it sounded a stern command. "Your Highness, duck."

On the other side the old man Franklin with clear blue eyes crouched and beckoned with harsh urgency, "Boy, come here."

Edward ducked.

The automatic cracked like thunder. Franklin's body plopped to the carpet. Tow barked at the prince to stay down.

Already he heard rumbling footsteps of guardsmen running this way. Tow dodged into a doorway and opened fire as the pack of them rounded the far corner. He did not ask their loyalty. Tow hadn't called them here, and from the way they came running all in a posse, it was evident that someone had. Tow assumed it was Franklin. But at the end of the firefight there was no one of the twelve alive to ask.

The last one had barely hit the floor when a second group arrived from the other end of the corridor. Tow recognized them as solid king's men. Tow and they were on the same side.

But they did not know that. Last they had heard, Franklin reported that Tow had made an attempt on the king's life. What they saw here was Franklin dead and the corridor awash with the blood of guardsmen in the same uniforms as themselves. And they saw Tow. They glimpsed him crouching in the doorway. They fully saw his automatic pointed at them.

"Halt and declare yourselves or I will fire indiscriminately," said Tow.

"How can you with an empty gun, General?" asked one haughtily; he had counted the bodies. Thirteen. Tow's automatic held thirteen rounds.

Tow fired. The speaker fell, a bullet between his eyes. "Any more questions?" asked Tow.

It was said in Farington that many were quick on the draw; being quick on the reload separated the living from the dead.

The guards had dropped back farther down the hall. Their commander declared, "We are His Royal Majesty's men. What are you?"

From the floor came an audible groaning sigh from the prince, who had flattened himself against the ground except for his arms, which curled protectively over his head.

Tow reached carefully with his wounded left hand into his pocket. "I assume you recognize this." He held out the king's signet for the guards to see. Their commander took a few steps closer to make certain of what he saw. He recognized the eagle signet. He nodded back to the others and a hushed silence fell over them. Tow continued. "Now, either this means that the king has given this to me and I act in his name. Or it means that the king is dead, in which case you take orders from his heir.''

All eyes turned without conscious will to Edward IV.

The child pulled himself off the carpet. He pushed his tangled dark curls off his face with its huge brown eyes and baby's red round cheeks.

The prince looked around at the bloody hallway and all the guns. And everyone was looking at him to give a command. The prince spoke to Tow in high yet unchanged voice. ''My father is alive?''

Tow nodded.

The prince straightened his white waistcoat and frowned a serious adult frown, his young forehead creased. ''Then carry on, Brigadier.''

Tow's brows lifted marginally in surprise at the child's startling good sense. Prince Edward had no idea what was happening, *knew* he had no idea what was happening, knew that Tow did, had reasoned that Tow acted with his father's authority, and so handed authority back to him. How old was this boy? Ten? He was his father's son for sure. But the king spent no time with the child, so who had been teaching him? The only person who ever had any time for the boy was Marion Martel.

The king's guardsmen put up their weapons and placed themselves under the brigadier's command. Tow sent them to flush out the last of the insurrectionists.

They found Secretary Shie treed in the bell tower with a few of his followers. After a short siege, his cohort defected and Shie himself was captured. That was good. They needed at least one leader to display at a public hanging.

The king's guards brought the struggling corpulence before Tow, bonds biting into fleshy wrists behind the secretary's back. Shie spat at Tow, swore and railed till he was purple in the face. The show was not defiant courage. Oh no, Tow thought further ahead than that—

and so did Shie. Shie did not want to be hanged. Shie wanted the quick single bullet Tow was infamous for. So he provoked, he insulted, he dug desperately for nerves. But he did not know where to strike. Tow's armor was difficult to pierce. The young brigadier holstered his .357 and smoothed back his light brown hair.

Tow gave orders for Shie to be thrown in the dungeon below the Capitol building; the place was dark and foul, little used. Then he went to tell the king.

The king walked the palace halls with his triggerman. Edward paused to pick up a smashed white porcelain vase and set it right on its alabaster stand. He looked at it sadly, at the bullet-riddled papered walls, the plaster-dusted floor, the rolled-up bloodstained carpets, the broken windows, and torn draperies. Picking up pieces was futility. The place would never be right again.

"How could this have happened?" Edward III murmured in honest bewilderment. "How could they do this to me?"

"You shouldn't have insulted them," said Tow.

The king was about to blast the brigadier for his insolence, then checked himself. *That* was how this happened. Tow was right. One could not afford to bruise the inflated egos that surrounded him. He was the king. He was sacrosanct. But that was only the ideal. In actuality one had to take into account human pride and ambition. Though he thought he *should* be, the king was *not* invulnerable. He rethought his intended rebuke and spoke to Tow without excitement: "I'll thank you to watch your tongue."

Tow accepted the reprimand airily.

The king was wary of this one and never stepped wrong around his dangerous pet. One step would be fatal. But the others—the respectable Franklin, Shie, Salten, Mack, and Kester—he had sadly neglected his step around those smaller, tamer creatures. "Oh God, oh God," he sighed. "They were stumbling like fools, what else could I have said to them?"

"Sire, you should have just pointed your finger and I'd have had done with them then, with much less mess," said Tow. He carefully toed a fallen framed picture out of his path. Plaster rubble was strewn all along the way.

At least I still have my viper, thought Edward. He'd never fully appreciated how much he needed his assassin. And he never quite realized how loyal the creature was. A perfect symbiont, Tow would just as soon cut off his own head as let harm come to King Edward III. Edward had always known Tow needed him. It was good that Tow knew it as well.

Edward counted the faithful. "I need a new Council. Who is left?"

"Lindy," said Tow wryly.

"Forget him."

"Your archbishop."

"Ah, Gregory."

"Martel."

"Good. Good." The king nodded, heartened by the last two names.

"And me."

"You," said Edward, and stopped his progress down the hallway. He faced the brigadier. Tow had saved his life and was smugly aware of it. Trouble was Tow was becoming difficult to reward, and that could be hazardous. The king did not know Tow as well as he used to. With lack of knowledge, control slipped. It had started with that damn aide of his, William Stanton. That was a peculiar development if ever there was one.

The king looked into steel eyes. "Tow, what do you want?"

Tow's smooth face moved to something like a smile. The eyes remained impenetrable. "Just remember I did this for you."

VI.

Schism

MARION WOKE IN ANGUISH AT BEING DISCOVERED ON the palace grounds. The dull sickness hung inside like a mortal wound. It was only a secondary distress that she could not feel anything below her rib cage.

She opened her eyes. She was in her own bed. Daylight was shining through the leaded-glass windows in beams. There was a ring of people around her: her father, a doctor, the white-robed figure of a clergyman that was Greg, her fiancé, Frederick, in his red palace-guard uniform, and the boy Prince Edward. She focused on them and burst into tears.

They were talking to her, but she did not want to hear, until she realized that they were speaking words of comfort to her not revilement, and it sank in very slowly that no one thought to question her presence at the palace last night. These people were not treating her like a criminal. And Marion found out that she was a heroine for putting herself between her fiancé and a turncoat's bullet. The flowers in the room were from the king.

The awful horror lifted and Marion smiled through her tears. She patted her father's rough hands, smiled at Frederick, who looked colorless and wounded. She pulled on Greg's cassock. His distress ran deep. His rugged weathered face was showing careworn seams and his dark eyes were strangely liquid. She had never seen him so undone. "Oh Father Greg," she cried, and pulled him down to embrace him. She felt his masculine presence over her, his strong hands on her arms. He rose. She kissed his ring and kept hold of his big hand.

Prince Edward was crying silently, tears running down his red cheeks, his shoulders sometimes caught in a sob. He had been told Marion would never recover. The doctor said she would never walk again.

The doctor was saying that they must let her rest, and he ordered everyone out. Marion asked if the archbishop might stay a bit. That request was allowed. She might need him yet.

Alone with her, Gregory checked himself before he could berate her. He alone paused to wonder what she had been doing in the palace courtyard when the violence had broken out. But done was done. He could only regret. He groaned, "Almighty God," less a pontiff's prayer than the cry of a man.

It was a comfort for Marion to see him distraught on her account. She did not enjoy his pain, but it was the only evidence of love she had seen in a long time. He had been so guarded with her lately that she thought he'd turned to stone; she would take what she could get from him.

"Do you want to hear my confession?" said Marion. "No, don't put on your stole. I love you, Greg."

Hot fingers brushed her dark hair from her face. She turned her face into his hand and kissed his palm.

"Could you love half a woman?" said Marion.

"Marion, if you could do nothing but blink your eyes, you'd never be half a woman."

She smiled. "You're not saying that out of pity?"

"Pity? Marion, I'm the one I'm feeling sorry for."

Marion smiled brightly. In the back of her mind her thoughts were edgy, for only a man who had been with many many women came up with such charming lines. But the past did not matter. He was with her now.

He leaned over close to her. "Child, what were you doing at the palace last night?"

She looked for the simplest way to explain. "I guess I went looking for a powder keg and it blew up in my face."

"Why didn't you tell me first?"

"You haven't actually been coming around much anymore."

"I'm sorry. You'll never know how much."

"Will I see you again?"

"I'll be here for you," said Gregory. "You know I will."

Detroit slid down the ladder, ignoring its rungs. She dropped into the bunker and rolled. The other rebels gathered around her, afraid she'd broken something, so breathless and flushed was she. She kept gasping one word. They thought she must have hit her head because she seemed to be doing bad bird imitations, then Scottie realized that "Coo coo" was "Coup! Coup!"

Scottie lifted her up by her shoulders. "What! By who! When!"

"Yesterday! King's own council!"

Shrieks rebounded within the closed underground walls, then the rebels silenced themselves to hear the rest.

"Tow shot them all! King's still in there, but Council's in shreds—"

She stopped, listened. The radio, which had been left on softly, interrupted its music and played now the customary trumpet fanfare that preceded a royal announcement. Detroit pointed and cried, "Get the radio! Get the radio!"

Lark turned up the volume. The announcer's voice was a study in casual annoyance.

"A number of exaggerated rumors have been circulating the Capital area. To set the record straight, the Crown has issued the following report. There has been an attempt by disloyal elements to harm the king. This attempt was in no way successful. The incident was a

minor one to everyone except for the perpetrators, who
were dispatched by the king's capable guards, and for
the world-be ringleader, who was apprehended and is
scheduled for execution on Potter's Hill. Detailed an-
nouncements will be posted for those wishing to attend
the hanging—''

"That's Secretary Shie!" Detroit inserted in a quick
whisper.

"In an unrelated story, the royal family is leaving us
for a well-deserved vacation at the royal residence on
the Isle of Maine—''

"Unrelated!" Ezra blurted.

"It's a retreat!" Chris-John cried joyously.

"Shhh! Shhhh!" Detroit hastily slapped her friends
to be quiet. She was nearly bursting with a wonderful
funny secret. "You haven't heard the best part!"

"During his Majesty's sojourn, petitions are to be
directed to his able coregents, General Lord Martel and
the archbishop, His Eminence Gregory Vandetti.''

A long jubilant screech ripped through the bunker.

Terese kissed Chicago Red's hands; Balt after her;
and one by one, all paid homage to their mortal saint,
though Chris-John said he hadn't done anything. They
told him that he *believed* and that was enough, that was
everything. They began to think that Chicago Red was
truly magical. Scottie Deerborne alone hung back.

The rebels popped the cork of a bottle they had been
saving and threw themselves a little party in the bunker.

While they were celebrating inside, Chris-John found
Scottie alone outside. Night quiet closed in around
them. The laughter and music were something apart,
seeming distant.

Their footsteps crushed loud in the weeds. Chris-
John's soft voice sounded behind Scottie's broad shoulder. "Scottie, why do you hate me?"

"I . . ." Scottie paused in pain, his big fists jammed

in his pockets. He finished with a huge admission. "Don't."

It had been easier to let him think he did hate him. The truth was harder. He didn't understand it himself. "You scare the hell out of me," he went on. "You believe in something, you make everyone believe in it, and it happens. It shouldn't. But it does anyway." His big bony shoulders were hunched as if against a cold wind. Chris-John could see his dark, handsome sculptured face with its deep hollows in the twilight-shaded forest, could see pain in it. Scottie turned to Chris-John. "Can I say without misunderstanding I love you passionately?" He wasn't speaking of physical passion. His voice was bald. "And it scares me to death."

Chris-John accepted it with an angelic smile.

Scottie shrugged. "I never wanted to say that. I feel like I've just lost my soul." And suddenly he seized Chris-John's hands and kissed them. Because he realized, no matter how hard he might try, you can't deny angels.

The royal family packed up its household in cars, carriages, and royal train cars, and made its move to Maine as the first snows were falling, blanketing the pretty Capital in white and settling a silent shroud on the body of Secretary Shie, dangling from the scaffold on Potter's Hill.

When they arrived at the royal estate on the Isle of Maine, winter was already here. The lake was frozen. The trees were frosted white like a ghostly fairyland. Palace servants had arrived ahead to light all the fireplaces and drive the chill from the great northern mansion. All the rooms were bathed in a cheery warm light by the time the royalty arrived.

As soon as they were settled in, the king took his daughters on a sleigh ride around the grounds, all of them bundled in wool quilts and a great white fur tucked under their chins. They peered through wind-narrowed slits of eyelids at the estate's wild isolated beauty as they went gliding across wide white fields of untrammeled snow. Startled deer lifted their tails like white flags and bounded away at the sound of sleigh bells and princesses' laughter. Ring-necked pheasants with emerald heads rushed out of hiding right from under the horses' hooves and took flight with rusty ringing cries.

The king was getting a rosy sting to his cheeks and nose. His daughters were laughing. Edward began to feel renewed. The bleeding pain of betrayal, of poor Marion Martel's crippling, of his weakening power, all began to ease and fade. The rabid patriotism that had greeted him here when he landed on the rugged northern isle was cheering.

His daughters journeyed into town and went on a spending spree for new cold-weather wardrobes. They came back in furs, heavy velvets and wools, and they tried on all their dresses and pirouetted for him in the parlor before a blazing fire in the hearth. They were very pretty. And it was so nice to see them excited.

Only young Prince Edward was unhappy here. He had wanted to stay behind with Marion Martel. But the Capital area was not safe. That was why they had fled. So young Edward sat in the window seat, one hand on his mournful hound, the dog's head on his knee, gazing out across the cold winter lake.

Edward III walked the hall with his daughter Juliet on his arm. He hadn't been up here to Maine in two years. He hadn't realized how much he missed it.

He stopped at a faint sweet sound, thought he was hearing things. He cocked his head back and listened. There came the melodic strains from a piano. "Ah, that's a sound I've missed." Tow hadn't touched the piano in weeks. Now the splint was off his hand. "He used to play all the time, and I always thought it odd a gunman should be a musician."

"Is that the general now?" said Juliet.

"Shall we see?" said the king. He patted his daughter's plump hand, tucked her arm in his, and they walked down the corridor toward the sound.

The piano was in the parlor. The door was ajar. The king pushed it slowly in, stepped inside with Juliet, and stood there listening.

Tow did not stop and rise at the king's entrance as anyone else would have done. And the king did not want him to stop. When Tow was finished and the last note vibrated out to still air, Tow stood up. "Your Majesty. Highness."

"You are recovered, I assume," said the king. What a tense time that had been, Tow with one of his precious hands broken.

Tow flexed his fingers. "Getting there, sire."

The king looked down at Juliet's honey-tressed head. He remembered a time a few years ago when she had come to him and said, "Daddy, I want to marry your brigadier."

My brigadier? he had thought. Why would she stoop to a brigadier? Then it had sunk in what she had said and his blood ran cold. *My* brigadier. No. No. Not Tow. *Not* Tow. She couldn't mean that. "Who?" he had said cautiously, trying not to sound panicked.

"David Tow."

"No!" he'd roared so loud she had actually jumped. Then he had forced a quieter voice: "You don't know what he is." He would sooner she take up with an ax murderer. Tow could be that, too, for all the king knew except that it smacked too much of manual labor, and Tow's signature was one fatal pull of one finger on a one-pound trigger.

"I know exactly what he is," she'd said haughtily. Did he think she was a naive child? "Everyone knows he's from Farington and he's your assassin."

"You don't know what he is," he'd said, and forbid another word be spoken on the subject. Edward III seldom forbid his daughters anything, but when he did, they did not dare talk back. Juliet had dropped the matter. She had also given herself to every uniform in the palace. He had always wondered if it was revenge.

Edward looked from her to Tow. At least that affair was over. Juliet was looking at Tow the way she looked at any man, with no more, no less interest. And Tow in turn exhibited no interest at all. The king knew where Tow's fascination lay these days. So when Juliet sat at the piano bench and demanded a duet, the king left them there together, secure that nothing would happen between them.

Once the king was gone, Juliet's fingers strayed from the keys. Tow stopped, looked up at the ceiling, and said tiredly, "Must you make a rabbit of yourself?"

Juliet straightened, indignant. "Now, did I make a rabbit of my*self?* Seems I had some help, David."

Steel eyes slid aside to her. She was fat. She reeked of gardenias. Her face was pasty, her nose was piggish. Desire her, he never had. Function with her, he wondered how he ever had. Of Juliet's long long catalog of officers, Tow had the dubious distinction of owning her virginity.

"At Your Highness's command," Tow replied.

"You don't find me attractive anymore." She pouted a full lip.

"I never did."

"Ooo, you have gotten arrogant and you have gotten mean. I can still go to my father."

"To accommodate you?"

"You think because you saved my father's life you can say anything now."

Tow nodded. "That's about it."

Juliet's pasty face turned livid with rage. She balled her plump hands with her tiny tapered fingers into fists. She was shaking and she was so angry she could not speak. She ran out so he wouldn't see her tears. She vowed to get him. Everyone had a weak point. One only needed to find it.

Lord Martel's heart was heavy. He had been named governor of the Capital area in the king's absence, a job he did not want. His daughter was paralyzed. He did not like to be away from her in this time. He leaned heavily on Cardinal Vandetti for help.

Given political power, Gregory wasted no time making changes. First thing he did was let go a number of greedy, sadistic tax collectors. He sent notices to some tyrannical provincial governors that certain practices must be curbed immediately. He cut some of the Crown's expenses and eliminated tax for the very poor or the farmers who'd had a bad year. Martel raised his eyebrows at such high-handedness but did not interfere. He did not like that Vandetti did all this in the king's name, but it seemed to endear the king more to the commoners and maybe wasn't such a bad idea to stave off the rebelliousness that was infecting the land. Some of the curtailed projects could be reinstituted once things calmed down again.

The ones who were most unhappy were the rebels. Even after Gregory lifted the controls on persons trying to enter the Capital City, the rebel Tina did not resume attending confession, so Gregory went to them one night, in Devil's garb, and was surprised at the cold, almost venomous reception that greeted him in the bunker.

When the silence broke, they said the last things Gregory had ever expected to hear: What in God's name was Gregory trying to do? The rebels had great momentum. Now this. Greg was soothing unrest. The rebels felt betrayed. "Whose side are you on!"

The archbishop was at first astounded, then angry.

"Whoever is on the bottom!" he answered. "My duty is the welfare of my parish, which is the Kingdom. Whether reform comes from you or from the Crown, I don't really care. If I can better their lives within the system, I will do it. I saw my chance to make changes and I took it.''

"In the king's name!"

"Was that so wrong?"

"We'll never unseat him now!"

Greg held his inhuman Devil's helmet under his arm, and he shifted it in agitation, his lips pursed tightly together as if refraining from saying something rash and irrevocable. His black garb made him a huge and sinister figure in the confines of the bunker. He raised one forefinger from a black-gloved fist. "I'm not an anarchist. I have no hatred for the Crown. Only certain of its practices. If the two are inseparable, then I am against the Crown. If I can get rid of the practices without unseating the Crown, that is well. Are you telling me I am to make the Crown look bad so you can overthrow it? I thought the idea was to overthrow the Crown because it was bad. What if it's not? It still has to go?''

"If it's not, that still leaves everything to the whim of the Crown," said Chris-John. "The *system* needs changing. You can't leave the fate of a nation in one man's hands. And point of fact, it *is* bad and it has to go. Carrie and Meredith can't marry or even live in each other's hometowns; Ezra can't worship his God in the daylight. But anyone can murder a child if he's wearing a uniform of His Royal Majesty's Service.''

"I can marry Carrie and Meredith," said the archbishop.

"That's putting a little strip bandage on a gaping gushing wound!''

"That's taking one step at a time. I cure the ills as I encounter them as best I can. I am a practical man. I don't share your zeal for ideologies. An unmarried farm girl with two bastard children needs a tax reprieve more than she needs a democracy.''

"How can you be so shortsighted!"

"How can you be so blindly idealistic?''

They parted with angry words. Greg swept out of bunker in a swirl of black capes. Anger billowed behind him like a wave. He replaced his grotesque mask on his head, mounted his black stallion, and wheeled away at a gallop. He was late for a visit to Marion Martel.

When Gregory reached the Capital Road, he gave the stallion its head and let it stretch out at a full run.

Somewhere in the woods he heard a crack, felt a blow to his side that nearly unhorsed him. The stallion staggered and reared. He held on, without breath. He knew he had been shot. He groped for the reins, found them, and kicked his stallion's sides. The stallion ran.

A quarter mile down the road he reined in. He pulled a flattened slug that might have been a .45-caliber bullet from his clothing. It had been stopped by the kevlar vest he wore as the Devil, but his entire side was a lancing red-hot mass of pain. His ribs were broken.

He rode on in agony through the forest, only stopping once at an untended chapel to stow his Devil's garb. He took a rag to wash the white streak from his stallion's forehead. The stallion tossed its head and butted him. Gregory's face screwed up and his breath caught in fire. *Please don't.*

But the creature decided to be difficult. As Gregory lifted the cloth to its brow, the reins pulled from his shaking hands and the stallion danced away. Gregory walked after it. Pain throbbed to his fingertips. It hurt to stand, it hurt to breathe. The cloth trembled in his hand.

"Come here," he croaked. The stallion looked at him, swished its tail.

He tried to whistle but the stallion walked away to nibble at some tender twigs in the underbrush.

Gregory waited till the beast was engrossed in its eating to walk over to it and take its reins. He pulled the stallion's head up hard and rubbed the white paint from its forehead. *I know God made you one of his*

*more stupid brutes, but why now do you choose to be
true to your kind?* He remounted in blinding pain and
rode, draped over the stallion's back to the Capital. He
slipped out of consciousness. The horse knew the way.

When he arrived at the city walls, the guards at the
gate were alarmed. Gregory told them that his horse
had kicked him and he begged them not to tell anyone
as it was very embarrassing. He sat up straight in the
saddle to prove that he was all right and rode away
smiling.

Arriving home, he opened his cassock to find his
whole side was a vicious bruise.

He taped his own chest with difficulty and lay down,
his face contorted in pain as he lowered himself on his
couch. He could not summon the strength to go upstairs to his own bed.

He lay there waiting for the pounding on the door of
the king's guards. An hour passed and no one came.
He dozed. He woke late into the night, and stayed
awake, deep in suspicion.

He did not know who had fired the shot. Not too
many people had guns. Few people knew how to use
them. It could have been someone's spy, a survivor of
the attempted coup. It could have been a soldier of the
king who had found him out, but since no one was here
to arrest him, he supposed not. It could have been a
bandit. It could have been.

He would probably never know. Snipers were seldom
caught.

He knew he could not trust anymore. Especially not
the rebels. Chicago Red and he were too different.
Maybe the rebels had come to the same conclusion and
this was it. He rolled the flattened bullet between his
fingers. Someone had tried to kill the Devil Rider. Well
then, let him be dead. The Devil would ride no more.
He grimaced. Maybe Gregory Vandetti would not either.

* * *

It was two o'clock in the morning. Marion Martel was still waiting for the archbishop, though her father was begging she sleep. Gregory would come, she said.

He had completely forgotten about her.

Early in the morning Brigadier Tow had gone out to tour the estate's grounds. He always liked to know the lay of the land wherever he was living. He returned to his room after breakfast. He thought he would find William there, so it was a rude surprise to discover Princess Juliet there instead.

He looked around the chambers, then turned to Juliet. "Have you seen my aide?"

"I sent him away," said Juliet.

"*You* sent him away?" said Tow. Icy cold gripped his chest and tightened high in his throat. He was furious and terrified. He tried to allow neither emotion to show. Sent him away? Fired him? Or sent him from the room?

"I thought we would be more comfortable by ourselves," said the princess.

She was all smiles. She had recovered from her setback and was ready to recommence the siege. Juliet always wanted what she could not have.

"Where did you send him?"

"Who?"

"My aide."

"Oh." She tsked impatiently as at something incredibly trivial. She flipped her silk scarf. "I told him to take the weekend off. How should I know where he went. Try a cathouse. Isn't that where they all go?"

"Only if one wants a cat," said Tow, relieved that she hadn't fired him. He dismissed the suggestion of where Will might be. The only way Will would be in a cathouse would be by naive accident. That was entirely conceivable. "And even then one needn't look there," Tow continued. "There's always the palace."

"Don't you dare, David Tow. You know I'm not for sale. I am only for whom I choose."

"Very virtuous, Your Highness. Except you've chosen exactly half the human race."

"Oh no. I can afford to be selective. You have that reversed. Exactly half the human race chooses me. I can have anyone I want. I happen to like a hairy chest. And that appears to discount you, Brigadier."

The old you-can't-have-me tactics. The woman was an extreme bore. Where was William? Tow smiled thinly. "I can't see the charm of them myself."

"Really?" Her smile was vicious. "I heard your fancies run that way from time to time."

He was supposed to be horrified as at the revelation of a great dark secret. If she *didn't* by this time know that Tow's tastes ran to either sex, she would have to have been incredibly blind and stupid. So she knew. So what? He looked her in her smug blue eyes. "Males, my dear, yes. Hairy beasts, good God no."

"I suppose that's because you aren't hairy and you love yourself very much."

"You are determined to make me angry today," said Tow, not very angry. "Why is that?"

She was looking for a nerve with which to manipulate him like her father did so artfully. Once you get a ring through the ox's nose you can lead him anywhere you want him to go. This ox's nose was difficult to find. She would get it eventually, though, she was certain. She kept stabbing. Besides, she enjoyed this conversation. Once prepared for it, she found she liked the abuse. To be so completely defied was exciting. Winning would be that much more fun. She need only find the proper key.

It came to her in an instant. It was right in front of her and so obvious, she started to laugh. She shook with gales of giggles. Then she would look at Tow and break out anew. How did the saying go? Not seeing the forest for the tree? She had been so impatient to get around that one tree she hadn't even seen it.

She gathered up her taffeta skirts and smiled sweetly. "I can see I'm wasting my time here. I think I'll work on something younger. If he doesn't like cats, we'll see what he does like." She saw she had scored a direct hit, though his facial muscles had not moved yet. "Or doesn't like. Does *he* know what you are?"

Tow did not move. He stayed carefully cool.

"What does he think of what happened to your other aides? He does know that, doesn't he? Or does he?" And Juliet started to leave.

Of course she did not get out the door. It slammed shut before her face; Tow's arm reached over her shoulder and pushed it closed. Juliet turned to see him wince. He had used his newly mended left hand. Oh, he *was* worried to do that. Not just a nerve she had struck. Mother lode. Oh God, and his aide was such a pale nothing!

Juliet turned and slid her arms around his firm waist. His heart was fast; it was the first time she had ever felt that. "Now that I have your attention," she murmured, blithe to peril. She thought she was like her father, the great puppeteer who maneuvered this dangerous man so deftly. The king always played close to the edge. He knew Tow and knew how to move him where he wanted him to go.

But Juliet was *not* her father; she had not lived half so long and she did not know Tow that well. Not well enough to be playing this game. Knowledge in this situation needed to be perfect. No mistakes were allowable.

She taunted him and his anger mounted till he grabbed her blond hair. "You bitch. You royal bitch."

"Ow! You're ruining my hair!"

He jerked her head to him and kissed her hard. He drew back his lips and snarled into her mouth heated obscenity and kissed again as if to devour her.

Juliet smiled when she came up for air and gave a throaty laugh. "You love me. You love me."

He swore at her, told her explictly what he was going to do to her.

Juliet tossed back her mussed blond tresses. "You talk like a Farington ditch," she chided, but her cheeks burned, aroused. "Keep talking."

She liked his aristocratic handsomeness and his uniform in contrast to his crude way and low talk. He was an animal in refined dress. He handled her savagely and she groaned in his arms. *This is my love. This is my love. And he knows it, too.* She took his beautiful head between her hands. "You and I are two of a kind."

"I daresay we are."

He took her upper arm roughly and dragged her from his room, walking with long strides, his breath coming deep and angry.

"Where are we going?" said Juliet, half running to keep up with him.

"Shut up."

He led her out to the shelter where the cars were stored. He threw her into one automobile and got behind the wheel. She snuggled next to him as he was driving and he put his arm around her and twisted his hand in her hair. She slipped her hands into his jacket, unbuttoned his shirt, and stroked his chest. Then she drew his automatic.

Tow hated people to touch his gun, and he never let them. Had Juliet not been a princess, she would not have been able to do so either. She used to lick the barrel and he would growl at her. Now she pointed it at his head and said in sultry voice, "What would you do if I pulled the trigger?"

His eyes glanced aside to the gun then back to the road. "Die," said Tow. "Question is what would you do?" He stepped hard on the accelerator and the car sped down the rutted icy road.

She laughed and lowered the barrel. "What if I pulled now?"

"What would *you* do with a eunuch?" he asked.

"Very good," she said, replacing the .357 in its holster. "I was about to do it."

She undid his clothing. When he stopped the car, he lifted her head from his lap by her hair. "Get out."

"It's too cold," she said.

He got out and came around to her side and opened the door. "I said get out," he growled.

"You'll freeze your prick off."

"Then I'll stick it someplace warm. Get out of the car." He hauled her out.

They were in a field far from anywhere. He pulled her out into the snow, threw her to the hard ground, and fell on her. She accepted him ferociously, put up a mock fight as he crawled and wrestled and talked dirty to her.

Then he got up. She waited, writhing on the ground for him.

But he was straightening his clothes, not taking them off. "What? What is it?" she said. "Is it the place?"

He was transforming before her eyes. All the Farington roughness slipping away like a mirage and he was the king's sleek cold-eyed aristocratic assassin general once more. He looked around. They were in the middle of nowhere. "No. The place is perfect," he said, and drew his gun.

VII.

Talitha

TOW FOUND HIS AIDE. THE BOY HAD BEEN BEWILDERED when Princess Juliet sent him away, but who was he to question a princess? It was days before someone found Juliet's frozen body in the barren field. William was horrified when he heard about it. He wondered aloud who could possibly have done such a thing. Tow said he didn't know.

The Kingdom went into mourning. The sad event even seemed to win some sympathy among the populace back to the Crown.

Naturally there was an investigation into the assassination, and within a few days Brigadier Tow received a summons from the king's inquestor to come out to the lakeshore. Tow answered the summons, leaving William behind.

Tow found the inquestor at edge of the frozen lake. The man's gray coat was flapping in the blustery wind. Tow nodded a greeting.

The man pushed his woolen muffler away from his mouth. He had a face like a hatchet. "Will you fire a shot into that hay bale, please," he said tersely.

Tow drew his shiny automatic. "May I ask what for?"

The man was a block of gray stone. "No sir."

Tow pointed at the hay bale and fired. He looked to the inquestor for further instruction or comment. But that was all.

''Thank you, sir,'' said the inquestor. He stooped to pick up the shell.

Ballistics was all but a lost science. There were not many guns in circulation in the Kingdom, and most of those were in the possession of military personnel. There were exceedingly few murders ever committed with guns, and little doubt as to which weapon was used when a murder *was* committed with a gun. Hence there was very little need to revive the arcane science.

Except for the death of a princess. No trouble, expense, or expertise was spared, even to the opening of forbidden Beforetime records to discover how the ancients, who were so practiced at killing each other with guns, tracked a bullet to its individual weapon.

The inquestor came to the king after comparing the bullets found at Juliet's murder site to the bullet from Brigadier Tow's gun. The king was pacing, a grim frown sunken into his face. The coroner had just told him that Juliet had been three months pregnant.

The inquestor stood in the doorway and cleared his throat, then waited for the king to acknowledge him. The king turned to him bloodshot eyes that pierced like flaming arrows. ''Who murdered my Juliet?''

''I don't know, sire,'' said the inquestor, expressionless as a concrete slab.

''Not Tow?''

''No sire. It wasn't a match.''

The king's shoulders slumped. He had been so certain. Tension fled and left him suddenly strenghthless and fatigued. He sat down. He bowed his head.

He had known, *known,* it was Tow. The shells were from a .357 Magnum. Never mind that it had not been Tow's signature shot—one fatal bullet—rather two, badly aimed, in the abdomen and groin. She had bled awhile out there in the cold. And in Juliet's pregnant belly, anyone could have done it. Still the king *knew* it was Tow, his faithful assassin turned on him. He was grateful to be told he was wrong. "Thank you." Edward dismissed the man. He slouched back in the divan and stared out the window.

The serpent's hole in the ground had many exits, many escapes. Tow was not a creature who could be trapped. Tow knew guns; he had access to Beforetime information; he knew what sort of science ballistics was. He knew that the assassination of a princess was not carried off easily. He had known before he shot her that someone was going to try to match those bullets to him even if he did shoot her twice. There were drastic measures to be taken.

Anyone who knew Tow at all knew that he and his .357 were inseparable. He would spend an unnerving amount of time cleaning it and paying attention to it. The damned thing even had a name, but no one knew what it was. The Magnum was Tow's only trusted friend. Now all the worst contingencies had come to pass and Tow knew what had to be done with his only friend.

Tow had always known the time would come when he would commit an act for which even he could not be forgiven. He had never let it be known that his infamous weapon had a double, and no one ever suspected, since a .357 semiautomatic was a rather exotic weapon even back in the Beforetime when it was being made. As far as anyone knew, Tow had the only one left in existence.

Tow had the only two left in existence.

Tow had found the two guns together, sequentially numbered, in a Beforetime bunker filled with guns and weapons and C-rats and a naturally mummified corpse dressed in camouflage fatigues clutching a Uzi submachine gun. Tow had taken both .357 automatics and secreted the second one away for a rainy day.

The rain had come. It was a deluge. Tow had murdered a princess.

From the desolate field where he had left Juliet bleeding, Tow had driven straight to the coast. He stood on the ragged rocks, gazing out at the wild gray Atlantic. Wet cold wind chilled through his woolen greatcoat and tossed his hair over his sloping brow. His face and ears were stung red by the wind off the Ocean. Salty, vaguely seaweed smell tinged the frigid air. He stepped carefully over the rocks, watching for the ice.

Out on the promontory he drew his automatic from its holster next to his side. The metal was warm.

He narrowed steel eyes at the sea. He felt the gun in his hand. This was difficult. It and he had come up from Farington together. It had gotten him out of Farington.

No, that line of thought had to stop, and the gun had to go. Juliet was the king's favorite daughter.

Juliet was a twenty-four-karat whore. Tow felt a rush of anger thinking of her coming *near* William.

You and I are two of a kind. That had been the worst thing she'd said. It was true. *But did anyone ever tell you, my dear Juliet, that "our kind" ought to be exterminated?* He felt disgust and loathing when he thought of her, when he thought of everything in himself that was like her. Breakers rolled and roared and crashed. White spume and salt spray reached him up where he was. The tide was low, halfway out. Stranded things were skittering in their tidal pools, abandoned in the forbidden icy wasteland on the rocks.

Tow fondled the smooth barrel of the .357 with gloved hands. Like a lover. A piece of him. It was hard to part with. Even now he caught himself trying to think of another way.

But no, that was folly and he knew it. *Ah, discipline, Tow, discipline.*

He gripped the Magnum by the barrel and smashed it against the rocks. Then he hurled it far out to sea. He watched it sink—in a flash like a rock.

Like a millstone.

An odd and amazing sense of relief rushed through

him. Eighteen years and he was glad it was gone. A stinking albatross. The shiny polished metal was dirty with the blood of countless murders of obscene pigs, of Juliet, of the filthy thing that had sired him. He watched it all sink into the gray waves and be gone.

He walked in from the rocks and replace the empty space next to his breast with the second automatic; this one was clean. It had never killed. It looked like the old one and it slid easily into its place. It weighed and felt like the old one. Only Tow knew it was brand new.

He breathed the cold sharp air. Business was done. He'd survived and at last he was free to think, his mind placid, heart peaceful.

Where is my aide?

The free people of Michigan were in vile straits. They could not sell their autumn harvest of corn, wheat, and apples to the loyalist territories all around them. Nothing was getting done under rebel control. Winter storms paralyzed the cities. Ships in distress in the Great Lake were not rescued by the king's navy. Streets were not plowed; garbage piled up and stank with the sudden thaws. No citrus fruits were arriving from the south. They desperately needed strong organization.

Then the rebel leader Alan Cervany declared himself King of Michigan.

He made the announcement over the radio, and the Crown rebroadcast it all over the Kingdom of America to twenty million stunned listeners: King of Michigan. Alan Cervany.

Cervany's move hurt the rebellion worse than anything Edward III could have done, both in Michigan and in the rest of America. What was the point of rebelling only to have a different monarchy—or worse, a separate monarchy? Something frightening dwelled in the concept of a second Kingdom. No matter how many days' journey one might live from Michigan, one could not help but feel the impact. As long as anyone had been alive, there had been only one Kingdom. America was all there was. It was the world and the world was one. The idea of another Kingdom was alien, unsettling, and wrong as a two-headed monster.

The effect of Alan Cervany's declaration was dynamic and immediate. The tide of opinion turned once again in favor of the Crown, the true Crown, King Edward III. And very soon the royal family could go home again.

Tow tossed one of his suitcases onto the bed in his old chambers in the palace and brushed the flowers off his shoulders. He went to the windows and threw the curtains wide. Will came trailing in after him with the other bags. Tow went to him and brushed the white petals out of his hair like snow. "Oh," said Will, realizing he was covered with them, and he flushed and smiled.

The townsfolk of the Capital City were cheering and throwing flowers out in the red-brick street to greet the royal family's return. The blossoms had been brought all the way from the southern Kingdom to welcome the king's homecoming. Will and Tow had been caught in the petal blizzard as they returned to the palace.

Will busied himself unpacking and putting everything back in order of normality.

Tow paced the room as if reclaiming the territory. He touched a few keys on the piano. It was in tune. Everything was clean and polished. The hallways had been recarpeted and painted and papered. Tow paused at the door to Will's side chamber and touched his fingers to the lock where he had shot it. There was no trace of the damage. The lock had been replaced while the repairmen were fixing the other gunshot damage done during the attempted coup of October.

Tow replayed in his mind the incidents surrounding his shooting off the lock. He remembered holding Will.

He wished he could arrange some less traumatic scenario for him to do it again.

Platonic love was odd to him, dizzying and kind of sweet. Fondness was so very new to Tow. It was soaring and nice. And maddening. Physical passion remained an aching demand, and Tow was having trouble resolving the two. Wanting and not taking had its rewards; but that situation was not meant to endure forever. Tow wanted him, and he couldn't figure out how to take him. He could imagine nuzzling that soft girlish cheek; he wondered if the boy even had to shave.

Will was gathering up all the empty suitcases and stowing them in his small side room under his narrow bed. Tow watched him as he passed in between the rooms. The room was brighter when he was in it; everything was more interesting.

The general poured himself a snifter of cognac.

He got himself slightly drunk that evening, on purpose. He lounged in the red velvet armchair, wet-eyed and languid, still very aware—just drunk enough so that if this plan backfired he had an excuse and a way to retreat.

He beckoned Will to him, reached up from his chair, and slid his hand around the side of his neck, his fingers in Will's hair. He gazed up into those bewildered brown eyes, then slid his palm down the boy's long smooth neck and beneath his shirt collar to rest on Will's shoulder and collarbone, watching his eyes. He saw no real horror, only a little astonishment and expected nerves. Will's pulse was quick, his skin heated under Tow's hand with a bright red blush. Tow withdrew his hand from his shirt, caressed the line of Will's chin, and with the tip of his thumb brushed lightly across his lips. Then Tow let him go. He was not going to do more now. Not drunk. He'd gotten what he wanted out of this tipsy venture. It was enough for now. Hope was soaring. He did not apologize. That would presume he'd done something wrong. The flustered boy straightened his shirt and retreated to his room. Tow's heavy-lidded eyes followed the blushing figure to the door, then he smiled into his glass. *I hope you play with yourself.* He took a drink. His own blood was running hot and fast, and he was uncomfortable. *Shit. I should talk.* He set his glass aside, touched the tips of his aristocratic fingers lightly to his brow. He did not like himself drunk.

He looked longingly toward the door now closed. *No,* he told himself. *Absolutely no.* He would be stone sober when he touched that boy again and Will would know he meant it.

Tow shivered and covered his face with his hands. He was terrified. *God, how did I get this way?*

He heard the sound of the side doorknob turning, and he looked up, his heart leaping the way it always did when Will came to him. Will's door slid open. Will was nearly recovered and realized what he'd forgotten in his flustered retreat. "Will there be anything else, sir?" There was no coldness in the question. It was the same question in the same sweet voice he used every night, with maybe a slight tremolo.

"No," said Tow gently, and put his hand over his eyes. "Go to bed."

"Yes, sir. Good night, sir." Will withdrew.

Tow got up from the red chair and played the piano awhile.

Marion washed her long black hair without help and dressed herself in a dark brown velvet dress with white lace. When she was done, she collapsed, winded, onto the bed in her room. It was wearying—more to soul than to the body—to drag her own lower carcass around like dead meat. She saw her legs gradually losing their taut muscle tone. Soon they would be thin toothpicks within a case of flaccid white flesh. She pulled her long dress down over them with a shudder. She brushed her thick midnight tresses, her hopes and spirits higher to-

day than they had been all autumn. The king was back;
today was Sunday. Greg ought to resume his Sunday
visits now. There was nothing else to keep him away.
She did not know why he hadn't come before. She refused to believe he was avoiding her.

Her fiancé, Frederick, had been doggedly faithful in
his visits. Every day. He brought flowers when they
were to be had, and sent a minstrel to play under her
window.

But there was a leadenness to his devotion. He was
here out of duty and debt. He swore he loved her and
he would marry her whether she ever recovered or not.

Every doctor in the eastern Kingdom had said she
would not. Father had brought every one of them here.

Frederick had given her a ring with many diamonds.
He sent her florists and dress designers so she could
plan her wedding. Women always loved planning wed-
dings and Father thought it was a wonderful idea to
keep her busy and lift her spirits.

Marion tried to play along—she wanted to see her
father and Frederick thinking they were succeeding—
but finally she couldn't anymore. All the infernal white
fabric and lace bored her senseless. And she was sick
to death of Frederick. She was sick to death of being
the cross to which he was nailing himself in selfless
martyrdom. She would ask Greg what she should do.

She pulled herself off the bed and into her wheelchair. She was going to have arms like a mason; she
had developed a formidable strength in her arms from
dragging her body around. All her things and her furniture had been moved to a first-floor set of rooms in
the mansion, so it was not too difficult for her to take
herself to the drawing room.

She lifted herself out of her wheelchair and arranged
herself on the divan in the drawing room to wait for
Greg's visit. She called a servant to take her wheelchair
out of sight.

The grandfather clock was striking two and the tea was cold when she realized he was not coming.

Trusty Frederick came.

He looked dashing in his captain's uniform with its scarlet split-tailed jacket with gold buttons, white breeches and black boots, and his sword at his side. His black hair was pulled back in a smart braid with a black satin ribbon and curled in two neat rolls at the sides of his head. He doffed his plumed hat, bowed, and kissed her hand. "Darling, you look lovely. But then you always do."

Marion was about to scream at him. Then all her anger drained away in uselessness. Her spirit was crushed. "Darling, sit down, I have something to tell you."

He sat with concern wrinkling his brow, his hands clasped between his knees. He leaned forward to catch her every word.

Marion took the diamond ring from her finger and held it out to him. "I am releasing you."

Frederick was astounded. He protested with tears in his eyes.

But in the end he took the ring and went when she ordered him away. Frederick, naturally, went to Lord Martel first to make certain. Lord Martel came running to his daughter where she lounged dispiritedly on the divan, her head rolled listlessly to one side on the cushions, her eyes staring into space, her hands folded in her lap.

"Marion, you don't know what you're doing. You're upset." He patted her hands.

Her eyes came to lift—sharp life. "And you'll never get another chance to marry me off! Well, so be it! Put me in a convent, bury me in the north field if you like, no one will ever miss me, just don't try to give me to Frederick! I was born your ball and chain! I won't be pushed off on someone else!"

"Good God, Marion. You're not a ball and chain—"

"Then what do you call this!" she shrieked, lifting one leg with her hands and letting it drop.

Lord Martel took her face in his hands. "Sweetheart, you were being so good. I should've known it wasn't all right. I'll send for the archbishop—"

Marion's black eyes blazed. *"Don't* call the god-damn archbishop! His Eminence would have *been* here if His Eminence jolly well *wanted* to be!"

"I'll send for him," said Martel. Gregory always knew what to do. "Can I do anything for you now, sweetheart?"

Marion pulled on the corners of a fringed cushion. "Get rid of Frederick."

"Do you mean that?"

Her eyes smoldered. Her sallow face was ugly in its menace. "Yes."

Martel nodded and sent the tearful—and relieved—young captain away.

Martel could not get a message through to Archbishop Gregory, and he was concerned.

"Of course you can't," said Marion. "And good! I hate him! I wish he were dead!"

Then another visitor came to see Marion. Lord Martel went into the drawing room and asked in a voice like walking on eggshells, "Marion, will you see Prince Edward?"

Marion answered tonelessly, "Why not?"

Edward came in, his new puppy in his arms. His hound had died in Maine. The new puppy was a miniature collie. Young Edward put it in Marion's lap. She almost smiled.

"I had a thought," said Edward tentatively. "I didn't tell anyone. They'd think I was a stupid boy. You might think so, too."

"Let's hear the stupid thought," said Marion. She held the puppy up to her face and it licked her nose.

"Do you think you could still fence?"

"That *is* stupid," said Marion, lowering the dog to her lap.

"You could still use the foil with one hand. You'd have to steer your wheels with the other. I know it would be very difficult, but that never stopped you from anything before." Then the prince shrugged. "Of course if it's too hard for you, you can always take up. needlepoint."

"Oh you royal brat," Marion said, steaming. She took the puppy from her lap and set it on the divan beside her. "Get my chair from behind that screen!" She snapped, rising to an upright sitting position.

Prince Edward grinned. "Should I get your foil?"

"I'll get my own foil! Get me my chair!" Marion blazed. The puppy was yapping. "We'll see who ought to take up needlepoint!"

All the recent grave reverses for the rebellion sent the cause reeling back on itself. A pall of trouble and danger hovered over Chicago Red and his band. They moved most of their equipment and all their records from the bunker, because they no longer trusted Archbishop Gregory. The archbishop wasn't seen much in public these days, only at high Mass, and his public smiles were strained.

Scottie still stayed in the bunker. Someone had to, to keep an ear on the radio, and his was a face best seen seldom in town—a supposedly dead doctor. The others kept moving from haven to haven with different allies in the surrounding towns.

Detroit and Tina came one evening to check in at the bunker. They brought Terese along with them. Detroit's burned eyebrows had never grown back in, and she wore big dark glasses all the time. She asked how Scottie was. Scottie had been up for three days and nights trying to make contact with *somebody* in Michigan. Everything was dreadful.

He was out of food, so Detroit and Tina made a run into the nearest village to get him some supplies. Terese had dozed off on the couch, so they let her sleep. They would pick her up when they came back.

Terese woke alone with Scottie and went into a panic.

Scottie was at the radio. He lowered his headphones so they hung around his neck and he looked round to see Terese cowering behind the ladder. He was tired. Nothing was going well. He needed to eat, needed to do laundry. There wasn't enough heat in this damn bunker. His woolen beige sweater was worn through at the elbows. Now he turned around and this girl was hiding from him under the ladder.

He ripped off the headphones, stood, and grasped the metal pipe they had installed to give the bunker running water—the walls were plastic or he would have used those—and he beat his head against the metal with frustrated snarling groans and tears.

One for the crackling radio.

One for Michigan.

And Terese.

Terese.

Terese.

A voice sounded through the banging, so strange and papery, and broken from long disuse, that he didn't know at first from where it came. "Stop."

He turned his ringing head and looked, eyes swimming.

There was only wide-eyed Terese crouched at the foot of the ladder. "Please stop."

Scottie stared at her. She stared back, voiceless again, crying without tears, without sound. Her shoulders moved with sobs.

He reached out his hand toward her, palm up.

She shook her head. She was crying real tears by now, her brow ridged and draw in toward the center. She spoke with no voice; her words looked like "I'm sorry." She scampered up the ladder.

Scottie was not sure if he ought to go right on banging his head. He sank to the floor in a crumpled pile of long big-boned limbs, and curled his arms around his head.

The king was in a good mood when Tow chose to tell him, "I know who Chicago Red is."

Edward set aside his new red coral bookends, which the governor of the southern province had sent him as a gift. "Who?" said the king.

"Lad by the name of Chris-John Stanton."

The king raised his brows, then lowered them hard over his blue eyes. "Relation to—"

Tow nodded.

The king spoke in urgency of a sudden. "We have to—"

"No, you won't," said Tow.

The voice was cold, firm without force. The king gave ground. No, he wouldn't.

Edward III knew what this was. Collection of a debt. The last time the two of them had been together in this study, the king's own council had been conspiring against him and only one officer stood between them and him with deadly force.

Remember I did this for you.

Edward knew what Tow wanted. Tow wanted to keep his pet—who just happened to be Chicago Red's kin, as it turned out. That was a steep steep price.

"How long have you known?" said the king.

"A time," said Tow. "Since you distributed Chicago Red's picture."

"That was months ago! You said nothing?"

"I didn't trust your staff at the time," said Tow.

A subtle sharp reminder, that. A valid point, besides. Edward sighed. "Are you sure he's not a rebel spy?" No one had spoken the boy's name. They both knew who they were talking about.

"I am sure," said Tow.

"I assume the lad knows he's Chicago Red's . . . what?"

"Brother."

"Jesus. Brother."

"Yes, he knows."

"Why didn't he report it?"

"He did," said Tow.

He did. To Tow.

"Brothers," said the king. "Tow, that's close kin." He felt he had to explain that to Tow, who didn't seem to have a proper concept of family.

"So is father and son, and Colonel Stanton is dead," said Tow.

Edward put a hand to his stomach as if feeling slightly ill. Evidently Tow did have the proper concept of family on the subject of Chicago Red. Edward had no more firm arguments. Still, "I don't like this, Tow."

"I doubted very much that Your Majesty would," said Tow.

Tow had prepared his icy calm facade this time. The king knew from earlier experience to tread lightly on the subject of Tow's aide. Mention the boy and out come all the quills; Edward smoothed them down with great care. Will Stanton was a dangerous topic, all the more touchy because the king knew he had his finger on a nerve, and Tow knew he knew. Tow *hated* to be read so deep.

But Chicago Red's brother!

Edward asked a few more cautiously worded questions for his own reassurance. He was told that the boy William was an innocent. The brother Chris-John had made a total break with the family; he was assumed dead, in fact. Will was as shocked as anyone to learn his brother's identity. Will was not useful as a source of information on his rebel brother; he didn't know anything. All of that was actually easy for the king to believe. Will was a pale weak young man. Tow's interest in him was baffling.

Tow had hitherto been asexual. Oh, he went to bed with everything that moved, but preference? He had none. He had sex out of contempt. It was an act of hatred for him. Desire, he didn't.

Now Tow had taken a love—was that even possible? The king didn't like it. Not that it was male; that was not the problem. The king put up with what he saw as vices and degeneracies. He didn't like what it was doing to Tow.

It was making Tow unpredictable, for one thing. Since he had always been dangerous, it was essential that the king be able to predict and control his viper.

Tow in love. *God forbid this creature I created ever become a human being.* It was not possible. True, the object of affection was abnormal, but the very idea that such feelings were within Tow's capacity was incredible.

Unpredictable and irrational.

It was also making Tow vulnerable. Human emotion was deadly to an assassin. Edward had seen him up in Maine, come in from the snow with the boy, and he'd been shocked by the warmth he saw in him. Vipers can't be human. The king was afraid he was going to find the attempted transition would destroy him.

The king was stern. "We are even," he said, request granted. He considered it one of the biggest, most precarious concessions he'd ever made. The debt was paid. In full. He looked exactly at Tow to make sure he understood that.

Tow bowed in leaving. "Sire."

Thoughts of hopeless and foolish obsession led Edward III to Marion Martel. When the king appeared at the Martel estate, the flustered maidservant said she would fetch Prince Edward immediately. Prince Edward had taken up residence at the Martel house, but the king said he had not come to see his son. He'd come to see Marion.

Marion was baffled by the monarch's visit. It had no purpose but kindness. Why the ruler should take time from his administrative burden and troubles with the rebellion to check on one of his officials' daughters was so thoughtful and so beyond expectation that Marion began to cry.

I threw a pumpkin on your doorstep for a man who can't give me a moment of his time now that I am crippled.

God has shown me who loves me.

She wanted very much to do something for the king. Something to express how deeply his concern touched her.

All she had to give him was one of his enemies. She could give him the Devil Rider.

She tried to speak. The words would not form. She could not betray her beloved. Even now.

The king saw her tears, said that he had upset her and that he would come again at a better time.

Marion sobbed and covered her face. She could not bear to look at him. Could not bear to be seen. "Your Majesty is too kind. I am unworthy."

"Nonsense, child," said the king.

When he was gone, Marion bent over double in her wheelchair like a stringless puppet. As long as she lived, for however many lifetimes, she could not be more wretched than she was now.

Thunder crash followed hard on blue-white cold illumination that for a split second froze the midnight landscape outside in ghostly daylight. It was odd, this storm in early December. Marion wished the whole Kingdom would wash away. She rolled her head on the pillow. She could hear the collie puppy in Prince Edward's room, whimpering in fear of the storm and dark.

Rain pelted the leaded windows. Where was Greg? He hadn't come to see her.

She knew where he was—thought she did—nestled

in a blanket before a blazing fire with a rebel wench
who had legs she could wrap around him. Of course
he wouldn't come see a cripple.

I need you.

Her tears were on the pillow. She stopped a cry with
her palm pressed to her mouth. When she took it away,
there were teeth marks on the fleshy edge. She tried to
stop weeping. She had sworn she was through crying
for him.

She fell asleep, bleeding tears.

Thunder crashing wove into her dreaming sleep. She
saw young Edward with a foil in his hand. Something
happened. He'd fallen on it and was whimpering for
help.

Marion threw off the bedcovers and ran to his room.

She stopped in the doorway. She was awake now. It
was just a dream. Edward was in bed; it was the puppy
who was whining. The house was sleeping and safe.

The young prince stirred, sat up in bed, and stared
at the figure in the door.

"Marion!"

"I—I thought you were in trouble," she said. She
hung on the doorjamb, trembling, fatigued, and weak,
the strength of panic leaving her.

Then she remembered she couldn't walk. She felt her
tired quivering legs. She *felt* her *legs*. "Oh my God."

Edward jumped up and hugged her, nearly bowling
her over. He led her to a chair and she sat laughing in
a kind of hysteria, wiggling her tingling toes. The room
was dark and she couldn't see to be sure, but she
thought the prince was crying.

She wanted to tell her father, but the general had
been sent to Michigan. She wanted to send him a mes-
senger.

Then she thought no.

This and the circumstances around it were a gift from
God. There was a reason for this.

"Edward. Promise me you won't tell anyone this happened."

The boy was astounded. "Marion . . . *why?*"

"Swear to me. This wasn't an accident, you can see that, can't you?"

The boy's eyes were huge and luminous in the dark, with the look of a child listening to a ghost story. He felt the near touch of the supernatural, of divine breath down his neck, and all his short hairs stood on end. He swallowed. "I swear."

Marion stood up. She was going to walk around and strengthen her legs while she still had the cover of night to shield her.

VIII.

Advent

ELEVEN REBELS MET IN THE BUNKER HEADQUARTERS.
Chris-John's name was known to the Crown now. It
appeared as if the archbishop had turned on them, but
why then weren't soldiers swarming over the bunker to
arrest them all? They agreed it was possible that the
Crown had found out Chris-John's name somehow else;
so maybe the archbishop was keeping his silence despite their quarrel. But then who had identified Chris-
John?

It was raining outside. The bunker had sprung a slow
leak where they'd put the water pipe through. The
caulking had somehow come loose.

King Edward III was back in charge at the Capital.
He was slowly undoing all the well-intended harm
Gregory had done to the rebel cause. Taxes were going
back into effect. People would become discontented
again very quickly. Chris-John reassured his rebels
things were not as bleak as they seemed.

And they seemed very very bleak.

The dismal little meeting ended. The rebels were
leaving for their hideouts in the surrounding towns.
Terese hung back as the others went up the ladder. She
looked to Scottie when they were alone.

Scottie gazed back at her, more than curious. The
girl had never sought his company, never to be alone
with him. He waited.

She appeared a little wisp of a woodland fawn, about

to bolt. She stared at him. She whispered, "You didn't tell on me."

Terese was still playing the mute to the others. She could talk. But only Scottie knew.

Scottie shook his head. No, he wasn't going to tell the others anything that wasn't their business. Just as he'd explained to no one the bruises on his forehead.

Terese moved to the ladder and looked back. A lock of hair had fallen in her face and she was peeking around it.

Scottie said, "I'm going to take a room tonight at the Carriage Cross Inn." He finished with a shrug.

Terese bit her lower lip as she peered from behind her lock of hair. She climbed up the ladder and out.

Scottie took a late dinner, seated with his back to the wall, facing toward the tavern door. Many people had come to the inn. They made a boisterous crowd. Smoke filled the dining hall. Men were singing, hefting tankards; women were laughing. The rain had stopped for a time and people were venturing out on the wet streets in search of refreshment and company. Scottie blended in with the thick common crowds. He kept watch on the door for soldiers, and for Terese.

At eleven o'clock he took a candle and went upstairs. They shut off the gaslights in the rooms at ten. The room was warm by then from the fire he'd lit in the hearth. He put on another log and stayed up awhile reading in the warm light. His book was nothing seditious; he dared bring none of that into town.

The room was a long way from the bunker in more ways than one. It was not rich but it was weather-tight and furnished with a muted carpet, soft pillows, and a thick quilt on the bed, and it had a private bath with running water—hot water too because he'd paid for it. Carriage Cross was a good place. He wouldn't have invited Terese to meet him there if it were not.

The red-yellow firelight gave the room a soft glow,

dry and snug. It made him sleepy. He looked at the clock on the mantel. It was past midnight and had started raining again. He guessed Terese wasn't coming.

He hadn't really expected her. He had hoped a great deal, though, and he was very disappointed.

The flames died, leaving the red glow of hot embers within gray ash. He put his book aside and pulled the covers over his head.

A knock on the door wakened Scottie from a sound slumber. "Who is it?" he called in sleepy mumble. There was no answer but another tapping. Scottie sat up. He would have been alarmed except it was so faint and timid. It was not a soldier.

Scottie tore the bedcovers aside. "Just a second." He took a handful of kindling and threw it in the hearth. The flames flickered and leaped, chasing away the darkness of the hour. It was two o'clock.

Scottie opened the door.

Round hazel eyes peered from behind a wet strand of hair plastered to her wet face that was framed in a hooded rain slicker. Scottie opened the door wider. She paused and crept inside.

She gazed up at him, at his face. He was naked. She wouldn't look down, only up in timid questioning.

Scottie took her face in his hands. A tremor passed through her at his warm touch. "I hoped you'd come."

White rings circled her lips. She was petrified. But she was here. Scottie drew his lips closer, close enough to share breaths, but afraid to kiss her. Distrust read on her face. Her glance was shifting from his mouth to his eyes. She said, "Do you want to fuck me?" The word was strange to her. She was not used to talking; but that word was altogether odd.

Scottie was startled; he hesitated to speak. He wouldn't put it like *that* exactly. The question was an accusation. It *was* what he wanted and it made him feel guilty. And she knew it or why do you meet a man at an inn? And even if she did not look down, she had to know. Scottie wanted to soften the words, to euphemize, but then he just admitted baldly to her eyes, helpless to own want, even if it drove her away and he was sure it would, "Yes."

"Oh." It was all so frank there was nothing to say.

Her wet hands rose to his dark handsome face, almost touching. Beginnings of lines traced from the corners of his eyes and across his brow. Her fingers brushed his straight black hair aside and touched his forehead, which was bruised purple where he had beaten it against the water pipe. She touched the hollows below his dark haunted eyes. Her touch was the light whisper of moth wings. Scottie was scarcely sure it was there.

She hadn't taken off her rain slicker.

He said, "Will you stay?"

She dropped her eyes from his. She lifted them again suddenly, as she saw what she had forgotten she was avoiding looking at. Her gaze was back to his face and he was waiting for an answer.

She nodded. Her eyes were round as gold sovereigns.

Scottie pushed her hood back and slid his hands under her hair behind her neck. He pressed his lips to her forehead. "Are you going to be OK?"

She shrugged. That was what she was here to find out.

He couldn't hold her in her raincoat; it was cold and wet and dripping on his bare feet. He undid the clasps while she just stood there like a little girl come to nursery school. He opened her coat and put his arms around her slender body within and pulled her in to him. She was a tiny thing, hard, without excess flesh, all her muscles taut. Scottie's face hovered over hers, barely parted, mouth to mouth. She lifted a rain-puckered palm to rest on his bare chest. He kissed her with gentle passion, careful, as if she would break. He felt her

stiffness melt against him. The little girl was fading,
and Terese the young woman remembered how to do
this. She was in a powerful aroused man's arms and
nothing horrible was happening inside; and she realized it was not going to. Like gaining back something
stolen, her arms flew around his neck—they were still
sleeved in wet plastic but he didn't care; they were
around him—and held tight.

She was going to be fine.

When Lord General Martel returned from Michigan,
he was pleased to see his daughter Marion in good
humor, so gracious and cheerful. That morning they
were laughing at breakfast, then played a game of
chess, and she beat him roundly.

Marion almost broke down and told her father her
secret. She hated to break his heart, making him think
she would never walk. But she needed to do this, at
least for a while. She hardly knew why, herself. Part
of it, the easily seen part, was a smug selfish sense of
power, bleeding pity from where it should have and
hadn't yet come. Part was something else she couldn't
explain, almost a premonition.

Then the archbishop came to call.

Marion damned herself for the way her heart caught
when she sighted him there in the archway, the form
she knew so well, the pontiff's silhouette in his cassock
and short cape, the tall man with craggy mature face
and close-cut dark curling hair. He came near and her
senses flamed with familiar masculine smell and
warmth. Her resolve quailed and she felt herself turning into spineless mush. But by God, where had he
been? She found her resentment again in time; it fed
off his infernal attractiveness and the heartrending nat-
uralness of being with him. She resented him more for
meaning so much to her. He should have been here.
And since he hadn't been, she should have betrayed
him to the king. No, it would not even have been be-

trayal, for there could be no betrayal where there was
no loyalty. She smiled and bid him greeting.

Gregory was amazed to see Marion so well. Her
black hair was coiffed just so and she was dressed in
pastel taupe with fine white lace spilling from her her
full sleeves at her elbows. A small gold cross glittered
at the base of her slender white throat. She was a bit
cool toward him, but color and liveliness and health
were in her cheeks. He had to blurt in surprise, "Marion, you look beautiful."

"You sound surprised," she said, pouring his tea.

"I admit I am. I expected—I don't know what I expected."

"No, I did not languish and wither in your absence.
But then my health is no thanks to your thoughtful attention either—I admit," she said, her tone sweet, but
it was all venom.

"Marion, I *am* sorry. Believe me I would've been
here if I could."

"I am certain," said Marion. She didn't sound certain at all.

"You must have felt terribly abandoned."

"Abandoned?" she said, as if the idea had never
occurred to her, as if it were the furthest thing from
her mind. Then she let loose. "Greg, I was never so
alone in my life. I never needed anyone like I needed
you these past months and *you weren't here*. Alone,
abandoned, rejected, suicidal, worthless—give me
some more words! So please forgive me if I don't jump
up and down for joy to see you now!" She took up her
tea cup again, icily civil. "And forgive the expression;
I *can't* jump up and down."

The lie burned her tongue but she tasted bitter
warmth to see Greg so remorseful. But then she had
seen his crocodile tears before and had believed them.
He looked so genuinely sorry. So had he before. She
would never be so taken in again.

She let down the delicate china cup with the cool

manner of a proper lady. "At what Mass do you read the Gospel when Christ bids the girl to get up and walk," said Marion. "I've been waiting for it."

Gregory did not touch his tea. He watched Marion. "I think it's one of the last Sundays after Pentecost."

It was already Advent now.

"I missed it," said Marion.

"You were bedridden at the time," said Gregory. "It was right after your accident. I recall having difficulty reading the words."

"How touching."

"Don't be angry." Gregory pressed his hand to his side, as if a pain troubled him there.

"No?" said Marion. "Very well, I will feel nothing. Why are you in purple? Did someone die?"

Greg did not know whether to answer her words or the frosted-over emotion running underneath. "It's the Feast of Saint Lucy," he said. "It begins an Ember Week."

"Ah, the Ember Days," said Marion. A time of prayer and fasting, and ordination of new priests, the Ember Days came four times a year. "You will be very busy, no doubt. Why do they name them for ash?"

"It's not Ember as in ash. Ember comes from a Beforetime word meaning a circuit or revolution."

"Revolution?" Marion nearly laughed.

"Revolution as in things that recur," said Gregory. "The four seasons. Events that go round. The cycles of the nature."

"Events do seem to go in circles. Is it true this country overthrew a monarchy once before?"

"You're not supposed to know that."

"Not knowing it is not going to stop it from happening again. Just as I won't shrivel up and die just because you won't look at me."

"That's enough, Marion—"

"Is it now?" she said, and Greg regretted saying exactly that. He hadn't meant it that way, but Marion would not let him continue. "You've had enough. Well, Your poor Eminence. You've had enough. You forget, this is my home. You may leave."

Gregory wanted to explain what he meant, why he hadn't been here to see her, the whole story, his being shot, his broken ribs. He had been in agony these last weeks. He had put up a public front of smiles and health for the endless dignitaries that came to him from all over the Kingdom, and at high Mass, so that whoever had shot the Devil Rider would not see the archbishop looking wounded. "Listen to me—"

"Why? Who wants you? Who needs you?"

And Greg realized she had no reason to believe him even if he explained. His public smiles were too convincing. Had he told her the truth while he was in trouble, she might have understood. But now that the storm was past and she could see only that he was well, she had no reason whatever to trust him. He had done nothing to make her believe otherwise. Softly he said, "Evidently you did, and I wasn't there."

"Get out."

"Do you mean that?"

She hissed, "Yes."

The archbishop stood grave and abashed, his face drawn. He inclined his head in a bow of parting and he left.

Marion bent her head to her hand, trembling in grim victory to have found strength enough to say she didn't need him.

Now she had to make herself believe it.

The winter snows returned. It was Christmastime in the Capital City. The streets were festooned with garlands and silver bells. Carriages and open sleighs were drawn by horses caparisoned with bells. Candles burned in the shop windows. Wreaths hung on every light post and every door. Church bells caroled from the cathedral on the hour.

Tow wore his light brown greatcoat open, a cashmere scarf hanging about his neck. His hands were protected in dark brown leather gloves. His short hair was wispy on his forehead, his cheeks rosy, eyes alive. He was looking human, and happy. It was twilight. He was coming in from the garage, walking through the snow behind the palace. He looked to see where his aide was.

Will was ahead of him, dressed in a short pea green battle jacket, climbing the brick stairs behind the palace up to the snow-covered terrace.

Tow impishly scooped up some snow into a ball and threw it at Will. Tow was beautiful in action, but there was no one around to see. He hit Will in the back. The aide turned, startled, and cranked his head around to look at the back of his jacket; yes, he'd really been hit with a snowball. Tow was laughing.

Not sure if he really ought, because Tow was a brigadier, Will scooped snow off the brick railing and pitched one back. Tow blocked it with his forearm, then charged at Will, who cried out and ran down the steps and across the snow.

Tow caught him and they fell to the ground together, Tow on top. Tow looked down at Will and kissed him on the cheek. Will looked back up, surprised. Tow took off his left glove with his teeth and caressed Will's face with one warm hand, one gloved. Then he kissed him on the mouth. Will didn't fight, didn't respond, but then he wouldn't know how.

Tow drew back, holding Will's white face. The boy was scared. Tow looked at him long, in want. He looked for something besides fear. He touched his cheek, and Will's eyelids quivered. Tow lightly brushed away wisps of hair from his forehead with his fingers. "Are you all right?"

"Yes, sir," Will whispered.

Tow laughed. He laid his cheek next to Will's and breathed into the snow, his eyes bright. He was terri-

fied. A nice kind of terror. The stars were very bright.
Lights shone in frosty halos from the palace. Colors
were deep and vivid, the dark evergreens laden with
white snow, the red brick of the palace, smoke from
the chimneys, shiny ornaments on green garlands, and
holly berries. Red blush on Will's pale face.

"You're a very charming young man."

He got up, helped Will to his feet, and brushed off
the snow.

They returned to Tow's rooms in the palace.

Tow tossed aside his scarf and threw his coat on the
bed. Will lit a fire in the fireplace.

Will was aware that the general was a very handsome
man, especially with the red shine in his cheeks and
smiling air and sparkle in his eyes. Tow sat down to
play the piano. Will went to his own small room and
undressed down to his shirtsleeves. He looked into the
mirror with his shirt open at the neck, cuffs undone.
His hair was disheveled, his face blotched red from the
cold outside. He was a skinny youth with a long neck
and none of the general's refinement and style. His
bones were good, but that was all. His wide-eyed expression staring back from the mirror was what he'd
had on his face in the snow, and he looked at it now,
embarrassed. The general was toying with him.

In the other room Tow was playing a passionate rendition of a winter song. Will leaned in the doorway,
his back on one jamb, his stocking feet braced at the
base of the other, his hands in his trouser pockets. The
brigadier looked up at him once, winked, and continued to play animatedly.

When Tow finished the song, he got up from the
bench. He exchanged a few words with Will regarding
the next morning's schedule, then said, "Good night,
Will."

"Good night, sir." Will started to turn back into his

little room, but the general beckoned him stay a moment and he walked to the doorway where Will was.

"Wait a minute."

Tow took Will's chin in his palm and tilted it up to him to kiss his lips, then he let him go.

Will curled up in his bed, tossing, sleepless, the sheet pulled over his head as if he were a small child and afraid. The other covers he'd thrown off because he was too hot. He was lost and confused and there was no one to ask questions of; he couldn't have spoken any of it anyway.

He replayed the evening in his mind over and over, reliving the kisses and caresses, surprised to feel such longing now. He didn't know what he was thinking, what he wanted. He was trembling, hoping and fearing Tow would come to his bed. And he was trying to think of what he would do if he did. Will had never made love—he thought that was where this was leading, but he wasn't sure. And he was not sure how it was done with a man, only that it was illegal. He tried to remember when he'd walked in on the twins years ago; but he'd run away then, trying *not* to see. He was aware that there was an awful lot he didn't know and wished to God he did now. He became angry at his own awkwardness. He hoped he hadn't turned Tow away. He cried, sat up in bed, pressed his cheek against the wall separating them, and touched it with his clumsy fingers, spilling silent tears.

He hoped Tow wanted him. He thought he wanted him. He had to. Didn't he? *This is what it all means, doesn't it? I'm not mistaken? I wouldn't fall apart if he came to me like that, would I?*

God, would he ever come? Or was he just being fond and kind? Will would have cracked his stupid head against the wall if Tow weren't on the other side. He curled back into the bed and closed his eyes to keep the tears in.

* * *

Dark. Dead of night. Not a gray ghost of dawn yet outside his window, not for hours.

Will was half-awake, the sheets bunched under his chin in a wet palmed grasp, when came a tap at the door. Pulse sped; eyes opened. Unreality gripped the moment. Will answered in shaky voice, "Yes?"

Tow opened the door. "Were you asleep?" He was a dark silhouette against the doorjamb, naked, hair tousled from restless sleep.

"No, sir," Will whispered. They were both speaking quietly, the night making every noise loud.

"Don't call me sir. This isn't an order. It's just a request from a very lonely man in the middle of the night; will you come to my bed?" The voice was open and hurt and even a little frightened.

A spear of feeling went straight through Will's gut to his groin. His heart was in his throat. Words stumbled out, always the wrong ones, "Sir, I—"

"I'm sorry. I shouldn't have asked," Tow whispered, and started to retreat.

"No, I—" Will sat up, shaking. "I want to. . . ." he blurted out. His mind was racing with uncertainties that needed resolving right *now* and he didn't know how. He was afraid to get out of the bed; he wore nothing and he had a very long erection. He wondered if he ought to put on his robe. What should have been natural and obvious was incredibly confusing when one didn't know the answers and was trying too hard. From the door he heard Tow's breath come deep. Will could barely see his face; it looked boyish and vulnerable.

Will got up, walked to him diffidently, aware of how gangly and skinny and naked he was, and how handsome and naked was the general. At the end of a long long walk of eight feet, a warm hand on his arm drew him in first-time-ever flesh to flesh the length of his body, just beginning an explosion of sensation. No longer lost at sea, he was caught in a power he didn't want to fight. Hands on him where he'd never been touched, tender outpouring of words that burned his cheeks, hot mouth and tongue on his skin and in his mouth surprised, filled him with a sheltered innocent's sweet horror.

The boy had no control, none. And he was not sure what to wait for if he'd had any. Will cried out and climaxed there, standing against him in the doorway. Tow caught him tight in his arms, "Sweetheart," he breathed, touched by the boy's utterly artless sexuality, and held him as he shuddered again.

Will felt all his muscles go weak, hysteria fading. When he came to his senses again, Tow was kissing his face. Will was mortally embarrassed; he'd just jacked off on a brigadier's leg. Tow took his face in one hand. "Are you all right?"

"Yes, sir. I mean—"

Tow laughed with a cry. "My name is David."

A strong arm firm against Will's back guided him to the general's bed; it was wide with fine cool sheets. Will went with expectant dread. This was uncharted country for him. He lay beneath his moving body, holding the man who sighed and moaned and kissed him, and groped and adored his gawky pale body. The general was warm and smelled and tasted nice. Will was grateful not to be lonely and so amazed this man could be brought so helpless in passion by *him*. He grimaced and groaned into the pillow when he finally came to it. Tow clutched round his shoulders, and in the second convulsion bit Will's shoulder, without hurt, a grazing of teeth on his bare skin. He kept coming till he was empty and shuddered again, then collapsed and relaxed, a heavy dead weight on top of Will. It was a pleasant way to be crushed. Tow was panting, recovering himself.

Tow turned Will over beneath him, rested his forearms on either side of the boy's head, and demanded, "Has there ever been anyone else?"

"No, sir—no."

"A girl?"

"No."

Tow kissed him possessively. He played at love for hours, a new toy he couldn't put down. The boy could keep it up all night. The general finally admitted defeat. "To be young again." He smiled. He was only thirty-four, boyish now, achingly attractive.

"Does it really fade?" said Will. He almost wished it would; until tonight desire had been nothing but a source of frustration and torment.

"Do I seem faded?" said Tow in gentle indignation.

"No. That's why I asked."

"Well, I am," Tow admitted. "When I was twenty— no, I don't want to think about being twenty."

He hunched over him, holding the boy's head to his chest protectively. He looked up at the stars through the window above the headboard, felt his heart beating, jealously guarding his joy, happy, and a little afraid something would happen to it.

Till a small voice underneath him said very shyly and reluctant, "I have to go to the bathroom."

Tow let him up. "Use mine." He guided him toward his own big luxurious bath instead of the little water closet adjoining the aide's room.

When Will came out, the general was there by the door. Tow started into the bath in his turn but paused to take Will's throat in his hand and gaze into his eyes before he went in. "Do me a favor." He kissed his cheek. "Change the bed."

The brigadier had always liked things clean. They had made a sticky, wet, and now cold mess of the sheets. Will felt a tight hand close in his chest. The enchanted night was over. He asked softly, crestfallen ritual, "Will that be all, sir?"

Tow tapped his cheek very lightly in a mock slap. "Change the bed and get *in* it."

Elation returned and Will obeyed.

Tow came out and slid between clean sheets. The stars had turned. Will fell asleep in his arms.

Tow stayed awake a time in wonder. *Happy, when have I ever been?* Lonely, he never realized he had been till suddenly he was not. Such perfection couldn't last.

And of course it didn't.

Part Three:
The Glory

I.

The Prisoner

WINTER PASSED, AND THE SPRING THAWS CAME NOT too soon for anyone.

King Alan Cervany of Michigan proclaimed that democratic elections would be held in his province-kingdom when the weather broke. He said that his kingship was never meant to be a permanent condition; it was a temporary emergency measure needed to get through the winter crisis. Now was the time to move toward forming a republic. He quoted from a pamphlet that Chris-John had sent him before the two rebel leaders had their falling out: "The progress from an absolute to a limited monarchy, from a limited monarchy to a democracy, is a progress toward a true respect for the individual. . . . There will never be a really free and enlightened State, until the State comes to recognize the individual as a higher and independent power, from which all its own power and authority are derived, and treats him accordingly."

The whole Kingdom was watching events in the renegade province with intense interest. The fate of the rebellion in the rest of America hung on the fulfillment of Alan's promise. It had yet to be proven to the Kingdom that democracy was a workable system capable of existing and functioning for itself. The Crown's propaganda corps was quick to point out that in nature there was no such thing as a creature with more than one head. And Alan's usurpation of power in foundering Michigan seemed to bear out that point with clear and painful force. If the rebellion was to have any hope whatsoever of surviving, much less succeeding in the end, it needed to prove its worth through an honest election.

And with the arrival of spring, Michigan in fact held the first presidential elections America had seen since the Beforetime. Everyone over the age of fifteen cast one equal vote—men, women, blacks, whites, Christians, heretics, convicted thieves, idiots, avowed supporters of Edward III, illiterates, doctors, priests, beggers—everyone. That Alan Cervancy won did not lessen the success of the grand endeavor—because Edward III had finished fifth. Democracy had taken its maiden flight and landed safely. The rebellion was still alive, and Chicago Red still had a fight before him.

The rebellion had no sooner survived its first major test when Chicago Red received word that the rebel leader Atlantis was arriving from the Pacific coast and wanted to meet with him. Atlantis was Chicago Red's West Coast counterpart; the name was a red herring.

Why Atlantis was coming in person, why not using the intricate communications net they had built so painfully over the last three years, Chris-John did not know. He didn't like it, though he did not guess it was about to set in motion the beginning of the end of the rebellion.

There was always a measure of mistrust in a rebel's meeting someone he had never seen. Chris-John agreed to it because Atlantis had more to lose than did he. The Crown, after all, already knew Chicago Red's true name and what he looked like. Atlantis was a total unknown.

They set up a meeting at the tavern of the Carriage Cross Inn. Chris-John took a table with Scottie, Balt, Ezra, and Tina.

As they were waiting, a prostitute sat in Scottie's lap. She was a tall willowy girl, taller than Scottie, with black hair to her waist, no curves, just a long slender body, miles of legs, and long white arms that fastened around Scottie's neck. Her enormous green eyes were bright and roving. She was wearing little; she could get arrested without even soliciting. And she was attracting too much attention to the nervous rebels.

"Look, miss, I'm broke," said Scottie; that always worked better than saying he was not interested. "You're wasting your time."

She nuzzled his ear and whispered a suggestion very low.

Scottie looked shocked. He took another drink of ale, then spoke, a little rattled, as he got up, one arm around the girl's long waist. "I'll see you all later. I got what I came for."

Tina twisted around in her seat to watch him go. She started after him, but Balt caught the edge of her coat and pulled her back down. Someone had to wait for Atlantis.

Tina called Scottie names into her beer. Ezra and Chris-John stared after Scottie strangely and shrugged to each other.

It wasn't like Scottie.

"Maybe he saw someone who recognized him and had to get out quick," Chris-John offered in defense.

They looked at the clock. Atlantis was late. The remaining rebels decided to wait awhile longer.

By 3:00 they decided Atlantis was not coming.

At 3:01 Tina realized Atlantis had already come and gone. She pushed away from the table. "I feel like an ass." She grabbed up her coat and threw Chris-John's at him. "Come on."

"What?"

"When you're being searched for everywhere, where do you hide but in plain sight. Would you recognize Atlantis if she sat in your lap?"

Ezra laughed in realization. "Bright as brass, right under our noses. In our very laps, you could say."

"Scottie's lap anyway," said Tina.

They returned to the spring meadow where their bunker was hidden. They found a very long blue automobile in the empty shelter where they used to keep the car they had lost in Farington. This new automobile was the first convertible top any of them had ever seen.

"Where's the rest of it?" said Ezra.

Scottie was already inside the bunker, with Atlantis, over whose shoulders he had put his jacket, deciding the woman needed more clothes.

Terese was huddled into the farthest niche of the small space, one of Scottie's faded green sweaters wrapped around her. The sweater was huge on her and she looked like a child bundled up in it, its sleeves bunched up in many folds so her little hands could show through at the cuffs. She'd clasped her hands around her ankles, her knees drawn up under her chin, and she watched the tall woman Atlantis stroking and hanging on Scottie the way Terese never did in public. Terese was still very skittish in front of others. Softness and show of affection were for Scottie—alone.

Scottie kept unwinding the arms—there had to be more than two of them—and glancing back at Terese as if afraid to find her gone.

Detroit sidled over to Terese and whispered an offer to punch out the tall woman, but Terese shook her head no.

Scottie had to wonder and did not dare ask if Atlantis had been the leader of the Seattle uprising in which Chris-John's father had been lynched. Scottie decided he did not want to know. Even after he knew better, he still thought that people who killed ought to look different from everyone else. He was continually disturbed when they did not. The woman looked like a side dish imported for a palace ball rather than like a guerrilla tactician.

Atlantis had brought a companion with her. He was not noticed right away because he was quietly drinking his tea and studying a map. His hair and eyes were dark, he was of middle height, and he looked like a thousand other men in the Kingdom. His name was a Tolan; he was Atlantis's right hand. Tolan was as calm and subtle as Atlantis was showy and outrageous. Atlantis had a grating habit of pretending to a lot more air than was actually between her ears, and the women did not like her much. Phoenix nearly fell down the ladder when he saw her.

When Chris-John arrived, Atlantis diverted her attention from Scottie to him. She took his face in her hands and cooed, "You're Chicago Red? Oh, aren't you just the most precious thing! You're prettier than your pictures." She plucked at a loose curling lock of his black hair and let it fall across his creamy brown forehead. He looked up with beautiful chocolate brown doe eyes, then blinked with rose-petal lids. She gave a squeal. "You're adorable! Tolan, buy me him!"

"We're democrats, my dear. We can't buy people," said Tolan.

Atlantis snapped her long fingers as if she'd momentarily forgotten. "Oh, but he's so cute." Then she turned to play with whoever had moved to the other side of her. Hardly even looking, she put her arms around Phoenix's neck, and said, "Oh and you're so . . ." She looked at his leering scarred face and yellow eyes. "Oh my."

"Ugly," said Phoenix.

"Ugly," Atlantis confirmed in wonderment. She kept her arms around his shoulders and just stared at him, mesmerized. Phoenix stared back. He thought he was in love.

Lark set down a teapot with a bang on the table and everyone looked. Lark was getting impatient. "Atlantis, why are you here?"

Atlantis disengaged her long arms from Phoenix, her face becoming serious. She interlaced her long white fingers under her chin. "We are in trouble."

"Who is?"

"We are. You are," said Atlantis, and bowed her head. She explained. "We made some very very very very very very very very bad mistakes. You see, in the process of coordinating the communications network between east and west, it came about that a couple of us, well, know too much. We were much safer in splintered little groups like we used to be. It seems now we coordinated too much."

"How is that bad, unless someone is caught?" said Tina.

"Someone was caught," said Atlantis, and a groan rose from the bunker.

"Is he loyal?" said Scottie.

"Martinez is loyal; he's dear and sweet, but he's weak," said Atlantis. "He'll fold right up under torture. He'll tell them everything he knows, and he knows everything. They have him out at the West Coast right now. It's everything they can do to hold on to him; my people have the place more or less under siege. They've decided to move him here, to the Capital, for interrogation."

"Then we just have to get him before he gets here," said Lark.

"If we only knew how they were bringing him," said Detroit.

"That, I can answer," said Atlantis, and Tolan brought out a map and unrolled it on the table. They held down the curling corners with teacups.

"With that much security involved, it was difficult to keep the route a secret," said Atlantis, one long white finger tracing a route marked in yellow on the map. "They aren't even trying for secrecy; it's all muscle. Lots of guards. *Lots* of guards, coast to coast."

"Maybe it's a ruse. They'll actually take him another route," said Chris-John.

"Thought of that," said Atlantis. "Wish they would. I don't think so. This plan is ironclad. I think they'll stay with it."

"Then we'll just have to hit it *some*where," said Detroit, bending over the map. "Where's a good place?"

They went over the route point by point then over again. It *was* ironclad, even to the boat across the Mississippi. The Crown wasn't risking the isthmus route so close to Alan Cervany's domain. There were no weaknesses at all.

"That settles it then," said Chris-John.

"What?" said Lark.

"Where we hit. There's only one place."

"Where?" said Lark. "I don't see it."

"Here." He was pointing here, the Capital itself, the end of the line.

There was silence, then Tolan spread his hands. "Sure. They'll never expect it."

"There's a reason for that," Scottie said.

I am going to die today.

The thought would not leave her alone. It came back again and yet again like a circling fly as many times as she chased it away.

"What's your business in the Capital?" the gate guard demanded.

"Lookin' for work," Detroit mumbled.

The guard's eyes raked up and down the small greasy woman. "*You?*"

Detroit wiped her nose on her sleeve. "I have the right t' look."

"Makes me sick when the likes of you talk about your *rights.*"

Detroit maintained a level dull gaze from under her long jagged black bangs. She wiped her nose again. "Got the right."

"Length of stay," the guard demanded.

"Morrow."

The guard glared. "You're not staying on the street. Where's your rent money?"

Detroit fished in her pockets and brought out, along with lint and black hairs, bunches of coins, the tiny cheap ones of soft metal. She began unfolding the bent ones.

"Get that trash off my counter!" The guard quickly stamped a one-day pass and pushed it at the pile of debris. "If you don't exit I'll come looking for you."

"I'll be out of here t'morrow," Detroit promised.

I am going to die today.

The plan had gone into motion as soon as it was conceived. That was yesterday. Martinez was due tomorrow, Thursday. He would arrive by train and be driven in a military convoy from the station into the Capital in the evening. There was no time to spare.

The risks were too high to use top rebels for the operation; but there was too much at stake to use anyone else. Chicago Red, Atlantis, and their inner circle would have to get Martinez out by themselves.

Detroit shuffled into the forbidding walls expecting to find things had been derailed already. She sat down on a bench and pulled an apple from her pocket and looked for a clean piece of clothing on which to polish it. She kept at this until she assured herself that no one was paying attention to her. Then she got up and shuffled slowly through the streets the long way to where she wanted to go.

She turned the last corner, expecting to find a horrid vacancy, but there it was, Tolan's blue convertible.

She froze where she stood. Did this signal success or ambush? She knew how the plan was *supposed* to go.

Yesterday afternoon, before Capital security could tighten too much, Tolan had taken the striking automobile into the Capital City. He was to tell the guards that the car was a gift for the king.

Lowly guards were not in the habit of looking royal

gifts too long in the mouth, and they should have let
Tolan pass without any questions.

The car was here, where it was supposed to be,
stowed under a rain tarp bearing the royal crest.

Detroit crept up the alley to it, pretending to be awed
by it. In case anyone were watching, she would appear
to be only a curious stray.

She touched it, paused, expecting the dreaded,
"Hold in the name of the king!"

Thundering silence surrounded her. Her pulse bellowed in her ears.

She was alone.

She reached inside, lifted the rear seat. When this
car had left the rebel hideout yesterday there had been
pounds of explosives stowed here. They were gone
now.

They had done it.

Beginning yesterday evening, relays of rebel volun-
teers from the surrounding towns entered the Capital
at various times and set the explosives around the foun-
dations of the Capitol building, which was to be the
prisoner Martinez's destination. Explosives were also
set at the foot of the North Wall of the Capital City.

At least that was where they were supposed to go.
There was every possibility that the king had the damn
bombs instead and was watching to see who came here
next.

Heart hammering, Detroit lifted up the front seat. A
brown burlap sack remained. She grabbed it and leaped
away from the car in a moment's panic.

She forced herself not to run. She shuffled down the
alley, dragging the sack in careless fashion to the poor
quarters. She went to the room that had been reserved
for her.

Mildew and dust made her sneeze. She waited.

Every tap on the door made her insides twist. One
by one they came, Tina, Lark, Balt, collecting from

the burlap sack a smaller sack containing the scarlet uniform of a palace guard.

The sun was down as Detroit waited for the last one. The rap came very loud. For an instant Detroit could not inhale to shout, "Whaddaya want!"

The voice was unfamiliar but the words were right, "Open the door, peddler, and you better be holding a current license."

Detroit exhaled in a burst. She cracked the door. It was Tolan. Relief came in a torrent. He was still free. And he would be her last caller this night. "On track?" she asked him, and she gave him his uniform.

"So far splendid," he said.

"Oh. Splendid." She curled up on the straw mattress and hugged the remaining palace uniform, a little sack of treason, to her leaping stomach. She chewed on a twisted lock of her hair. It was going to be a long night.

Tolan paused at the door. "What's wrong?"

"Nothing."

I am going to die.

Thursday morning, outside the city, Atlantis armed Chris-John and Phoenix and Scottie with Beforetime submachine guns. The guns were Uzis. "Careful with these," she warned. She showed them a switch. "This is your selective fire. On fully automatic they don't just shoot, they positively throw up. Its rate of fire is six hundred rounds a minute, but you'll wreck your barrel if you keep up a continuous action—not that you'll be able to hit anything like that. You can't really aim when it's kicking back. Bust up an ambush real quick though. Here's your magazines." She gave them four each. "There's thirty-two rounds in one."

Chris-John frowned. "That's less than twenty seconds of ammo."

"Twenty seconds is a long time to be firing, friend. Keep it on semiautomatic if you want to control it."

She also gave them a loaded grenade launcher. "I hope you appreciate that you are holding the heart of the west's arsenal."

"We don't have anything like these," said Chris-John.

"You only find them in the interior. The desert is kind to artifacts."

"I hope we can make this is worth it."

"We have no choice."

Thursday afternoon everyone was in position: Terese at the North Wall with a detonator; Chris-John, Scottie, and Phoenix in the rebel car disguised as a medical vehicle parked outside the South Gate; Tina, Detroit, Lark, Balt, and Tolan dressed in uniform of palace guards patroling near the Capitol building; and Atlantis inside the South Gate in the blue convertible with the motor running.

Some police officers came to Atlantis, attracted by the astonishing automobile and the pretty lady at the wheel. She smiled and chatted with them. She had an Uzi under the dash with which to end the conversation in case they did not leave when their cue came.

At 6:33 P.M. Martinez's train pulled into the Capital station. A military convoy picked up the prisoner and started toward the city itself.

At 6:55 the prisoner's convoy entered the Capital City walls via the East Gate.

At 6:56 there was an explosion at the North Wall. The police who had been flocking around Atlantis at the South Gate abruptly abandoned her and ran north. All available guards rushed to the scene of the explosion, while the military convoy hastened toward the Capitol building to deliver their prisoner.

As the convoy pulled up in front of their destination, the entire back of the Capitol building exploded.

Suddenly there was nowhere to deliver the prisoner.

A group of what looked like five palace guards

rushed to take the prisoner. "There's a big breach in the North Wall! Rebels! Look out!"

A grenade exploded inside one of the vehicles of the military convoy and everyone ducked.

"Quick, they're here!" said one of the palace guards, and five of them hustled the prisoner away from the burning vehicle as the military guards looked all around for rebels.

Someone barked after the fleeing guards, "You! Wait!"

"Keep running," Detroit told the others. "I'll get out on my own." She turned back to divert whoever was challenging them.

At seven o'clock, while most of the Capital guards swarmed to the breach in the North Wall, the few Capital guards that remained in the guard post at the South Gate fell to Uzi fire; and a grenade launcher took out the South Gate.

A blue convertible full of four bogus palace guards and one prisoner and one pretty lady crashed through the debris and sped away. No one expected an automobile that obvious to be used as a getaway vehicle. Its obviousness had worried the rebels as well, but they had to use it because nothing the Crown had could catch it.

"We did it," Chris-John breathed as the blue car disappeared in a roaring cloud. He threw the empty grenade launcher away from him. "We did it."

"No, we didn't," said Scottie at the wheel of the rebels' medical car. The car wouldn't start.

A scarlet flash of a palace guard's uniform appeared through the ruins of the South Gate and came running at them. Scottie nearly shot her before he realized she was too little to be a real guard. It was Detroit. She ran up to the car and pounded on it. "Come on, Scottie, you're not supposed to still be here. Go! Go! Go! You shouldn'ta waited for me!"

Scottie got out of the car. "Detroit, I love you, but I didn't wait for you. Battery's deader than we are."

Detroit breathed a curse. "Can't be the battery." She started to open the hood but already guards and soldiers were running through the smoke toward them, and Scottie gave Detroit his Uzi and a push. "Go. Run." He pulled Chris-John from the car. Phoenix was nowhere in sight. Scottie took Chris-John's arm and ran, pulling the little rebel chief along with his giant stride. Chris-John's feet barely touched the ground. He flew in Scottie's tow.

They ran into the forest, through whipping branches and clawing thorns, leafy boughs batting at their faces and trying to hold them back. Chris-John stumbled. Scottie yanked him up, feeling about to pull his arm from his socket. They ran.

The forest opened to the road. They had lost direction in the wood.

Suddenly there was a commanding bark to halt and a bright light in their eyes. They'd been outflanked and cut off.

"Where's your gun?" Scottie hissed.

Chris-John swallowed with dry throat and answered in whispered stammer, "It's empty."

II.

The Erinyes

CHRIS-JOHN STOOD MOTIONLESS BESIDE SCOTTIE under guard in the giant hall for over an hour. It was a cold cavernous place, hospital white but dingy with age and ground-in grime. This was the lowest level of the old Capitol building; it was not used anymore, not until now.

Not far away, at the bombed-out new Capitol building, the fire had been brought under control and the shouts had died down.

The guard in the white hall kept redoubling. The windows were high and small, some of the small panes broken, all dirty. Outside, night had fallen. Inside, artificial electric fluorescent light seemed dim and dismal, glaring hard off the white walls. Gasoline smell and racket of an old generator chugging were giving Chris-John a headache to go with his other hurts. The dungeons were down here, in the interior of the building, away from the windows and the light.

Chris-John felt the cold in his joints, in his skin. He thought he was getting a fever. An aching feeling pained him all over. He bled from a wound in his foot he did not remember receiving.

His eyes wandered the hall, looking for a clock.

He was just beginning to feel secure that all his other companion conspirators had escaped when Phoenix was marched into the hall, hands tied behind his back, his ankles shackled with a short length of rope between them. The guards snarled at him, threw him at Chris-

John's and Scottie's feet, and barked at him to stand up
and shut up.

Phoenix stood and cast a sheepish almost grin to
Chris-John.

Guards were shouting to one another. "That"—one
guard pointed a hairy finger at Phoenix—"was under
the car seat. Somebody pry that trunk open; see what
other baggage is in there."

Chris-John met Phoenix's yellow eyes, and Phoenix
shrugged.

The guard kept changing and increasing. A brigade
of Capital police came through, demanding everyone's
papers—the palace guards', the military officers', the
soldiers'. The police asked everyone who knew who
else in the room by name, then demanded identification
to prove it.

The proceedings made Chris-John hold his breath
until he was dizzy.

Then, behind Chris-John, two police officers came
into the hall dragging a limp figure between them. They
gripped it by the arms that seemed disconnected from
the rest of the small body, dressed in the bright red
jacket and gold braid of a palace guard, leaving a dirty
rust red smear tracked on the floor behind it. Chris-
John turned his head around to see. The officers
dropped the body on the floor and kicked it over. Ragged cut black hair fell across a pasty bloodless face,
dark eyes open and staring. Chris-John would not have
recognized her except that she had no eyebrows. Detroit.

One of the guards looked over and saw Chris-John
watching. "Turn around!" he barked.

Chris-John was frozen, staring at Detroit, his eyes
enormous. He thought he would pass out. He didn't.
He could not move. If he could have moved, he would
have thrown his arms around Scottie and cried.

Someone slapped his face around to the proper direction.

Something pounded through his brain to the beat of his heart, words. They seemed to make his heart go and without them he would be lost.

> *We are living free,*
> *Though there's blood been shed,*
> *And we'll always be,*
> *Be Chicago Red.*

Henry Iver's words. He heard them over and over again until he was aware of nothing but the words, and he had to believe them. Otherwise he had murdered Detroit. And Stephanie. And would cause the deaths of Scottie and Phoenix. And himself as well most likely.

The words repeated, then changed slightly, screaming inside him.

> *I am living free,*
> *Though there's blood been shed,*
> *And I'll always be,*
> *Be Chicago Red.*

Then he was aware of a rapping echo through the cavernous hall, pushing back the voice inside his head, and a clarion-voiced chamberlain was announcing. "His Royal Majesty King Edward III. Long live the king."

"Long live the king," the guards and police and soldiers all repeated dutifully, standing at attention.

Of course the king hadn't come sooner, not until the area had been secured, all guards identified, and the fire in the nearby new building under control.

And of course they'd had to get him out of bed, wigged, powdered, and perfumed. Edward III had come in his state. His ermine-lined, light green velvet cape dragged on the floor. He was aware that you can't get blood out of velvet, but he had other capes. In fact he was fast becoming annoyed with this one, and he unfastened the heavy gold chain at his breast and let it fall on the floor. Attendants hurriedly gathered it up and faded into the background.

Without the cape, the king was arrayed in a green-gold frock coat with fan pleats at the sides headed by gold buttons, the same design of gold buttons that held back the coatsleeves' wide cuffs. He wore a gold cloth vest and silk shirt with lace cravat and cuffs. His crown was centered and secured atop his long curled white wig.

Phoenix gave a wolf whistle between his teeth. A sword pommel smashed into his nose and Phoenix dropped to the floor, doubled over. Someone kicked him and snarled at him to get up. Phoenix stood up, blood streaming from his nose, his eyes watering.

The king was looking away, ignoring the exchange, his eyes nonchalantly on the bare white wall as if there were a work of art hung there and he was admiring it.

The king was slow to move. He sauntered in a great circle that just happened, or so it seemed, to bring him past the rebels. He paused before Chris-John and studied his pretty face, noted the light brown baby's skin, delicately cut mouth, and lovely eyes. He was so young. This was the face in the sketches, the accurate ones. This was Chris-John Stanton. Chicago Red.

Edward III spoke to him, "Your life and your own estate if you say, 'Long live the king.' "

He received no reaction. Sweet eyes were just looking at him. A slight crease appeared in his youthful brow, but not a real expression. Chicago Red didn't smirk, didn't swear, didn't spit, didn't answer.

This was very bad indeed. One could not deal with such.

The king looked to the next one. Not the one with the bloody nose, that one was hideous. But the tall dusky-skinned handsome man. "Your life and your own estate if you say, 'Long live the king.' "

Scottie said nothing, but his face was an open glass and his emotions reflected clear—torment uppermost. The king continued with this one.

"You could still have a bright future. 'Long live the king.' "

Scottie shook his head.

"If you are to have any future at all," said the king, all threat now.

"No," said Scottie.

The king turned from him. This one was obvious. The boy, Chicago Red, he was frightening. The king spun abruptly to face the rebels again and said to Phoenix, " 'Long live the king.' "

Phoenix smiled with half his mouth—the motion pulled on his nose and brought tears to his eyes. "Sure," he said cheerily, exhaling blood from his nostrils, "Long live the fucking king."

The king walked away. Much as he had suspected, that one was worthless. Guards had closed in his wake to pummel Phoenix to the floor.

The king snapped his beringed fingers to someone beyond the door and, with that, a team of white-coated medical personnel wheeled in a gurney. There was mud on the wheels, for they had come from the half-smoldering new building. This place was the old torture chamber; it was never used anymore, but after the rebel bombing, the Crown had to make do with what it had left. The medics brought also a metal tree hung with bags of clear liquid.

Chris-John's eyes lifted in question to Scottie, who muttered, "Pentothal, probably. Anesthesia, but they call it truth serum."

A guard poked him in the back and made them stand apart from each other.

The king turned back to face Chris-John. "Mr. Stanton."

Chris-John's eyes lifted in wary attention.

"I think it is very obliging of you to trade for my

lost West Coast prisoner," said Edward. "I like having Chicago Red better. There can be fortune from disaster."

"Oftentimes," Chris-John breathed, an otherworldly look in his eyes.

The king nodded to the medics—he hated to call these henchmen doctors. They were members of the inquisition; they used medical knowledge to drug and torture information out of people. Not doctors, by God.

With the aid of two soldiers the medics strapped Chris-John onto the gurney and put him under sedation.

As they were proceeding, members of the king's council were shuffling in, sleepy, red-eyed, roused from their beds at their estates outside the city. "You're late," the king growled. "Where's Tow?"

"Oh Jesus," Phoenix mumbled, one eye swollen shut from the last beating. He was leaning on Scottie to stay on his feet.

"The brigadier is waiting for his aide," Lindy answered the king, his voice full of contempt.

The king let out an impatient puff of breath. "I oughtta hang him," he muttered, looking heavenward.

Lindy, the only one close enough to hear the remark, said hopefully, "It could be arranged, sire."

"No," said the king. He looked straight at Lindy. "No." He turned to the medics. "Are you ready?"

"Yes, sire." The ranking physician straightened. "The preliminaries are very good. He answers to his name and he admits to being Chicago Red. He should tell us anything we want to know."

Scottie shut his eyes. *Of course he will. He talks in his sleep.*

But luckily, the infamous Chicago Red did not know much about the rebel information system—probably less than Martinez. He could give codes and passwords, but few names and few locations. The king thought he was being stubborn. Edward bid the medics keep trying.

Chris-John told where the bunker headquarters was. Scottie hoped the others would have the sense to clear out. Carrie and Meredith were ready to move and destroy the place in case anything went wrong. It had gone wrong in a grand way.

At last Brigadier Tow came in, late, wide-awake, well groomed, as haughty and unrushed as a cat and with as much compulsion to explain his tardiness.

At the same time, through another door, a fourth prisoner was brought in kicking and silently screaming—a young woman without a voice, clawing and struggling in the grasp of the police.

"Terese!"

The wild-eyed girl looked toward Scottie's voice. She broke from her guards and ran into his arms. Gun barrels followed her dash across the floor, but she stopped harmlessly enough, and did not seem about to move from where she was, so no one shot her. And no one tried to pull her away from Scottie.

When he saw the four prisoners, Tow's face lost none of its serenity. Inside was all turmoil.

I know I have led a villainous life. But oh, that I should be paid back in spades.

Here was a gaggle of rebel prisoners and Tow knew each and every one of them. The tall dark one named Scottie Tow had killed, or thought he had. He had shut him in a burning bunker. *Should have used bullets*, Tow thought. That ought to have been rule one: never switch techniques. Tow's trusty Magnum never failed.

He gave a glance to the body on the floor, clad in a crimson palace-guard uniform. Burn scars marked the pallid face. She was another one. She had been shut in the burning tomb with Scottie, Tow was sure of it.

Tow was not used to having bodies come back to haunt him.

And there was the girl Terese. Tow hadn't recognized her until Scottie had spoken her name, Terese. Then Tow remembered knowing her. Terese had been a palace maid. That was years ago. She was the little wretch who had scratched his piano. Tow had ordered two of his guards hold her down and he'd had dreadful things done to that girl. Then he'd told the guards to take her into the Black Forest and do whatever they cared to do to her as long as she was dead when they were done.

They'd mucked it up. Rule two: always do it yourself.

He remembered an unwritten rule from Farington—all rules in Farington were unwritten: there are no second chances.

Tow blinked slowly in mental pain. How all his mistakes could have come back to roost now and all at one time.

His biggest mistake was black and blue, bleeding from the nose and uglier than ever. The creature was so ugly Tow had to catch in his breath. *Phoenix, my brother, my son.*

Tow was surprised to see Phoenix in high rebel company. Tow had supposed him to be nothing but a harmless self-serving coward. The deceitful bastard turned out to have a hero's streak in him. Tow should never have let him live. Tow forced himself to stay cool and pray Phoenix wouldn't let out a "Hi, Daddy," in front of Will.

The last rebel was on the table. Chris-John Stanton. Will's brother. He looked exactly like his photograph; he hadn't even aged.

Chris-John was not Tow's mistake, but was Tow's misfortune. William was the mistake, but could not be helped. Tow had not chosen to lose his heart. He had tried not to care for him.

Tow looked down at Will. The boy was pale, very pale, standing as close to Tow as he dared in public. Will looked up at Tow, pleading, as if the brigadier could make everything right.

Tow would that he could make everything right,

make all those rebels disappear. They were hanging around his neck and strangling him, corpses of old murders rising from the dead and pointing rotting fingers at him in front of his beloved.

Then the archbishop came into the white hall. The king's voice rang across the big chamber: "Greg!"

The king went to him and ushered the archbishop to the table where Chris-John was sedated. "Is this the rebel whom the monks put in your custody?"

Gregory looked at Chris-John's sleeping face and hesitated. He could not get away with a lie and it would do no good now. "Yes," said Gregory.

The king pointed to the other three rebels. "Recognize any of them?"

Gregory paused. The rebels were staring at him hard. Gregory tried to remember whom he was supposed to know and whom he supposedly had never seen before. His breath stopped in his throat to see little Detroit dead on the floor. "Dear God," he murmured.

"See someone?" said the king.

Gregory pointed to Phoenix. The monks would identify Phoenix even if Greg didn't. "That one, I believe. I don't know these other people."

He saw the guarded look in Scottie's eyes, distrusting and asking for help. Greg wondered if the rebels would turn on him.

The king was talking to him. "Greg. You said the Devil Rider took Chicago Red out of your hands. He should know who is the Devil Rider, shouldn't he, Greg?" The king turned to the medics. "Ask him who is the Devil Rider."

The medics asked who was the Devil Rider. Chris-John said, "Greg."

The medics scowled and hissed, "Sire, please, Your Majesty is contaminating the results!"

Brigadier Tow raised his brows. "Indeed?"

The medics were becoming frustrated. What had started so promisingly had grown difficult. Their gushing well dried up and they were not getting many answers out of Chicago Red. They told the king that Chris-John was either very ignorant of rebel workings or was very stubborn. The king nodded. He believed stubborn. He could not conceive of Chicago Red being ignorant of rebel systems. Other methods could be used to get the information out of him. Edward was satisfied anyway that he at last had possession of Chicago Red.

The medics brought Chris-John out of the drug. Chris-John sat up groggily. He saw faces. Scottie, Phoenix, Terese—what was Terese doing here?—the pit viper Tow, and one very familiar face, from a distant time. "Billy!"

The king's guards were all looking to see whom Chicago Red called with such familiarity. The rebel leader's sight was focused on Tow's aide.

Young Lieutenant Stanton looked absolutely sick. A guard tried to arrest William, but Tow drew his automatic and threatened to blow out whatever brains the man had.

The king intervened. He told the guard, "Leave the boy alone."

"But sire, Chicago Red knows him!"

"I know he does," said the king.

Chris-John's head was spinning, stomach swimming from the drug. He saw his brother in military uniform at the side of Satan himself, General Tow. The archenemy, the king was defending him. It was too much to decipher before the white floor came swimming up into his face.

Tow hustled William out of the white hall. The commotion over William's acquaintance with Chicago Red made a good excuse for Tow to get Will out of there and away from those damned and damning rebels. Tow was still a saint in the young man's eyes. And Tow would not have his image tarnished in them.

The two of them walked back to the palace. The air

outside was thankfully cold with nightfall. Tow inhaled deeply, filling his head with spring scents, trying to shake the sick feeling. The ground felt soft and spongy way down deep, as between earthquake tremors.

Will was too ill himself to notice the general's disquiet, and Tow feared that the boy would faint before they even made it upstairs. Will held back his tears until they were up in Tow's chambers. Tow sat Will down on the velvet couch and poured him a small liqueur glass of sherry, a sweet kind Tow seldom touched himself.

Tow handed him the glass over Will's shoulder from behind the couch. "Here."

Will looked. "What is it?"

"Just wine."

"I don't know," Will said, voice unsteady. "I never drink."

"It's not strong. I just want to calm you down, not snuff you out."

Will took the glass and hesitantly tasted the sweet warming sherry.

Tow paced.

The trouble with having was that it brought in the possibility of losing.

The last months had passed like a dream in days of revelation, nights of wonder. It was all new and splendid, even to Will's icy toes that shocked him awake in the middle of the night. Tow had never slept with anyone, never closed his eyes on anyone. He shared his Beforetime music, and the poetry—Shakespeare's works were from the forbidden time, but they were the prettiest words ever written, so Tow had a collection on blatant display on his shelf. Tow, who'd never said anything pretty to anyone and hardly knew how, read the sonnets to Will and Will blushed.

Tow watched him now so pale.

Will waited a long time before he said anything. He inhaled a wavering breath, exhaled almost a sigh. "It's terrible to say, but I'm glad my father's not alive to see this.''

"Natural," said Tow.

"No," said Will. "Because it's not because he'd be hurt . . . It's because he'd disown me, he'd kill Chris-John, and he'd blame the whole thing on our mother. Isn't that a terrible reason to be glad someone's dead?'' He raised guilty light brown eyes to Tow.

Tow ran his fingers through the youth's soft hair. "I should have such guilty secrets," he said sadly, tender.

Will gazed into empty space and his eyes welled tears. "How could he order our father killed?''

"You don't know that for certain," said Tow.

"I know for certain my brother is Chicago Red," said Will. He paused, then said, "And I know for certain there's a guard outside the door.''

Tow set down his own glass of cognac and went to the door to deal with this indignation himself. He seized both doorknobs and swung the white doors wide. There were guards flanking either side of the entrance. "By whose order are you here?'' Tow demanded in his lowest tenor.

"General Lindy, sir.''

"Well, this is my room, not General Lindy's, so *get the hell away from here!*''

"Yes, sir.''

Tow slammed the doors. Seething, he couldn't sit down. He paced the room. He came to stand behind Will. The boy looked up. "Thank you.''

Tow smiled mildly. "For what?''

"Not letting them arrest me.''

Tow's hands caressed his throat, his chin. "I would do anything to keep you with me," he said.

III.

Ash Wednesday

MIND TRIPPING AND STAGGERING, CHRIS-JOHN SAT ON the cold stone floor, propped up against the stone wall, his hands and feet bound. It was dark, dark beyond the blindfold that served no purpose but to unnerve him. There were no windows but for the small barred opening in the door that led to an interior corridor. The air in the cell was stale. Chris-John felt hot and cold. It was hard to breathe. His body was one great shivering ache. His ribs were sore where someone had kicked him. His foot was numb. Someone had kicked his wound. He wondered if it were a bullet wound. He had forgotten to check and hadn't the strength to work off the blindfold and look now. When he moved his foot, stabbing pains streaked up his leg like hot metal wires strewn through every fiber of his being.

Where were the others? Where was Billy? Chris-John had seen him; it *was* him. In military uniform. With *Tow.*

Oh God, don't let them hurt Billy.

Billy didn't have sense to come in out of the rain. Someone had to look after him.

Thirsty. Very thirsty.

Chris-John thought he heard scratching and rustling. Listened. He did hear scratching and rustling.

He hoped guards scratched and rustled. Because if they didn't, that meant there were rats in here.

* * *

Woke again. Didn't remember drifting out. Thirsty. *I am going to be very very sick.* He forgot he was already sick.

Stink. Sitting in his own urine.

Mouth dry. Can't swallow. Hot. Burning hot. Floor cold beneath him.

Felt something moving around his feet. *It feels like a dog, but it can't be a dog, because it's a RAT.*

He shook his feet. The knives went up his leg and he passed out again.

Somebody get me out of here.
Somebody please get me out of here.
For the love of God, get me out of here. Free me free me free me free me.

> *We are living free,*
> *Though there's blood been shed,*
> *And we'll always be*
> *Be Chicago Red.*

We are living free though there's blood been shed and we'll always be be Chicago Red.
WearelivingfreethoughtheresbloodbeenshedandwellalwaysbebeChicagoRed.

"Chris-John, it's me." The familiar voice dragged him from the abyss up to consciousness. Firm hands lifted him away from the stone wall and held him. A cool glass pressed to his lips. Water trickled into his dry mouth. He drank.

Soft male voice was talking to him. He connected that voice to its owner. Billy. William.

"Bil-ly." Chris-John called him, voice cracking. "They arrest you, too?"

"No." A cool hand was pushing back his wet black curls. "Oh Chris-John." The way he said it told that

he was horrified by what he saw, his distress uncon-
cealed in his cry.

"Billy . . . how long?"

"Um, almost twenty hours now."

"Can you get rid of this blindfold for me?"

"Can't," said Will like an apology. "I was lucky to
see you at all." There was a catch in his throat and he
spilled out tearfully, "Chris-John, you look miserable."

"Where are the others? Are they all right?"

"I don't know," said Will at a loss.

"Don't know or aren't telling?" Chris-John had a
wounded way of calling someone a traitor and tearing
his heart out.

"I didn't ask about them," said Will. "I don't care
about those people."

"Billy, get me out of here."

"I can't."

Chris-John's lips curled back and he snarled with the
venom of the hurt and abandoned, "You're not even
trying."

The reply was soft, in a reasonable cold calm that
was unlike Billy: "What did you expect?"

"That, I suppose," said Chris-John in deep resentment. "You're wearing the uniform of the people that
killed our brother."

Walt had been killed by a king's soldier.

Bewildered, Will's eyes watered up. He had no answers. He tilted his head back, trying to contain his
tears. He saw the weeping limestone walls and rats,
and Chris-John's wounded swollen foot. He hadn't expected the encounter to go like this at all. All Chris-
John had was for the rebellion. There was nothing left
for his younger brother, nor even for himself. Voice
quavering, Will said, "Is that why you killed our father?"

Chris-John started to sob. He curled into Will and
cried.

Will started to cry, too. He took off the dirty blindfold and pressed his cheek to Chris-John's brow that was burning with fever.

Then, from the cell door came a guard's gruff command, "Time's up, bingo. Let's go."

"No," said Will.

"Hey. Your rank don't mean piss down here, Lieutenant. You had two minutes. Out."

"I'm staying," said Will.

"OK, bingo. It's your butt. The brigadier ain't gonna like it." The guard pulled out. "And I'd get that blindfold back on if I was you." His key-jingling walk receded down the corridor.

Chris-John tensed up in Will's arms. "The brigadier! Tow?"

"I'm his aide," said Will.

Chris-John choked, tightened, and writhed to sit bolt upright. "Oh God, Billy! Oh God!" He thought of all he'd heard of Tow's aides. And his brother next in line. "Oh God! Never mind me, get yourself out of here. Go far away, Billy. Now, right now. Get out!"

But already he heard a sharp clicking of heels in the prison corridor, a lighter stride than the guard's, even like a metronome. The walk of someone who knows music. Chris-John grew hysterically urgent. "Bil-ly!" he whispered. "He's going to kill you!"

"No, he's not," said Will, and Chris-John moaned.

Even Will was not so calm and certain as the footsteps reached the door and the key turned in the lock. Will huddled closer; Chris-John could feel his heart pound and quake.

A voice he knew spoke in beautiful chilling tenor: "Come, William."

Chris-John was thunderstruck to hear his brother's meek, "No, sir."

Chris-John screwed his eyes shut. *That's it, that's it, that's it.* Tow was going to draw out that monstrosity of a Magnum and kill both of them right now. No one ever ever said no to Tow. Not even "no, sir."

There was evil silk in the voice. "William. Now."

"No, sir."

Chris-John hunched his head against Will's chest. He braced himself for the end and held his breath. And ran out of breath before the shot ever came.

He cracked an eyelid to peer out. The shot was not coming. An ominous slim shape darkened the dim light in the doorway. Chris-John saw consternation in the cold handsome face. Chris-John was perplexed by it.

Tow stepped inside, and Chris-John shrank as from the devil himself.

Tow stood over them. He seemed to bring fresh air with him, the clean scent of some soap. The cloying filth and dank wouldn't touch him. Chris-John not only saw but *sensed* him over them. He was surprised by the brigadier's low, almost gentle tone: "Will, look at me."

In barely a squeak now, Will said, "No, sir." It was frightening enough to disobey, impossible while gazing into those steel gray eyes.

Tow crouched. Smooth plastic face wrinkled so slightly at the smell. In gentle concern he said, "What is it?"

Will was weeping. He couldn't look. "He's sick. They don't feed him, they haven't given him water. There isn't even a toilet in here. There are rats in here. He's burning up, and I can't—" He couldn't talk.

Chris-John felt Tow's hand on his brow. Tow turned Chris-John's face and looked into his eyes. It was a firm touch, without roughness, dispassionate as a doctor's touch, looking for sickness. Tow saw lice and he pulled his hand away quickly.

Then he took Will's chin in his hand, saw a tremor on his lips, and made him look at him. His gaze held Will's. Then suddenly he spied a louse on Will's neck and he crushed it. He rose, wiping his hands in disgust. He spoke in impatient beseeching command: "I'll see what I can do. Will, get up."

And Will carefully settled Chris-John back against the wall. Tow moved toward the door as if the ground here itched his feet. He spoke to Will: "Go to the kitchen and get cleaned up. The servants will know what to do about the lice. Burn those." He meant his clothes. He was looking at his own uniform; it was still clean. He would burn it, too.

Will obediently started out toward the kitchen.

Once outside the cell Tow straightened his shoulders. He stood tall but was feeling weak with relief. He had weathered that storm. Tow had known he would have to let William see his brother sooner or later. He judged that sooner was safer. And he was right, as it turned out. Will had been so concerned with Chris-John's failing health that they hadn't time to discuss the evils of General Tow. Now the assassin was feeling victorious and satisfied with himself. He had gambled big and won.

As for his promise to Will, Tow was fairly certain that the king would move the prisoner to better conditions shortly anyway and Tow could take credit for that. He did not want to be seen as the persecutor of a once-beloved brother when Chris-John was swinging from the gallows.

Maybe yet it would prove to be Providence that brought all these old mistakes of Tow's to the palace at once. Having come all at once, they could be destroyed all at once. Tow need only ride out these next days, and the king's hangman would dispose of all his old sins for good, never to threaten him again.

Chris-John woke in a soft bed. He'd thrown back a quilted coverlet in fevered sleep. Sun outlined the heavy draperies of the tall windows. The ceiling was very high, with ornate cornices. Tinted and frosted globes fit over the lights in their bronze sconces.

Chris-John tried to get up. He leaned over the side of the bed and let himself fall. He tumbled a long drop from the mattress to the thick pastel carpet, unhurt. He staggered to the window and pulled back the rich drapes.

He saw exclusive shops and neat brick streets, fine carriages, and a flowered courtyard. He knew this view. Rather he knew the reverse view.

I'm in the palace.

He crawled to the huge double doors and grasped the rings. They were not locked. He opened them and looked up from his hands and knees to see guards.

Of course there were guards.

They lifted him up—there wasn't much to Chris-John to lift—and put him back in the bed and shut the doors.

Chris-John closed his eyes. He suspected he would have visitors soon.

Well enough to walk about, Chris-John paced his room, his royal prison. Finally he heard approaching footsteps down the hall, a single set, not the herds that meant a changing of the guard. Chris-John faced the door and squared himself to meet the dictator.

But it was not the king. Chris-John *thought* the cadence of the stride sounded familiar. It was Tow.

The doors shut behind the brigadier assassin. Chris-John was penned in with this creature.

He was a handsome bastard, trim, everything in place. There were smooth lines to him and his clothing, and a refined polish on him. His face looked artificial with high sculpted cheekbones and straight nose almost sharp in its crisp definition. Steel eyes were studying Chris-John.

Himself, Chris-John was an ageless beauty, a dark little enchanter. His sickness had not taken much from him. His velvet lips had healed, and still, always, he had his bewitching eyes. Full-grown but childlike, he was appealing even to his enemies—all but this one.

Tow spoke: "You're a short son of a bitch."

"You're a son of a bitch," said Chris-John.

Tow moved, sudden, swift—or maybe not so sudden, but so smooth and unexpected, with no preliminary gesture to signal what he was going to do, that Chris-John flinched when Tow merely walked to the window. Tow stopped at the window and smiled coldly.

Already having betrayed fear, so he would lose no ground now by speaking what was on his mind, Chris-John said, "What are you going to do to me?"

Tow's eyebrows moved apart, slightly elevated. "If it is up to me, you'll have an accident."

"It's not up to you," said Chris-John. Chicago Red knew his own importance. Only the king could decide his fate.

Unless, however, the king had thrown him to his favorite wolf. Chris-John was guessing, praying, he had not.

He hadn't. "You're to be hanged on Potter's Hill," said Tow. "Unless of course you recant."

"Henry Iver died on Potter's Hill. I would be honored."

Tow made a shrug with his perfectly shaped head. "I dislike the association myself. Putting popular figures on the gallows is a bad idea."

"Why am I being kept in this gilded cage?" said Chris-John.

"Now, I would have thought you'd have guessed that," said Tow. "You were getting too much sympathy down in the dungeons, poor child. The king decided you would get much less sympathy with royal treatment."

" 'Under a government which imprisons any unjustly, the true place for a just man is also in prison,' " Chris-John quoted from his favorite tract, *Civil Disobedience*.

"Just so," said Tow. "And besides, the king recognized the martyr in you and guessed you would be more miserable here." *And Will is happier, and I'm delighted.*

Tow moved away from the window, eyes in steady focus on his adversary. "You're not at all like your brother."

"Neither are you," said Chris-John.

There was a wry pull to the side of Tow's mouth. "It appears my family has a penchant for yours."

"You leave my brother alone!" Chris-John cried.

Tow smiled, baring small but perfect and even pearly teeth. His smile was cold in the pit-viper eyes, as if at a private joke, and he said nothing. Chris-John's worry reached hysterical pitch.

"You ditch. You bastard. So help me, I could kill you!" Chris-John was looking wildly around the elaborately furnished room for something to throw at him.

Tow remained undisturbed. "Yes, no, and no, you could not. And save your bombast for the king; I'm not interested."

Chris-John made fists in the air, furious in his powerlessness. He cried out, "Why are you even here? What are you doing here?"

"I *am* the king's assassin."

Suddenly unnerved, Chris-John's angry momentum deflated and crumbled from under him, and he was left standing here frightened for his life.

Had it been a lie about Potter's Hill? Like a cat batting his victim about before he killed it to break its spirit? It worked. Tow had dangled a heroic dream in front on him—which Chris-John was too willing to seize at—then yanked it away. He lied. Tow lied. Of course he lied, he was a viper. Chris-John backed up to the bed and hugged the heavy carved post in dread.

Tow glanced at his watch; he wore his on his wrist, not on a chain like most noblemen. "You're too easy, Chicago Red. The king will tie back his wig with you." And he started for the doors.

First confused, stunned, then relieved, Chris-John rediscovered his wrath. "Goddamn you, you aren't going to kill me! Why the hell did you come! You get your thrills this way, *Brigadier?* Why?"

Over his shoulder Tow gave a wicked smile, with a low-lidded side glance, and voice so sweet: "I promised William I would look in on you."

The doors shut and Chris-John ran to them and yanked at the handles, but they were locked this time. He pounded with both fists. The mocking "promised William" still echoed inside. *Like hell.* Tow was going to kill Will; Chris-John knew it. And he had come here just to rub Chris-John's nose in that fact.

Chris-John fell against the door and closed his eyes, his cheek to the painted wood, leaning on the locked gates of his ornate prison.

Then he heard a key in the lock and Chris-John stepped back. The doors opened once again. With no chamberlain, no announcement, no ermine robe, the man walked in.

King Edward III.

IV.

Crown of Thorns

THE KING ENTERED AND STOPPED. BEHOLD THE CHI-cago Red. The rebel leader was a beautiful thing but not imposing. Wild-eyed, he might inspire others to insane zeal. Tow had said the youth was high-strung but not physically violent; it was safe for His Majesty to come into the room alone as long as there were guards in quick readiness outside the door.

The first words from the legendary rebel leader were a demand: "Where are the others?"

The king was slow to answer. He deigned to reply at last: "Well kept."

"Where's my brother?" said Chris-John.

The king almost said, "You mean he wasn't with the brigadier?" That boy was Tow's shadow. Tow took him everywhere. But not here. One would almost think Tow had a guilty conscience.

"About his duties, I trust," said the king.

"With Tow!" Chris-John was aghast. "The man is an atrocity!"

"Mr. Stanton, if it were not for my brigadier's in-tercession, your brother would have been in the dun-geons with you and the rest of your lot. I would not be too judgmental of the brigadier, were I you."

"He commits capital crimes; why isn't *he* in the dun-geons with me?" said Chris-John.

"I am not shackled to words on parchment," said the king. "I need Tow alive."

"So the law bends to a whim."

"To discretion."

"That's assuming the one in power has any!"

The king sighed. He suspected he should not have dignified the image of Chicago Red with this visit. It seemed Edward III had come just to be insulted by a pretty young man. There was nothing here for the king. He did not know what he had hoped to find. And he started to leave without a word.

Chris-John said, "This wouldn't happen in a democracy."

"And what is so magical about a democracy? What do you think one is besides a mob rule?" The king had reached the doors and was about to open them.

Biting sharp came words Edward had read somewhere before but was surprised to hear now: "Government of the people, by the people, and *answerable to the people.*"

The king stopped. What sort of child is this? The king turned.

Edward started to address him, "Mr. Stanton—or do you prefer Chicago Red?"

"Chicago Red."

"I thought so. Chicago Red, I did not come here to discuss the welfare of your coconspirators, your brother, or my brigadier. What I have is a very bad situation of your making—"

"The rebellion would be here without me."

"Even rain does not fall if it does not have a dust core to form around. You are dust and you will not interrupt me again. You have chosen to be disloyal on supposedly philosophical grounds; one can almost respect that; but there is no excuse for being ill bred."

Chicago Red bit his lip, debating whether to contest that. It was not a matter he had given much thought to and he was not about to make a slip in front of the king. Tow had, in so many words, said that the king was clever. Chicago Red was not going to be used to tie back King Edward's wig.

Chris-John noted by the way that the king was not wearing a wig now. Edward III was a man of simple tastes when allowed to be. Perfume bothered his sinuses and cordials laced with gold dust gave him a bellyache; but a monarch must look and behave as a monarch or else cease to be. However, Edward III deemed it better now to come to the demagogue in less grandiose aspect.

Edward III was watching him for a reaction. Chicago Red answered with silence. "Good," said the king. "Let us talk then about democracy.

"You want this nation to be a democracy? It *was* a democracy. They destroyed themselves—ah, I see you did not read that in whatever Beforetime sources you got your hands on."

"I read enough to know that this Kingdom was once a democracy and as such it was the greatest nation on Earth out of *many* nations," said Chris-John. "They flew in airships every day. There is a flag of theirs on the moon! Everyone had an automobile and anyone could become president—the people elected him. I didn't read about the destruction—I don't think anyone was producing books when the disaster came—but it looks to me like it was a natural disaster. I can read a map. A good quarter of what was once America is now underwater. Your Majesty is trying to tell me democracy did that?"

"What you say is very logical," said the king. "Reasoning from limited information. But be aware that your information is limited. How much do you know about those marvelous airships people flew every day, and those automobiles everyone had? You had a car, Mr. Stanton. You know what exhaust is. Multiply that exhaust by millions. I have read predictions from the Beforetime that enough exhaust could raise the world's temperature a half a degree and melt the polar ice caps. You saw ice caps on the old maps. I have sent ships to the north pole, and do you know, Mr. Stanton, there is no ice in summer. There is no permanent ice pack. So you tell me what happened.''

"A volcano could've done the same thing," Chris-John countered. "Car exhaust didn't drop the West Coast into the sea—that land was too high to be flooded with the rest of it. That was an earthquake. Did cars cause the earthquake?''

"I could argue," said the king. "We could talk about nuclear reactors built on fault zones. But let us for the moment say you are right, it was volcanoes, it was an earthquake. That does not change the fact that this democracy was fouling itself at an alarming rate despite warnings of the consequences—all for the sake of immediate convenience and monetary gain. Those are the priorities of democracies—because those are the priorities of the common person. He does not care about ideology. He cares about his own immediate wants and needs first, not about the nation, not even about his own future.''

"That's a low opinion of your subjects," said Chris-John.

"So it may be. But it is realistic. And realism is something of which you are in short supply. Democracy is an unwieldy beast. It cannot function in crisis. And so it was that the people turned to monarchy when this nation was wobbling on its new legs after the disaster—whatever the exact nature of that disaster happened to be. It was monarchy that pulled them together and up out of chaos.''

"But our legs aren't new anymore," said Chris-John. "And we don't need the monarchy anymore. We've grown up.''

"Have you indeed? Do you want to know something? The people would never tolerate a democracy. Give them absolute freedom and they will be begging for a leader in no time. And if they cannot find a king to follow, they will follow a minister. They will enlist in an army and follow a general.''

"At least they would chose their rulers. There's no choosing you and the serpents you put in your governorships."

"People can never choose their rulers," said Edward III. "Rulers rule. You only think you've chosen. You've actually found a man who has built a pen for your lost sheep. And all those sheep will gratefully trot into their new corral and not even hear the gate lock behind them. They have been brought up from childhood to follow—'Yes, Mother,' 'Yes, Father,' 'Yes, teacher,' 'Yes, Reverend.' And when they become adults, they say, 'Yes, sire.' Very few people are born to be leaders. And in a democracy everyone must be one. Most are inadequate, so they flock around the ones who are capable."

The king crossed the room slowly, hands clasped behind his back. Then he turned. "Tow," he said. "Do you know what he is to me?"

"Your assassin," said Chris-John.

Edward III nodded. "When Tow first came to the Capital, all he could read was music and all he could spell was his name. Embarrassed—you could see it in his eyes, back when you could see something in Tow's eyes.

"I still remember the day they brought this eighteen-year-old slug out of Farington into my throne room and threw him at my feet to be sentenced to death. There were two things I noticed about him. First, he was the most evilly handsome creature I had ever seen. Second, there was not a scar on him. No one can spend any time in Farington and not be sliced. I told the guards to strip him, and he looked at me very indignantly, laughed, and called me by a number of then-popular gutter terms. The guards threw him back down and read off the list of his crimes—twenty-five known counts of murder including his mother and father, nineteen counts of rape, including his mother and sister. And one count of assassination, for which he was hunted down and brought in. He had assassinated my assassin—in a shoot-out. And the remarkable thing was how cleanly he'd done all these murders. One shot, fatal. He did not brawl or street-fight—that I could see from looking at him—he had no scars anywhere. He shot before anyone could come close enough—with an accuracy that put my assassin to shame, not to mention to death.

"And I thought to myself: I need an assassin. This creature could be cleaned up and added to my staff."

"Someone who killed his own mother and father?" said Chris-John.

"Ah, you see I knew how this creature's mind worked," said the king. "I let him put his clothes back on and had him brought in here." He waved his hand around the rich chamber. "Just as you are, unrestrained. And he did not kill me for the same reasons you don't—curiosity and knowing that there are six guards outside the door and that it is four stories down from the window. He did not look suicidal. He looked hungry. He was less dangerous than you are now. I could not be sure you wouldn't make a martyr of yourself, shout 'death to the tyrant,' bludgeon me with that candlestick, and die heroically in a shower of bullets. Tow definitely not. He was enchanted. He prowled around this room as if it were a cathedral—though I am sure he would have shown less respect for a cathedral. I asked him if he would like a room like this. He didn't say anything, but I knew he was interested. I told him I needed a man killed. I was going to set him free to do it. There would be no profit in his running away, not when I offered this and all he had to go back to was Farington. He asked how he could be sure I would not have him killed after he did my bidding. I put a gun in his hand and said, 'Defend yourself.' He was invincible with a gun on him. The only way we caught him in the first place was that he ran out of bullets before we ran out of soldiers. He was a very shocked creature. He stared at the gun, checked to see if it was loaded with real bullets not blanks—he could tell by the weight that it was loaded with *something*. The creature knew his guns and he has a remarkably sensitive touch. Look at his hands and you can tell he has never hit anyone with his fist. And I knew he would not shoot me. I was worth more to him alive than dead. If I died, he died. And he sensed I was not a paranoid little rodent afraid to let him live simply because he was very very dangerous.

"I showed him the room of the assassin he'd killed and offered it to him with a large salary. And with that, I had him in my hand. I pulled his strings and he obeyed. So began his first instruction in maneuvering. The creature is now Brigadier General Tow and he has gotten hold of some of *my* strings. He could kill me and get away with it now—make it look like you did it. I don't know why he doesn't except that he enjoys playing with me. Revenge, I suppose. I used to laugh at that creature.

"The point of all this is: should this country suddenly become a democracy, men like Tow will not disappear when all people are suddenly made equal. The minute you have equality, someone will set about correcting that situation. Have you thought of what you are going to do after you—if you—depose the monarchy? Then what? Gather everyone together for a vote? Twenty million people? Or maybe you will have representatives speak for them—like my provincial governors. And maybe to keep these organized, you will have one man over everyone—like me. Or is everyone going to make up his own mind—like in Farington? Now, there is a democracy for you."

"That's anarchy."

"How did it get that way? Because they threw out authority and there is no organization left! So who's going to organize twenty million people after my downfall? You? Democracy will not just happen. Organization does not happen by wishing. You are going to find building a democracy far harder than destroying a monarchy. And what happens in the interim, before you have formed the laws? It must be anarchy.

"You are trying to make this country into one big Farington and I won't have it. I am here to guide and protect my people and you are the worst evil that could befall them. My rule is flawed—I will give you that. Injustices happen—gross injustices—like your twin's death—yes, I know about that—but can you say your democracy—should you be able to form it even though I think it is impossible—will be any better? Decision, I assume, will be made by a majority vote. Now what happens if the majority keeps making decisions against a smaller group? Is that more just? Tyranny of the majority?"

"That's unlikely," said Chris-John.

"Really? You *are* naive."

"Stop calling me that."

"I'm afraid it's true. I have ruled this land longer than you have been alive. I know how this Kingdom works, its economics, its needs. You, on the other hand, are a hurt child who lost his brother."

"You've the makings of an excellent propagandist," said Chris-John. "Include that in your credentials. The way you simplify me down to one factor."

The king tapped two fingers against his chin thoughtfully. He said, "Should your new democracy elect *me*, what will you do? Did you ever think of that? Maybe you will have another revolution till you do approve of who is in charge? Who is simplifying, Chicago Red?"

Chris-John sank onto a chair and curled up his legs beneath him and bent his head to rest on his knees. "I have to think. You fence too well with words. Just because you are a clever talker doesn't make you right."

"You don't do badly yourself," said the king. "I can see there is nothing to be changed or proven here." He walked toward the doors. He paused, and spoke with his back still turned: "Do you require a priest?"

Chris-John lifted his head. For the first time the gallows felt near and real. He blinked. "You're going to kill me."

"Tell me how I can afford not to," said the king. He turned. He had heard fear in the young man's voice. "Make your amends now, today from the balcony of this palace, and you and your companions will live."

"I want a priest," Chris-John said, glowering over his knees. Then, as the king turned away, Chris-John was on his feet, grasping at far chances. He cried, "I want *your* confessor!" He had an idea who that might be.

Edward III sighed what might have been consent and went out.

When the doors opened next, Chris-John ran to the white-robed apparition standing there. He seized the archbishop's hand, kissed his ring, and whispered, "Greg, get me out of here!"

Greg shook his dark head. "The only help I can give you now is for your soul."

Chris-John felt his face drain of color. He sputtered, *"What?"*

"I mean I *can't* get you out," Gregory said just above a whisper. "I'm only a heartbeat from the gallows myself. Did you know you named me as the Devil Rider when you were under the drug?"

"You're still free," Chris-John said accusingly.

"The circumstances made your answer ambiguous. If it weren't for a very stupid stunt Marion Martel pulled last fall, I would be at the end of the same rope as you. I can't get you out. I am only here in the capacity of a confessor."

Chris-John's eyes widened in disbelief, then narrowed. "Fine," Chris-John said harshly. "Just fine. I hope my people can do the same for you sometime, *Father.* Don't ever be in need."

Gregory's broad shoulders stooped. He turned away and went to the doors.

"Oh, and Greg." Chris-John spoke at his back. "Don't pray for me. I doubt your words carry much weight in heaven."

Tall flat forehead bowed and forward like a butting bull, eyes fixed downward on his shined expensive shoes striding on red brick, Gregory walked, mesmerized by the sound of his own quick heel strikes and his short cape flapping from his shoulders, snapping behind him, like all the ghosts beating at him: Chris-John's as if he were already hanged, Marion's in her wheelchair, all the poor people of his parish. All those people begging him for help and he could not do anything for them.

Gregory had never been a revolutionary, only a reformist. Both sides hated him now. Compromise was doomed to disappoint everyone. Everyone wanted him to take a stand. *He that is not with me is against me.* Even God detested a fence sitter.

Gregory reached the cathedral a broken man beneath the weight of accusation and despair. He marched up to the sanctuary and threw open the ambry wherein were the sacred vessels. "Where are you now? Where are you now?"

He wheeled on the crucifix above the altar, raised his hands in anger and anguish, but the words he would speak caught in his throat.

The great painted wooden carving of the emaciated and skeletally thin man dying on the cross hung in sorrowful acceptance. The figure's head was dropped onto one shoulder, deep-set eyes upturned in a face of woe. Drops of age-darkened red paint had been let to trickle from the nails in his hands and feet, from his wounded side, and from his crown of thorns. The carving was very old, its colors faded and chipped. It had never been redone for fear of losing the expression on the face.

It took his voice away.

Gregory fell on his knees and beat the altar with his hands, a helpless servant commanded to do what was beyond his power. *God, how can I help them all?* The poor, his king, the rebels, and Marion—for the love of God, Marion.

Tow was in uniform, the dark green military one with straight-leg trousers and hip-length jacket, not a court dress uniform, which he did not even own. Tow liked fine things, but he would not dress up in silk breeches and gold bullion cords like somebody's window sash. Nor would he let his hair grow long or wear a wig. That was all right for the king, but Tow still had some vestigial Farington ideas on his own dignity.

Dark green was a more sober color for an execution anyway.

This was a somber occasion. Tow tried not to appear too spirited. By evening all his troubles would be over. And he could spend the night comforting Will. It was difficult not to smile.

Tow stood before the mirror and positioned his tie. Then he looked to his aide. The boy's eyes were puffy. Tow knew he cried when Tow was not looking. As if he could hide it. "Coming?" said Tow.

Will shook his head. He answered in a hollow whisper, "I can't." He looked so forsaken.

"I won't make you," said Tow. He kissed him on the mouth and left his chambers. It was odd to be without him.

A rap on the door surprised Will. He looked at the clock. Tow was fifteen minutes gone. Will had watched his car drive down the street below. Will wondered if the brigadier had forgotten something. But Tow wouldn't knock; these were his chambers. Will opened the door.

In the hall stood a king's Royal Guard in full regalia. Will thought he was under arrest—he felt suddenly helpless and alone without his strong protector. But this was not an arrest. Only a summons.

"It was the last request of the condemned to see you," said the guard.

"Chris-John," Will breathed. "Where is he?"

"They're holding the prisoners in the guardhouse. The truck is waiting to take them to the gallows, so you'll have to hurry."

Terese, Scottie, and Phoenix were already in the truck. Chris-John was in the guardhouse. The outside door was open, but a ball and chain around his ankle kept Chris-John where he was. He stood by the door, keeping eye contact with his comrades in the truck. They drew silent strength from each other's gaze. It was hard to die, even for a cause.

Chris-John's gaze was pulled away from them as another door opened. His soul leaped to see his brother William. "Billy!"

Now in the full light of day, not in a dark prison cell, Chris-John could really see his brother, and he became disturbed. Will's hair was shorn and he was scrubbed so clean he squeaked—trim, neat, manicured and groomed, austere. Like the brigadier—or a possession of his, kept polished like his gun. There was a subtle air to his mannerisms that was shocking to Chris-John. Will had taken on an unconscious grace that was not from himself, and Chris-John recognized too well its source. It was spooky to see the viper's ways seeping into his guileless brother.

"Where's Tow?" said Chris-John.

"He's already at Potter's Hill," said Will.

Chris-John grabbed Will's shoulders. The guards outside started in alarm at the motion, but relaxed again

on seeing that it was not an attack. "Good!" said
Chris-John. "You'll have time to get away."

"Chris-John, I'm not going anywhere."

"Billy, you don't know what he is!"

Quietly Will said, "He's my lover, Chris-John. I
sleep with him."

Chris-John covered his eyes. He hadn't ever suspected.

Will continued, "Was that what you were going to
warn me about?"

Chris-John dropped his hands. "That was the start.
The rest has got to make your blood run cold."

"No, I don't know what you're talking about." Will
was only certain that there was nothing about Tow that
could possibly horrify him.

"Do you know about all the people he's killed?"
said Chris-John.

"He's a soldier, Chris-John. He's a general. What
do you want?"

"Jesus. He's a real brigadier like you're a real lieutenant!" Chris-John spat.

That struck under Will's serenity. Will knew he'd
done nothing for his rank. He was beginning to come
unnerved.

"I'm not talking war dead," said Chris-John. "Tow's
never been in battle. And I'm not even talking the secret killings ordered by the king. I mean the free-lance
whims. Tow had twenty aides before you. Half of them
are dead. I think he raped all of them. What happens
when he gets tired of you?"

"It's not like that at all," said Will, relaxing again
upon hearing Chris-John talk blatant tall tales.

"What? What? You think you're different? Do you
suppose he's *in love* with you?"

The way he said it made Will squirm inside. He said
it as if the idea was the most absurd in the world. Will
had supposed. But hearing it spoken so revived an old
insecure self-doubt, a question Will constantly asked

himself, *What can he possibly see in me?* Chris-John's challenge made everything clear. The obvious, logical answer Will had always known in his heart of hearts—what anyone could ever see in him, especially a man like Tow—nothing.

Will floundered. He felt like he was drowning.

Chris-John was speaking, going on and on with a list of heinous crimes supposedly committed by the adored brigadier. Will protested weakly, "It's all vicious rumor."

But even while Will was shaking and grasping to regain solid ground, Chris-John pressed home. "Billy, that man had Terese taken out to be killed because she scratched his piano. Because she scratched his goddamn piano!"

At that charge, Will blanched to pure white. Will had seen the scratch. His stomach turned. He tried to maintain composure, holding on by frayed threads. He looked outside to the other rebels under guard in the truck. "Is that Terese?"

"Yes."

Will walked woodenly to the door and ordered the guard to let Terese come to him.

Terese came and Will presented a tremulous challenge to her: "Tell me where the scratch on the brigadier's piano is."

Mute Terese glanced in confusion to Chris-John, then she crouched on the floor and traced a grand piano's shape in the dust. She looked up at Will, who said, "Well?"

Terese drew in the scratch.

Will's hand flew to his mouth. His eyes shut. He knew now that it was true.

And the rest of it had to be true, too.

Outside, the guards were beckoning to Chris-John and Terese. Time was up.

Will didn't even watch them go. He barely heard the dragging ball sound moving away from him, the truck's doors slamming, and the truck driving away toward the gallows, leaving Will with the outline of a piano in the dust.

Tow watched the gallows as the hangman placed the nooses around the necks of the condemned. Chris-John was first. He had refused a hood. The crowd cheered. Tow was positioned apart and above the thousands in a reviewing box with the other important personages. The structure had been built for this occasion. They had known that a mob would turn out for this one. They hadn't expected quite this many.

Tow was plagued with disquietude. He was about to be released of all his troubles and something was bothering him yet. He thought at first that Phoenix was the cause, that he might be feeling some regret that his own kin was about to be killed. But no, that was not bothering him. He would be relieved to have Phoenix off his hands and out of his life.

He racked his brain in all vain directions, trying to avoid looking where he ought to look, but at last his thoughts came back, as always, to Will. He tried to visualize him. He pictured him with puffy eyes. He wished he hadn't left him like that.

On the scaffold they were asking Chris-John if he forgave the hangman.

"No, actually," said Chris-John.

The crowd's cheering erupted again for another two minutes.

Tow spoke aside to the general on his left; it was the stout old General Lord Martel leaning on his cane. "They're dispensing with the last request?"

"Already had it," said Martel, eyes not varying from their grim straight-ahead stare at the scaffold. "Wanted to talk to his brother."

Tow felt a ripple like a rolling aftershock of a great explosion through his guts. Very carefully he asked, "When was that?"

"Back at the palace. Just now."

Tow shifted. He was beginning to fidget on the viewing stand. He glanced over at the king. He bit his lip, glanced at his watch several times, looked around. Looked to the gallows.

His gaze caught on Chris-John's defiant pretty face. Dark luminous eyes flashed daggers at the reviewing box, a trace of a smile on the condemned's face. For a moment Tow had an unsettling sense that the boy was looking at *him*.

Finally Tow pulled back and left the reviewing stand. He asked no permission. He just pushed his way out to find his car at the edge of the mob and told the driver to take him back to the palace as fast as possible. The driver started the engine and closed up the windows as the drumroll began.

Fear that had gripped Chris-John in cold coils all night was gone in a weird elation. Up to this very moment he had entertained a fantasy of Atlantis, Tolan, Meredith and Carrie, Ezra, Tina, and Lark coming to his rescue. Now, with the prickly rope noose around his neck, that fantasy faded like the stars in daylight. His fate was sealed. This would be quick. He was shivering, nervous as if with stage fright, but something in the moment, in the very reality, banished the apprehensive terror of imagination and waiting. Henry Iver had gone this way before. There was a purpose to this. Thousands of people were watching. If the king thought trouble had started with Henry Iver's death, let him watch now the death of Chicago Red. He was a martyr to the cause, and young enough to find the idea romantic. He gave his head a cavalier toss within the noose, flipped a coiled black lock off his smooth girlish brow. Yes, he was frightened, but he could still curl back his lips and smile at the king. At that he could hear the crowd cheering him over the drumroll. Even those who were here just to see death couldn't help but carry away with them an impression of something else.

The drums stopped abruptly and so did the voices. The first creaking warning from the trap underfoot signaled the end and Chris-John snapped his eyes shut.

The trap clattered open to sudden nothingness underfoot.

A short quick drop, bounce, and burning noose. Exhaled with a hard snort through his nose. Jaws clamped shut. Sway and slow spin and pulsing blood buzzing in his ears. The spin slowed to a stop then went the other way.

Became aware that he was still aware and realized:
Oh HELL it didn't work!

V.

Kingdom Come

STILL ALIVE, A BURNING RING AROUND HIS NECK, breath a little strangled, blood pounding hot in his temples, Chris-John felt for other damage within himself, but nothing whatsoever was wrong—except that rotating on the end of the rope was making him nauseated. He reached his bound legs out to the edge of the trap to stop his spinning. He opened his eyes.

The multitude gasped and stepped back in one motion. Dead silence settled over Potter's Hill.

A single voice called, "Sire, he's not dead."

The king pushed to the front of the reviewing stand and commanded, "Finish him." His face was grave. He did not like this and he should have foreseen it. The boy did not weigh enough.

The hangman stepped up on the scaffold. He meant to jump on Chris-John to add his own weight to his. But Chris-John riveted his great eyes toward his would-be executioner and the man stopped.

Something in the other-than-human gaze. The man reeled back, gabbling. He climbed down, bumbling into the crowd, his voice a flood of disconnected sound. When he spoke in words, he said he saw a shining nimbus around the prisoner's head.

Others cried that he was speaking in tongues. The report spread through the crowd: they had tried to kill an angel. A messiah.

The archbishop covered his tired eyes. This nonsense was the result of not educating people. Such were the hazards of keeping religion a mystery. It bred superstition and belief in the unreal. The ignorant always turned away from the rational in favor of the irrational. What was mystical sounded more powerful, and so more real. The king had kept religion shrouded and arcane so he could have only a few—his chosen few—who could lead and interpret religion for the masses. It made the masses more controllable than if they could decide questions of divinity for themselves. But it was a dangerous game—like handling a serpent.

Here the serpent turned in his hand and struck.

The crowd surged onto the scaffold to cut down God's chosen one and his apostles. They tore the hoods off Scottie and Terese and Phoenix and cut their bonds. The guards that tried to stop them were thrown from the scaffold—or else their heads were put in the nooses meant for the rebels and the traps opened from under them.

Martel touched the king's arm. "Sire, I'd advise Your Majesty go now. This is very bad."

The king nodded and let himself be guided from the reviewing box. They made their way through the crowd that was already hostile but still tentative toward the Crown. Martel smelled violence about to break over them. It crackled in the air like ozone before lightning. They were almost to the king's limousine when the first cry of "tyrant" came and the first rock was thrown.

The king's guards moved in to shelter the king—those that were still loyal. A few of them had been caught over in the tide of revelation. And those took their guns with them.

Gregory watched from the reviewing stand in dismay. Someone grasped his pontifical robes—a peasant with a mad glow on his face. "Father, Father, it's a miracle!"

Gregory just shook his head. "He didn't weigh enough."

The peasant recoiled, first confounded, then suspicious, and he backed away from the king's archbishop, muttering to the others about him and pointing to him behind his hand.

Gregory gathered in his robes. It was best he be away from here, too.

General Martel had managed to get the king to his car and off, shielding his retreat with but a handful of loyal guards to assist him. Gregory forged his way to where Martel was under siege. He took the old man's arm and had to shout in his ear to be heard, a press of ugly faces all around them shouting and gesticulating with fists. "My friend, I urge you to go now, too."

But Martel told Gregory to go ahead without him. "Take my horse," said Martel. The old general said he would try to keep the lid on this mob as long as he could.

"For the love of God, you come, too. They've already killed."

"In a minute. See to the king. Someone has to," said Martel. He put his horse's reins into Gregory's hands and gave the pontiff a somehow reverent push. "I'll be right behind you."

Gregory looked toward where the king's car had gone. Edward had made it through the mob. But Martel was right; if ever Edward needed him, it would be now. Greg took the reins and mounted. The horse reared, and the angry peasants ducked. Gregory called down to Martel, "Be careful."

"I'll be right behind you," Martel shouted.

Gregory kicked the steed's sides and the war-horse charged toward the edge of the angry thousands.

As he cleared the crowd, he heard shots behind him. He could not see Martel anymore. The end had begun.

Brigadier Tow arrived at the palace before the storm broke and started up to his room. By the time he was on the second flight he was taking the stairs by twos.

He opened the doors to his chambers to reveal Will jamming a suitcase shut.

"What are you doing?" The stony voice from behind made Will whirl around in terror to face the general who was supposed to be at Potter's Hill for the next few hours. The boy was white as death, eyes so dilated in fear they looked smoky. The scene was a dagger in the gut to Tow.

Steel gray eyes slowly shifted down to the suitcase on the floor. Not his usual methodical aide, Will had been pulling out drawers and dumping them in. He knew. He knew. Chris-John had told him and Will believed.

Tow came inside. Will backed up. Tow was not a big man, but he seemed to fill the room and push at its boundaries. His visage was a long-practiced, now instinctive, part of him—a serpent's mask, with changeless hard eyes that bored deep and did not blink. Cold came off him like an arctic wind or malevolent spirit. He terrified, was aware of it, and yet could not drop his mask—because it was his own reaction to terror. He couldn't show a glimpse of the sorrow or panic he felt. It was physically impossible. Brokenhearted, his only armor was his alter ego, barely distinguishable from himself, the viper.

Will had never seen Tow like this, and it instantly reconfirmed everything his brother had said. The slightest doubt was gone now. Without question, this was a ruthless killer. Worse than that. What he was was unspeakable.

Tow couldn't talk. Gentle pleading was wailing in the pit of his stomach, but he could only maintain his stony stare. He took another step in.

Will backed into a lamp table. He knocked over the lamp, caught it with fumbling hands, set it aright, and backed around it.

Tow's voice was very cold, too smooth and soft: "Where are you going?"

Will could never stand up to Tow's commanding presence. It took all his courage now to answer, "Far away."

"Why?"

"You know why."

"No, I don't. You will have to tell me," the assassin said smoothly.

The quiet force made Will vacillate again. A tremor ran through his body and he blurted suddenly, "Did you really kill a girl because she scratched the piano?"

Tow came in closer, cornering Will. Will just stood there frozen. It was almost a plea to be talked out of leaving. Tow took heart. He allowed himself to soften a little with this tiny flicker of hope. He could yet take control of this situation. He could always control this boy. He could tell him anything, make him believe anything he said. Tow lifted his hand haltingly to touch Will's shoulder, then he put his arms around him and laid his cheek to the boy's temple. *You can't leave me now.* "That's a rumor—"

Will broke free and struck him as hard as he could. Tow drew back in surprise, touched the bruise forming on his handsome face.

Tow could tell him anything—anything but that.

If there was only one thing Will was sure of, it was that *that* was a lie. If Tow had said *anything* else, Will might have stayed and listened. But he'd lied, and Will was terrified. Will could have handled a full confession. The lie so utterly unhinged him that he thought anything was possible now. He believed he was as his brother said, one more on a chain of used and murdered victims.

Tow saw he had made a mistake. There was no recapturing a sound that was already out and shrieking *liar,* reverberating through the air. He tried to touch Will again. But the boy shrank from him and was edging around him toward the open doors.

"Will, please."

Near fainting, childlike, incredulous and betrayed, Will bleated, "You lied."

"*Yes*, I lied!" Tow cried, all his reserve crashing down. The boy's panic was infectious. Tow couldn't think. Everything resolved to one thought: *Stay.*

Will tottered with dizziness and blinked. He was trying to ease between Tow and the couch.

Tow caught him roughly by the arm and swung him around to face him again. "You're not leaving," he said, but then wondered how he could prevent it.

"I am," said Will, his chin quivering. "You wouldn't want me around anyway, because I hate you."

Tow searched for something to say. Lacking words of his own to express what he felt—had never felt and never had to express before—he fell back on an ancient line from the Beforetime poet. " 'These words are razors to my wounded heart,' " he said softly.

"Now don't start talking like that." Will, already terrified and distraught, began to cry and struggled for freedom.

Tow didn't want to fight him. He pinned him against the couch, touched his cheek, and held him till he stopped thrashing and slumped against him. Tow breathed a little freer. "There now. We're all right." He loosened his hold and nuzzled his cheek. "Do you want some wine?"

"Yes."

Tow let him go, and Will bolted for the door.

"Stop," Tow commanded uselessly. One thought struck the panicking Tow—he had to stop him and, almost by instinct, he executed the only method of stopping a person he'd ever used in his career as King Edward's triggerman. He drew his Magnum and stopped him just as he stepped into the hall.

The king needed his assassin. He was shaken from the scene at the gallows. *Horrible. Horrible.* He was still disbelieving. He had feared for his life among his own people. He had seen the little orphan harpist, the blond girl who sang so sweetly at his harvest ball. She had picked up a clod of dirt and thrown it at him. He wiped his face with his hands. Dirt came off on his fingers. He stared at it, utterly undone.

He could not let himself believe the mobs that had crushed in all around him and boiled over to deadly violence with terrifying speed. His car had driven through them. They hung on the door handles and beat on the windows. He nearly hadn't made it through. Such venom unleashed, hitherto unimagined—where had it come from? Had he been so blind to them? Had he been such a bad king? Everything that his family had built was breaking down and out of control. They'd killed Martel. He knew that without having seen. The trusty old war-horse who wanted to retire had died defending him. *My right arm.* Edward found himself actually clutching his right shoulder as if blood were spilling from it, a physical wound.

He needed Tow.

He ran up to the third floor. With dull dread he beheld the forms on the floor at the end of the long hall. The king approached cautiously. Tow crouched over his aide, who was sprawled out motionless. The king could see blood under him. Tow stroked back his hair. The king had seen once a bereft vixen trying to coax its dead young back to life. Tow caressed the boy with intimate touch. If ever Edward felt embarrassed for someone, it was now. "Is he dead?"

He stepped forward, but Tow looked up with red-shot eyes and growled, and the monarch stepped back, wondering if Tow were irrational enough to take a shot at him also. Tow glared at him, then turned his attention back to Will.

So he's killed him at last, true to form, thought the king. Maybe now he could get back to his top efficiency and predictability. Edward III needed him that way.

This tenderness and regret were not usual in the least. It was disconcerting to see him crawling on the floor like that. Edward hoped he would get over this spell quickly. But Tow ignored the king's very presence. He propped his elbows on either side of Will's head, his fingers laced in his hair, his arms forming a tender cage around him, and he bent over him in private communion. Edward thought he kissed him but couldn't see. Of the king, Tow was oblivious.

The king was impatient but would sooner rush a wounded badger. "When you're done here, I want to see you. We have a serious problem."

He turned away and walked back down the hall. Of all times for this to happen.

He had arrived at the head of the stairs when the gun fired. The sound brought him back to the site immediately.

He knew what he was going to find but couldn't help feeling shocked. He had known Tow too long as a survivor. He would sooner have expected water to fall up. But then the Kingdom was upside down, so why not?

"Oh Tow," he said. "You poor lovesick fool. I gave you more credit than that. I thought you were stronger."

Edward crouched down on one knee to make sure he was dead. Tow never missed. One shot. In the heart. There was blood on his back; the bullet had gone through. He had fallen over the boy. The king touched his face; still warm. There were tears on his cheeks. *Tears!* Eyes that never shed them. The king shuddered. Emotion was incompatible with the viper. Serpents can't become human. He could only self-destruct. Edward passed the back of his hand over his soft hair. David Tow had always been coldly attractive. Edward remembered him as a youth, back when they were both a lot younger. One of the colossal mistakes Edward *hadn't* made was taking Tow to bed.

God knew he'd made others. And he was trying to

save his Kingdom now despite them—with his right and left arms cut off. Martel and Tow. He was furious with Tow. *Damn you.* He'd failed him in his hour of need. Edward hurried down the two flights of stairs.

Pain in his chest stopped him near the lowest landing. Breath came short.

He tried to inhale, but everything was frozen. Hands raised to his chest in dire disbelief. *No.* Not now.

He could hear an urgent voice somewhere in the palace calling in search, "Your Majesty! Your Majesty!"

He wanted to cry, "Here!" but nothing issued forth but a hiss of strangled air from his throat. Lungs would not move. He was grasping at the banister and falling.

"Your Majesty!" the voice called in the next corridor. He heard quick vigorous footsteps, doors opening and shutting, and the muffled voice calling into rooms, "Your Majesty?"

Clinging to the railing and swaying on his knees, Edward opened his mouth, straining to speak. He lost his grip and dropped to the carpeted floor on his back, clutching at his waistcoat, wanting to open it and let in air. "Greg," he whispered. He could barely hear himself.

He stared up at the painted ceiling, high, high, so far away. There were rose garlands, and pretty pastel birds with ribbons in their mouths cavorting on the ceiling above the crystal chandeliers. Edward closed his eyes.

He heard the footsteps come into the foyer, stop, and run toward him. He heard Greg's voice, felt Greg's hands on him. "Majesty."

Fingers pulled back his eyelids, opened his shirt. An ear pressed to his chest. Then came words. He'd heard Greg speak them over others. So unreal that he be speaking them over him. *"In nomine Patris, et Filii, et Spiritus Sancti. Amen."* And a crucifix pressed to his lips. Eyelids fluttered open to see violet stole around Greg's neck, violet for penance—and extreme unction.

I am dying.

Greg was giving him the last rites in the hall, granting absolution in his last breaths. Greg asked if he was sorry for all his sins. Edward answered without voice: "yes." He recognized the Latin "I absolve you," and then drifted away at peace as words tumbled over him like heedless timeless surf.

Pater noster, qui es in coelis: sanctificetur nomen tuum; adveniat regnum tuum. . . .

VI.

Line of Succession

THE MOBS MULTIPLIED. RAGE THAT HAD BEEN A LONG time building exploded and overran the land around the Capital in a molten flow. They brought torches to the palace and found the king was not there. Maddened, they divided to hunt down the tyrant. They descended in hordes upon the rich aristocratic estates, crying death to the sons and daughters of privilege.

A splinter group of them raided the Martel estate. They pulled the heiress Marion from her wheelchair and dropped her on the floor, pushed at her with heavy farmers' boots, and told her to crawl in the dirt like everyone else. They twisted her wheelchair into a knot of metal and threw it through an ornamental screen of painted silk.

Prince Edward they dragged outside, tied his hands, and seated him on one of Lord Martel's prize Thoroughbreds. They made a noose from a silken curtain cord and threw one end over the thick branch of a shady maple tree from which a swing was tied in summer. They were leading the Thoroughbred toward the hanging noose when Marion appeared in the doorway to the house—on her feet—a revolver in either hand. She shot everyone who did not run away.

At the first shot the Thoroughbred bolted. Prince Edward, his hands bound, held tight with his knees and kept his seat until the horse stopped running. Marion mounted another horse and rode out to get him. "Edward! Edward, are you hurt?"

The little prince was confounded. He tried to shake his long bangs out of his eyes. "Marion, what happened!"

Marion did not reply. Prince Edward knew the answer. He just wanted someone to contradict what he knew.

Marion unbound him and they rode back to the house. There, Marion loaded a horse cart with dried fruit and meat, and clothing and guns. She gave Edward the reins and said, "You know my father's ship. The crew should be loyal. If they're not, use this for real." She gave him her own revolver. "Wait for me as long as you can, but don't lose the tide or you'll never get out of the Seaway. If I'm not back in time, you get yourself away from here. I want you to promise me. Go."

"Go *where?*"

"Europe."

"Europe is a myth!"

"No, it's not. The pilot will know how to find it. We've talked about it before. We always wanted to look for it."

"You could get hanged for talking like that," said Edward. America was the only land on Earth. The outer Ocean was a vast desert of water, forbidden to travel. It was dangerous and nothing was out there, everyone knew that.

"We could get hanged for *not,*" said Marion.

"Is my father dead?" said Edward.

"He could be," said Marion softly.

The boy nodded soberly and picked up the reins. "What about you? How are you going to pass though the streets?"

"I'll get through."

Prince Edward did not challenge her. He had met her will before.

* * *

Scent of beeswax and incense filled the Cathedral. Candles burning in bronze candelabra around the closed coffin shed an amber glow on the rich wood and gilded fittings. The archbishop in black robes and tall miter swept down the center aisle, waving the censer while doleful strains of the great pipe organ resounded in the high vaults. The organ itself was silent; the threnody was a recording. Gregory had sent the organist, as well as all the brothers and nuns, away. He was alone in the Cathedral. It was dangerous to be honoring the King this day.

The expected tumult arrived, first as a muffled unresolved noise beyond the great doors, a rumbling beneath the music, then the muted candlelight was washed out by cold daylight as the great doors flew wide and the disorderly mob trooped in. They brandished farm equipment and smithy's tools and a ready-made noose. They wanted the king.

Gregory was kneeling at the altar when they broke in, his back presenting a gold cross embroidered on the back of his chasuble. He stood slowly and turned at the altar to face them, stern and lordly. He answered them from the raised dais of the sanctuary, standing beneath the woeful figure on the cross, "He is gone to his Maker. This is a house of worship. Leave this place."

But all the trappings of deity and authority daunted them not at all. They wanted to do sacrilege. This was the *king's* cathedral. The *king's* God. They felt no debt to *Him*.

Seeing that they were too late to work their wrath on the king, they wanted the king's body. They couldn't kill him, but they could desecrate what was left, the temple that his soul had fled. Maybe he would see their work from hell.

The archbishop strode forward and blocked their way with his own person, his arms spread protectively before the coffin. But the militants were not impressed and they roughly pushed him away and ripped open the coffin.

And there was revealed, nestled in the rich satin lining, a little urn of ashes.

The archbishop was standing by in grim calm waiting, his hands folded, his chin raised. "So."

A rawboned scarecrow of a peasant plunged claw hands into the casket and snatched up the urn. He hurled the ashes down—the urn cracked dully on the Byzantine-patterned floor—and he turned on the archbishop with new eyes of anger. *"You!"*

Wrath must have its way. The mob would vent theirs upon another target. If the king were out of harm's reach, then the king's archbishop would do. He had sent the king to heaven. He had absolved Satan and let him escape his due. This one must pay. Vengeance would yet be served.

The crowd closed in on Gregory, grabbing, tearing, their savage faces twisted out of their very humanity.

Jostled and prodded and jabbed, Greg tried to keep his balance and he searched for some face in their swarming numbers that he could recognize and could address by name. If he could break the ravening pack into individuals, he could disperse this madness.

But he did not know anyone. This was not his congregation. There was not even anyone he knew from his country rounds. These were all strangers to him. *Who are these people?* He was mystified. *Where did they come from? So many.*

And, God, the anger.

His tall miter toppled. The rope scratched at his face as it went over his head and tightened round his neck. The mutineers pulled off his gold rings. "How much are these worth while your people are starving?" a rotten-toothed mouth shouted into his face so close he saw nothing but those teeth.

Someone jerked the rope taut at his throat and he fell to gagging and rasping for air.

An old woman's thin crying voice came from somewhere. "No! No! Not him! Not him!" But her piteous shrieking grew distant as she was pushed from the church.

The executioners were looking up for a cross beam over which to throw the rope.

Then darkness blotted the daylight that had been streaming in the wide doorway.

A black-cloaked figure on a pawing stallion filled the high-arched entrance.

There was sudden stillness in the Cathedral, the rioters frozen in murderous tableau, staring at the faceless feared ally of the poor, the Devil Rider hooded in black like an executioner.

As the peasants thawed from shocked motionlessness, they gave ground, edging backward.

Weird dark lenses gave the Devil's mask eyes like a giant insect looking down at them from its tall mount. Black-booted feet kicked, and the Devil rode the stallion right up the aisle into the church. At the coffin the giant black reared and the mob parted, scattering into the pews.

The dark rider steadied the stallion, and the insectoid eyes scanned the throng. Armed mutineers shrank beneath the vacant smoked-glass gaze. It—the rider was inhuman—reined the stallion around in a tight circle. The great beast snorted and lifted sharp hooves in prancing steps, protesting under the inflexible hand that directed its head. Having turned full around, the rider brought the steed to a standstill and gazed again over the deadly congregation. It was said that bullets passed right through the Devil Rider.

Suddenly the Devil stood in the stirrups and pointed a condemning black-gloved finger at the archbishop. Sinister voice came strained through the ungodly mask: "Give him to me."

There was a pause of slight reluctance. The hunters were not sure they wanted to give up their prey. But no one wanted to cross the Devil. And as they thought about it, they became eager. This was a proper end for the king's archbishop, and so much more ghastly than anything they could do, they were sure. The bravest of them gingerly placed the end of the rope into the black-gloved hand.

The archbishop was led out stumbling on his leash, stupefaction imprinted on his face. The rioters followed them to the doors of the church. Then the Devil reached down and pulled the captive up and across the horse's back like a grain sack, whipped the steed, and galloped away with a strident gale of awful laughter so high-pitched that it really couldn't be human.

No one of the townsfolk ever saw the archbishop or the Devil Rider again.

The black stallion panted hard with guttural sounds deep in its windpipe, froth dripping from its mouth. The Devil reined left and the stallion turned off the paved way into a fallow pasture and galloped up over the embankment, away from sight of the road.

It came to a stop on a windy hillock ragged with tall grass and an outcropping of gray stone, where three other horses were tethered. The black shook its bridled head and nickered.

The dark rider let the archbishop slide from the stallion. He was scarlet in the face and dizzy; his ribs hurt from the wild upside-down ride during which all he could see were the stallion's feet, the stallion's white feet. Regaining his footing, the first thing Gregory did was take the noose from his neck. Then he stared at the Devil, who almost had to be *the* devil, because it certainly was not Gregory, and the only other person who had ever ridden as the Devil was crippled for life.

He watched the black-robed stranger dismount. On the ground the Devil's stature diminished. The rider bent over and pulled the gas mask from her head, then straightened, letting tumble a shock of long black hair.

"Marion!" The slender young lady was padded big as a bull, she was strong as an ox, and she could *walk*. "Marion, I thought you couldn't—"

"I couldn't," Marion verified abruptly, her eyes

flashing dark and fiery. "It was a miracle. In *your* absence, Archbishop. *Without you*. What does that say?"

Gregory stuttered, then blurted, "Why didn't you *tell* me?"

Marion dropped her mask at their feet. "Because I was so angry I could have killed you! The king came to see me and I almost turned you over! Can't you understand!" She pushed back her hair jerkily. It didn't need pushing back.

She turned away suddenly and tended to her black stallion. She took off its saddle and bridle, yanking at the buckles and straps with sharp angry pulls. Then she smacked its hindquarters and sent it free.

As she saddled up another horse she snapped at Gregory, "I thought the rebels were your friends."

The archbishop rubbed his neck sadly. "There's no room in the world for compromise. In any revolution it's the moderates who go to the wall first."

Marion looked for the sun in the sky. It was already low to the west. "The tide's going out. I'll miss my ship."

"You came back for me?" said Gregory.

"No," said Marion. "I came back for the king, the queen, and for my father. The queen won't come. I guess I found the king. But I can't find my father." Her facial muscles were twitching to refrain from expression. She had to fight the horse to put the bit in its mouth. Her rough haste defeated her and the horse refused the bit. She dropped it, grabbed a fistful of mane, and cried into it, "Where is my father!"

"He's dead, Marion," said Gregory. There was no time or way to blunt the words. "They killed him at the gallows. He was guarding the king."

Marion let out a long hoarse shriek of pure grief. She leaned into her horse's withers and sobbed. Then she shook her head and fiercely knuckled the tears from her eyes. She threw her shoulders back. She clamped her teeth on her upper lip and squinted at the horizon. "What time is it?"

"Seven o'clock."

"Oh God." Marion made the horse take the bit. She tore off her Devil's garb and pulled out two brown-hooded cloaks she had hidden under a wind-beaten pine tree. They were ragged garments such as the poorest peasants wore. She threw one cloak at Greg and put on the other one.

Gregory took off all the fine silk and wool pontiff's vestments trimmed in gold. He could no longer actually be called archbishop. Without the Crown, there was no more Church of the Kingdom of America, no pontiff.

Under all the liturgical vestments Gregory wore plain black trousers and a white shirt. He glanced at Marion. She was staring at him oddly.

It was so curious to see him as just a man.

And she—Gregory found himself staring back. She was disheveled in her brown peasant's cloak, her black hair a wild tangle, her eyelids swollen and red, her lips wet crimson, unconsciously sultry in distress. Gregory seized her by her arms. "Marion, you're a walking angel. Why do you bother with me?"

Marion screamed at him. "Damn you, I'm not an angel. I'm a woman, which seems to have escaped your notice!"

His hands slid from her arms to encircle her and he stepped closer. Deep crumbling voice she'd never heard before burned her ears and brought her breath shallow in her chest, "No, it hasn't, Marion." The way he said her name, it was a private touch.

She was going to push away and screech at him, but she clutched at his shirt instead. "Don't you leave me again, Greg! Don't you dare leave me again!"

"If I do, I swear I am dead."

He pulled her in hard against him. Her head fell back, her face tilting up to his, her arms up around his broad shoulders feeling instantly as if they belonged there. His big hand behind her head trapped her there and his mouth came down on hers.

Their lips parted. Marion whispered, "The tide's out."

Gregory took her hands. "And you can't walk." He untethered two stallions and cut the third free. He mounted, looked back to see she was mounted, then kicked the great stallion's sides and they ran like they never had, cutting cross country in a straight line to the coast. Behind them grew an eerie light on the horizon, red like a fiery sunset, but the glow was in the south. The picture-pretty Capital was in flames.

The horses' ears flattened back, their nostrils narrowed, smelling danger, a sense so strong Marion felt it, too. They raced across fields against the wind, cloaks flying out like wings behind them, as the world was ending.

All was quiet around Potter's Hill now. Mobs were running riot elsewhere.

Terese pulled her shawl around her. She was leaning against the scaffold that was nearly hers. She watched Scottie digging holes. "What are you doing?"

"Looking for bones."

"Whose bones?"

"Henry Iver's. Chris-John thinks he buried them around here somewhere." He stopped for a moment, jabbed the shovel into the dirt, leaned his elbow on it, and wiped salty beads off his upper lip. He looked at Terese, his palace-pretty lass, holding a wide-brimmed hat before her in both her hands. "Where's Chris-John?" said Scottie.

She shrugged.

Scottie looked up at the scaffold. If he closed his eyes, he could see the crowds again. He wondered if anyone was disappointed. *They came to see our eyes pop out and watch us bite off our tongues and shit. We gave them a new nation instead.* He wondered if they were disappointed.

Terese had turned her head toward the red incandescence low in the sky in the direction of the Capital.

"Oh," she said.

Everything that was was in flames. She shivered. She

pushed off from the post on which she was leaning and dropped her pretty hat. She went to Scottie, took his shovel from him, and set it aside so she could cuddle to his broad chest and hide her eyes. He stroked her hair. "Don't look back," said Scottie.

There was only forward now.

Chris-John had run away. Not for good. He was euphoric in victory, America's acclaimed liberator, but still he felt need to take time to go apart and walk in solitude.

He touched his neck. The skin around the wound was outraged, a raw ring around his throat. The scar would be with him the rest of his life.

He thought of poor Detroit without her eyebrows, wearing those big dark glasses.

He wondered if he truly was a liberator. It was too soon to know yet if this uprising was a localized event or if it would spill over to the rest of the Kingdom. It would almost have to spread—without a king. So who now to put in control?

Just like King Edward had said, the people wanted a leader with all the answers to make decisions and care for them. He'd been right about that. All the hammering questions were thrown at Chris-John. The people wanted him to tell them what to do. He answered them, "Why are you asking me? This is rule by the people. Do I look like all the people to you? It's your country. What do *you* want to do?"

Phoenix had said glibly, "They could elect you king. They're ready to elect you *God.*"

At that Chris-John fled.

This was a quiet place. He squatted by a headstone in a country churchyard. Ivy rambled over the moldering limestone, its epitaph weathered so he couldn't make out the name. He rested his back against it.

They would make me king and I am crazy. There were great gaps in his memory. *I don't even know who*

I am. He could imagine the chamberlain announcing him: *King Chris-John or Walter the First!*

He carried Henry Iver's book with him. He opened it and thumbed through it, holding it up to share it with the unknown tombstone as if it were reading over his shoulder. The pages were tattered, ragged, wrinkled, dog-eared, and almost memorized. Some answers were in there but not all of them. Not near all of them.

Chris-John rose and walked alone. He thought of the king. And he understood how lonely it was way up high. At last he thought he could understand the old man. And forgive him. He wondered if there was consciousness after death, and could the monarch see from whatever place he was.

And forgive me.

Two stallions ran down the beach, spurred faster by their riders, sand sprayed up from their pounding hooves.

They slowed as they drew near the wharves, for there were peasant fishermen on the shore. The two aristocrats pulled their brown hoods up to hide their faces and they looked out into the harbor.

The tall ship was not there.

There were sails on the horizon. Gregory pointed, sighting three masts far down the Seaway.

Marion stopped a cry with the edge of her fist. Common folk were all around them on the wharves, and she couldn't cry out loud; she couldn't know who might want to harm them. Marion had a quick eye and she had noticed that the fishmongers weren't separating the sheepheads for sale to the poor from the perch for sale to the better classes. All the types of fish were thrown together. These people were democrats. The rebellion was here, too, and the two aristocrats were in danger.

Already they were drawing curious looks because of their horses. But for all these people knew, the fine steeds were stolen, so no one moved against them yet.

Marion bowed her hooded head. Tears slipped down her nose.

Their horses had come to stand where a little fishing boat was tied off. Two fishermen in it, bent over in their hooded rain slickers, were busy untangling a net. One of them recited aloud, to no one, the voice youthful, the tone almost a question:

"And he took the damsel by the hand and said unto her 'Talitha cumi'; which is, being interpreted, 'Damsel, I say unto thee, arise.' "

The Archbishop's face within his hood jerked aside to look at Marion. Her back had straightened in startlement. The fishermen hunched over their nets.

Marion took her horse at a walk near the little boat. She peered down at the fishermen. A boy peeked up from the slouched brim of his rubber slicker. It was Prince Edward.

Without words or quick motion that would draw the eye, Marion dismounted and climbed into the little boat. Gregory followed her. When they were seated on the thwarts, Edward and his companion tossed aside their fishing nets to reveal a motor.

A boat with an engine was an astonishing thing. It was an extravagant royal toy lavished on the little prince for his tenth birthday. He started the engine.

At the sound, the peasants on the dockside stood up and looked, but if anyone thought of doing anything, the boat was already speeding away in a white wake to catch the tall ship bound across the sea.

The little powerboat came alongside the clipper, and the sailors helped the passengers aboard.

The captain of the clipper was a sturdy broad seaman, the master of his ship, nobody's servant, but no democrat. He called Marion "Lady," Edward "Majesty," and Gregory "Eminence." Once he had them safely aboard, he bellowed for more speed. The deckhands unfurled more sails. The great ship heeled over hard and sliced through the waves.

Greg and Marion were shown cabins below. They settled in and came back out on the deck. No one wanted to stay below just now. This would be the their last sight of America.

Gregory braced against a mast, his arm around Marion's waist. Marion leaned back against him, her head resting against his chest, her hand on young Edward's shoulder, gazing to the horizon. Man, woman, and child, they made a strange little family—the archbishop, the lady, and the young king.

Edward IV. They had told him his father was dead, for certain this time. He still showed no emotion. He did not feel like crying. "I am fine," he said. He'd never been close to the king.

Marion told him that his mother wouldn't come. He nodded. He hadn't thought she would.

He listened to the creaking of ropes straining against wood. The clipper was flying full sail with a good breeze on the beam. A fine mist of sea salt settled on his face. The waves deepened and he broadened his stance to keep his footing on the listing deck. It was cold out on the open water. Their clothes were snapping in the wind.

Edward shivered and pushed his hands in his trouser pockets. He felt something in one and pulled it out to see.

It was a handkerchief.

Looking at it, he felt a peculiar numb twinge, or rather felt something breaking through numbness. Suddenly it was curiously hard to focus and he kept blinking to stare at the handkerchief. It was pure white, of the finest linen, and embroidered with the letters: EIII.

And Edward IV cried.

About the Author

Rebecca M. Meluch graduated from the University of North Carolina at Greensboro with a B.A. in drama. She also has an M.A. in ancient history from the University of Pennsylvania and a black belt in *tae kwon do*. She worked as an assistant in the classics department at Greensboro. She has also worked as a data processor, artist, and fashion model. She is involved in the theatre and active in a playwrights' workshop sponsored by the Ohio Theatre Alliance, and has helped inaugurate a Readers Theatre program at Beck Center for the Cultural Arts. She travels at any excuse and has worked on an archaeological excavation in Israel. She has a passion for World War II fighter aircraft. Her other novels, *Jerusalem Fire*, *Sovereign*, *Wind Dancers*, *Wind Child*, and *War Birds*, are available in Signet or Roc editions. Miss Meluch lives in Westlake, Ohio.